# H E L M

TOR BOOKS BY STEVEN GOULD

*Jumper*
*Wildside*
*Helm*

# HELM

STEVEN GOULD

TOR®
A TOM DOHERTY ASSOCIATES BOOK
NEW YORK

This is a work of fiction. All the characters and events portrayed in this novel are either fictitious or are used fictitiously.

HELM



This book is printed on acid-free paper.

A Tor Book
Published by Tom Doherty Associates, Inc.
175 Fifth Avenue
New York, NY 10010

Tor Books on the World Wide Web:
http://www.tor.com



Book design by Ellen Cipriano

ISBN 0-312-86460-4

First Edition: April 1998

Printed in the United States of America

0 9 8 7 6 5 4 3 2 1

## Acknowledgments

Thanks are due to my *sempai,* Ron Druva, for screening the aikido scenes in this book for accuracy. Any mistakes that remain are my fault. More general and heartfelt thanks are due to all my teachers and fellow students at Southwestern Aikikai and in the Western Region of the United States Aikido Federation.

*Depending on the circumstance, you should be:*
*hard as a diamond, flexible as a willow,*
*smooth-flowing like water, or empty as space.*

—Morihei Ueshiba

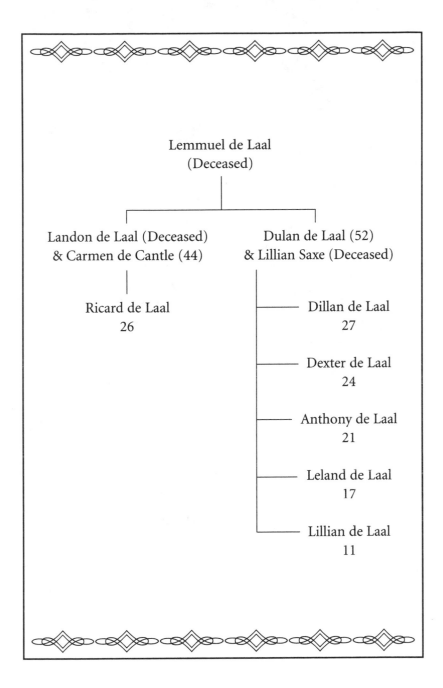

- Lemmuel de Laal (Deceased)
  - Landon de Laal (Deceased) & Carmen de Cantle (44)
    - Ricard de Laal 26
  - Dulan de Laal (52) & Lillian Saxe (Deceased)
    - Dillan de Laal 27
    - Dexter de Laal 24
    - Anthony de Laal 21
    - Leland de Laal 17
    - Lillian de Laal 11

# H E L M

# PROLOGUE

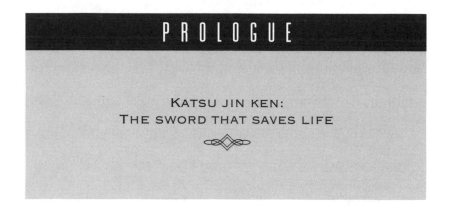

## KATSU JIN KEN: THE SWORD THAT SAVES LIFE

They huddled on the floor, shoulder to shoulder, in a rock pocket off the main corridor, moving their heads carefully to avoid banging them on the low roof. A single low-wattage light shone down on dirty hands clutching notes and data screens. Unkempt hair floated above wrinkled brows and sunken cheeks. The fresh, sharp tang of acetic acid from caulk-covered cracks mixed with the ever-present smell of sweat, ammonia, and feces.

Those crowded into the corridor outside envied them.

"Is the recorder on?"

"Yes."

"This meeting of the executive committee is in session. Minutes are accepted as filed. The only item on the agenda is the emigration vote."

A minor quake shook the rock slightly and Dr. Herrin stopped talking. Eyes widened and down the corridor somebody started screaming and thrashing around. Dr. Herrin ignored the noise and concentrated on her breathing.

She was sitting *seiza,* on her shins, composed, her shoulders relaxed, a sharp contrast to the others, who were sitting cross-legged or leaning back against the rough rock walls. Many of those clutched their knees and squeezed their eyes shut.

If the section was holed badly, there wasn't anything that could be done. There weren't enough pressure suits to go around. She hoped that the panic in the corridor wouldn't spread. They had to keep the pathway clear so that the emergency squads could get to smaller leaks—the ones that *could* be repaired.

The month before they'd lost forty-nine men, women, and children when a quake holed a corridor. Vacuum decompression is a violent death, and any death was hard to face after so many dead on Earth. Two of the clean-up crew went back to their niches and poisoned themselves.

The quake subsided and the screams down the hall died to violent sobbing.

Dr. Herrin continued. "There is high confidence in the accuracy of this data?"

Novato, a woman wearing a faded pair of NASA/ESA coveralls, nodded.

Herrin swallowed convulsively, then put her fingertips to her temples and closed her eyes. "Let's reiterate." She opened her eyes and held up five fingers. "The probe data is more than conclusive. Epsilon Eridani has an Earth-sized planet with a $CO_2$ nitrogen/water vapor atmosphere. The probe has initiated phase one seeding and initial results are excellent—the tailored bacteria are reproducing exponentially and already producing detectable oxygen. And, as you know, these results are twenty-five years old. Based on this data, current estimates indicate that by now, though there are still toxic levels of $CO_2$, the atmosphere is at least ten percent oxygen.

"However, in the hundred and thirty years it will take the ship to reach the system, the bacteria will finish the job. The atmosphere will be fully breathable. Resulting temperatures will be in the Earth-normal range.

"These are not only encouraging results—they're optimal."

Stavinoha, a middle-age man with a shaved head, said, "It's certainly better than we can get from *this* solar system." Stavinoha had been the last person off Planet Earth, launching from the Baikonur Cosmodrome in a converted ICBM six weeks after the Earth's mantle was breached at Tehran and, miraculously, snagged at the peak of his ballistic arc by an American Epsilon-Class orbital tug. Unlike the rest of them, he knew firsthand how bad conditions were on the planet.

The temperatures at Earth's equator hovered around 4 degrees Centigrade. Snowstorms and high-altitude dust clouded the planet.

Herrin continued. "There are seven thousand humans on the

moon in facilities designed for six hundred. If we don't do something about reducing the load on our current resources, *everyone* will die. Given our current status, we might die even if we do reduce the load."

More nods.

"So, we send four thousand in the ship in cold sleep for one hundred and twenty-five years. However, since it was designed for one thousand, we'll have to use cargo space as well. This is acceptable because we can't afford to send all that equipment and supplies away. We need it *here* to survive on Luna and, eventually, to rehabilitate the Earth."

"But they'll need that equipment!" said the NASA/ESA rep. "It was in the original mission specs!"

Dr. Herrin shook her head. "Yes and no. They'll need that equipment if they're to have a high-tech society at that end. It's been estimated that they won't need it to survive. It's a certainty that we do need it *here* to survive."

She paused to look around the room. "So . . . our main problem is how to insure they have the highest chances of survival given a low-tech environment." Dr. Herrin looked now at Dr. Guyton, a small man wedged into the corner outside the circle of the executive committee. "I'd like the Focus Committee to summarize the proposal."

Dr. Guyton, an anthropologist, leaned forward and cleared his throat. "We feel that there are three areas we must concentrate on: nutrition, hygiene, and literacy. As you know, the ship already holds a comprehensive and nearly indestructible library. If we can get the colony to retain literacy while surviving the initial colonization effort, we think they can build back to a comparable technology within three hundred years. In the meanwhile, maintaining good hygiene and nutrition will take care of ninety percent of their health problems. Other problems can be taken care of by practical nursing, but, no matter which way you stretch it, they'll lose people that we could save with our current technology."

He looked around to make sure everyone understood. "What is needed is a strongly enforced code of behavior that will insure good nutrition and hygiene as well as keep succeeding generations literate.

"Codes of this kind have been a part of every viable culture in our planet's history, but the most striking example is that of the Talmudic Laws followed by Judaism. Not only do they provide specific instruction on nutrition and hygiene, they also require a Jew to demonstrate literacy as he comes of age."

"We don't have four thousand Jews on the moon," said Spruill of Logistics.

"No, of course not. Besides, we need a much more abbreviated version than the Talmud. It contains much that is inapplicable and, frankly, countersurvival under these circumstances. My staff has prepared the basic tenets, and we are fleshing them out. We will be ready by the time the ship is."

Bauer, a former congressman from Connecticut, spoke. "What's to make them follow your code? When they're scrambling to stay alive on that distant world, what's to make them take the time to teach it to their children? Are you going to hand it down to them on clay tablets?"

"No." Dr. Guyton exchanged glances with Dr. Herrin. "We propose using the imprinter."

Bauer recoiled. "Jesus Christ!"

Another voice said, "You want to do *what?*"

There was a moment of chaos as everybody tried to speak at once. It subsided almost immediately, but faces betrayed rage and fear.

Herrin raised her hand and let the silence stretch a bit before she spoke. "Consider carefully, please. *Everything* depends on what we decide here today." She waited a moment. "Bauer, you object to the imprinter?"

"Our fellow humans destroyed each other because of the imprinter! I'm outraged that there's even one on the moon! How could this happen?"

Dr. Guyton shook his head. "There isn't an imprinter on the moon . . . but we know how to make them." He leaned forward and held out his hands. "Look, it's true that the French dropped Mag Bottle Seventy-four on Tehran because the Iranians were using the imprinter to forcibly convert Muslims and non-Muslims to their particular brand of Shiite fundamentalism. But this is an argument against antimatter as much as it is against the imprinter. We can't ignore the fact that it could make the difference between life and death for the human *race!* If we imprint the tenets on the colonists, they'll adhere to them automatically—with almost religious fervor. This will assure that they pass it on to their children at the earliest age. It's not as if we're inducting them into a particular political or religious philosophy.

"And we must also consider the imprinter's ability to drop a lifetime of experience into the user's mind. If we were to send loaded imprinters with the crew, we would have a further hedge against failure."

Bauer exploded. "At what cost? You know that information instilled by personality dump is useless without adequate preparatory education. You do that to an ignorant man and you'll end up with a dangerously confused ignorant man. Besides, no matter whom you choose for the template, there's no such thing as slant-free information. A political bent will still be imparted!"

The chairman leaned forward. "We are wasting time."

"It's important!"

"As important as the survival of the human race?" Dr. Herrin turned to the Dr. Guyton. "Is that the extent of the proposal?"

"I just want to point out, again, that this also gets all the antimatter manufactured to date out of the system. But yes, that's the extent of the proposal," the anthropologist said.

"Then I call for a vote."

The tally of the main committee was seven in favor, one against.

Dr. Herrin looked at the next page of her clipboard. "Very well. Prepare the catapult. Initiate the ship modifications after the cargo has been removed from the holds and put in stable orbits. We currently don't have the fuel to bring it down to the moon's surface, but it'll be safe up there until we do. As soon as the passenger bags are ready for the launch buckets and the ship is moved to the L 2 point, we set up a catcher crew. As proposed earlier, imprinting will be done after the first stage of cold sleep prep. If they wake up at the other end"—she spread her hands and exhaled—"well, they'll have religion."

After the vote, Bauer had rested his face in his hands, but he looked up at she said this. "You're not going to tell them?"

"No," the chairman said.

Bauer's face turned white. "You *must!* If you don't, I will!"

The chairman looked at his furious face and thought about her two daughters, now among five billion humans dead. "Consider how many lives your announcement would end. Panic leading to riots could kill us all."

"Nonsense," said Bauer. "That's the sort of argument that's been used to control people through the ages. The *only* way I'll keep quiet is if you abandon this plan to use the imprinter."

She placed the palms of her hands together, fingers up, and bowed from the waist. "Then I'm sorry."

He frowned, puzzled. "Sorry? What do you mean? If you think for one minute that an apology will change my—"

She moved, then, forward in *shikko,* samurai knee-walking, skimming the floor, really, in the low gravity.

He raised his hands as she closed, uncertain, surprised. She was a small woman, unarmed, after all, and he was a large man.

She brushed her right arm against his right wrist and then pivoted, sliding beside him, faster than he could turn to follow. As he tried to twist around, she swept his right arm down with both of her hands, to the floor and back, then the edge of her left hand cut down into the back of his shoulder as she moved behind him, twisting her hips. He bent over abruptly, facedown, his own arm a crowbar levering his torso down.

She reached across the back of his head with her right hand, slid it down across the side of his face, and reached under, to cup his chin. Then she pulled, twisting her hips and shoulder back in one abrupt movement.

Bauer stared up at her, his torso still facing down, his neck twisted one hundred eighty degrees.

Everyone in the small chamber heard his spine snap.

Dr. Herrin laid him on his back, carefully, folding his hands across his chest, then backed away, still on her knees. She bowed again, to the body.

The rest of the committee stared, shocked, shifting their eyes between her and Bauer's lifeless form.

When Dr. Herrin finally spoke, her voice was calm. "The vote on emigration stands. I depend on you, Dr. Guyton, to handle the imprinting procedure with appropriate candor. As to my behavior in this incident"—she nodded toward Bauer's body—"I tender my immediate resignation."

She slumped then, her hands folded on her lap, her eyes downcast. In a quiet, empty voice she said, "I have betrayed my training. If the committee decides I should live, I would like to go with the colony."

# ONE

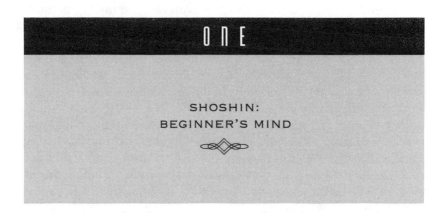

## SHOSHIN: BEGINNER'S MIND

First there was the cyanophyta, the blue-green algae, a hundred different kinds, tailored to float at various strata of the atmosphere, to lie in puddles of water, to infest the shallow seas. They were injected into the upper atmosphere in ablative capsules that exploded when they'd sloughed off enough heat and velocity and floated on the winds.

Some varieties went extinct, never finding their needed habitat, but others thrived, harvesting carbon out of the all-too-plentiful $CO_2$ and releasing oxygen and, at an exponential rate, reproducing.

Next, when the temperatures began to subside, came the lichens, desert, arctic, jungle, temperate—tiny filaments of fungus surrounding algae cells. These soredium fell like fine ash, scattered through the atmosphere to fall gently to the rocky surface.

In some regions the fungus couldn't attach to the rock, or there wasn't enough water, or sunlight, or there was too high a concentration of heavy metals, or it was too hot, or too cold, or any of a hundred other versions of *just not right.* But elsewhere, in the cracks, in drifts of crumbling rock, and in basins of dust, they thrived, the fungal layers absorbing minerals and water while the algae did their photosynthetic magic with $CO_2$ and sunlight.

Right behind the lichens came the decomposers, bacteria and fungi critical to the breakdown of biological material. The fungal filaments of lichen found tiny cracks and flaked off bit after bit of rock.

And as parts of the lichen aged, or conditions changed, they died, and the decomposers went to work, mixing with the dust and water—a simple sort of topsoil was born.

Later the grasses, clovers, and other complex groundcovers came, along with simple aquatic plants, and desmids and other freshwater plant plankton, more ablative capsules put in deliberately decaying orbits and entering the atmosphere like clockwork—ten, twenty, thirty, forty, fifty years after the lichens. Freeze-dried bundles of bacteria, fungi, and seeds encased in nutrient pellets fell like rain to die, flourish, or lie in wait.

These early arrivals were limited to those varieties that could self-pollinate or spread asexually, by budding and branching. Their root systems were, for the most part, shallow. Except for pockets and basins where natural forces had concentrated dust and rubble before the arrival of life, the new soil was thin and tenuous, easily disturbed by wind and water.

The first insects arrived by parachute, in capsules targeted on the highest concentrations of reflected chlorophyll spectra. While the capsules still floated high above the ground, small openings ejected newly revived impregnated queens of the honey bee, the Asian carpenter bee, and the bumblebee, as well as fireflies, caddis flies, nonbiting midges, cockroaches, and lac bugs. Closer to the ground, the capsules scattered earthworms, butterfly larva, crane fly larva, and crickets.

Specialized capsules delivered animal plankton—rotifers, copepods, and cladocerans—to bodies of water large enough to detect from orbit.

The next spring came the predators: praying mantises, ladybugs, ground beetles, and other insects. Spiders included the orb weaver, trapdoor, tarantula, jumping, and wolf. The capsules scattered them wide, ejected kilometers above the surface in gossamer packets of protein webbing that slowed their fall. On the ground, the webbing broke down, oxidized within minutes of creation, freeing the spiders and insects to hunt and eat.

To the waters came protozoa, minute crustaceans, hydras, dragonfly larvae, diving beetles, and other aquatic insect predators.

The vertebrates came with man.

In Agatsu's more turbulent past, a freak crack had formed in brittle crust and iron-rich magma had thrust its way up a narrow fissure in the seabed, trying to reach the lesser pressures above. Fifty million years later, after wind and water had done their work with the surrounding shale, the hardened rock raked the sky, a dagger of rusty granite sixty meters across at the base and over three hundred meters tall. When the sun neared its zenith, the tip of the spire would flash brightly, reflecting light that could be seen clearly over five kilometers away.

They called it the Needle, and Guide Dulan de Laal had forbidden any man, woman, or child, on pain of Dulan's wrath, to climb it.

Lit by the planet's ring, the Needle was an ivory tower against a dark sky. It sprang abruptly from the forested side of a low hill and climbed sharply into the night sky.

Three kilometers from the Needle, below the massive structure of Laal Station, the town Brandon-on-the-Falls was brightly lit. It was the last day of the fall harvest, and festival had begun. The Station was also ablaze with lamp light, and a steady stream of traffic curved down the mountain road from the fort to the town.

Leland de Laal wiped sweat from his brow as he watched the castle and the town begin the festival. He smiled for a moment, picturing his three older brothers dancing and drinking in the town. Even little Lillian would be there under the watchful guidance of Guide Bridgett. And where would Father be? Oh, yes—the judging and blessing—spring ale, fruit, and grain. Doubtless he'd drafted Guide Malcom to help.

The rope was biting into his chest. Leland decided he'd rested enough and shifted on the tiny ledge, bringing the rope over his head. He edged his way over to the six-inch vertical crack he'd chosen earlier and begin working up it, jamming his boots sideways and reaching his hands back as far as they could go. Centimeter by centimeter, he climbed his way up the rock face.

Prohibitions or not, he was already three-quarters up the Needle.

His grip began slipping from moisture on his fingertips so, every time he pulled one hand from the crack, he'd wipe his fingers across his shirt. This left dark streaks across the white cloth—blood from abraded skin.

Step up—set the foot. Free a hand—wipe it—reach higher. Repeat as needed. Don't waste any strength on moans or grimaces. Ignore the grinding of rough stone into raw fingertips. Just climb.

Fifty meters from the top he paused. The wind pulled at him, a gentle breeze that cooled his sweat-soaked clothes and threatened to pluck him from his precarious handholds. He freed one hand and took another iron spike from his belt. Carefully he wedged it in a small crack on the right, then took up the hammer hanging from his neck on a lanyard.

His aching arm muscles twitched as he swung at the spike, causing him to strike the head off center. He cursed as the spike flew past his right shoulder and fell into the dark. The sound of it bouncing off the face of the Needle far below came to him once, and then nothing.

Tiredly he groped for another spike and his hand closed on two sticking out of the loops in his belt. Two? He groped further. Only two out of the thirty spikes he'd started with remained. For the twentieth time since he'd left the trees below, he considered quitting and going back down.

He leaned out and craned his head back, gripping the crack tightly. The tip of the needle floated above, ethereal in the moonlight. *So close!*

With far greater care, he placed and drove in the next to last spike.

Hanging from the spike in the rope and plank chair, he collapsed against the rock face and let his muscles shake.

Time passed and the wind died softly to the barest sigh. Leland's muscles began to chill and stiffen from inaction. He forced himself to eat cheese and bread from his belt pouch, chewing automatically after muttering the categories. He was mildly surprised when his blindly searching fingers came out of the pouch empty.

In the distance, the town and Station still swarmed with activity as the festival neared its peak. On the flat plain between the town baths and the castle moat, a bonfire blazed and three rings of dancers circled the flames while the castle band and town symphony played. Leland could just make out the high seat where his father should be presiding and, if he held very still, the music floated gently to him.

*Enough, sluggard.* He eased back to the crack, almost crying when the dried blood on his fingers cracked open again. His muscles screamed protest as he recovered the plank chair and began climbing again.

Five meters from the top, the crack narrowed to a hairline fracture too fine even for his last spike. There were no hand- or footholds within reach.

*So close?* The Needle was less than two meters thick where Leland perched, and it narrowed rapidly up to the narrow, meter-wide circle that was the Needle's point. *Only another two meters and I could get my arms around it.* He started to slump against the rock, disappointed.

*Arms around it . . . why not?*

The trick was going to be tying a knot with one hand.

Leland reached behind him for the rope that hung coiled from the back of his belt. It was his way out, a length of rope twice sufficient to lower him from spike to spike. He stuck his head through the coil and used his teeth and free hand to untie the knot that held it together. Then, a free end in his mouth, he pulled the last spike from his belt and tried for several frustrating minutes to tie a knot around it. By the time he'd succeeded, his legs and arms were trembling and he'd had to switch his grip several times to wipe off slippery blood.

Lowering the rope slowly, he began swinging the spike from side to side, banging it against the stone first to one side, then the other. He played out the line as the speed increased, gradually wrapping farther and farther around the circumference of the Needle as the period became larger and larger. As the rope's length neared what was needed to circle the Needle's diameter, the violence of Leland's swinging threatened to pull him from his perch. Just as he felt sure he could hold no longer, the rope completed its farthest swing and slapped across the back of his leg. He flipped the lower part of his leg up, leaving him perched dangerously with one foot and one hand wedged in the crack, but also with the rope stretching from his right hand all the way around the Needle to end up hanging from the back of his left knee.

Sweat trickled into Leland's eyes. His heart pounded heavily in time to quick, deep breaths. Still holding tightly to the rope, he worked his right hand back to the crack and wedged it, rope and all, above his other hand. Then he released his left hand and groped for the rope trapped in the crook of his knee. When he had it in hand, he was able to return the left foot to the crack.

He flipped at the end in his left hand, alternately pulling and flipping the rope, getting it to climb the sloping rock until it was slightly above him on the other side of the Needle. Then, maintaining the tension, he moved his left hand as far out to the side as he could and pulled his right hand from the crack.

His heart seemed to stop as he leaned backwards, then thudded to clamorous life as the rope, one end in each hand, held him, logger style to the Needle.

So far, so good. Leland walked up the crack, maintaining tension on the rope to keep him from falling away from the face. When he reached the top of the crack, he took up the tension in the line and flipped it higher on the far side. This entailed leaning forward quickly, flipping the rope, and then taking up the tension again just this side of disaster. Luck was with him for the rope found some projection higher on the other side and caught. Leland took his right foot out of the crack and planted it on the rough, sloping granite.

Up he went, not daring to pause, for his arms were trembling and his nerve was almost gone. Soon it became more of a scramble, as the Needle narrowed to a mere meter and a half. Then foot- and handholds appeared near the top, and with a last desperate lunge he was over the edge and hugging the shining metal post that cradled the Glass Helm.

Leland trembled, shook. His legs and arms cramped and his eyes stared vacantly at the Agatsu's ring. The rope and assorted climbing paraphernalia draped over the sharp edge and dangled, like his feet, over the abyss. At first he was just drained, empty of all feeling. Even the cramping in his arms and legs seemed remote, like they belonged to someone else. He concentrated on just getting air into heaving lungs.

*I won't spoil this minute by throwing up!*

Then, along with biting pain and nausea, the exhilaration flooded into his body.

*Not bloody bad for the bookworm!* He struggled to sit, still hugging the ten-centimeter-thick post where it sprang from the rock. This movement brought his head level with the Glass Helm.

*I am looking at a legend,* Leland thought, awestruck. *By the Founders, it's beautiful!*

The gleaming metal post terminated in a stylistic model of a human head, full scale, with mere suggestions of facial features represented by smooth depressions and curves. With crystalline grace the Glass Helm crowned the metal head, a brilliant cascade of reflected moonlight and odd patterns buried deep within the transparent matrix.

*When was the last time a human looked at this? Did the Founders put it here with their flying cars? Does the legend come from them?*

Leland reached out and gently ran a fingertip over the surface. *Smooth, so very smooth.* "*What!*"

Blood from his torn finger had seeped onto the glass. Almost immediately, the Helm began to change. Minute flashes of phosphorescence seemed to run along the patterns (wires?) buried deep in the glass. From cold immobility to warm, barely perceptible pulsing, the Helm seemed to come to life. There was a visible movement as the part of the Helm that gripped the metal head's temples spread a full centimeter. Leland touched the Helm again, and it moved freely, no longer bound to the post. He shrank back from the Helm as far as he could without actually going over the edge or releasing his grip on the post.

*How many have made this climb and stopped at this point?* He squeezed his free hand into a fist and winced at the pain this caused. *Father be damned, fear be damned, and Founders be damned! Not me!*

He stood (because it seemed right) and lifted the Helm from its stand. Then leaning firmly against the post to steady himself, he lowered the Glass Helm onto his head.

Guide Dulan de Laal, Steward of Laal, Sentinel of the Eastern Border, and Principal of the Council of Noramland, was relatively content. The summer's harvest had provided a large trading surplus above and beyond satisfying the categories, and the sugar in this year's grapes was very high, meaning good wine by spring—even better for the trading. The Festival was winding down for the night, though it had two more days to go, and he and Guide Malcom de Toshiko, Steward of Pree, were listening to the town symphony play a requiem for the day.

"A good festival, Dulan. You treat me like this every time I visit and you'll have a permanent house guest." He looked sideways at Guide Dulan, smiling.

Dulan snorted and shook the huge mane of silver hair that closely framed his face. "Do it, dammit. What keeps you in that drafty hall of yours? Kevin is holding it quite well."

Malcom sighed. "And when I'm there, we fight tooth and nail. Don't think I'm not tempted. It's been two years since Mary died and I still can't walk into any room in the place without expecting her to be there."

Dulan nodded at his old friend's confession. "I know. It's the same for me with Lil, and she's been gone these eleven years. It's almost heartbreaking to look at Lillian and see her mother's eyes looking back at me." He lifted a pitcher of ale from the table beside him and freshened both their tankards with a muttered *grain.* "Perhaps we should remarry?"

"Ha! And inflict our ghosts on innocent women? Better to take a harmless tumble when the need becomes too great. Like your sons, eh?" He pointed to the edge of the green where Dexter, Dulan's second oldest son, was walking into the dark with a town girl.

Dulan frowned, then smiled slowly. "I saw Dillan and Anthony vanish likewise, earlier. They better be careful . . . if the wrong lover got hold of them. Well, even Cotswold's fingers reach this far."

Malcolm frowned. "Surely you've trained them against that?"

"Oh, of course. Just an old man's fears."

"And even little Leland, eh?" said Malcom, sipping from his tankard.

"Doubt it. He's old enough—fifteen? No, by the Founders, sixteen, and seventeen next month. Where does the time go? But Leland is a strange one—more likely in the library wasting candles."

"Dulan!"

"All right. Not wasting. And I wish his brothers had half the time for the scholarship. But there's the other side, too. He's timid—doesn't get out enough. Well, he did work in the fields this harvest—like a dog. He does pursue whatever interests him with a passion. But he never stands up for himself."

"Oh? Is he beaten regularly?"

"No, he backs away when there's any sort of confrontation."

Malcom smiled. "Maybe he knows more about fighting than you think."

Dulan snorted. "I doubt it. Anyway, it makes him look weak, and that only makes him a more likely target." He stretched his arms and looked up at Agatsu's ring, then looked carefully around for listeners. "My agents in Cotswold are nervous. The people are hungry and the Customs are being twisted. Siegfried is directing their attention this way. This may lead to a confrontation that Leland cannot avoid."

"When?"

"Well, next harvest at the earliest. Even as poor a farmer as Siegfried Montrose was able to harvest enough this season for the coming winter, though he's hardly filled the categories. The rains have never been better. But next year will be much dryer, and Cotswold doesn't have the watershed we do. They'll probably strike after we've done the work of getting in the harvest."

"Risky, that. Then you're stocked for a siege and they won't have supplies to outlast you." Malcom looked thoughtful. "Laal Station has never been taken, either by storm or by siege."

"True—but how long has it been since someone tried? Eighty years. Our population has doubled since then—they won't all fit in the Station now. Even half would cause problems with *sanitation.*" Both men touched their foreheads automatically.

"Enlarge the Station?"

"Well, we could go *into* the mountain, I suppose. But the manpower . . ." He shook his head. "Doing it by next autumn would require skipping next year's harvest."

Malcom frowned. "Then what will you do?"

Dulan tapped the gray, curly hair that covered his temples. "I've a few ideas," he said with a surprisingly boyish grin. "I've a few ideas."

The music changed to a waltz and several of the crowd came forward to dance. Malcom stood and asked Guide Bridgett onto the "floor." After entrusting Lillian to Dulan's care, she accepted.

Little Lillian crawled up in her father's lap and promptly fell asleep. Dulan cradled her and smiled, stroking her hair and watching the swirling dancers on the grass. He was as surprised as any when the music died discordantly, one instrument at a time, ending with a lonely flute note that hung in the air leaving a phrase achingly incomplete.

Dulan stood and carefully placed the still-sleeping Lillian on his chair. Then he looked over the heads of the crowd, trying to determine the cause of the interruption.

There must have been fifteen hundred people in the clearing, fully ten percent of Laal's population. The muted roar of that many people talking, wondering aloud, and supposing filled the air. Then Dulan heard a shout from the forest side of the clearing, near where the musicians sat, and he saw the crowd at that edge split and spread apart, forming a path leading in the direction of his seat. The steward frowned and stood on tiptoe, but he couldn't see what the crowd made way for. And he was damned if he'd clamber onto a chair like a child to see, so he waited stoically for whatever was coming.

Moments later, the crowd in front of the high seat parted. At first he didn't recognize the figure that walked toward him. The great bonfire had died to embers so torches and ringlight were all that lit the festival field. The steward could see that the man was small and walked stiffly, almost unnaturally. Then the figure stepped nearer one of the torches and Dulan caught a glimpse of a blood-streaked shirt and a coiled rope draped awkwardly across one shoulder. Another step closer to the torch and the figure's head seemed to catch fire as the gleaming headgear he wore caught the torchlight and threw it at Dulan.

He staggered as if hit. *The Helm!* His hands went automatically to his own temples, to the crescents hidden beneath his hair. Then, and only then, did he recognize his youngest son, standing rigidly before him, swaying slightly, staring fixedly at Dulan with a face empty of expression.

Dulan stepped forward. "What have you done?" He shouted the question with anguish in his voice. Those nearby stared in shock, for Guide Dulan had last been heard to raise his voice the day his wife had died. His calm was legendary.

Leland blinked, then slowly shook his head as if befuddled. Slowly, clumsily, he raised his arms and lifted the Glass Helm from his head. As he did, a tremor passed through his body and he collapsed full length across the trampled grass. The Glass Helm bounced once on the ground and rolled to a stop at his father's feet.

Dulan's question went unanswered.

For three days Leland lay unconscious in the confines of his room, attended always by a one of the Laals or Guide Malcom. The servants' gossip was full of the tale of Leland's climb. By the first evening, the exact extent of Leland's injuries was known by the youngest kitchener, from his torn and bloody fingers to the half-circle burns on his temples, where the Glass Helm had marked him.

"I've never seen the guide look like this. I don't think he's slept in two days—he just sits in his study and stares out at the mountains," Captain Koss told Bartholomew, the kitchener manager. "Even at the battle of Atten Falls, with Noramland's army in pieces and the Rootless pouring across the river, he exuded confidence. You'd have thought it was a picnic. It scares me to see him like this."

Bartholomew smiled at the thought of Captain Koss scared of anything but said, "As one ages, cares aren't handled as well."

From Dulan's study window, the Needle was a finger pointed at the sky rising from behind a green hill. He stared unseeingly at it and brooded.

*Damn it all to hell,* he thought. *Two decades of charging wasted! Why, oh why, Leland? Dillan was going to be ready soon, I could feel it. But not now, not for twenty more years, if the house survives that long. If* civilization *lasts that long!*

*Leland, oh, Leland. You were a treasure to me. A child of love without worry of utility or station. You were there for me to treasure as a child and a son—not a weapon I must hone, a tool I must shape.*

Dulan grieved. He grieved for himself. He grieved for Dillan, his eldest. He grieved for Lil, his late wife. But most of all, he grieved for Leland.

*I hope you can survive the forging!*

There was also much speculation as to the nature of the Glass Helm. Guide Dulan himself placed it on a helmet stand beside Leland's bed, where it sat lifeless, lusterless, and cloudy. He bound it in place with wire and sealed it with wax and his signet.

"Undoubtedly magic," Sven the junior kitchener assured his peers. "How else would the weakling have made it up the Needle if not assisted by sorcery?"

"Fah! He's strange, but he's no weakling. He worked the full harvest in the fields, and it was no sham. I saw him sweat. You have magic on the brain."

"Sure I do. That's why he lies in a trance."

"Listen, twit. If I'd climbed the Needle, though I doubt I could, I might sleep for three days myself!"

Sven laughed harshly. "And the exertion would leave the demon brands on your temples, too?"

There was no answer to that.

On the fourth day, the patient opened his eyes and stared blankly at Guide Malcom. "Uncle Malcom?" he croaked, intelligence returning to his eyes.

"Yes, Leland. Here, drink some of this."

Leland tasted it and made a face, then he saw the Helm on the table beside him. His eyes widened. "It wasn't a dream, was it?"

"No," said Malcom, "definitely not."

A haunted look came to Leland's eyes. "It put something in my head." He touched his hair gingerly.

"What sort of something?" Malcom asked.

The haunted look became one of frustration and pain. "I don't know! I can feel it in there, but it's all dark. I can't get a *hold* of it."

"Don't try. Don't let it bother you. Don't even try to think. Drink."

After the boy sipped half of the offered medicine, Malcom went to the door and sent a servant for the steward. Scant seconds passed before he arrived.

"So you're going to live, eh?" Dulan's first words as he came into the room were spoken forcefully, without a hint of kindness. Leland's tentative smile died before it touched his lips and his face froze to stony immobility.

Dulan went on. "You have a month to recover your health. One month—no more. And then, my fine climber of rock, you're going to wish you'd never been higher than your head. When I'm done with you, you'll probably wish you'd never been born!"

# TWO

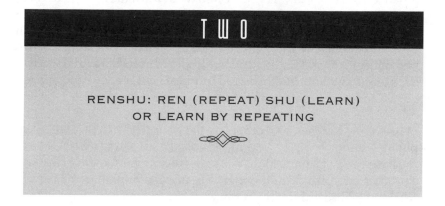

## RENSHU: REN (REPEAT) SHU (LEARN) OR LEARN BY REPEATING

Leland shoveled snow. He shoveled great quantities of snow. And ice. And occasionally refuse from the kitchen. Twelve hours a day, seven days a week. Oh, well. Last month it had been manure, as his father had him handle the output of every domesticated animal in Laal Station. At least snow didn't *stink.*

He was clearing the walkway on the east wall today, trying to ease his shovel loads of snow over the outer wall without the stiff wind flinging it back in his face. Ice rimmed the hood of his coat and coated the outside of his scarf where it passed across his mouth. But though the wind and minute flying crystals stung his exposed skin, he was warm enough in his exertion.

As always, his mind worked, prodding and prying at the dark and confusing mass of half-seen knowledge locked in the back of his mind. Sometimes, during the six hours he was allowed to sleep, he dreamed of amazing things—steel towers large as the Needle rising into the sky on glowing pillars of blue light. And once he'd seen the ring as if they circled another planet—not the one he was on.

Pain exploded from his shoulder and he found himself falling forward into the snow. *Damn, damn, damn. Will I never learn?* He rolled heavily to the side and the bamboo cane fell again to rap painfully across his shins. Leland scrambled back and stood facing his assailant. "Hello, Dexter. So it's your turn today, eh?"

Leland's brother stood rigidly in the snow, leaning on the bamboo cane thoughtfully. He seemed about to say something, but Leland held up his hand. "No. Don't say anything—you know you're not supposed to. And don't shuffle your feet to try to warn me like you did last time. That only makes me careless and gets me beaten twice as hard when Anthony has the cane. *He* enjoys it."

Dexter pulled his hood closer about his head and tucked the bamboo under his arm. Then, with a curt nod, he turned away and walked back toward warmth and light and brothers he was allowed to talk to.

Leland stared blankly after him and rubbed his shoulder.

Dexter hung his coat with others by the door to the Great Hall, then put the bamboo behind it, leaning against the stone wall. As he entered the large room, he noticed that he kept rubbing his hands against his shirt as if trying to clean them off. He stopped himself, clenched his fists, and looked around the room.

Anthony and Dillan were standing before the fire, talking quietly. Lillian and Guide Bridgett were seated on lounges beneath a double-paned window, where the light was strongest, playing cards. A few tradesmen were meeting in a corner, a practice encouraged by Guide Dulan.

*Father has an inordinate interest in successful trade,* Dexter thought. *Not like the guardianship in Noramland proper who'd as soon spit on a tradesman as talk to him.* He smiled in their direction and nodded. They waved briefly and continued their bargaining. *The attitude pays off. They've swarmed to Laal from Noramland since Arthur de Noram took the high seat. His tax on craftsmen was the last straw.* Dexter shook his head in admiration. The Laal treasury was fuller than it had been for years, and just from a one-in-twenty tax across the board—no favorites. In Noramland and Cotswold, taxes reached eight in twenty for richer craftsman and the settled landowners. And their treasuries were getting smaller. There was no doubt about it, Guide Dulan had a good reason for his every action.

*So why the hell is he making us treat Leland this way?*

He walked over to Anthony and Dillan and stamped his feet by the fire. Snow fell from his boots and began melting on the hearth. Dillan looked sideways at him, his eyebrows raised in question.

"Number-one attack of the day accomplished." He paused. "Five more to go."

Dillan's eyes widened. "*Six in all?* That's double the number he's been requiring!"

"Yes, he changed it this morning," Dexter said, but he was looking at Anthony. He didn't like the half smile on Anthony's face. He spat in fireplace. "So, Anthony, it's true—you do enjoy it."

Anthony looked startled. "Enjoy it?" He stared into the fire, then lifted his eyes challengingly back up to Dexter's. "In a perverse fashion, I suppose I do, but mostly because he makes me so angry."

"Father?" asked Dillan.

"No, Leland! I started out light enough, but he just took it—didn't fight back, didn't whimper, didn't cry out. So I figured I must be doing it too lightly. So I started hitting him harder, more often at each attack. He reacts the same way. Nothing, no matter how hard I hit him. Oh, he scrambles quick enough to get away, and I've seen him limp out some mornings, barely able to move after I've beaten him, but still no reaction to the pain. He just stares at me with those green eyes of his and doesn't make a sound.

"It's a test of will, and I'm going to win it."

Dillan's eyes met Dexter's and, as one, they shook their heads.

In early spring Leland worked in the new fields, walking the irrigation waterwheels, moving rocks to build terrace walls.

At least this was better than working in snow that muffled footsteps. Now he could hear them coming with the cane and dodge. On the other hand, he was wearing less clothing and the blows that did land hurt more.

There were nights without sleep, as bruised muscles wracked him with pain. Meals lost every morning as the anxiety of facing another day of beatings sent him vomiting to the privies. Meals not touched from exhaustion, pain, or nausea. Leland grew thin and haggard. His skin became sallow, hollows appeared under his eyes, and lines appeared at the corners of his mouth—lines that shouldn't have been on a seventeen-year-old's mouth.

For a time he became a shambling scarecrow of a human, stumbling to the tasks assigned him and cringing inwardly every time the cane fell, always from an unexpected quarter.

Then he changed. One evening he went from hopelessness to curiosity. The cause of his downfall in some small way became his salvation.

First, he asked, *Can I avoid the blows?*

So he tried, and fewer blows landed.

Then he asked, *Should I avoid the blows?*

He couldn't think of a reason not to avoid them, and several reasons he should.

Even fewer blows landed.

His appetite improved and, though he didn't gain much weight, he became quicker, more agile.

Sometimes, to make Anthony mad, he'd stand perfectly still until the last moment—then sidestep the blow and dance away. Invariably this would result in more pain later, but he gained a certain grim satisfaction from it.

At night he would read in the kitchen while he ate. To the rest of the family and most of the servants, he was a pariah. Bartholomew was the only one allowed to talk to him, both because he saw to Leland's feeding and because he passed on Guide Dulan's latest whims of labor.

One night Bartholomew pushed his glasses down his nose and peered over them at Leland's small table. They were alone in the corner of the huge main kitchen, where Bartholomew had his desk and kept track of the enormous quantities of food necessary to feed his charges. "Tell me, young Leland. What are you thinking about your father?"

Leland stared at him. Bartholomew would tell all the gossip that passed in the castle but had always shied away from discussing his father's motives. He placed a marker in the text he was reading, *Practical Medicine,* and carefully set it to the side.

"I don't know what to think about him. The man won't even talk to me. How can I think anything?"

"Well, what do you feel?"

Leland laughed, but it was a harsh sound, verging on bitterness. "Don't ask. Don't ask. The man has loved me all my life—everything a father should be. Then he turns on me. But I did something he had expressly forbidden. No matter what I feel about the last six months, I should remember the first seventeen years."

Bartholomew leaned back. "You must hate him."

Leland put his face in his hands and said miserably, "I don't *know!*"

He didn't see Bartholomew's smile of satisfaction.

* * *

In late spring, High Steward Arthur de Noram, ruler of greater Noramland, visited Laal en route to Cotswold. He was traveling there for peace talks with High Steward Siegfried Montrose, who had been raiding Laal's borders and those of the other Noramland stewardships. It was hoped that Arthur could win an end to hostilities on Noramland's southern border so he could concentrate on his annual war with Nullarbor, to the east.

Leland wouldn't have noticed the visit except Bartholomew was too busy to talk to him. The high steward traveled with an entourage of seventy-five. Leland found himself ignored by his father and actually had time on his hands. So one morning he put a chair in the back of the library, in a corner hidden by the shelves, and read beneath a sunny window.

Most of the books in the library predated the Founding. They were made of near-indestructible materials—pages thin as gossamer yet untearable, waterproof, fade-proof. Leland had grown up in this room and had probably read over half the twelve hundred volumes on the shelves. Many of the books, though, were useless, needing knowledge from other books not in this library to understand them. *Like learning to run when one has never been shown how to walk.*

Leland occasionally dreamed of going to the Great Library of Noramland and the tiny university starting there. *Only two hundred kilometers. Why not?* He laughed bitterly to himself.

Someone entered the library and Leland listened carefully, but the footsteps weren't his father's or any of his brothers', so he slumped back in the chair and propped his feet back on the window ledge. By the Customs, all of Laal was allowed access to the library. Proving literacy was an important part of the Rites of Thirteen, when boys and girls were declared adults. And stealing a library book was punishable by shunning or exile.

Leland was lost in his book, deep in a complex algebra word problem, when the same footsteps walked up behind him. He sat up with a guilty start and found himself staring at a young woman he'd never seen before.

"Excuse me," she asked. "Do you work here?"

Leland continued to stare. She was amber-eyed with black hair and couldn't have been much older than Leland. Her clothes were embroidered green, from bodice to slippers. She was not beautiful, her features being slightly too small for her face, but there was something about her—perhaps her still, confident posture—that Leland found very attractive. He found his tongue. "I suppose you could say that. I work everywhere else." He stood slowly and replaced the book in its shelf. "How may I help you?"

"I was looking for books on medicine." Leland stared, silent. She added, "As we travel to all the stewardships, I've been cataloging their libraries. When there's a book on medicine we haven't seen before, we have a copy scribed and send it to the university—it's a hobby of mine."

"Then you're with the Steward de Noram's party—it must be nice to travel." He turned and led her up the aisle. "These three shelves are all we have," he indicated. "But I wonder, have you been considering the biology and biochemistry texts? Ultimately, they are going to teach us more about medicine than these practical primers."

She raised her eyebrows and Leland thought about how he looked—the sun-browned skin from working in the fields. His rough clothing. She probably thought him one of the servants.

"At one time I hoped to do that, but no one can follow the trains of knowledge required to understand those texts."

Leland shook his fingers at the ceiling. "That's because the books are spread from Cotswold to Kzi Lung and nobody has ever taken the effort to consolidate them, as you are doing with these medical works." He stepped back. "Excuse me. It's long been a dream of mine to be able to walk into a library that was complete—not just a collection of fragments as this one is. Forgive me for getting excited."

She smiled at him suddenly, a burst of sunlight in the shadowy room. He wondered, if he were to turn suddenly, would he see his shadow cast on the wall. She spoke. "It's a good dream." Almost under her breath she added, "I share it."

For the first time in months Leland smiled naturally with no trace of irony or self-derision. It felt strange on his face.

Two hours later found them still talking, comparing books, pointing out the obvious and less obvious gaps in the collection. Leland opened the chest beneath the window seat and brought out the cheese and fruit Bartholomew had provided for his lunch.

She blinked. "What a clever chest—I thought it was part of the wall.

Leland winked. "You are now privy to the best hide-and-seek place in the Station. This was my favorite hiding place as a child."

They shared afternoon rites on the closed lid.

At one point he found her looking at him oddly. "Have I been eating with my mouth open again?"

"Oh, no. Nothing like that. I just realized I don't know who you are—and you don't know who I am, do you?"

Firmly Leland said, "Of course I know who you are. You've spent half the afternoon telling me, just as surely as if I could read your mind."

She blushed and looked out the window. Leland grinned. After a moment she turned back and stared frankly at him. "And I suppose I know you, too. But it would be nice to have a label for what I know."

Leland stared down at his hands, at the calluses and the scars on his fingertips. Slowly he said, "Names are heavy labels—their baggage can weigh one down so."

She blinked uncertainly. "Well, first names then. Surely that couldn't hurt."

"I suppose not. They know me as Leland."

"And I am called Marilyn."

He smiled and she returned it.

Other footsteps entered the library and Leland froze. One of those sets belonged to Dillan, his oldest brother. An older female's voice called out, "Marilyn? Are you in here?"

Marilyn raised her voice, "In the back, Aunt Margaret."

A plump, matronly woman walked around the corner. "Ah, there you are, child. You've promised to go riding with your father and Guide Dulan. Can't keep them waiting." She saw Leland then and smiled. "Well, introduce us, child, or I'll tell your father on you."

Dillan stepped around the corner then and saw Leland. His face froze halfway between a frown and a smile. Then he spoke. "Allow me. Guide Margaret, this is my youngest brother, Leland de Laal, Warden of the Needle. Leland, this is the Guide Margaret de Jinith, the Steward de Noram's sister."

"Warden of the Needle?" asked Marilyn. "Is there a grant of stewardship around the spire?"

"A small one. My father bestowed it upon Leland after he climbed the Needle six months ago."

*He did?* Leland stared at Dillan.

Guide Margaret and Marilyn looked at Leland oddly. Leland looked oddly at Dillan.

"By the way, Leland. Anthony has been looking for you all day—

something about a piece of bamboo. I must tell him where you are."

Leland grinned. "Thank you." He bowed to the ladies and said to Marilyn, "Thank you, Guide Marilyn, for your time today. I've never enjoyed a conversation more." He tried to catch her eyes as he said it and succeeded for a timeless second. He thought, *For a moment there, you delivered me from hell.*

Marilyn dropped her eyes suddenly, slightly flustered. "Well, why stop talking now? Why not come riding with your father and mine?"

Behind her, Dillan began coughing, a sudden, explosive paroxysm.

Leland's face froze, and Marilyn sensed walls snapping into place within him. With careful lightness, he said, "Inescapable duties. I'm sorry . . . very sorry."

Marilyn frowned, then said, "As you must, Warden. Good-bye."

Leland bowed again and the ladies left, escorted by Dillan.

The room seemed suddenly dark.

Dillan walked quietly along behind Guide Margaret and Guide Marilyn, deep in thought. The sight of Leland actually *grinning* had surprised him a great deal. He was amazed at how quickly he'd gotten used to the lined, silent face of the last several months. For a moment there he'd seen Leland as he remembered him from a clumsy childhood of just a year ago. Not awkward though—just a piece of that good cheer he used to carry for everyone to see.

He suddenly remembered Anthony's boast at midwinter.

*Don't be too sure, Anthony. Don't be too sure.*

Guide Margaret was maintaining a three-way conversation in which she supplied all the parts.

"My, yet another handsome son of Laal? Where does your father get them? Oh, everyone knows how beautiful your mother was! What the high steward would give to have a son. Ah, but then that's life, isn't it, Guide Dillan? Of course it is. Well, Marilyn, don't keep back what you and Warden Leland discussed—how long were you with him, by the way? Surely just a moment—after all, you said you were going up to the library right after midday rights . . . my goodness, that was two and a half hours ago! I suppose he just showed up right before we did, eh, Marilyn?"

Marilyn nodded distractedly. "I suppose. It seemed we were together for just moments."

Guide Margaret went on chattering away.

Marilyn thought, *We've been here a week. Why didn't I meet War-*

*den Leland at meals in the Great Hall? Is he some kind of recluse? Maybe he's in disgrace.* She shivered involuntarily as she remembered the depth of his green eyes and the trace of something dark in them when Dillan and Guide Margaret had shown up. Something almost tragic.

*I wonder if I'll see him before we leave.*

Arthur de Noram, High Steward of Greater Noramland, Protector of the Customs, and Guardian of the Sacred Plain, was a small man, favoring his mother rather than his father, the famous William.

"Your health, sir," said Dulan.

They were standing in one of the four small courtyard gardens that were tucked high up in the Laal Station—on top of the basaltic outcropping that formed the Station's backbone and north side.

Steward de Noram sipped the wine and sighed. "When will we see this wine in Noram, Dulan? It's incredible."

Dulan smiled slightly. "I'm glad you like it—we made it from the very last grapes of the harvest, the ones that froze on the vine. I've heard tell of a similar wine that was made on old Earth. They called it *Eiswein*, a word from a language called German."

Arthur frowned, as he did at all mentions of old Earth. He had a sneaking suspicion that all that stuff was nonsense, but, as Guardian of the Sacred Plain, the landing place of the Founders, he paid overt respect to the legends. He also resented being lectured to.

Guide Dulan went on. "I'll prepare several cases for you to pick up on your way back to Noram City."

Arthur smiled. "That would be very generous of you, Dulan."

Dulan shrugged. "Your due."

"Nonsense, Dulan. You double-tithed the last three quarters. We are in debt to you." *Your generosity makes me ill*, Arthur thought furiously, hiding an incipient frown by taking another sip of the wine. *You lure away my craftsman with lower taxes and have the gall to give me back a portion of the wealth. You and your damn generosity have been a boil to me since that time on the plain. Why the hell couldn't you have let me die? I would have been sung about for a thousand years, instead of sneered at for blowing the battle of Atten Falls, killing three hundred of my own troops, and then being rescued by the damn upstart house of Laal. My father William stood there and looked at me like I was a worm after that, and you had the gall to intercede for me.* Arthur smiled sweetly. "I don't know what the Noramland would do without citizens like you."

Dulan shrugged. "It's the duty of the better-off stewardships to make up for the poorer ones. Surely I wasn't the only one to double?"

Arthur seethed beneath his smile. "Of course, you probably know that Guide Malcom did." *Your crony!* "A few of the other houses tithed and a half."

Dulan nodded and raised his glass. "Prosperity to the stewardship and luck on your mission to Cotswold."

They drank deeply.

"I flatter myself that I can work something out with High Steward Montrose," Arthur said. "These border affairs are draining all of us. We need to stop them so we can go after the real enemy—Nullarbor."

"It's a good sign that Montrose has offered to treat," said Dulan. "But watch him. I've know him for over thirty years and he's crafty, sly, and not above some deception."

Arthur frowned openly. "Teach your mother to make baskets. I'm sure I'm up to it."

"My apologies, sir—I didn't mean to patronize. Forgive me if I offended."

Arthur turned his smile back on. "Of course, of course. I'm a cranky bastard, aren't I? Don't worry, Dulan. Between the two of us, we'll handle Siegfried of Cotswold." *And Siegfried and I will handle you!*

Ricard de Laal, Captain of the Laal Mounted Pikes, waited in the shade of the Floating Stone, the great gateway of Laal Station. Ricard was the only child of Guide Dulan's late brother, dead in a Nullarbor/Noramland skirmish when Ricard was three weeks old.

Dulan, the second son of Lemmuel de Laal, had been twenty-five then, with Dillan a laughing two-year-old and Dexter a slight swelling in his mother's figure. *Bide your time, child,* Ricard's mother would whisper. *And one day you'll be a force in the world.* He frowned at the memory.

Once more he walked down the squad of soldiers he'd picked for today's escort. If it had been his uncle alone, there would have been a small unit of eight, either his Mounted or Captain Koss's Falcons. But today they rode with the High Steward of Noramland, and that meant a larger honor guard. He paused before one of the men and said pleasantly, "Slouch like that when Guide Dulan walks into the courtyard and I'll kick your ass all the way to the Black. Your tongue and eyes I'll leave here for the crows."

The soldier, a young boy of seventeen, jerked erect, his face going white. There were other minor alterations down the line as the more nervous straightened by their mounts. Captain de Laal was at his worst when he smiled like that. When he shouted you could end up with extra duty, personal fines, cuts in pay. When he smiled you ended up with bruises and broken bones.

Ricard turned and looked at the Floating Stone. It was a single piece of granite carved in the shape of a half cylinder. It stood four meters high, its diameter was five meters, and it weighed thirty-seven metric tons. The half cylinder revolved around a vertical axis on a pivot of iron that rose from the stone below and another iron beam that went into the rock above. The gate opening was a full cylinder of the same dimensions. When two men pushed on one side of the half cylinder, it rotated freely around the pivot, either filling the gate or half filling it, as now, leaving a two-and-half-meter-wide doorway, four meters, high.

But, if the gatekeeper stationed below were to throw the lever, a lock would open in the stone causing the waters of the underground reservoir that forced the iron pivot up to drain. The floating gate would drop a hand's breadth, coming to rest in locking grooves, and no force on Agatsu could rotate it open or closed against that friction.

There was a noise from the passage to the stable yard. Ricard pivoted on his toes and watched Guide Dulan and High Steward de Noram emerge from the shadows into the light. Marilyn and Dillan followed them with grooms and horses last.

"Present!"

The twenty men bowed at the waist, their helms flashing in the sun. Arthur de Noram ignored them while Guide Dulan nodded gravely and looked down the line. The men were dressed identically, as all of Ricard's Mounted Troop were, in dark-green pants and blouses, black leather boots, and scale vests. *Not like Koss's Falcons,* thought Dulan. *They're a motley bunch if ever there was one. But I'd not pitch two of the Mounted against one Falcon. One could lose an awful lot of Mounted that way.* "The men look good today, Ricard."

"Thank you, Uncle." Ricard turned his head and barked, "Squad, at ease." The men straightened. "What's your pleasure today? Down by the river or up to the hills?"

Guide Dulan glanced over at Arthur de Noram. "Sir?"

Arthur shrugged. "Whatever."

Dulan turned to the Guide Marilyn. "Was there anything you wanted to see, gentle lady?"

Marilyn smiled. "Why, yes, there is. Could we ride out to the Needle?"

Guide Dulan's mouth tightened briefly, then he smiled. "Of course—wherever you wish. Whatever you wish."

"You talk like a courtier, Guide Dulan." She laughed. "All agreement while the price is low enough."

Guide Dulan smiled. "No, truly. If it's within my power and conscience's dictates, I'll do anything for Noramland's second fairest flower."

"Second fairest! You cad."

Dulan laughed. "Your older sister will rule Noramland one day. Prudence is called for."

Marilyn shrugged. "It's more than prudence. Zanna's got our mother's face. You're forgiven. But you'll really give me what I ask?"

He nodded.

"You'll regret it, then," she said.

"Try me," he said, mounting. The rest followed his example, the soldiers at Ricard's command.

"My choice of dinner partner tonight."

Guide Dulan laughed. "Oh, ho! One of Laal's own has caught your eye, has he? Who is it, someone from the town? If you thought I'd be upset at having one of the settled at my table, you've not been observant. I host the cadre often."

Marilyn shook her head. "No, Guide. You're famous for your treatment of the people. And wise in that, for they're your greatest resource."

Guide Dulan nodded, suddenly serious. "Wise as well as fair."

Arthur, only half following the conversation until now, suddenly frowned and looked at Marilyn. *Was that an implied criticism, daughter?*

Marilyn went on. "No, the person I had in mind is of the guardianship. One of your sons."

Guide Dulan was surprised again. "You do us much honor. Any of my sons would be delighted."

She bowed from her saddle. "I was wrong, then. Your words aren't just empty promises. You are too kind to me."

Guide Dulan smiled, her obvious delight too genuine to ignore. He nodded and headed his horse out the gate. Ricard immediately sent five riders out to ride point down the curving path down the mountain face. "And don't kick up the dust in their faces," he muttered at they went by.

Guide Dulan and Marilyn rode through the gate then, knees touching to squeeze their horses through. Guide Dulan thought, *Her father won't like this much.* Turning, he asked her, "Well, which one is it? Dexter or Anthony?" As she remained silent, he said, "Surely you're not interested in Dillan here, are you? He's fifteen years older than you."

They emerged into the sunlight and started down the road to the town. He looked at her expectantly.

"Oh, look," she said. "It's so clear out I could just reach out and touch the Needle. How far is it?"

Guide Dulan reined his horse to a stop, a frown beginning to gather his hairy brows together. "Child, I believe you're toying with me! I've given you my word; which one is it to be?"

She sighed, then turned to face him squarely.

"Leland," she said.

# THREE

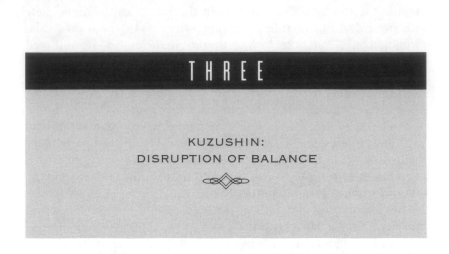

## KUZUSHIN: DISRUPTION OF BALANCE

Dillan found Anthony pacing furiously up and down the Great Hall, the shattered end of a piece of bamboo sticking out of his wildly waving fist. "Look at it!" he shouted when he saw Dillan. "Look at it! He stood by the wall and ducked. It shattered on the corner. By the Founders he makes me mad!"

"Where is he now?" Dillan asked, fighting hard to suppress a smile. He had learned from his father that laughing at frustrated people seldom endeared you to them.

"He was heading for the baths. At least he was in that hallway. As soon as Martin gets back with my new bamboo, I'm going to go down and smash his testicles!"

Martin was the household manager of Laal Station, a solemn man who kept the household functioning smoothly despite all external and internal disasters.

"You should not have told Martin to get you a new stick. With the banquet tonight he has better things to do with his time. Are you so lazy that you can't ride down the hill to get a stick?"

Anthony's eyes got darker, and he started to shout something into Dillan's face, but a calm voice from the door stopped him.

"Of course I had a groom go for the stick, Guide Dillan. I'm sure Anthony didn't expect me to go myself."

Both Anthony and Dillan turned to see Martin standing in the door, a new length of green bamboo held loosely in his hand. Behind him stood a waiter with goblets and a pitcher on a tray. "I took the liberty of bringing ice tea. The afternoon is warm." He poured a glass for Dillan while Anthony took the bamboo and shattered the air with vicious, two-handed swings.

"Good," Anthony said shortly, accepting the waiting glass. "Thank you, Martin. I'm sorry if I caused any trouble. I was so angry, I forgot about the banquet." He avoided Dillan's eyes when he said this.

Dillan allowed himself a small smile and winked at Martin. "Delicious, Martin," he said, draining the glass. Then he turned back to Anthony. "Father relieves you of *the duty* until the high steward's party leaves. Martin, Leland will be attending the banquet tonight. Please inform Bartholomew and make the necessary arrangements."

Anthony stared at Dillan, shocked.

Martin took it frozen faced as always. "Yes, Guide. And will Leland be at the main table?"

"No, like all my brothers, he will head his own table. The Gentle Guide Marilyn de Noram will be his partner." He set the goblet down on the tray and thanked the waiter. "Peter, isn't it? The glassmaker's son?"

The boy nodded. "Y-yes, Guide," he stammered.

"Keep up the good work. After the high steward is gone, we can drop all these airs again and get back to life." Dillan walked to the door. "Oh, by the way, Martin, Leland will need something suitable to wear. Any of my clothes that can be made to fit are at his disposal."

Martin nodded. "I'll work something out."

"Thank you." He left.

Anthony stared after him for a long time.

Leland floated on his back, content with the world. *Oh, the anger on Anthony's face!* He watched the lamplight reflect off the water and onto the ceiling above. This was the main pool of the men's baths, cold and clear as the underground river that fed and drained it. It felt good after soaking in the fire-stoked hot water. He lifted his head and settled his feet to the bottom of the pool.

He listened for a moment, then lay back again, hearing only the flickering echoes of rushing water. The memory of Marilyn sitting on the windowsill of the library came back to him again, bright as the sunlight that had surrounded her. *In the name of the Founders, she's something. I wonder if I'll see her again.* He sighed and drifted, reliving the afternoon. He closed his eyes and shook his head sadly. *Probably not. Dillan will tell Father and I'll have more work and more beatings in the blink of an eye.*

He opened his eyes and gasped. Dillan stood on the edge of the pool looking down at him. He was about to kick violently to the other side of the pool when he noticed that Dillan's hands were empty. He stood and let the water drain out of his ears.

"Careless, Leland."

Leland nodded gravely in agreement, furious with himself.

"After your bath, please go see Bartholomew—he has some instructions for you."

Leland shrugged. "I knew it was too good to last. So what is it this time? Back to shoveling manure? Or more stump pulling? I knew that when you saw me in the library, word would get back to father."

Dillan stared at Leland, the humor he held within not touching his face. "Oh, no, Leland. Not stump pulling, or wall building, or ice hauling," he said. "It's something far worse. Report to Bartholomew." He turned on his heel and walked out.

*Yes, word did get back to Father,* Dillan thought as he wound his way up the stairs. *But it wasn't from me—not initially.* He remembered his father's consternation earlier in the day when he'd reined aside to speak to Dillan as Guide Marilyn and the Steward de Noram had ridden ahead to view the Needle.

"Have you or your brothers been talking about Leland?" he had asked.

"No, Father. He met her in the library this afternoon. They were talking when Guide de Jinith and I entered. I can't say how long they were together, but it could have been as much as two hours."

Guide Dulan had been silent then, his face impassive, staring unseeingly at the Needle. Then: "She seems to have been at least amused by him. How were his feelings toward her?"

"From what I could see, unusually warm."

"Elaborate."

Dillan had been flustered. "They were laughing together. Leland's been like a rock, lately—cold, withdrawn. He's shown very little feeling in the last several months."

Guide Dulan had nodded. "Understandable, given the circumstances." Then he gave Dillan instructions regarding the banquet.

*Yes,* thought Dillan. *Our father shows even less than Leland. I wonder what's happening.*

Two servants passed Dillan on the stairway, their arms laden with towels for the baths. Dillan nodded as he passed.

Their voices echoed up the stair after he'd passed.

"I wonder what he was grinning about."

"Something they're going to do to Leland, no doubt."

Dillan laughed out loud. *No doubt.*

Bartholomew stood in the middle of the kitchen, a shouting rock in a sea of chaos. "Hurry with the salads, Sven, and if you drop one I'll chop you up for sausage. Robert, ready the waiters to collect the soup, but *not* before Guide Dulan pushes his bowl aside. Allan, more wood for the fire. Irma, we'll need to broach another cask of ale. Pay special attention to Dexter's table, that mob is always thirsty. After the salad, don't forget to take ale and small foods to the musicians. Also, leave them a pitcher of the chilled tea."

Irma poked her finger into his substantial belly as she walked by with a cask over one shoulder. "Why don't you go jump out a window? Everything's arranged, everything's being done. Margaret has the musicians' refreshments stored in the cabinet by their alcove."

Bartholomew pushed her hand away and roared with pretended rage. "Ha! Incompetents! Imbeciles! If I didn't keep on top of you, nothing would get done!"

Sven tossed a damp towel across the kitchen. Bartholomew ducked, sidestepped, grabbed a tankard of ale off a passing tray, and left to see how things were going in the great hall.

*The Founders deliver us from mistakes,* he thought, largely content with his help and the way things were going. Earlier that afternoon things had not gone so well when Martin had come to him with the changes.

"Is Guide Dulan trying to drive me mad?" he'd shouted to Martin. "He set the table arrangements a week ago. What are we to do?"

Martin had laughed. "You improbable bag of wind! You know what to do and you'll accomplish it in fifteen minutes—but only after an hour of complaint!" He handed Bartholomew a list. "Here, I've already rearranged the seating list so you have no real headache. Just adjust the waiters for the extra table and increase the service by one. Simple. The hardest thing you have to do is tell Leland that he's attending."

Leland had shown up just a half hour before the dinner, in the midst of banquet preparations. "Dillan says you have more work for me."

"Oh, that I do, my boy. Why should you sit and read when we're all working?"

Leland shrugged. "What do you need me to do?"

Bartholomew had wrinkled his nose in distaste. "It's dirty work, a job I'd not have my lowest kitchener do."

"Enough already! What is it?"

"Hold down a chair."

"What?"

"There's been a terrible rash of chairs flying off into space, so I need you to hold down a chair in the Great Hall. Tonight. Soon. So, by the Founders, go get dressed! The seamstress is waiting in your room to fit something on you!"

Leland had started to say something else, but Bartholomew had pointed at the door and roared, *"Now!"*

Leland had left quickly.

Bartholomew walked up the stairs and peeked in one of the balconies overlooking the hall. The reception line was barely half done, those who'd already extended their greetings milling about on the floor conversing or taking drinks and small foods from the circulating waiters. Bartholomew scanned the crowd for Leland but didn't see him. The brothers, however, were in evidence, each the center of attention of a small group of friends and would-be friends of both sexes.

The Guide Marilyn stood between her father and Guide Dulan, greeting the guests with practiced charm. He saw her acknowledge a compliment from Captain Koss, now at the head of the line with his wife and daughter.

Martin came up behind Bartholomew. "Are things going well in the kitchen?"

"Eat feces and die slowly," Bartholomew said mildly.

Martin laughed. "Ah, good. I wouldn't want anything to go wrong tonight, eh? Wouldn't help things with the high steward."

"No, may he trip down a stairwell. Where's Leland?"

"The seamstress modified one of Dillan's formal outfits to match the size of one of Leland's old suits. Stupid. His shoulders must be eighty millimeters broader than they were last summer. We had to get another of Dillan's outfits and shorten the length a touch. They were just finishing a few moments ago . . . ah, there he is now."

Bartholomew looked and saw Leland step up to the end of the line. The person in front of Leland glanced back over his shoulder, saw who was standing there, and stepped aside and waved Leland forward with a small bow. Leland shook his head, but the man insisted. Leland smiled and said something, then stepped up in line. The process repeated until Leland stood at the head of the line, bowing deeply to his father, Steward de Noram, and the Guide Marilyn.

"Ah, but to overhear that conversation, eh, Martin?"

Martin nodded. "Your waiter Peter is near. You'll tell me when you hear, won't you?"

Bartholomew smiled. "Perhaps, Martin. Perhaps."

Marilyn de Noram smiled at the latest notable and curtsied in response to his bow. *Where is Warden Leland?* She put away that thought, anxious to counter her father's barely civil hauteur. "Oh, what a stunning dress," she said to the next in line, a matronly woman who ran Laal's school system. "Was it made in Laal?"

"Yes, Gentle Guide. Rolf Toscin was the designer."

Marilyn nodded. "Ah, yes." She didn't say anything else. Toscin moved to Laal from Noram City to avoid the taxes, and his exodus had been considered a great loss. She hoped her father hadn't heard the name.

She turned to the next guest, but he stepped back, as had all the line before him, and Leland walked forward nodding his thanks for their courtesy. She took her father's arm suddenly, no longer sure of herself.

Leland bowed deeply. He held the bow for a full second, then straightened. His brother's modified clothes fit him surprisingly well. His shirt was black cotton with a stiff half collar accenting the almost whipcord muscles of his neck. Gray embroidery crossed the front in an asymmetrical pattern running from left to right. He wore a gray sash and black pants bloused into gray calf-high soft boots.

He looked first at his father, but Guide Dulan was already talking to the next guest.

"Father," said Marilyn. "This is Leland, Warden of the Needle, Guide Dulan's youngest son."

Steward de Noram nodded and smiled briefly. "Ah. Yes, I last saw you when you were seven, at your mother's funeral. Clearly, you've grown."

"I would hope so, Father!" Marilyn said. "I'll join you later, Leland, at our table."

Leland blinked. *Our table?* He nodded slowly. "Of course, Gentle Guide. At our table." He bowed again and left.

"So that's the young man who's caught your fancy, eh, girl." Steward Montrose watched Leland walking off. He especially noted the way nearly everyone in the room watched the young man circumspectly. He didn't see Marilyn blush in response to his question.

"He's a scholar, Father. He asks questions I didn't know existed."

"Oh, ho! You want to suck his mind out, eh? Like you do to those poor people at the university?"

Marilyn chuckled thinly. "Perhaps, Father. Perhaps."

Anthony stopped in midsentence to stare across the room, to where his younger brother stood by himself holding a glass awkwardly.

"You were saying, Guide Anthony?" asked Clarissa Koss, daughter of Captain Koss.

Anthony looked back with a start, a strange expression on his face. "Uh, I seem to have lost my train of thought." He glanced back at Leland. "Well, never mind, it was probably boring anyway."

Clarissa shook her head. "Nonsense. I'm sure I would have been fascinated. Try to remember."

With an effort, Anthony remembered what he'd been talking about and finished, but his mind was still on Leland. *What's happening here?* He didn't understand this reversal in his father's behavior. Of course, he hadn't understood the last reversal either, but things had been *consistent* for months, so Anthony had accepted the conditions as normal. *Is this a switch or a temporary halt?*

He noticed the reception line had finally finished and watched Guide Dulan and Steward de Noram move to the main table on the dais. He saw the Guide Marilyn take Leland's arm. Glancing back at Clarissa Koss, she saw her watching Leland and Marilyn, also. *In fact,* he noticed, *nearly everyone in the hall is watching them! Small wonder—it's the first time Leland's appeared at a public event in six months. Everyone around here must know how we treat him.*

Martin himself came out into the hall to lead Leland and Marilyn to their table. *Ah, I wonder if Father ordered that? Oh, well, he can't treat*

*Leland too badly without insulting Guide Marilyn.* Anthony turned back to Clarissa and offered her his arm. "Shall we, Clarissa?"

She smiled shyly and slipped her hand into place. For the first time that night, he really looked at her. Something stirred inside him. *The hell with Leland! He's dominated my thoughts enough!*

"I'm glad you came, Clarissa. It's been too long."

*Why is Martin honoring him?* Guide Dulan watched Martin holding first Marilyn's chair, then Leland's. *I didn't order that.* He didn't know whether to be pleased or upset.

*Bend her to your cause, boy. You'll need help if things go as badly as they could.*

Seated next to Guide Dulan, the Steward de Noram toyed with his mustache and smiled at his dinner partner, Carmen Cantle de Laal, Guide Dulan's sister-in-law, the widow of his late brother and Ricard's mother. She was an attractive women, looking at least fifteen years younger than her forty-seven years. Arthur was toying with the idea of taking her into his bed tonight.

She in turn was considering letting him. "And when do you leave for Cotswold, Sire?"

He shrugged. "It's not a tightly scheduled thing. I'll see how things go here first. It's my responsibility to personally inspect every aspect of my stewardship's domains, eh?" He let his gaze drop to the low-cut neck of her gown for an instant. "Every aspect."

She laughed. "Clearly, a man whose duty knows no bounds."

He smiled, liking her earthy reaction. Others at this naive little court had blushed and fled at similar statements. "What else would you expect of the high steward?"

"Nothing else. Nothing less."

Arthur looked over at his daughter, where she sat next to Leland at the head of one of the four floor tables. She was toying with her salad, not talking. Leland was also quiet, apparently listening to the conversation of others at their table. Arthur saw Marilyn glance at Leland for an instant, when Leland was nodding at something another had said. For a moment he saw something in her eyes that disturbed him a great deal.

*She's attracted to him.* He mulled over the possibilities and ramifications of that fact. *Not good,* he decided. He continued to watch them as the dinner progressed.

At one point, Leland seemed to ask Marilyn something. She lifted her eyes from the table and answered him. Leland's face drained of blood, and he stared suddenly up at the main table where his father was talking with the Guide de Jinith. Arthur glanced at Guide Dulan to see if he'd noticed but couldn't tell. Leland stared back at his own table and flushed, then said something to Marilyn that caused her mouth to drop open and eyes to flash angrily.

Neither of them said another word to each other the rest of the dinner.

At the end of the banquet, Arthur said, "As usual, a wonderful host, Dulan. Still, I shan't drain your resources with my party much longer. We leave tomorrow at noon."

Guide Dulan lifted his eyes in surprise. "As you will, Steward. I'd hoped we'd have the pleasure of your company a little longer."

"Of course I'd like to stay, but this Cotswold business should be concluded as quickly as possible." *Before your Leland finishes snaring my daughter. She's obviously half snared already. Why else did she react so strongly?*

"I'll arrange an escort to the border," said Guide Dulan.

With the high steward gone, Leland's work and the random attacks began again. Late spring was a bad time for Leland.

Since his brothers were having a hard time carrying out their assigned number of attacks, Guide Dulan detailed four of the Guard, Captain Koss's Falcons, to help. They would lay traps with exquisite care, letting one of their number drive Leland to where the others were waiting. Then they would surround him and drive him to the ground, the air alive with the sound of singing bamboo.

Leland became more haggard—also thinner, causing Bartholomew alarm. The boy also became more wary, more alert, and, slowly, much tougher.

The Helm's legacy was also troubling Leland that summer. Tantalizing bits of knowledge were slowly surfacing in his mind. Infuriatingly, the bits were not unlike the more esoteric books in the library. What in the hell were population density indices? What was antihydrogen? Without definitions, he was as confused as the time he tried to learn tensor calculus without a single introductory calculus book in the library.

Frustration piled on frustration, and he came closer and closer to running away from Laal, but always a voice seemed to tell him, *Endure, wait. Why let them succeed?*

He considered cutting a bamboo stick of his own and attacking in turn, but this seemed a failure of a different kind. By accident, one day, he discovered a way to fight back.

He was planting trees on the upper slopes—hauling compost to natural pockets in the stony ground, planting seedlings, and then building rock retaining walls to discourage erosion and trap water. The Falcons and Anthony fell on him as he was walking back through the trees below. Leland dropped his tools and tried to run, but they had moved into a rough circle around him. Desperately he feinted toward one side then dove between Anthony and one of the guards. Quick as a snake, the Falcon twisted his cane in midstrike and swung it toward Leland. Instead, the bamboo smacked solidly into the side of Anthony's head.

In the resulting confusion, Leland ran deep into the wood and hid, but Anthony's howl of pain rang cheerfully in his memory the rest of the day.

The next time the Falcons struck, Leland repeated his trick, getting one of the Falcons hit in the process. Again he was able to escape in the resulting turmoil. That evening, trying it again, he was beaten badly and crawled into bed that night with groans of pain.

But, as the days grew shorter, more and more he managed to turn his tormentors' blows on one another. One day, in a bout that would stick in his memory forever, he hurtled himself between Dillan's legs and heard *two* canes smash into his brother's legs. He turned to see the Falcons coming after him. They looked mad.

He grinned at them and thought, *Why not?* He ran back at them yelling at the top of his lungs. The first Falcon looked startled, then swung his cane at Leland's midsection. Leland dived forward, over the cane, and rolled under the next one. Then, for spite, he leapfrogged over Dillan, where his brother crouched holding his legs. With a whoop, he ran on.

"And now a blow struck Leland?"

"None, sir."

Dillan sat on a bench and pressed cold compresses against his shins. Guide Dulan stood at the study window and looked east, toward Cotswold. His voice was low but curiously tense. He swayed from foot to foot. "Can you walk?"

Dillan looked up. "Painfully."

"Fetch Dexter and Anthony to the hall. I will join you there after I've written some messages."

Dillan set the compresses to the side and stood slowly. He hobbled across the room. Before he reached the door, Guide Dulan added, "And get Leland, as well."

Dillan froze, still facing the door, silent. After a moment he said, "Yes, sir," and went on.

Anthony found Leland in the kitchen, reading in the corner by the light of an oil lamp.

"Come to the hall," Anthony said. "At your father's command."

*My father's command? I suppose.*

He followed Anthony to the hall with calm exterior and shaken interior. Guide Dulan hadn't talked to him in seven months. Leland had seen him only at a distance. Leland was quiet because it was taking all he had to maintain an air of calm indifference.

It was dark in the hall. The drapes were drawn and only the oil lamps around the high seat were lit, making a pool of light against crouching shadows. Dillan sat on the stone steps leading to the high seat. His pant legs were rolled up, showing red and blue marks on the shins. Dexter stood above him, leaning against the high table, hands resting lightly on the edge of the table. Anthony paced, his arms first locked together behind him, then crossed in front of him.

None of them looked at Leland.

Leland stood on the edge of the circle of light, feet spread slightly, arms hanging to his sides. He stared straight ahead, at the back of the high seat.

Then Guide Dulan was in the room with a stirring of air and the slam of the door behind him. Leland flinched at the sound and cringed inwardly. In Guide Dulan's hands was a bamboo cane.

He stopped before the high table and threw the bamboo at Dexter, who caught it awkwardly, almost dropping it.

"Dexter," said Guide Dulan. "Try to hit Leland."

"What, sir?"

"*Try* to hit Leland! Are you deaf, or just disobedient?"

Dexter swallowed and hefted the cane. He slowly walked down the stairs and moved across the stones toward Leland.

*Not before them all!* Leland took a half step back involuntarily. His skin, bone, and muscle screamed at him to run. Then he took a deliberate step forward, at Dexter, and stopped in the same spread-legged stance.

Dexter swung then, feinting from on high, then slashing from the side at rib height. The open end of the bamboo screamed in the air of the hall, a shrill whistle. Leland pulled his hip, twisting, and the tip of the bamboo passed a finger's breadth from his arm, still hanging limply at his side. Dexter skipped forward, bringing the bamboo around and down at Leland's shoulder. Leland simply leaned aside and the bamboo passed even closer to his arm, but still not touching him. He stepped forward then, past Dexter and behind him, pivoted and stood still.

Dexter grinned tightly and swung around, the bamboo at shoulder height. Leland dropped to one knee, his hand lightly touching the floor before him. The bamboo passed harmlessly overhead.

"Enough," said Guide Dulan.

Leland slowly stood up and turned to face Guide Dulan.

"Give me the cane, Dexter."

Dexter took several quick steps forward and handed the bamboo to his father, glad to get rid of it, apparently.

Guide Dulan eyed Leland, slowly slapping the bamboo into his right hand. Then he walked forward. Bap, bap, bap—the bamboo slapping into Guide Dulan's palm was the only noise in the hall. He made one slow circuit around Leland—very slow.

Leland stared straight ahead, his face impassive, still as stone. In truth, petrified—fearing not pain or injury but hurt dealt out from this man—by this man himself. Leland concentrated as hard as he could on the back of the high seat—at the Seal of de Laal worked into the back with multihued pieces of carved wood.

The crest was an open book with a candle flame above it. Below it were the words LITTERA SCRIPTA MANET.

Guide Dulan came back around in front of Leland. Slowly, deliberately, he raised the bamboo over his head, poised. His eyes searched Leland's face, probed into his eyes. Leland stared at the seal over his father's shoulder, stone faced, like a graven image—frozen without because he was petrified within.

The cane whipped down, almost too fast to see. Leland closed his eyes. Then jerked them open again, furious with himself. The cane had stopped before it touched his head.

Leland stared at the seal.

Guide Dulan slowly lowered the raised cane—his eyes still searching Leland's face. He shifted his grip on the bamboo until he held it with one hand in the center of the cane. Holding it out at arm's length, he dropped it at Leland's feet where it clattered on the stones, a harsh, hard sound in the silence of the hall.

Leland continued to stare at the seal.

Guide Dulan walked briskly back to the high table and turned. "Dillan, Dexter, and Anthony. Leave us."

Dillan stood slowly and started to walk toward the door. As he passed in front of his father, he stopped and stared at him for a moment. Guide Dulan stared past him, into the dark end of the room. Dillan walked on, shaking his head. Dexter and Anthony followed.

After the door had shut again, Guide Dulan spoke to Leland for the first time in over seven months.

"Sit if you want."

Leland said nothing, made no move.

"All right then—sit, I command it!"

Instead of moving toward the chairs of the lower tables, Leland sat cross-legged on the floor where he stood, arms resting on his knees and his back stiff as a board.

"I wonder why you didn't dodge my blow," Guide Dulan asked.

Leland licked his lips but said nothing.

"Well?" Guide Dulan looked at Leland expectantly.

Leland shifted his head for a moment, looking in Guide Dulan's direction but not lifting his eyes above knee level. "You didn't ask me a question," he whispered. In the silent hall it was loud enough to be heard.

Guide Dulan winced then and turned his face back toward the shadows. "Why did you dodge Dexter's blows?"

"I did not wish to be hit."

"And why did you not dodge mine?"

Leland was quiet for a moment. A tear formed at one eye and slid down his cheek, making him furious at his weakness. In the darkness of the hall, Guide Dulan did not see it. "You are my father and my steward. If it is your will to strike me, then I will not stop you." *And if it is your will to strike me, what is the pain of flesh? The damage is done by the willing.*

Guide Dulan stood in front of Leland for an instant. "What did the Guide Marilyn say to you at the banquet that caused you to insult her?"

Leland blinked at the sudden change of subject and winced

slightly at the remembered pain. "She told me why I was at the banquet. That you allowed me to attend as a favor to her."

"And what did you say in response?"

"I asked her to mind her own affairs."

Guide Dulan grunted. "I see."

*You do?* wondered Leland. *I sure don't.*

"I'm sending a heliogram to Denesse Sensei at Red Rock Station. He'll expect the day after tomorrow. Stay there until I call for you. Obey him as you would me," Guide Dulan directed.

He stepped forward and took the stick of bamboo off the floor, then leaned it in the nook behind his chair. While his back was still turned, he said, "There will be no more beatings." Almost as an afterthought he looked at Leland and added, "Any questions?"

*Why? Why? WHY?* Leland screamed inside his head.

"No questions," he said.

Guide Dulan turned and walked to the door. When he'd opened it, the light from the passageway without silhouetted him as he paused and half turned, as if to say something.

But, with a shake of his head, he went on, slamming the door behind him.

# FOUR

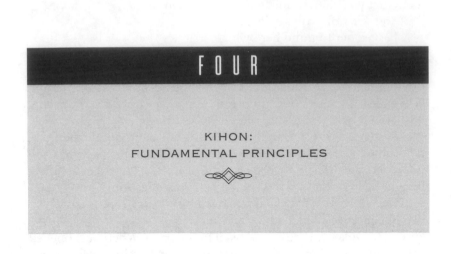

## KIHON: FUNDAMENTAL PRINCIPLES

Leland left Laal Station at dawn leading a string of six pack llamas—three bays, two gray roans, and a dilute agouti. They were all geldings except the lead, the agouti whose name was Bonkers.

"Long as you're going," Bartholomew told him, "you might as well take this month's supplies. The string belongs to Red Rock, but Louis, the boy who brought them in, broke his leg and won't be traveling for a while."

"He break it on the trail?" Leland asked.

"Dancing at a wedding."

Louis, bedridden in the men's guest dormitory in Brandon-on-the-Falls, was skeptical. "You handle llamas before?"

"Yes. Cart work and packing. For a while this summer I packed the supplies to the heliograph stations."

"Well, Bonkers—he's the agouti, the one with the black head and reddish body, he's dominant *and* he prefers to be up front. He likes to be scratched, but the others weren't handled that much as crias so they're not into touch. You can handle them all right—they just don't like to be petted. Melvin, the roan with the torn ear, is the most nervous, but if you put him behind his buddy Pumpernickel, he does fine. Pumpernickel is the fresh-shorn bay. He's got more undercoat than most pack llamas but he's really strong. I put the water bags on him."

Leland didn't take a horse—the low road suitable for horses required going the long way around, a weeklong trip, and the pace of horses was different from llamas.

The first three hours he and the string climbed steadily, moving up the valley, passing planted fields, groves, pastures, and greenhouses. He kept crossing the Tiber, the valley's small river, and the many mountain-born streams that fed it, on stone and wooden covered bridges. Then, as he got higher and the broad fields of the valley floor were replaced with wall-lined terraces, the bridges gave way to stepping-stones or felled trees paralleling rocky fords that the llamas splashed through. The terraces were replaced by forest interspersed with pastures, and the road, narrowing yet again, gave way to a broad rocky path.

The few people who saw him raised hands in greeting or touched their heads in deference if they recognized him, but went about their business—driving sheep, pulling weeds, fishing, or just passing on the road.

Once he pulled the string off to the side when a cart of soybeans pulled by a three-llama team went by. He'd checked that all the pack string had their fighting teeth filed down but still didn't want any trouble—the packs could get dumped.

By noon he cleared the timberline and the path narrowed, a thin trail worn down through the grasses, edelweiss, rock flora, sedges, rowan, creeping pine, and dwarf shrubs that covered the gentler slopes. In the distance he could see occasional clusters of sheep or long-haired angora goats, driven up for the summer grazing by shepherds and dog teams, but no one passed him on the trail.

Just before the Khyber Pass, he made the string lie down. "Kush, kush. Kush, kush." Then he sat on the lead rope while he ate his lunch on a rocky shoulder that overlooked the entire Tiber valley. He could see the great stone station and Brandon-on-the-Falls, the Needle, multicolored fields, groves, the flashing reflections from greenhouse roofs, the thin gravel lines of road, and the meandering liquid silver of streams. Then the forested slopes above leading to the high meadows, and then the alpine tundra, and, finally, bare and lichen-splotched rock marred only by the stone towers of the heliograph stations on the ridgelines.

Much of Laal was like this—a series of fertile valleys, like fingers spread between crags of barren, volcanic rock, a happy accident, where alpine freezing and thawing had collected pockets of rubble, dust, and volcanic ash, and the right mixture of summer temperatures, spring rains, snow melt, and dry autumns had proved receptive to the Great Seeding. Only the Plain of the Founders, the richest delta of farmland on Agatsu, and areas of the great Noram plain rivaled the Tiber valley's fecundity.

He turned his back on it and climbed the last hundred meters to the pass. Here was a completely different world.

Only yellow and green lichen, the occasional clump of scrawny grass, and a surprising cluster of rhododendron were in the pass itself. He kept an eye on the llamas as he led them past. Rhododendron is poisonous and llamas hungry for leafy browse have been known to eat it. Between lead ropes and llamas, the entire string stretched back almost twenty-five meters, so he had to crane his neck, but none of the animals so much as glanced at it.

Beyond the pass was much the same, though the grasses were more common. This side of the mountain was in the rain shadow and received far less snow and rain. Which is not to say life stopped outside of the main valley. Here was low brush, even a bristlecone pine. Here were isolated clumps of Indian rice grass. Here a gnarled, stunted cedar. Above floated red-tailed hawks, so there must have been smaller animals, prey that lived in this drier place.

His path took him along ridges, through long dry washes, and then finally, as the sun was setting, north again, climbing a series of tight switchbacks toward another high pass. As he walked, he collected dry llama dung from previous trips, putting it in a bag on Bonkers's pack.

Several times he had to break up the string and lead them over and around obstacles one animal at a time. He thought about horses on the same ground and shuddered.

He stopped as the sun dropped below the horizon and the wind picked up, making camp in the shelter of an overhang.

He unloaded the llamas, switched their lead ropes from halter to collar, and staked them out—close enough to socialize, but far enough apart to avoid territorial disputes. He fed them a mixture of parched corn, cottonseed meal, and alfalfa pellets from their packs. They watched everything he did and hummed at each other, making him feel as if his every move were being discussed. Before and after eating, he let them drink from a collapsible bucket.

The temperature dropped quickly with the sun, and he sat before a small fire of dried llama dung, sheltered from the wind, his bedroll draped across his shoulders.

The ring was bright tonight, casting shadows among the rocks, and for a while Leland stared at it. Some said the ring was the work of the original probe, remnants of ice moved from the system's outer planets and used to increase the water on Agatsu. Others said it was made of seeds, pods of frozen life, waiting eventual orbital decay to rain down on soil made ready by the passage of time. Leland's reading suggested the rings were the product of planetary formation, a moon that either never formed or was pulverized by some ancient collision.

He lowered his gaze to the southern landscape, where he could just see the faintest glimmer in the distance, kilometers to the south, where the Rubicon River separated Cotswold from Laal. He thought of Marilyn then and frowned.

*Why did I do that? Why did I attack her for being kind to me?*

He had no more answer for that than he did for his father's behavior.

He used a small amount of his water for evening rituals and, after burying the remnants of his fire, stretched his bedroll over the warm earth and slept, sung to his rest by the wind in the rocks and the muttering of llamas.

He was up in the predawn glow, stamping his feet and swinging his arms to warm himself. The wind was lighter, but his breath formed clouds in the cold air and when he took his first drink, ice clinked in his canteen. He loaded the llamas quickly as he could, taking care that the packs were balanced, then moved up the pass, chewing trail bread as he walked.

The sun cleared the walls of the pass as he crossed the high point of the saddle, almost four kilometers above sea level, and the air warmed substantially, letting him remove his sheepskin vest. On the north side of rocks little pockets of snow and ice lingered. Even lichen was scarce here, and he had trouble catching his breath. Then he felt the slope change and knew he was headed down again.

Almost immediately there was an increase in vegetation. This was the wet side of the range and, like the Tiber valley, it received ample rain. When he dropped below twenty-five hundred meters, he encountered alpine tundra—grasses, flowers, and sedges—just like the heights above Laal Station. Below, though, there wasn't the same rich forest.

Here soil hadn't collected and formed as it had in the Tiber valley system. Below was a landscape more typical of the planet. Topsoil was patchy and thin, slowly building, but also subject to erosion. Foliage was sparse, shallow rooted, and prey to variations in rain patterns since the soil held very little water.

This was why humanity was both a scattered and concentrated affair on Agatsu. Laal's villages and communities were concentrated first in the Tiber valley system, then spotted in smaller islands of fecundity—pockets and basins and canyons where topsoil accumulated and thrived.

But between these pockets were the barrens—rocky desolate, sometimes arid, sometimes wet stretches of landscape hosting only lichens, scattered grasses, and negligible topsoil.

There was a stream now, or, more accurately, a rivulet, running between meter-wide pools. Here life was a little more concentrated. Algae on the rocks, caddis larva, diving beetles, some simple aquatic plants, and a few rushes. The path followed the water's twisting plunge into a canyon, and Leland paused to let the llama drink, wetting his bandanna in the waters and wiping his exposed skin before moving on.

By midmorning he reached the turnoff—a place where his trail met a small road coming up the canyon from the flatlands below. The road turned and entered a side canyon with high, reddish walls.

Leland looked down the road. It was the longer way to Laal Station, leading to a lower pass and a longer road that looped up into Noram proper before cutting back to the Winter Pass into the Tiber valley. But Bonkers, the lead llama, didn't hesitate, edging past Leland and trying to turn up the canyon. When his lead rope pulled up short, Bonkers clucked and looked back at Leland, as if to say "Well?"

Leland laughed and walked up the road, side by side with the llama.

Red Rock Station was an oasis of biota, one of the areas of fecundity that had "taken" during the seeding, but was too small and geographically isolated to settle until recently. A low volcanic caldera, opening deep on the side of a line of shield cones, formed a natural dam. Over the years, this lake collected particulate stone fractured by temperature variation and, after the seeding, organic materials.

When Leland led the pack string up a rise in the road that turned out to be the rim of the original caldera, he could see that the lake was still there but was now a tenth of its original size, reduced by silting. A small settlement, fields, groves, and a scattering of woods now lined the lake on fertile former lakebed.

Several small valleys and canyons opened into the area, and Leland could see the beginning of wooded slopes. He continued along the road, trying to keep up with Bonkers, whose pace was now accelerating. Just before the settlement—it would be excessive to call it a village as there were less than ten buildings—the road entered the shade of a tightly spaced grove of peach trees. When he walked out of the trees, the sun had touched the canyon rim and the reddish rock of the surrounding hillsides turned shades deeper—truly red.

Ahead, a figure stepped into the road from the porch of a large, low rammed-earth building. "You made good time. We were a little worried that you wouldn't be in until tomorrow."

Leland shaded his eyes with his hands and said, "Louis broke his leg."

The woman was in her late thirties, a little taller than Leland, with short, dark hair and a sun-weathered face. She nodded. "Yes." She gestured a small wooden tower beside the building. "We got it on the heliograph."

"Then you know that I'm Leland."

"Yes, Warden. I'm Charly." They shook hands. "Come on—we just have time to unload the string before supper."

They put the pack frames on the porch of the building, then turned the llamas out into a large fenced pasture at the other end of the settlement. Bonkers, the first one released, went bounding off to where a taller fence separated the pasture from a cluster of female llamas.

The geldings followed, making their short musical humming sounds deep in their throats.

Leland and Charly put the lead ropes, collars, and halters in a nearby shed, and, as Charly turned away, Leland asked, "Who will feed them?"

Charly shrugged. "Good question—it's Louis's job normally. His little brother's been doing it while Louis was gone. Maybe he'll continue."

Dinner was held in the "hall," the large building where they'd unloaded the packs. It was communal dining room, library, meeting hall, and school. There were thirty or so adults in the room seated at long tables with benches or standing. Several children played around the edges. The drone of conversation dipped as they entered and Charly said loudly into the gap, "This is Leland de Laal, Warden of the Needle. He brought Louis's pack string. I'll let you introduce yourselves to him at your leisure."

Leland raised a hand and nodded, then said, "Just Leland, really," but the resuming conversation covered his voice.

At one end of room a shutter opened revealing a large kitchen. The man who'd thrown the shutter open said, "It's food!"

There was a general movement toward that side of the room and a line formed, people picking up utensils and wide shallow bowls from a shelf, but the person at the head of the line stopped short of the window and they all looked at Leland.

He blinked. "Oh. Thanks, but after you, please." He walked over and joined the line at its end. The man at the front of the line inclined his head then stepped up to the window. The line moved on.

Supper was brown rice, stir-fried vegetables with or without duck, and a salad of mixed greens. The drink was chilled mint tea, and Leland drank several glasses.

"That was well done," Charly said.

Leland blinked. "Well, surely you've seen other people drink tea before."

She smiled and the lines around her eyes deepened. "There are many who came here to get away from the guardianship. The fact that you arrived by foot and you didn't claim any special privilege set well with them."

Leland shrugged. "A bit ironic."

"What?" she said.

"Where do they think the guardianship came from? It was people who pushed out from the established settlements and founded new Stations—just like this one. Of course, they've become something else now, I guess. In Noram and Cotswold, it's much more formalized. Ritualized, I guess."

"Especially in Noram," she said.

"Is that where you're from?"

She nodded.

He poured himself more tea from an earthenware pitcher on the table. "Why did you come here?"

"To study."

Leland looked around at the bookshelves. "We have a much bigger library in Laal. And there's the Great Library in Noram City."

"What I study doesn't come from books."

"Aikido," Leland said.

"Yes."

Leland looked around. "Which one of these people is Denesse Sensei?"

"Sensei occasionally eats here but usually he eats with the *uchideshi* up at the dojo."

INSIDE STUDENTS, Leland translated to himself, then froze, staring at the table. He'd never heard the word before in his life. Aikido was one of several martial arts practiced on Agatsu, but he'd never studied it—never really known someone who had. Why did he know what *uchideshi* meant?

"Are you okay?" Charly asked.

"I don't know," said Leland.

"It's a long walk from the Tiber valley. Maybe a bath before bed?"

"I was supposed to see Denesse Sensei."

Charly shook her head. "He knows you're here. I'm to take you to him at breakfast."

"A bath, then."

She showed him where the public bathhouse was and, when he was clean and steaming in a fresh set of clothes, walked him up the road by ringlight to a small house set in a grove.

"This is my place. The spare bedroom is yours while you're here. Please leave your shoes by the door." A bench seat by the front door held a shelf beneath, half filled with shoes, boots, and sandals.

She lit an oil lamp and Leland looked around.

Inside the place was even smaller as the walls were almost half a meter thick. "How cold does it get here in the winter?" he asked.

"Quite cold. We're at thirty-two hundred meters."

There were only four rooms—the front living room, the two bedrooms, and a small bathroom with a wash basin and a composting toilet. A tiny iron stove sat between the two bedroom doors. The floor was mortared flagstone strewn with sheep and llama wool rugs. A small loom and a spinning wheel sat before one of the room's three windows. A shelf in the corner held baskets of uncombed wool, large spools of dyed and undyed yarn, and other oddments of weaving and spinning.

Leland set his bag down and took off his shoes.

Charly kicked her sandals onto the shelf and entered one of the bedrooms with the lamp. She used it to light another lamp within.

"This is your room." She brought the first lamp out and placed it on a table near the loom.

"Sensei eats breakfast when sunlight first hits the peaks. We'll have to wake in time to dress and walk up the hill, so I'd get some sleep."

Leland bobbed his head in a half bow and carried his bag into the bedroom. The room was a bit like a cell, a straw tatami mat along one side with a thin hemp mattress on that, then a quilt and a pillow. There was a nook in the wall near the head of the bed for the oil lamp and more empty shelves on the wall above the bed. There was a wool hanging on a dowel across the doorway for privacy.

Leland stacked his few things neatly on the shelves, then did evening rituals in the bathroom.

Charly was weaving, throwing the shuttle back and forth with a practiced, casual motion as she raised and lowered the shedding bars, pausing every six or so rows to slip a slim rectangular wooden bar in and beat the threads tight.

"Good night, Charly," Leland said, pausing awkwardly in the door to his room.

"Sweet dreams," she said without pausing. "I'll wake you before dawn."

He pulled the drape across the door, blew out the lamp, and fell asleep to the soft clacking of the loom.

Leland followed the dim figure of Charly and her shoulder bag up the path. He could see stars and only a dim glow in the eastern edge of the sky told him it wasn't the middle of the night.

After ten minutes he kept expecting them to come to Denesse Sensei's house, but they kept walking, working up progressively steeper switchbacks. Leland thought about asking how much farther but decided it didn't matter—they'd get there when they got there.

Finally, about thirty minutes after they'd started, Leland smelled smoke and they rounded a shoulder of the hill and the path opened onto a mostly flat nook, an inset gully some hundred meters deep, facing south. There were three buildings adjoining a large paved square. The largest building was wide and long with several doors facing the pavement. Across from it was a narrow greenhouse, almost as long as the square, but not as wide as the larger building. The smallest building, at the far end of the court, looked much like Charly's house with the addition of an ornamental garden in the Japanese style beside it.

A cloud of steam rose from the back of the greenhouse, curled around the edges, and drifted away in the light breeze.

"What's that?" Leland asked, pointing.

"Geothermal hot spring. It's why the dojo is here."

As they walked across the square Leland heard laughter, conversation, the sounds of cooking and washing from the far end of the larger building. The sky was positively gray now, and he could see that most of the remaining area of the nook was terraced gardens. And he saw that there was someone standing in the ornamental garden besides the small house at the end of the square.

The figure, a man wearing a long kimono and a thick woven wool overjacket, was trimming a small bush with a pair of iron shears and dropping the leaves into a basket at his feet. He glanced their way at the sound of their footsteps, then dropped the shears into the basket and turned fully to face them.

Charly stopped at the edge of the garden and bowed deeply. "Good morning, Sensei. I've brought Guide Leland."

Leland stopped beside her and bowed.

Denesse nodded his head. "Thank you, Charly."

Charly bowed again and left abruptly, going across the square to a door in the larger building. Leland looked after her, surprised, then back at Denesse.

Denesse smiled and gestured. "Come into my garden."

*Said the spider* . . . Leland stepped off the paved square and followed the man back to where two tatami mats sat on raised area of tiled paving stones. A low table sat in the middle. To one side was a small charcoal brazier with an iron kettle upon it.

Denesse slipped off his wooden sandals at the tatami's edge and kneeled by the brazier, one tabi-covered foot folded across the other at the instep. He pointed to the other side of the table. Leland sat on the edge of the platform and removed his boots, then sat on his knees opposite the man in the kimono.

There were households that lived like this, he knew. He'd visited a few as a child, but there was something happening here—something totally familiar about the way he folded his stockinged feet right over left, dropped his hands to rest on his thighs, and arched his back ever so slightly, causing him to sit upright without tension.

Was it Denesse Sensei? He looked at his face as the man poured boiling water into a partially glazed teapot at the end of the table. The face was unfamiliar, not resonating like some of the other new things. He was not as old as his father, but older than Leland's eldest brother Dillan, perhaps in his mid-forties. His hair was dark brown with the faintest graying near the ears, and Leland saw a pronounced bald spot at the crown of his head when he bent over to pour the water.

"We'll let that steep," Denesse said, looking up. "How was your trip?"

Leland licked his lips. "I enjoyed it. The barrens are such a contrast after the Tiber valley."

Denesse shifted sideways, so he could look up at the peaks above, a series of black and red cliffs formed by the collapse an underground lava chamber. Leland followed his gaze in time to see the sunlight hit the tallest point.

Denesse was silent for a few minutes, watching the line of light crawl down the face of the cliff. The basin grew lighter and birds and insects began to sing.

Denesse finally turned back to Leland. "I was surprised when I received your father's heliogram. I've been expecting your brother Dillan for the last few years."

Leland didn't know what to say. "Perhaps I shouldn't have come. Should I go back?" *Is this another thing I screwed up?*

"Do you want to?"

"My father sent me here but he also told me to obey you as I would him. If you send me back, I will go. But, no, I don't particularly want to return." Leland began to shiver slightly as the heat of exertion from the climb began to wear off. He wished he'd brought his vest. His legs, below the knees, were also going to sleep.

Denesse clapped his hands suddenly, causing Leland to blink.

Footsteps clattered across the court pavement and Leland turned his head to see two young men round the corner of the house and enter the garden carrying a tray apiece. They were wearing off-white cotton gi and voluminous, dark-blue divided skirts, like enormous culottes.

HAKAMA, supplied that dark part of Leland's mind—the part he associated with the Glass Helm's legacy. KEIKO—PRACTICE—GI. He froze for a moment, reeling.

They kneeled at the edge of the tatami, set the trays before them, and bowed. Then they lifted the trays to the edge of the table.

Denesse nodded to them. "Thank you. Go on now. You don't want to be late for class."

The two bowed again and left.

The trays contained a bowl of wheat, rice, and oat porridge with nuts and dried pears, a chunk of bread, a thick dollop of honey, and a slice of goat cheese. A covered pot on each tray held a steaming hot washcloth, which both Leland and Denesse used to clean their hands.

Denesse picked up the teapot. "The tea should be ready now. I wonder if you are."

"Sensei? Ready for what?"

"When did you put on the Helm?"

*Does everybody in the world know about the Helm?* "Last fall—Harvest festival."

"Well, we'll just have to see if it has steeped long enough." He poured tea into the cups.

Slamming sounds, echoing in an enclosed space, came to them across the courtyard, as if several rugs were being beaten, but Leland recognized it as *ukemi* practice—the sound of palms and forearms slamming into the practice surface during forward and backward falls. *Why do I know what it is?*

Denesse set a steaming teacup before Leland. "Are you sure you want to stay?"

"It's my father's wish." He said it softly. "Therefore, I stay."

"Well, it's a reason to come here. Let's hope you can find a reason of your own to stay." He lifted his cup in a toast. "Good *keiko* to you."

Leland lifted his cup. "MASAKATSU." A certain detachment was coming over him—almost as if he wasn't in charge of his own body anymore. *Masakatsu* meant "true victory" and, at least in the practice of aikido, referred to a victory over oneself—over one's defects and imperfections. Leland hadn't known the word a few minutes before but he was beyond surprise now.

Denesse's eyes widened slightly. Then he drank from his cup and said, "I think the tea is ready."

# FIVE

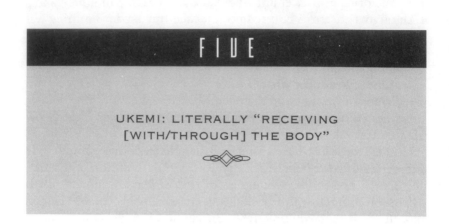

## UKEMI: LITERALLY "RECEIVING [WITH/THROUGH] THE BODY"

After breakfast, Denesse led him back across the square, to the large building—the dojo, he now realized—into the door that Charly had entered. A hallway stretched back past the initial alcove, a place to remove shoes with shelves to store them. Denesse slipped off his sandals and waited for Leland to slip out of his boots.

Small, rough-glazed skylights dimly lit the interior.

As they walked back, Denesse pointed to doors leading to the smaller end of the building. "That's the kitchen and dining room." They reached the end of the hall, and it branched left and right. "Here are the changing rooms," he said, indicating two doors in front of them. "The *uchideshi*'s rooms are that way"—he pointed down the long arm of the hall—"and the entrance to the mat. Here we have the baths, and that door on the end is the toilet."

He pushed a curtain aside to reveal some shelves set into the hall wall. Bundles of clothing sat in neat rows, marked by size. Denesse selected one and held it out to Leland. "The men's changing room is on the left. There are shelves for your clothes."

Leland bowed and retreated to the changing room, a narrow room with pegs and shelves for clothing. He stared at the bundle, then untied it—a white cotton belt wrapped three times around a rolled gi and knotted. He undressed, pulled on the pants and tied the drawstring tight around his hips, put the jacket on, then looped the belt twice around his waist and tied it in front, a tight square knot.

All of this was automatic, but after he tied the belt, he felt *wrong.* The gi was on correctly. IT JUST DOESN'T FIT THE WAY IT USED TO. A wave of dizziness swept over him and he leaned heavily against the wall for a moment.

He'd never worn a gi before.

He stepped back into the hall. Denesse was waiting, wearing a gi and a dark-blue *hakama.* Leland wondered how he'd changed so fast. *Maybe he was wearing them under the kimono all along.*

Denesse walked down the hall to a double doorway opposite the entrance to the *uchideshi*'s rooms. Inside the large room five men and three women were throwing each other on a tatami-covered floor. Charly, wearing a practice gi and a *hakama* was sitting *seiza,* on her knees, near the far wall, to one side of an altar—a niche set in the wall.

"After you," said Denesse.

Leland started to step onto the *tatami* but something inside made him freeze. He exhaled, dropped to his knees on the stone flagstones outside the door, and said, *"Oneigaishimasu!"* He felt dizzy and faintly nauseated.

Charly looked at him and lifted her hand.

Leland bowed, then knee-walked onto the mat. He bowed to the altar—THE KAMIZA—and then slid to one side, out of the doorway, but remained seated.

Denesse stepped onto the tatami and kneeled, flipping the inner edges of his *hakama* back as he sat, then bowed to the front of the room, toward the altar.

Charly clapped her hands together and the people practicing stopped, knelt in *seiza,* facing toward Denesse, and bowed. He bowed in return, then said, "Please continue."

Charly stood and said, "Let's change."

Immediately the students formed a seated line across the back of the room, lining up on the seam between one row of tatami and another. Charly gestured at one of the women, and she jumped up, moving to one side. They bowed to each other, then Charly touched her wrist. The woman took a sliding step forward and grabbed Charly's right wrist.

Charly stepped ninety degrees to the side striking at the woman's face with her left hand. The woman leaned back, taking her face out of range, and Charly used the same hand to cut down into the inside of the woman's elbow while drawing her held arm back. Then she took the woman's wrist and hand with her free hand and shot the captured wrist up, breaking the grip and taking the elbow. She brought her arms forward, extended, and then down, bending the woman over, her elbow bent down by one arm, the hand of the same arm twisted at the wrist. Then Charly stepped into the woman, toward her exposed ribs, and the woman went over, slapping the tatami hard with her free arm. Charly finished with a diagonal step away, drawing the arm toward her, and dropping to her knees, pinning the woman face-down, with pressure at the wrist and elbow.

She rolled the arm forward until the woman slapped the tatami again, hard. Charly released her and stood. They did it three more times, switching from left to right.

"Try that. Keep your arms extended. And keep your center expanded!" This last seemed to be directed at one person in particular. The students bowed and paired up, practicing the technique.

IKKYO, THE FIRST TECHNIQUE. THE BEST TECHNIQUE.

Denesse cleared his throat and pointed to the right back corner. "Go warm up. Stretch."

Leland bowed, stood, and went to the corner. He knew some stretches from schoolyard activities, the warmups preceding calisthenics, but as he bent to start them, that other part of him took over, leading him systematically through a series of stretches that worked his joints from neck to toe.

His muscles and tendons screamed from some of the stretches, as they took his body in totally unaccustomed directions. From that dark place inside came surprise and dismay, a sense of betrayal. HOW DID MY BODY GET SO TIGHT?

Leland shook his head, bewildered, and continued the stretches, working for some degree of flexibility. His muscles, hardened by months of labor, felt like they were betraying him, limiting his joints' range of motion, though he'd never been particularly flexible. IT DOESN'T MATTER. WE'LL WORK WITH WHAT WE HAVE.

Denesse who had been watching the class, turned his head to Leland and said, "*Ukemi,* please."

"HAI," said Leland, bowing.

He took a step and leaned forward, relaxed, until his head almost touched the tatami. When his balance was gone, he threw his hip forward, swept his arm back, and rolled from his left shoulder to his right hip, slapping with his right forearm and palm, and came upright again, knee, toes, and foot. He fell backward, then, reversing the process, slapping, rolling diagonally across his back, to stand again.

*What on earth?* He stiffened in the middle of the next roll and banged his shoulder hard. GET OUT OF MY WAY! the inner voice said. STOP THINKING ABOUT IT—YOU'LL JUST HURT YOURSELF.

He stopped and took two deep breaths, then began again, trying to think of nothing in particular.

At first, there were a few bumps, his shoulder banging the tatami, or his hip, or his elbow, but, after a few moments, his contact with the surface of the tatami was like a wheel, a smooth transition—almost a gliding—as he fell forward or backward. He went from back-rolls to back-falls, arching his back until the point of unbalance and twisting, slapping first with one arm before actually hitting, and using that torque to roll across the back before slapping again with the other arm.

Then forward falls, breaking a forward fall with a slap, arching the back, and absorbing the shock.

Leland was rather amazed and feeling pleased with his ability when the inner voice said, BARELY ADEQUATE, YOU'LL HAVE TO DO BETTER.

"That's it," he heard Charly say. "Stretch your backs!"

Denesse gestured to the tatami beside him and Leland knelt, to sit in *seiza.* The pairs of students were grasping each other's wrists, then turning, arms overhead, until they were back to back. Then one would bend forward at the waist stretching the other across his back and hips. When they'd each taken a turn, they straightened their gis and *hakama* and lined back up, sitting in *seiza.*

Charly spoke again. "If there's a point to today's class, it's extension. Please think about this." She turned to face the front of the *kamiza* and sat upright for a moment, then bowed. The rest of the class, Denesse, and Leland, followed suit. Then she pivoted again and bowed specifically to Denesse who returned it, then to the class. "Thank you."

"*Domo arigato,* Sensei!" the students said, bowing.

Charly stood, walked behind the line of students to where Denesse and Leland waited. "Please thank your partners," she said, and sat beside Leland.

The students, still seated, bowed again, then, knee-walking, paired up again, bowing to each other, thanking each other, going to the next student, bowing, expressing thanks.

Then they jumped up dashed for the far corner, where three brooms hung on pegs.

Denesse raised his voice. "I need the mat. Please sweep later."

They looked surprised. "Yes, Sensei." They filed out, bowing at the doorway, to the *kamiza.* The last one, the woman that Charly had pinned with Ikkyo, did a sitting bow to Charly and said, "Will you need your *hakama* folded, Sensei?"

She shook her head. "No."

The woman bowed again and left—as she did, she stared at Leland with open curiosity.

The three of them bowed in, formally, Denesse in the spot recently occupied by Charly and Charly now beside Leland, where the students sat.

The light from the skylights was brighter now and more of the *kamiza,* the altar at the front of the mat, was visible. It was an inset nook holding an unlit oil lamp, an arrangement of spring flowers, a bowl of salt, a small wooden platter with three parallel stripes of dried rice, corn, and wheat grains, and a bowl of sand with incense sticks standing. Above this was a parchment scroll with an ink painting—calligraphy in Chinese, thought Leland—and a triangle above a circle above a square.

JAPANESE, BUT IT'S THE SAME.

Above the nook were two pictures in charcoal and chalk—one was of an old Asian man, balding, with a bushy goatee. The other was an old Caucasian woman with short hair and heavily etched smile lines around her eyes and mouth, though in the picture she wasn't smiling.

The picture of the old man was expected, or at least that inner voice wasn't surprised, but the sight of the old woman shocked him to his core. He felt numb inside, almost bludgeoned.

And he didn't know why.

THEY SHOULDN'T HAVE!

Denesse said, "Charly—Leland will be *uke.* Begin with variations on *kokyunage* from *gyakuhamni katatedori.*"

Charly pivoted on her knees and bowed to Leland. " '*gashimas,*' " she said. MAY I HAVE THE HONOR OF PRACTICING WITH YOU?

He bowed back and stood, still numb, operating on some strange kind of autopilot.

She stepped toward him, extending her right hand toward him. He slid forward and grabbed her wrist with his hand. She turned smoothly, pivoting on her forward foot, raising her right hand and extending it forward, toward the far wall, and then down.

Leland moved with it, tucked, rolled, slapped. He stood, turned back to her, and took her left wrist with his right hand. She threw him again, slightly harder. Leland rolled smoothly and turned again to take her wrist.

Denesse said, "Stop."

Charly and Leland sat.

"Charly," he said, looking at her with a frown. "I want to know his limits. Leland *needs* to know them. Do you understand?"

Charly's eyes widened. "Yes, Sensei."

"Very well. Continue."

They stood and, once again, Leland stepped in to take her wrist. She moved as he neared it—leading him, keeping just out of reach—his fingertips just brushing but never grasping her wrist. He accelerated and she threw him, whipping the wrist around in a small circle. He landed harder but rolled back to his feet, turned, and moved, this time taking her wrist despite her quicker movements. She slid across his front, *omote*, and he pivoted smoothly, flying. The next throw was harder, and the next harder still.

Part of Leland tried to pull away, was frightened to death every time this demon woman moved. RELAX, STAY LIGHT, STAY ALERT! NO! DON'T BE SO TIGHT IN THE SHOULDER. SHE'S VERY GOOD. BE THE SORT OF UKE SHE DESERVES!

He froze again and fell, hard, but stood quickly, shaking his head angrily. *If I could do it before, I can do it now. Relax!*

After several of these throws, Denesse called out, "*Iriminage.*"

Leland grabbed Charly's wrist, she took him around, broke his grip, and grabbed the collar of his gi, forcing his torso down, then sweeping up, under the chin with her extended arm. He flipped over backward, into back-falls and back-rolls depending on the throw. She varied her execution, sometimes coming directly to his chin, sometimes pivoting, leading him around and down, then up and back. It was almost like a tango, requiring him to stay light on his feet and move with her.

He didn't know which was harder—the falls or the ongoing internal critique.

The circles of her arms got smaller, tighter, the downward impetus shifted, became a whirlwind that sent his feet arching high overhead as his head dropped toward the ground—turning the fall from a back-roll to a break-fall.

Leland's breathing labored, but he stood up each time, as quickly as before—to take up the attack.

Denesse stopped them five minutes later. "Catch your breath."

Leland glanced sideways at Charly and was relieved to see she was noticeably sweating, breathing deep, measured breaths. He followed her example and soon his racing heart slowed.

"*Shomenuchi,*" Denesse said. "All the immobilizations."

Leland and Charly stood again and bowed to each other.

Leland attacked with an overhead strike, like a vertical sword cut or club blow. Charly met his arm before he'd begun the downward stroke and pivoted, turning his elbow over and guiding it down. He was forced to the mat, slapping hard with his free arm, then twisting to lower that captured arm's shoulder to the ground as quickly as possible, to take the pressure off of it. Next came *Nikkyo,* the second technique, a joint manipulation technique that worked against the wrist. Leland moved with it, dropping his center when Charly dropped hers, keeping the pressure off the joint.

*Ikkyo, Nikkyo, Sankyo, Rokyo, Gokyo, Kotegaeshi*—immobilizations of elbow, wrist, fingers, shoulder, pins, takedowns. Leland thought his heart would explode, that the next fall would break his neck, that his wrist or elbow or shoulder would be dislocated. Inside, though, the voice kept saying RELAX—IT'S EASY IF YOU RELAX AND EXTEND.

*How can I relax when you keep shouting at me?*

Still, he kept rising to his feet and attacking yet again, as if he meant it, trying to connect with Charly's forehead.

His hair was plastered to his scalp and sweat was dripping down his nose. He'd thought that he was in good physical condition after his winter and summer of manual labor, but his muscles and tendons were burning. Charly threw him—an *Ikkyo* projection that took him into a side roll. He came to his feet, turned to face her, and stumbled as his burning thigh muscles gave way, going to one knee and steadying himself with a hand on the tatami. He straightened then and started toward her again.

"*Ma-te!*" said Denesse. STOP. "Stretch your backs."

Leland blinked and wiped his sweaty palms off on the pants of his gi. Charly seemed to shrink slightly, and the intent focus of her expression dissolved into a tired grin. She stepped forward and offered her extended arms to Leland. He bobbed his head and took her wrists, and they pivoted together until they were standing back to back with arms overhead. She bent her knees, then leaned forward, lifting him onto her back. He felt vertebrae crack and pop. Then he did the same for her.

They backed away from each other and bowed, then turned to the back of the room and straightened their gis. They lined up, seated, facing Denesse.

Denesse looked at them. "Come back the day after tomorrow, Leland. Start with Charly's morning classes. When your body is up to it, take as many of the daily classes as possible."

Charly bowed. "Excuse me, Sensei, but why wait? His *ukemi* is up to any of our classes, isn't it?"

Denesse smiled. "Yes and no. His mind is ready—but his body won't be, not for a while." He gestured at Leland. "Tell her how many times you've practiced."

ALL MY LIFE.

He turned to Charly and said, "I've never done this before."

Charly stared at him, frowning. "I find that hard to believe."

"I'm having a hard time with it myself," he replied, "but it's the truth."

She turned back to Denesse. "How can this be?"

Denesse said gently, "It's not my place to explain it, *kohai.*"

Leland heard a sharp intake of breath from Charly. "Yes, Sensei," she said, her voice neutral. She bowed.

Denesse looked back at Leland. "Hot baths are good."

Leland blinked. "Yes, Sensei."

They bowed out formally and Denesse left the room.

Charly bowed to Leland, an odd expression on her face. "Thank you very much, Leland, for the *ukemi.*"

"Thank you, Charly."

She stood. Leland tried to. It took him two tries. Charly walked to the door and, much as Leland wanted to follow her, that inner thing steered him to the corner, where the brooms hung. Charly saw what he was doing and followed him.

Together, working in rows, they swept the mat.

Halfway down the hill, Charly took Leland's rolled-up gi from him and carried it with her own bag. He was stumbling by the time they got to the crater floor and leaning on Charly by the time they passed her cottage.

She helped him sit on the low rock wall by the road, dropped their bundles, and said, "Wait right here."

He half laughed, half groaned. "I'm not going anywhere—really."

She trotted up the path to her house, then came back after a few minutes with another bag. "I took the liberty of bringing your spare shirt and pants."

"Uhmm."

"Come on—let's go to the baths."

Groaning prodigiously, he levered himself off of the wall and onto the road. "Lay on, Macduff, And damn'd be him that first cries, 'Hold, enough!' "

"I suggest you save your breath for walking."

At the bathhouse she dropped him on the grass, in the sun. "It will take some time to heat the water. Rest here."

Leland's hip wasn't moving right and he flopped back, facing the sky, to relieve it. "Just leave me something to read and, in the fall, bring me a blanket."

She disappeared inside, laughing.

Leland closed his eyes. The sun's warmth felt good and he tried to sleep, but the aches were extensive, like the worst flu he'd ever had. It was more like that than his worst beating, for the pain centered in his joints.

He tried to think about the morning, but his thoughts veered away to Laal, wondering what was happening with his brothers and sister, or what his father was doing. *Don't worry, Anthony, I'm still getting my beatings. They're self-inflicted.*

"Are you laughing or groaning?" Charly said, sticking her head out the window.

"Yes."

"Ah. Well, come on in. I'm doing the wash and I need the clothes you're wearing."

Leland tried sitting up but his body just wasn't letting him. He ended up rolling over, facedown, and climbing to all fours, then using the framework of the bathhouse windmill to help him to his feet.

The bathhouse was divided into the men and women's washrooms and then a large common area divided between the soaking tub and a laundry area. A wood fire was burning briskly in the cast-iron stove that made up one side of the soaking tub. "Too bad," Leland said, "that there aren't hot springs down here, too."

Charly had changed out of her clothes and was wearing a large towel wrapped around, over her breasts and hanging down to midthigh. She pointed at the men's washing side and said, "Get out of those clothes if you want them washed." She dipped her hand into the soaking tub. "It's getting there—if you take your time washing, it'll be ready when you're rinsed."

Leland handed his clothes out from the men's side, then ran water from the cistern into a bucket and poured it awkwardly over his head.

"Aaaaagh!"

"A bit cold?" Charly's voice asked from the other side of the partition. "The chimney goes up through the cistern, but it hasn't really had time to affect it yet."

"Tell me about it," muttered Leland. He lathered himself down with a bar of vegetable oil soap.

"There is *some* geothermal warming down in the valley. It protects the crops from early frost and keeps the lake from freezing completely over in the winter. They've been talking about trying to drill down into the hot rock and circulate water to heat homes and greenhouses during the winter, but the drill heads would have to come from Noram and they're very expensive."

"What about piping it down the hill?" Leland said through chattering teeth.

"There's barely enough for the dojo. Some winters they have to supplement with stoves."

Leland ran another bucket of water, gritted his teeth, and poured it over his head. "Aaaaaaagh!"

He wrapped a towel around his waist and walked quickly into the common room, to stand by the stove.

Charly was draining the soapy water from their clothes in one of the laundry tubs. Without turning around, she said, "Go ahead. It's not quite hot, but it's warm."

He hung his towel on a peg and awkwardly climbed over the edge and sank down to his chin, pushing his feet out toward the iron heat exchange fins projecting from the stove. He groaned with pleasure. "I'm never moving again. I'm just going to stay in this tub forever."

"Ewwwww. Guide soup. Almost half the people here at Red Rock are vegetarians. I don't think it'd go over very big." She replugged the wash basin and ran clean water in. She wrung the clothes, piece by piece, and piled them on the drain board. When she was done, she drained the basin and went into the women's wash room.

Leland listened, and, though he heard the splash of the water and the sounds of washing, he didn't hear her gasp, or curse from the cold water.

She came back in a moment, a towel carried casually in front of her. She hung the towel and, naked, put another split log in the stove.

Leland closed his eyes and leaned back. He felt the water rise as she stepped into the tub and shifted up to keep his mouth out of it. She was probably twice as old as he was but her body didn't seem old at all.

"That"—Charly sighed—"is a bit of all right. I don't usually take a soak in the middle of the day, but then I don't usually get such a workout." She was silent for a moment and Leland opened his eyes. Charly was opposite him, sunk to her chin, but she was regarding him thoughtfully.

"Yes?" he said.

"You meant it, right? About never practicing before?"

He nodded.

"Did you read about it? Did you observe classes?"

"Not aikido. Only the unarmed combat classes they teach the militia. Karate and a few throws and chokes."

She shook her head. "It takes years to develop *ukemi* to your level. I've been doing aikido for twenty-two years and I'm not sure my *ukemi* is as good as yours."

Leland said, "If I'm so good—"

YOU'RE NOT.

"—then why does my body hurt so much?"

"Maybe because you're a *tuklu?*" she muttered, then shook her head.

"What's a *tuklu?*"

"Never mind."

Leland tried not to watch when Charly climbed out of the tub, but he wasn't completely successful. At least it moved his attention from his aching joints and muscles to a different part of his body.

The stiffening (both kinds) had lessened by the time they went back to the cottage. Leland was able to carry some of the laundry and to help hang it in the afternoon sun, but then he went inside and collapsed on his pallet.

At noon and supper, Charly cajoled him into stumbling stiffly down the road to the hall, but his appetite was low. He tried to participate in the dinner conversation but dropped out gratefully when Charly started a long conversation with a woman about flax and hemp fibers.

Back at the cottage she boiled water. "I think you'd better drink this." She handed him a cup of bitter-smelling liquid.

"Willow bark. Yuck. Got any honey?"

"It's sweetened."

"When I was a kid, we got honey *and* milk."

"You're still a kid. But if you want milk, you'll have to go back to the hall for it. They've got goat's milk in the cellar." She damped the stove and began winding a new set of warp strings on her loom. "Drink it or don't. It's your body."

He did. As before, he fell asleep to the sound of Charly's loom.

She woke him midmorning, after returning from the dojo. "Did you go to breakfast?"

He shook his head and groaned.

"Well, get up. You're probably stiff as a board."

He used the toilet with difficulty, then hobbled outside to sit in the sun. From inside the cottage, Charly's voice said, "Go beg some food from the hall. If I give you any more willow bark on an empty stomach you'll get sick."

The act of walking loosened his muscles and, after some minor coaxing, the kitchen staff gave him some bread, honey, and one quarter of a greenhouse cantaloupe. His appetite was better but the muscles groaned.

Back at the cottage he drank his bitter dose of willow bark tea, then sat in the open doorway and carded llama wool while Charly worked at the loom. He had trouble standing, and limped when they walked down to the hall for a light lunch.

When they returned, Charly gave him more willow bark and said, "Take off your clothes and lie down on your pallet."

He blinked. "Pardon?"

She went into the bathroom. "Go on. Lie facedown."

He did as she directed, lying down as she came into his room. "It's your lower back, isn't it? On the left side? Spasming?"

"Yes—that's the worst place."

She sat a small ceramic bottle on the tatami and removed its wooden stopper. "This is oil of peppermint. You ever use it?"

"Only in candy."

"It'll feel cool at first, but after a while it'll produce heat and will reduce the pain. This, and a bit of massage, will help loosen those muscles." She poured some of the fluid onto her hands and spread it onto Leland's back. Then she dug her thumbs into the knotted muscles on the sides of his spine.

He tensed.

"Try to relax into it," she said. She worked over his entire back, then his shoulders and upper arms. "You are tight *everywhere.* Relax a little. Does this hurt? Does it feel good?"

"It feels good." *Very good.* He was blushing and hoped she didn't notice. His body was reacting to her touch in more ways than one.

"Well, groan a little. Relax. It's okay to acknowledge pleasure. Turn over and let me work on your quadriceps."

"Uh, that's okay. Really." He tried to think cold, withering thoughts but it didn't seem to be doing any good.

She must've sensed what was troubling him for she took a towel from the shelf and draped it across his buttocks. "Here—go ahead, turn over."

He twisted over, moving carefully to avoid dislodging the towel, and stared studiously at the ceiling. She dug her thumbs into his thighs, working from the towel's edge to the knees, then working on the muscles and tendons around the knees. If she noticed the bulge under the towel, she didn't say anything.

She stopped when the smell of mint filled the room and covered him with a thin sheet. "Relax—rest. Sleep if you can. I'll wake you before supper."

An intense wave of sorrow swept over Leland and he felt his eyes began to water. *It must be the mint. Where were you when I was being beaten every day?*

"Thank you, Charly."

Leland was still sore the next morning, but he swung his arms briskly on the walk up the hill and, by the time class started, he was feeling something approaching normalcy.

Charly led them through warmup, then started the class with *Ikkyo,* a basic immobilization.

The woman who paired with Leland was *nage* first, the one who throws or pins, and she performed the technique with vigor, straining Leland's sore muscles.

SHE'S CHALLENGING YOU, said the voice.

When it was Leland's turn, he hesitated for a second. He'd never performed these techniques. NOT IN THIS BODY. RELAX. He extended his arm for her to grab. She took it and his fingers spread, alive. He moved, performing the technique with precision and just enough force. As he sank down for the pin, he felt her start to resist, but the arm with which he held her elbow was extended, and the wrist of the same arm was held above that, giving her no leverage. He let his center drop and she slapped hard with her other arm to break the fall. He completed the pin and stood.

She came back even stronger, but he didn't fight force with force. He just performed the technique with precision, working no harder than necessary—never pushing against her force—working across it or blending with it.

When it was her turn to pin again, he went with her, blending, moving as fast but no faster than she did. When she moved her knee into his ribs, he simply moved with it, so that, at most, it merely brushed his side. When she came down with all her weight on his elbow, he slapped hard with his free hand, arched his back, and dove his captured shoulder for the mat, keeping the stresses off it.

As he stood up, he saw Charly watching them with a smile on her face, but she didn't say anything. When it was his turn to be *nage*, he continued to use good technique and minimal force.

Charly stopped them. "Prudence," she said, to the woman. "Is your *ukemi* up to more *kokyu?*"

The woman looked surprised. "Yes, Sensei."

"Very well. Leland, more *kokyu.*"

Leland bowed. "*Hai.*"

Prudence moved to take his arm and, as she made contact, he moved abruptly to the side, cutting down into her elbow and dropping his center. She fell forward so fast that she was forced to take a forward break-fall, but she scrambled to get back up, still holding his wrist. As she rose he took her elbow over and straight down, into the tatami. She tried to slap, but the side of her head and shoulder hit the mat first with an unpleasant thud.

Leland let go immediately and sank to his knees. "Are you all right?"

Prudence was blushing and carefully prodding her shoulder. "Uh. Yes. I'm okay."

Charly's face was neutral. "Perhaps you should *both* hold back a bit."

Prudence was less challenging after that.

After a week of the morning classes, Leland started walking up the hill for the late-afternoon class with Denesse Sensei. Several people from the valley came up for this class, and the tatami was crowded, requiring constant awareness to avoid throwing one's partner into other students.

Denesse had a different teaching style than Charly. He'd laugh, cajole, roar, shout, and joke. When he threw people they flew hard, slamming into the tatami. He didn't use the same *uke* for an entire class, calling up a different student each time he demonstrated a new technique.

The students were different, too. There were some without *hakama,* like Leland, and others, with *hakama,* who were obviously more experienced than the *uchideshi.*

Some of these reacted to Leland as Prudence had, throwing him hard and resisting when they were *uke.* He ignored them, simply blending with their motions and jumping right up. When they resisted his technique, he ignored this, too, depending on proper extension and *kokyu* to override their rejection of the technique. This caused their *ukemi* to be rougher than necessary.

After one evening class Leland returned to the cottage and asked Charly about them.

She laughed. "Nobody knows what to make of you. You've got better *ukemi* than any of them but you're not wearing a *hakama.* I've been asked more than once where you studied and why you aren't wearing a *hakama.*"

"What did you say?"

"I told them to ask Denesse Sensei."

Leland remembered Denesse's answer to Charly, when she asked. *It's not my place to explain it.*

Wednesday nights, Charly joined Leland for the advanced class. This was *hakama* wearers only. Leland felt awkward being the only one on the practice surface without one. He relaxed, though, and watched carefully, that dark part of him muttering things like THAT IS A DERIVATION—IT FOLLOWS FROM THE FUNDAMENTAL PRINCIPLES, KIHON, BUT IT WASN'T TAUGHT IN MY TIME.

The level of *ukemi*—the vigor of techniques—was higher in this class. He tried to take his partners to the edge of their *ukemi* but no farther. More than once he shook a higher belt's complacency, as they expected his lack of *hakama* to indicate lack of technique.

Slowly his body became used to the practice. He no longer ached through the night, and at the end of a practice he wasn't drenched in sweat.

But the inner voice was never satisfied. YOUR FEET WERE OFF THE LINE. YOU WERE TOO FAR AWAY FROM THEM. YOU WERE TOO CLOSE. YOU DIDN'T TAKE THEIR BALANCE SOON ENOUGH. YOU WERE THREE CENTIMETERS OFF THE ELBOW.

The voice never criticized *during* a technique. But almost always afterward.

During the days, between morning and afternoon practice, he began working at the hall, first cleaning dishes and washing tables. Later, after the school coordinator saw him working through a mechanical engineering text, he began tutoring older kids in math and elementary mechanics.

He saw that they also didn't know what to make of him. If they tried to treat him like a guide, he went back to doing menial chores. If they tried to treat him like one of their own, a piece of that *other* would slip out—a phrase of language, a piece of knowledge—and they couldn't help but regard him as strange.

He understood this. He didn't know what to make of himself, either.

A little over six weeks after he'd arrived, the heliogram came. The boy in the tower shouted and a cook fetched Leland from an algebra tutoring session in the hall. He walked outside and looked up.

"Message for you, Warden," said the boy. "From Laal Station."

"Okay." Leland's stomach felt odd. "Read it, please."

"To Warden Leland de Laal, Red Rock Station. From Guide Dulan de Laal, Laal Station. Return soonest. Escort at K. Pass. Advise ETA there." The boy looked up from his message slate. "That's it."

Leland stared at the dust by his feet. He could leave now and, if he walked well into the night, he could make it to the Khyber Pass by the following sunset, but he didn't want to leave without making his goodbyes at the dojo.

"Send 'Arrive pass noon, Friday,' " he said.

The boy nodded. "Anything else?"

Leland gave a sour smile. " 'I hear and obey.' "

He watched the boy bend back to the heliograph, adjusting the mirror for the current angle of the sun, then flipping the shutter back and forth to send the Morse message. Leland shaded his eyes and looked to the west, to the ridgeline where the relay station was, but it was too far to make out the tower. After a minute, though, he saw the flashes of reflected sunlight: MSG. RCVD.

The boy said, "It's on its way."

"Thank you."

There were four relays between Red Rock and Laal Station, but the message would be there in less than ten minutes. Leland thought about his father reading the message—brought by runner from the heliograph platform on the Station's northwest tower—and he felt the hair on his scalp tingle.

He returned to the hall and finished the tutoring session.

When it was time to go up the hill, for his last class, Charly opened a low chest in her room and took out a fresh gi and a *hakama* so dark and blue it resembled the last edge of the twilight sky. She put them in her bag and said, "Let's go."

"But it's not Wednesday."

She nodded. "That's right." She slipped on her sandals and walked outside. He gathered his gi and slipped on his boots, then hurried to catch up.

They climbed in silence, but, at the last switchback before the dojo, Leland said, "I need to tell Denesse Sensei that I'm leaving."

She said, "You don't have to. There were several heliograms received and answered today."

"Oh."

The changing rooms was packed with bodies. Leland dressed carefully, trying to avoid poking his elbows into those around him. LIKE DRESSING IN A PHONE BOOTH. Leland shook his head. *What the hell is a phone booth?*

The mat was also crowded when he bowed in. Every student he'd seen over six weeks of classes was there and a few faces that were strange to him. There were so many people on the mat that they formed two lines instead of the usual one. So many bodies warmed the air that the skylights were tilted opened, for ventilation.

Leland joined the line in back and concentrated on his breathing, eyes half closed, one hand cupping the other in his lap. After a few minutes he heard a shifting sound, as those seated straightened their posture. He was on the end of one line so he could see Denesse Sensei, accompanied by Charly, bowing in. Charly sat beside Leland, at the end of the back line, and Denesse continued to the front.

The class bowed in and Denesse led them through warmups. When they were done with the stretches and *ukemi,* he demonstrated the first technique—*udegarami,* an elbow throw. Practice was difficult on the mat since it was so crowded, but Leland took it in his stride, modifying his *ukemi* to avoid striking anyone, and, as *nage,* changing direction in midtechnique to find an empty place on the mat to throw his partner.

Whenever it was time to change partners, he found people jumping to tap his shoulder or knee. He noticed the same was happening with Charly, the upper belts scrambling to be the first to choose one or the other.

BE FLATTERED.

*If you say so.*

Substantially before the end of normal class, Denesse Sensei said, "Stretch your backs!"

Leland was surprised. When they were seated again, to bow out, Denesse Sensei said, "A short break while the lamps are lit. Shall we say a quarter stick?"

He turned on his knees and bowed to the *kamiza,* then to the class.

After he'd left the mat and the students began bowing to their partners, Leland asked Prudence, the *uchideshi* who'd challenged him the first day, "What's happening after the break?"

Her jaw dropped. "You don't know?"

"I wouldn't have asked if I did."

"You're testing. You and Charlina Sensei. I can't believe they didn't tell you. That's why everyone is here."

I CAN.

"Oh," said Leland. *What's testing?*

BETTER YOU SHOULDN'T ASK. YOU REALLY NEED MORE PRACTICE. DRINK SOME WATER.

The *uchideshi* had lit and adjusted the wicks of the lamps and replaced their glass chimneys. There was still the dim glow of dusk coming through the skylights, but the lamps, set in beveled niches around the room, lent a yellow glow to the room. One of the seniors, watching the burning of a stick of incense at the front of the room, clapped his hands and they lined up.

Denesse Sensei reentered the room carrying a small book. They bowed in and he said, "*Shidoin* to the front. Everybody else, to the sides."

The two lines split in the middle and moved to the ends of the room. Leland found himself at the other end of the room from Charly. She looked composed, but her face seemed slightly pale.

*She's nervous. Uh-oh.* He felt his hands begin to tremble, and he pressed them firmly against his thighs to stop the shaking.

There were five other *hakama* wearers at the front of the room, beside Denesse Sensei. Denesse Sensei opened his book and placed it on the ground before him, then took a pair of half-glasses from inside his gi and perched them on his nose.

"Charlina Rosen. Leland de Laal. Come forward."

Simultaneously Charly and Leland came out in *shikko,* knee-walking, and lined up beside each other in the middle of the room, facing the *kamiza.*

"I'm sure that many of you would like to do *ukemi* tonight but I only want *shodans* and above."

FIRST-DEGREE BLACK BELT.

"So," continued Denesse, "*ukes,* please."

Leland saw motion out of the corner of his eye and heard the sound of multiple feet racing across the tatami. Someone thumped to the mat behind him and he heard the slower feet withdraw back to the sides of the room.

They bowed to the altar, then to Denesse Sensei, then he turned to face the person behind him, one of the older *uchideshi,* Peter was his name, and bowed to him. Leland turned back to the front.

"Variations on Ushiro Ryotedori Hamnihandachi kokyunage," Denesse Sensei said.

And so it started.

Leland lost count of the times they changed ukes, and when they went to *jodori*—staff taking techniques—he almost panicked. The wooden staffs were the length and width of the bamboo poles used by his brothers over the last year.

PULL YOURSELF TOGETHER. THEY'RE ONLY STICKS. TAKE THEM AWAY. YOU DON'T HAVE TO PUT UP WITH THAT.

He threw his attacker very hard, necessitating yet another change of ukes.

Knife and sword taking went easier, and he was more under control.

At the end, totally drenched in sweat, first Charly, then Leland took turns with five-person *randori*—multiple-person attack.

He was too tired to be nervous. FIVE IS EASY. THEY GET IN EACH OTHER'S WAY. He kept turning, moving forward to the next attacker, turning, moving forward, throwing attacker into attacker, entering their space so quickly it felt more like he was attacking the five, not the other way around.

And then Denesse Sensei clapped his hands and they stopped coming. Leland staggered slightly, then sat beside his ukes. They bowed out and Denesse Sensei said, "A short break." Then he led the other black belts out of the room.

Leland didn't know what to do. A short break before what? More testing?

There was a collective groan as the students who'd been sitting *seiza* throughout the class straightened, massaging their knees. *Maybe I was the lucky one.* But he felt limp, drained.

Charly walked over to him and sat. "I didn't see much of your test, Leland, but your *randori* was lovely. I particularly liked the *sankyo* projection at the end."

"My *uke* seemed surprised. Hope I didn't hurt him."

"Worry about the two he collided with. But they're all fine."

Leland remembered something. "Hey! Why didn't you tell me about the test?"

Charly stifled laughter in the back of her throat. "If you'd known, would you have taken it?"

He blinked. "I guess."

"And would you have worried about it?"

He remembered that intense stab of panic in the pit of his stomach when Prudence told him. "Well . . . yes."

She grinned. "Then I did you a favor, didn't I? Believe me, I was nervous enough for both of us."

"How long have you known about this test?"

"I've known about mine for months. It's why I'm here at Red Rock, after all. I found out this afternoon that you would also test."

WHAT WAS SHE TESTING FOR? "What were you testing for?"

"GODAN. And my SHIDOIN certificate."

FIFTH-DEGREE BLACK BELT AND HER INSTRUCTOR'S RATING.

"What was *I* testing for?"

The smile dropped from Charly's face. "I don't know."

A student seated near the door clapped his hands and the lines re-formed. Denesse Sensei came back in with the upper black belts. They bowed in formally and Denesse Sensei turned to face them.

"Charlina Rosen." He gestured to the mat before him.

Charly came out in *shikko* until she was before him, then bowed.

"It is with great sorrow . . ." said Denesse Sensei. There was a gasp from the students and they shifted en masse.

*Didn't she pass?*

Denesse glared at the students and they settled back. "As I was saying—it is with great sorrow that I . . . award you your *godan* rank and *shidoin* rating. For it means you will leave us." And now he smiled and there was muffled laughter from the students.

THAT OLD SCUMBAG!

Denesse Sensei said, "Good test, Charly." He led the applause, which went on for quite a while. Then they bowed to each other again and Denesse Sensei gestured to a spot by his side. Charly slid forward and sat beside him.

"Leland de Laal."

Leland knee-walked out and bowed.

"When we promote it is to acknowledge something that has already been accomplished—something that already is—but it is also to acknowledge the work, effort, and *time* that has gone into attaining that level of technique. Do you understand what I mean?"

PERFECTLY. "*Hai,* Sensei," Leland said.

"We find it inappropriate to rank you at this time. This does not reflect upon your test, which was excellent, but only on the amount of time you've practiced. We do award you your *shidoin* certificate, though, for to do otherwise would be to deny *us* what you have to teach."

Denesse gestured to Charly and she bowed, then turned to a corner of the *kamiza* where a dark bundle sat. She took it and turned back to Leland, knee-walking forward and putting the bundle down in front of him, then bowing. In a low voice she said, "I wove the cloth myself."

He bowed low and took the package. It was a midnight-blue *hakama* folded in the formal style.

Denesse spoke again. "Charlina Sensei and Leland Sensei will be leaving tomorrow. It is my hope that Leland Sensei will teach the morning class before he leaves."

*Me?* YOU? Leland blushed to the roots of his hair. "*Hai.*"

Denesse Sensei said, "For those of you who can stay, we'll be having a dinner immediately after. In the meanwhile, let me be the first to congratulate Leland Sensei." He began a round of applause.

*I didn't do anything to deserve this.*

PERHAPS THEY'RE APPLAUDING FOR DINNER.

*Cynic. They're applauding—it's enough.*

Later, when he was feeling his way down the hill with Charly, he asked, "So you're leaving tomorrow also. Where to?" The sky was overcast, blocking the ringlight, but he'd been up and down this path so many times in the last six weeks that his feet knew the way.

Charly said, "I'm from Noramland, though I've been here for the last nine months. Almost like a pregnancy, eh? Gestating a *shidoin* certificate." She laughed. There'd been a lot of toasts drunk to the departing pair and they were both light-headed from the wine.

"Oh. Where in Noramland?"

"The city."

Leland blinked. "I went once—when I was seven. The whole family made the trip. My father has an estate and a townhouse there."

"Yes. He's a Principal of the Council, after all."

The thought of his father chilled Leland. "Ah. So he is." He tried to change the subject. "Will you be taking the horse road into Noram?"

"No. I'll be going to Laal Station with you and travel with the next trade caravan. It'll be good to get back to my dojo. There are people I miss. And heliograms are poor substitutes for flesh."

"What'll happen to your cottage?"

"It's not mine. It belongs to the dojo—for visiting instructors. I've been told that there'll be two this winter. I hope they keep the *uchideshi* hopping."

When they reached the cottage the lamps were on and the fire was lit. Charly's weaving supplies and clothing were packed in hampers, lined neatly up in the space her loom had recently occupied. The loom itself was disassembled and lashed into bundles. Leland's clothing was laid out neatly, next to his bag, ready to pack when he'd selected his clothing for the next day.

"Who did this?" Leland asked.

"The *uchideshi.* They left before the toasts."

"They were back before *we* left!"

"Well, they ran up and down the hill. It's good for them. But remember, when you teach in the morning, if they seem a little slow in class? Take it into consideration."

"I will." He grinned wickedly. "Believe me—I will."

Putting on the *hakama* was like going home after a long absence—both intimately familiar and passing strange. He was surprised to see more than the *uchideshi* on the mat. Several of the evening students were there, too.

He led the class in warmups, including some stretches strange to them. Then, after *ukemi* practice, he called on Prudence as his *uke.*

It was like dancing.

He ran through techniques from *ushiro ryotedori*—an attack where *uke* grabs a wrist with one hand, then circles behind to grab the other wrist and pin *nage*'s arms behind.

He started with ikkyo, the elbow immobilization, then proceeded through a series of projections: *iriminage, jujinage,* standing *kokyuho,* and finally *udegarami.* As he walked around correcting technique and *ukemi,* he felt like an impostor, a fake.

YOU'RE HERE FOR THEM—NOT YOURSELF.

He tried to ignore the doubts. At the end, when he was bowing to the picture of the great teacher, he lifted a prayer. *Make me worthy . . . in my* own *right.*

ONLY YOU CAN DO THAT.

*Oh, shut up.*

# SIX

## KOSHIN: MOVING BACKWARD

The walk back to the Khyber Pass was much like Leland's first trip to Red Rock. Bonkers and the rest of the llama string were with him, though this time they carried Charly's household goods and loom. Also, the night stop was in the low barrens between the two passes. And, of course, there was Charly.

"I saw a lynx! I'm sure of it." She was bouncing up and down.

"This is awful low altitude for a lynx. Did it have tufted ears?"

"Uh, I'm not sure."

"It was probably a bobcat. It's the same genus, but smaller, though it has the tufted ears. Have you ever seen a lynx?"

"Yes. Not alive, though. There's a stuffed one at the Steward's Palace in Noram City."

"They call Noram House a palace?"

"Well, it is a bit big to be called a house. The steward started calling it that and it stuck."

*When will "high steward" be replaced with "king"?* He changed the subject back. "We get lynx above the Tiber valley, sometimes, especially in the winter. They come down after the snowshoe hare."

On the Tiber side of the Khyber Pass, they were met by three mounted squads of the Falcons and Louis, the boy from Red Rock who'd broken his leg.

The man in charge sketched a quick salute. "Warden Leland," their leader called. "Coronet Gahnfeld at your service. Captain Koss sends his compliments. We've been assigned as your bodyguard."

Leland returned the salute. "My bodyguard? Whatever for?"

Gahnfeld was a big, dark-skinned man with heavy bones. He seemed in his mid-thirties. He shook his head. "I've no idea, Guide. After your father met with the messenger from the high steward, I was told to meet you here and stick with you, if you'll pardon the expression, 'like a stud to a mare.' "

Leland frowned. "Those weren't my father's words, were they?"

Gahnfeld grinned. "Captain Koss."

"Ah. This is Charlina Rosen. She travels with us to the Station. Why are you here, Louis?"

Louis, who was scratching Bonkers's neck vigorously, grinned. "I'm here to take my string back. I'm going home."

Leland glanced back at the llamas, loaded with Charly's stuff.

Louis said, "Oh, don't worry about the loads. These guys brought pack mules for your stuff."

"And mounts for you and Guide Charlina," Gahnfeld added.

"Uh, Charlina isn't—" Leland started to say, but then he looked at Charly, who laughed.

"Well, actually, Charlina is," said Charly. "It's de Rosen but it's not important. I don't usually use it. Was it an assumption, Coronet?" she asked Gahnfeld.

"No, Guide. My orders specifically mentioned 'Guide Charlina de Rosen of Noram City.' "

"Oh, well," said Charly. "Your father knows mine. They're on the council together. He probably recognized my name in Denesse Sensei's heliogram."

Leland tried to picture Charly dressed for a court function but couldn't imagine it. He shook his head. "Well, let's transfer the baggage."

"At your command, Guide. If you'll be seated—there's lunch waiting." Gahnfeld turned. "Petrach, Liu—have your squads transfer the baggage. Grambort, perimeter watch—both sides of the pass. Bungy—ride on back to that line-of-site and signal Laal Station."

"What message?" asked the soldier who must have been Bungy.

"To Koss, Falcons. Haystack. Gahnfeld."

The soldier repeated it back, then mounted a horse and rode back through the pass.

"Haystack?" said Leland.

Gahnfeld grinned. "As in finding, Guide."

Charly said, "I don't understand."

Leland blushed. "I'm Warden of the Needle. The message means they've found me. A needle in a haystack."

"Oh," Charly said. "So, *shidoin,* why do you need a bodyguard?"

"Ix-nay on the idoin-shay, if you please. I've no idea."

Gahnfeld steered them to the side of the pass, out of the way of the soldiers moving the bags.

"Do you know anything about the high steward's message?"

"Yes, Warden. The high steward's party crosses the Black tomorrow morning. With them rides Siegfried Montrose." One of the soldiers carrying luggage spit at the sound of Montrose's name. The coronet stiffened at the sound but kept his eyes on Leland.

Leland's eyebrows went up. "Montrose, eh? My, oh my." *Peace?* He sat down on a boulder in the shade and blinked. "Well, I guess we should eat this food and get going then, shouldn't we?"

"Steward, I must protest!"

Dulan de Laal raised his eyebrows and looked at Captain Koss. There was a silence in the room, rigid and furious. Captain Koss clenched his jaw and stared back. Martin and Dexter stared wide-eyed at both of them, shocked not only by Captain Koss's outburst but also by the statement that had caused the reaction.

Guide Dulan sighed and looked aside. "Please excuse us, Martin, Dexter."

Dexter stood immediately, followed more slowly by Martin. They both bowed and left Dulan's study, closing the door behind them.

Captain Koss was still glaring angrily when Dulan turned back to him. "Machiavelli had advice for situations like this," Dulan said quietly. "He suggested that a prince should have a council of a few wise men who feared not to tell him the truth *but only when he asked for it!*" He raised his eyebrows again. "Did I ask your opinion of my orders?"

"Stuff Machiavelli! You'll throw your sons into open revolt if you give the new unit to Leland!"

"You take a great deal upon yourself, Leonid!"

"Then remove me from my post or kill me! If de Noram calls on you for troops to fight the Rootless, then the new unit will be all that defends Laal. If Montrose attacks, despite whatever agreement he's cemented with Arthur, the new unit will need a commander that's been proven in battle. That means you, Dillan, or Dexter. Ricard and I will be on the other side of Noram, fighting for that stupid plain, and your guides will be harrying the enemy's flanks with their few professionals and their militias! By the Founders, man, he's only seventeen!"

"Ah," said Dulan. "That's why you're upset. Well, don't worry. When and if Cotswold crosses the Black, the Falcons and the Mounted Pikes will be here to meet them. The new unit goes to the plain."

Captain Koss sat back in his chair, astonished. His mouth opened twice to say something, but each time he shut it again. Finally he pushed his chair back and knelt on the floor. "I apologize abjectly, sire. I beg you to remove me from my post. I am not worthy to hold it."

"Oh, shut up and get us some wine. Think what's going to happen when I tell Dillan!"

Captain Koss hesitated for a moment, then got up and went to the sideboard. He returned with two goblets. "Nothing will happen when you tell Dillan—he will say 'Of course, Father' and that will be it. Anthony, on the other hand, will be furious. Dexter will be confused."

Dulan nodded. "Yes, you're right. That's why I sent Dillan to escort Arthur in. Nothing Arthur or Siegfried can say or do will get a rise from him." He accepted the goblet from Captain Koss. "I'm still surprised you don't object more about Leland's appointment. Aren't you worried about the men?"

Captain Koss shrugged. "Yes, but less than if Dexter held the command. Leland is more likely to bring them back alive. Dexter takes too many risks. Also, when you received that head wound at Atten Falls, I was the one who bathed and bandaged it. I saw the scars on your temples, and I've seen the scars on Leland's head in the same place."

Dulan grunted. "There is that . . . I hope." He turned back to Koss. "How many of the men are from the old troops?"

"All five halvidars and fifteen of the coronets. We have chosen provisional coronets for the other eight positions." He paused then, keeping his eyes on the table. "I would offer a suggestion."

Dulan looked at Koss gravely. "Please—I *ask* it of you."

"I'll appoint a master halvidar for the unit. Someone the troop halvidars have confidence in."

Dulan considered. "No," he said finally. "I might as well give that man command. Instead, give him a good halvidar for his headquarters unit—someone who'll give good advice, *when* advice is asked for."

Captain Koss winced. "Yes, Guide."

* * *

Leland offered Charly quarters in the station but she said, "I'm staying with the Druza family in Brandon-on-the-Falls. It's arranged."

"The Druzas? They have a bookbindery. Have you been here before?" Leland asked.

"No. But their son is a student of mine in the city. His mother is the sensei at On-the-Falls Aikikai."

She hugged him when they parted. "Come practice before I leave."

He thought about going back to the Station—his father's house—and hugged her back fiercely. *Please come with me.* "I will."

Leland's first action on returning to Laal keep was to dismiss the bodyguard. This didn't work.

"I beg your pardon, Guide, but Captain Koss was quite insistent! He ordered us to stay on this duty until relieved by him or your father."

Leland considered this. "Well, dammit, man, I can't have twelve men following me all around the Station. The hallways aren't that big!"

Coronet Gahnfeld nodded. "Of course, Guide. With your permission, I'll relieve two squads for supper, post two men at your quarters, and the other two with your person. I also ask that you give me advance notice of your intentions, so we can check the way ahead of time."

"You are kidding, aren't you?"

Gahnfeld looked surprised. "Oh, no, Warden! It would be worth my skin to disobey Captain Koss's orders."

Leland winced at the use of his title. *Fornication!* He steamed quietly for a moment, taking quick, short steps across the stable yard. Finally he snapped out, "As you will, Gahnfeld. Right now I'm going to the library. Then I'm going to take a bath, and then I'm going to eat." His voice, raised in annoyance, stopped suddenly, and he seemed to take hold of himself. When he spoke again, it was quietly and calmly. "Is there anything else I should brief you about?" he asked the soldier.

The coronet took a step back and saluted. "No, Guide."

Dillan de Laal waited on the bank of the Black River, a solitary figure on a gray horse. Ten meters behind him was his standard-bearer, and fifty meters behind him the Third Mounted Pikes stood at attention beside their horses, a disciplined line of a thousand kept all the straighter by Ricard de Laal's constantly moving eye.

From politeness, Dillan had invited Ricard to wait with him at the front, but Captain de Laal had declined. "No, Cousin. This rabble of mine needs constant attention."

Dillan had been relieved. The two disliked each other, a mutual antagonism that had started in childhood but had resolved itself into a cold truce in adulthood.

On the other side of the river a distant dust cloud marked the movements of the High Steward's party across Cotswold's Gray Plain. A small scouting party, well in advance of the main column, came galloping into view, paused at the top of the far bank, then came trotting down the cut to the ford.

The Black was a deep river in most places, flowing south from the Hearth Mountains in the east and forming Greater Noramland's eastern border with Nullarbor, then flowing west to mark Noramland's southern border with Cotswold. Here, at Jaren's Ford, the Black spread wide instead of deep, flowing over bedrock. In the spring it was too deep to cross, but for the rest of the year, it was usually passable.

Now the main party came into view, five hundred mounted troops riding to the side of the carts, wagons, and mounts of the steward's retainers. Near the front of the group, Dillan could make out the banner of High Steward de Noram and beside it, the clenched fist of Cotswold. Passenger coaches followed and the baggage carts brought up the rear. The mounted troops spurred ahead then and came down the cut and split, lining the far bank to each side of the ford.

Dillan turned his horse and nodded at Ricard, then trotted down to the ford, his standard-bearer following. Behind him he heard Ricard shout, "Prepare to mount! Mount!" Dillan rode on into the shallow water and splashed his way across the half kilometer to the other side. Ricard's Mounted Pikes stayed where they were.

Once out of the water, he nodded to the captain of the Cotswold mounted troops and waited.

The first four riders down the hill were High Steward Arthur de Noram, Guide Marilyn de Noram, and two others whom Dillan had not met but knew to be High Steward Siegfried Montrose and his son, Guide Sylvan Montrose. Immediately behind them came the two standard-bearers.

Dillan dismounted and knelt in the road as Arthur rode up. "Greetings, Steward. I carry my father's compliments and wishes for your well-being." He stood then.

Arthur waved his hand in half salute, arrogant, barely polite. “Greetings,” he said shortly. “Are we ready to proceed?”

Dillan ignored the slight and continued politely. “Certainly, Steward. May I offer my father’s greetings to the Guide Marilyn and to the family Montrose?” He performed a half bow to Marilyn, Siegfried, and Sylvan.

Marilyn, surprised at her father’s rudeness, said quickly, “Thank you, Guide Dillan. I trust your father and the rest of your family are well?”

Arthur frowned at his daughter’s words but said nothing.

“Yes, Guide. My father is quite well. I hope your road has been easy since we last saw you.”

Marilyn smiled. “It has. May I present High Steward Siegfried Montrose and his son Guide Sylvan.”

“Honored, Steward. Guide.”

Siegfried smiled slightly, his eyes going from Arthur to Dillan. “A pleasure to meet the eldest son of Dulan de Laal.”

Sylvan yawned and looked at the river.

Dillan mounted then and said, “At your command, Steward.”

Arthur turned in his saddle. “Are you ready, Siegfried?”

Siegfried Montrose smiled. “A moment, if you please, Arthur, while I give my captains their orders.” He reined aside, accompanied by Sylvan, and conversed privately with his officers for a few moments.

Dillan waited quietly, studying Siegfried Montrose.

The High Steward of Cotswold was a tall, thin man, with craggy, bony features and thick, ragged eyebrows below a receding hairline. His hair was dark and shot with streaks of gray. His dark clothing, though simple of cut and ornamentation, was made of the best fabrics; his boots shone in the sun. His appearance suggested disciplined power.

Arthur, with his brilliantly colored collars, lapels, and sleeves, looked foppish when contrasted with Siegfried.

Sylvan was somewhere in between, both in dress and features. He had something of his father’s discipline but some of Arthur’s liking for fashionable clothing. As tall as his father but without the thinness, he had muscles that his clothing didn’t hide. He wore a curved sword in the Cotswold fashion, on the waist for a cross draw. A long dagger was in a sheath across the small of his back, and Dillan spotted another sticking out of the top of a boot.

Arthur sat without speaking, a sour expression on his face. After a moment he turned to his standard-bearer and said, "Have wine brought. This dust will be my death."

Dillan thought, *Would that you'd been more like William.* There'd been no trouble with Cotswold when William de Noram had ruled. Nor had Nullarbor ever held the Plain of the Founders for even a season. Dillan shrugged. "And how did you find Montrouge, Gentle Guide? I've heard it has many impressive buildings."

Marilyn nodded. "Indeed, but it's hot and dry there, and the dust storms are terrible. I'll be glad to get back to somewhere *green!*" She glanced at her father, who had ridden back up the road a bit to meet the servant with the wine. With a lowered voice she asked, "And how are your brothers?"

Dillan kept a straight face as he toyed with her. "Dexter is fine. He's drilling with Captain Koss's Falcons and loves it. Anthony is working with the harvest masters. They have to build more granaries this year since the surplus from last year hasn't been exhausted. The work seems to agree with both of the them."

Marilyn frowned. "And Leland? What of Leland?"

Dillan raised his eyebrows. "Leland? Oh, yes, Leland." He looked at the river for a moment. "I hope you'll find him well."

"What's he doing?" she asked quickly, since her father was riding back toward them.

Dillan sighed. "His father's will, Guide. His father's will."

Anthony and Dexter reached the Great Hall together. Each had returned to the Station just before the banquet and had hurried through bathing and dressing.

The High Steward de Noram's party and escort had arrived shortly after midday. There'd been a brief greeting ceremony in the Great Hall, with refreshments all around, then they were escorted to the guest halls and given access to the baths.

Bartholomew, stationed at the door, bowed formally as they hurried into the room. Dexter slowed so suddenly that Anthony bumped into him.

"Easy, brother. With dignity now."

Anthony took a deep breath and glared halfheartedly at Dexter. Then he winked at Bartholomew and followed his brother into the room.

Guide Dulan, the High Steward de Noram, and the High Steward

Montrose sat on the dais that normally held only the high seat. Now de Noram sat in the high seat and de Laal and Montrose sat to each side of him. They appeared to be talking quietly and sampling small foods from passing trays.

Dexter looked around the great floor. He saw Dillan waiting near his table talking to the Guide Marilyn and a tall, dark man wearing green and black with a jeweled dagger prominently on his waist. Dexter paused and stared at him for a moment. *Ah, that must be Sylvan Montrose. Big fellow, isn't he?*

Anthony headed for his table and the group of guests waiting around it, so Dexter did likewise. "Evening, Leland," Dexter said as he passed Leland's table.

Leland, whose eyes had been staring across the room, turned his head quickly at Dexter's voice and smiled faintly. "Good evening."

Dexter walked on but couldn't help wondering why Coronet Gahnfeld, the "bad boy" of the Falcons, was standing behind Leland looking uncomfortable in formal clothing. And why two more Falcons in dress clothes stood by the wall near Leland's table fully armed.

Captain Koss smiled as Dexter hurried up. "Ah, there you are. Did you give the second troop a good workout?"

"Hah! They wore me to a pulp. Next time you send me on a forced march with that group, I'm taking a horse. Their legs are too long."

"Tsk, tsk. I've already received a report from Halvidar Morton. He's of the opinion that 'Guide Dexter should be given a pack full of stones.' I think you gave as good as you got." Captain Koss's eyes wandered to Anthony's table and his daughter, Clarissa.

Dexter followed his gaze and saw her, head close to Anthony's, deep in conversation. "Oh, oh. You really should talk to Clarissa about the quality of the company she keeps."

Captain Koss smiled halfheartedly. "She's old enough to make her own mistakes—if mistakes they be. Be quiet, the high steward is about to speak."

Up on the dais, Arthur de Noram stood and raised a hand. Conversation ceased and all assembled turned to face the high seat. "Greetings and good fortune to all present," Arthur said in his reedy voice.

The crowd responded with a murmured "And also to you."

The High Steward continued. "I am pleased to be able to make the following announcements." He paused and motioned to Guide Dulan and High Steward Montrose to stand. "First of all, this afternoon, in closed council with me the Stewardship of Cotswold and the Guardianship of Laal signed articles of peace and cooperation. This leaves Greater Noramland free from hostile forces on its eastern border!"

Martin, standing to the side of the dais against the wall, signaled the applause by starting it. He stopped ten seconds later.

High Steward de Noram beamed. "Yes, yes. Thank you. As evidence of his good faith, the High Steward Montrose is sending his only son, Guide Sylvan Montrose, to reside in Noram City for the next two years, both to study our justly famous University of Noramland"—the high steward paused here to point out into the audience at Guide Sylvan—"and to pursue his suit with his newly betrothed, my daughter, the Guide Marilyn de Noram."

Dexter's jaw dropped. While the stewardship wasn't automatically hereditary and Marilyn's older sister came first, the son of a high steward married to the daughter of the ruling steward would join the list of qualified heirs. *A son of Cotswold on the throne of Noramland!* Dexter barely had wits about him to join in the applause. No matter how he considered it, he couldn't look at it as other than disastrous.

When the applause died down servants rushed to supply everyone with a goblet of wine. Guide Dulan stepped forward with his goblet raised. "As host I offer this toast, the traditional blessing of the Laals."

*Damn,* thought Dexter. *He might have warned us!* He readied himself.

Guide Dulan bowed toward Sylvan and Marilyn, then shouted, "Long life."

"Good health," continued Dillan.

"Good fortune," shouted Dexter.

"Many children," added Anthony.

"And great happiness!" finished Leland.

"Great happiness!" echoed the entire hall.

Dexter stood among the cheering crowd and thought dark, depressing thoughts.

*So much for Leland's prospects,* thought Anthony, eating more of the squash. He wasn't displeased. Speculation about Leland's interactions with Marilyn had run from the grandiose to the silly, but he'd been uneasy. He washed the squash down with a swallow of ice tea.

At Anthony's left, Clarissa picked at her food. Anthony looked at her and the problem of Leland faded, as usual, to the back of his mind.

"Ah, Clarissa. What do you think of the news? Peace, a new name in the ranks of heirs, eh?"

Clarissa frowned, then shook her head. "It's not my place to comment, Guide."

Anthony blinked. Her use of his title was unusual. Was it a subtle hint that this was a formal, public occasion and that perhaps her opinions were not suited for public display? "Perhaps we'll talk of it later," he said.

She nodded slowly.

Anthony settled back.

He watched his father talking with high stewards where they sat on the dias. He saw them smile and occasionally laugh at one of Arthur de Noram's jokes, but there was something unnatural about the way the high steward sat. Dulan and Siegfried seemed perfectly at ease, but there was something uncomfortable in the way Arthur kept shifting back and forth in his seat. No matter how much he smiled and laughed, something seemed to be bothering the High Steward de Noram.

"Hmmmphh."

"Pardon, Anthony?"

"Nothing, Clarissa. At least I hope it's nothing." He twisted around in his chair and looked at Dillan's table. "Guide Sylvan is eating well, I see."

Clarissa smiled. "I'd noticed. That's his third helping of the mutton."

Anthony looked at Marilyn de Noram, where she sat on Dillan's right. "Marilyn seems cheerful enough. I hope they have a happy marriage."

Clarissa raised her eyebrows. "We'll see. She certainly has good self-control. I haven't seen her eat a thing."

Anthony blinked. "Probably too happy."

"No doubt," Clarissa said slowly. "No doubt."

Over at Leland's table, Coronet Gahnfeld was passing Sylvan Montrose. He was working on his fourth helping of mutton, his third helping of wheat pilaf, and his sixth roll. Those also seated at Leland's table stared at Gahnfeld in open-mouthed amazement. When he'd polished that off, he looked around for the attendants circulating with more food, but Bartholomew had told them to stop serving Leland's table since the only one eating was Gahnfeld.

Leland watched Gahnfeld bemusedly, grateful for the distraction. When it became clear that no waiter was going to respond to the coronet's gestures, Leland slid his own nearly untouched plate in front of Gahnfeld.

"Why, thank you, Guide. That's very kind of you."

Leland replied dryly, "I can't have my bodyguard fainting from hunger, can I?"

The two guards standing against the wall behind Leland had been replaced so they could eat in the kitchen. Leland looked across the hall to Dillan's table and Marilyn. He felt a sharp pain at the sight of her laughing at something Sylvan Montrose had said. He looked away quickly.

He glanced up at his father and found him looking back. For a moment their eyes met and held, then Dulan nodded slowly and turned to answer a question from Siegfried Montrose.

Leland blinked and felt oddly comforted. He started paying more attention to those around him and, by the end of the banquet, had even managed some feeble flirtation with the daughter of a visiting guide.

But, after the banquet, his bodyguards wondered why he climbed to the east wall and watched the Needle until the moon went down.

# SEVEN

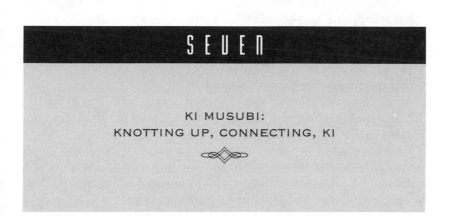

## KI MUSUBI: KNOTTING UP, CONNECTING, KI

The morning after the banquet was clear and cool, with a pleasant breeze out of the east. On the west wall, High Steward Siegfried Montrose paced slowly back and forth while he waited for his son. Two of his guards stood at each end of the walkway and his body servant waited with tea on a brazier.

He paused now and then to watch the activities beginning in the courtyards below and out in the town. Yawning groups of men and women headed for the fields to get the weeding done before the heat of the day. Children, laughing and playing, walked, skipped, and otherwise made their way to Morning School. Montrose frowned at this.

He heard steps behind him and turned. Sylvan was walking slowly toward him, one hand to his head and the other shading his eyes. He was wincing.

"Good morning, Sylvan," Siegfried said loudly.

Sylvan covered his ears. "Oh, malnutrition! Do you have to speak so loud?"

Siegfried laughed. "You idiot. If you want to overeat and overdrink, you deserve the consequences."

Sylvan turned so his back was to the rising sun. "Well, you could at least have had this meeting inside!"

"Idiot I said and idiot I meant! How would you know there weren't any ears behind the walls? Or worse? Who knows what devices these people have for remote listening? They teach their peasants to read and let them have full access to their libraries!"

"I know that! But what harm has it done? Laal is one of the richest stewardships in Noramland. Can you tell me what it's done in harm?"

Siegfried's amusement had changed quickly to anger. "You mean besides blocking Cotswold from further expansion? Do you mean besides luring all our best craftsmen away?"

Sylvan flinched.

Siegfried continued. "Tell me how far Laal's borders have expanded in the last hundred years."

Sylvan started to speak, but Siegfried said, "Oh, shut up! Laal's borders are exactly the same. They're not going anywhere. They're a dead end. We control our people, not the other way around. They work for us! Dulan de Laal as much as told me that the guardianship exists to serve the people! He's as much an idiot as you!"

Sylvan looked hurt. "Their borders haven't shrunk, either," he said under his breath.

Siegfried didn't hear him. "Oh, never mind. What have you learned about this Warden of the Needle and the whereabouts of the device?"

"Damn little. Nobody will talk about him. Why do you want to know about him anyway? If I were you I'd be concentrating on Dillan, or Dexter. They've hurt us before in border actions. Leland's a child."

Siegfried took a deep breath and tried to calm himself. "Then why did his father give him that wardenship? Didn't you listen when I told you about the Glass Helm?"

"So he climbed the Needle and put on the Helm. I'm impressed. But I don't see how that threatens us. Is he going to climb back up and drop rocks on us?"

Siegfried stared at his son. "If you weren't my son, I'd stake you out on the Anvil and leave you."

"What did I say?"

"The Glass Helm is the last of the imprinters left from the Founding. All the others were destroyed by Townsend's cult—deliberately, because they conveyed too much power to their wearers."

Siegfried walked casually past Sylvan, then turned suddenly. Sylvan took a sharp breath as his father's dagger appeared suddenly at his throat.

"Careful," Sylvan hissed.

"Quiet! And listen carefully for once—*as if your life depended on it!*" Siegfried twisted his free hand around the front of Sylvan's shirt and moved the dagger closer.

Sylvan's eyes went wide and he blinked several times.

"Knowledge. Is. Power." He scraped the tip of the dagger over Sylvan's Adam's apple. "Can you say that?"

Sylvan tried to speak, but his voice cracked. He finally managed "Knowledge is power" in a croaking whisper.

"I knew you could," said Siegfried. "Again."

"Knowledge is power."

Siegfried pulled the dagger away and released Sylvan's shirt. "You don't put knowledge in the hands of your enemies or potential enemies. Never forget it."

Sylvan slid down the wall and sat staring at his father.

Siegfried looked over the wall and sighed. "Find out everything you can about Leland and the Helm. Put your servants on it. Servants gossip—they probably already know more than you could ever find out by asking the guardianship. I want a report tomorrow morning."

Sylvan stood shakily.

Siegfried looked at him with dead eyes. "On your way out, tell Niels that I'm ready for my tea."

Gahnfeld stuck his head into Leland's room shortly after midmorning. He found a three-meter cube with the bed a built-in nook on one side. A shuttered meter-high window opened high above an inner courtyard. A table with two chairs sat below the window, and a dresser and three chests against the wall opposite the bed held his clothing and other belongings. An unlit cast-iron stove stood in a corner.

Leland was buried under covers, a pillow across his face.

Gahnfeld cleared his throat. Nothing happened. He cleared his throat a little louder. A hand appeared from under the covers and pulled the pillow closer.

Gahnfeld opened the door completely and motioned one of his men in with a covered tray. He wondered if he was doing the right thing, but considering the right thing had never stopped him in the past.

"Put it on the table," he indicated. The soldier closed the door behind him as he left.

Gahnfeld opened the shutters and let light stream into the room. "Good morning, Guide."

Leland sat up, shedding pillows and quilts. He stretched and yawned. "And I thought you were Bartholomew, come to get me for another day of labor in the fields. How old is the morning?"

Gahnfeld stopped holding his breath. "Several hours, Guide Leland. I've brought breakfast."

Leland sniffed. "Hmmm. So, this is what it's like to have a bodyguard, eh? You may not be such a nuisance after all." He stood up in a nightshirt and kicked his feet into old leather slippers.

"You should get a rug for your floor. It would keep the cold away."

"Yes, but then it would have to be cleaned. It's hard to mop a rug." Leland sat down and uncovered the tray. "I don't know why I'm so hungry this morning." He picked up a roll and began buttering it, then stopped with his hands in midair. "Oh, yeah. I guess I do remember. Well, just don't stand there, Coronet. Sit."

"Thank you."

Leland noticed that there were two cups by the steaming teapot, so he said, "Pour us some tea, won't you? Are you going to make a habit of this breakfast-in-bed thing?"

Gahnfeld smiled slightly. "It's hardly breakfast in bed."

"Yes, but then I've gotten used to scrounging breakfast in the corner of the kitchen or going down to a communal hall. Have a roll."

"Thank you."

"So, how much longer do I have a bodyguard, eh? Have you heard anything from Captain Koss or my father?"

"No, Warden. However, when Captain Koss put me on this assignment, he said I was to be extravigilant when any of the Cotswold bunch were around. Maybe that means it will stop when they go back home."

Leland tried the porridge and frowned.

"Is the porridge cold?"

"Oh, no. It's fine. I just wonder why I rate a bodyguard while Dillan and Dexter don't? They're more in Father's confidence than I am, and they both have command positions with our forces. And what's to fear from Cotswold? They've been nasty in the past, but we're at peace now."

Gahnfeld frowned. "I'm just a simple soldier, Warden, but what the High Steward of Cotswold says and what he does have been known to differ in the past."

Leland nodded.

Gahnfeld sipped his tea. "In any case, you might find out more tomorrow morning. Your father has called a staff meeting for ten o'clock. You're on the list."

Leland looked up from the porridge. "Really?"

"Yes, Warden."

"Please stop calling me that."

"Pardon?" Gahnfeld asked.

Leland waved his spoon in the air. "Warden. It bothers me. Might as well call me knight or bishop. That's what it means—I'm a piece in some game my father is playing." He pushed what was left of the porridge away, suddenly not hungry.

Gahnfeld grinned. "Aren't we all? At least you're a piece of some importance. Not like the rest of us pawns." *And don't be surprised if you're more like a rook, Warden. Strange things are happening.*

"When you met me at the pass the other day, you looked more than passing familiar. You weren't one of my tormentors from the summer, were you?"

"No, War—Guide Leland. I was on the border most of the summer."

Leland pursued it, grateful of anything that took his mind off Marilyn. "I remember now. You were one of those decorated after the border incident last summer. After the defense of Mangle Ford."

Gahnfeld looked pleased. "You have a good memory, Warden."

Leland frowned. "Not really. I remember you as a halvidar."

Gahnfeld shrugged. *A very good memory.* "What are your plans for today, Warden?"

Leland smiled. "A bath, followed by some time in the library. Then a ride this afternoon, into town to see Charly—Guide Charlina."

"Good. May I ask that you don't tell anyone until right before you leave?"

"Afraid of ambushes, Coronet?"

Gahnfeld waved one hand airily above the table. "Why take chances? It can't hurt to do it my way, can it?"

Leland thought about it. "I suppose not. I'm surprised you don't have me go around claiming a different destination."

Gahnfeld smiled. "A good idea. Perhaps some other day?"

Leland pretended surprise. "You'd have me lie?"

Gahnfeld shook his head. "Not at all. Just exaggerate."

"Disinform."

Gahnfeld thought about the strange word and all it implied. *That seems to imply something deeper, more pervasive.* He blinked. "I suppose so—to mislead, to mask, to disinform."

Leland nodded. "To disinform."

In the early afternoon Leland took down a book from the library shelf and experienced an acute attack of déjà vu. Footsteps sounded from around the corner, and he looked up as he automatically listened for the footsteps of one of his tormentors. Almost as soon as he realized that he didn't have to fear attack, he recognized the footsteps. And he was afraid.

"Guide Marilyn," he said as she rounded the corner. He bowed his head briefly.

She stepped back as she saw who it was, her eyes going wide momentarily. "Warden." Her face was impassive. "I trust you are well?"

He nodded. Leland studied her features, the way her nose and close-set eyes seemed too small for her face, the thinness of her lips, any trace of roughness, desperately looking for defects. *Oh, damn, she's just as attractive as last time.*

He finally found his voice. "Did you find any more medical books in Cotswold?"

She shook her head. "Cotswold has no libraries. Hardly any of the people there read."

Leland blinked. "What about the rites? The reading?"

She shook her head. "They memorize a passage from the Code. Something their parents' learned by rote. And washing is more a ritual dipping of the fingers than a true cleansing."

Leland blinked. "It's been so long since we've had open contact with Cotswold. I knew it was bad, but I'd no idea."

"Hopefully this new alliance will change that. As soon as I get back to the capital, I'm sending a delegation of teachers to Cotswold."

"Yes? I wish you luck."

"What do you mean?" she asked. She moved over by the window and sat on the ledge.

"Back before our open conflicts with Cotswold, my father sent a caravan of teachers and books there. Their bones were found on the Anvil and there was no sign of the books. Siegfried said it was bandits, but traders brought word from bragging militia that it was done on his orders."

Marilyn went pale. "I don't believe it! Kill teachers? Why?"

Leland shrugged. "I don't know, Guide. It happened before I was born."

"I'm not sure it happened at all!"

Leland felt blood go to his face. He said, tight-lipped, "Perhaps you're right, Guide. I've only my father's word for it."

Marilyn blinked. "I don't mean to cast aspersions on your father's word. I just find it hard to believe that anyone would steal a book or kill a teacher. Perhaps he was misinformed."

Tonelessly Leland said, "I would be a fool to argue with you."

She turned white. "What do you mean by that!"

He shoved the book he'd been holding back onto the shelf. "Whatever you like, Guide. The truth comes in many forms. Just be sure that you don't choose one version just because you like its bearer more."

She stood up quickly and walked to the end of the shelf. "And be sure your version of the truth isn't chosen out of jealousy!"

With great effort, he grinned at her. "Or wishful thinking."

She left, shutting the door behind her with a bang that made Leland's ears ring. He walked around the bookshelf and looked at it.

The door, a massive, iron-bound, wooden affair that had hung in the library doorway since Laal Station had been built one hundred and thirty-five years before, was cracked down the middle.

WELL, THAT WENT WELL.

*Oh, shut up.*

Leland crouched down on the floor to examine the break. The two Falcons who were his bodyguard exchanged grins over his head. Leland whistled softly, wondering what Martin would say. Then he heard footsteps from up the hall and looked up to see the High Steward of Cotswold walking with his manservant a few paces behind.

Leland stood and bowed, the two Falcons echoing his salute.

Siegfried smiled. "I heard the most horrendous noise, Warden. It almost made me think somebody had been using explosives."

"No, High Steward," said Leland. "It was just a door shutting a little too hard. Nobody here would break the Code."

"I would hope not! Who wants to go down that path? Our ancestors were wise to ban its use, eh?" Siegfried toed the door with his boot.

Leland nodded. "Yes, High Steward."

"Wait here, Niels. So, this is your library, eh?" The high steward walked past Leland and into the room.

Leland saw the guards exchange glances. "Yes, High Steward." He followed Siegfried into the room.

"I love to read," the high steward told him, picking out a book at random. "I wish we had as many fine books in Cotswold." He looked up at Leland, as if waiting for him to say something, but Leland refused to take the bait. Siegfried continued. "Have you ever read the works of Machiavelli? Or Sun Tzu?"

Leland nodded. "Certainly, High Steward."

"Masterful minds, those. The principle of economy of force seems so simple after one has read it. Your father is a master of it."

"Is he?" Leland asked. "I've heard it said he knows his way around a council meeting." *And a battlefield.*

Siegfried nodded. "Yes. What are *your* plans, Leland? What are you going to do with your life?"

Leland shrugged.

"Perhaps another soldier? Or are you going to be a builder?"

Leland looked out the window. *What does he want? What do I want?* "I suppose I'll do whatever my father requires."

Siegfried nodded. "Admirable. A father needs loyal sons, no matter how he treats them." He watched Leland closely as he said that.

Leland just raised his eyebrows. "My father commands loyalty."

"I'm sure he does, Warden. I'm sure he does." Siegfried put the book back on the shelf and chose another. "If you ever find yourself wanting to do important work, I could use a man with your education. You are rare even in this enlightened land. Perhaps I'll see if your father would post you with me for a while. An administrative position would give you experience with the real world—let you see how the world of ideas relates to the world of rocks and tears."

Leland half smiled. "Perhaps. If my father felt that was a good idea."

Siegfried nodded. "I'll ask him."

Leland half bowed as he watched the high steward move back to the doorway.

"I'll talk with you again," Siegfried said, and left.

Leland waited until Siegfried's receding footsteps could no longer be heard before he went to the window and looked out at the rising hills of Laal.

*Suddenly,* he thought, *the world seems less safe.*

* * *

*Why are you so nervous, Arthur?*

The view from Guide Dulan's study looked toward the west, where the Cloud Scrapers broke the setting sun into ruddy fingers reaching to the sky. The High Steward of Noramland had commented on it. "Do I see some white on Mount Bauer? Your harvest is two weeks off. I hope you get it in before the first freeze."

Dulan poured tea for them both. Arthur's hand shook slightly as he accepted the cup. "With luck and hard work we'll get it in, Guide." He walked around the conference table to his chair and waited for Arthur to sit.

Arthur paced instead. "I need to talk to you about the troops, Dulan. Now that snow has started falling in the mountains, the Black will soon drop."

Dulan nodded.

On the east side of Noramland, the Black and Ganges rivers came out of the Herrin Mountains and merged to form Noramland's border with Nullarbor. The Plain of the Founders, a rich section of land in the delta of their junction, was the original landing site of the colonists. It had been a source of contention between the two countries for the last hundred fifty years. However, because the Black flowed fast and deep for most of the year, the warfare was confined to autumn, before the winter storms, but after the water had dropped enough to ford.

"So, Dulan, my spies tell me that Roland is putting five thousand men in the field. I'll need at least five hundred provisioned men from you by the end of the month." He stared challengingly at Dulan.

Dulan walked to the window and mentally cursed this uncivilized brat who didn't have the manners to sit down so his subject could take a seat. His right leg, broken thirty years before in a climbing accident, was aching badly. He looked down at the green, verdant fields of Laal, the trees, the foothills, and finally the mountains, and sighed quietly.

Arthur, for once, kept his mouth shut. He toyed with his tea and waited.

Dulan turned around. "Certainly, sire. I'll send eight hundred, and they'll leave with you at the end of the week."

"You will?" Arthur looked surprised. "I mean, that's excellent. Truly excellent." He looked around as if confused.

"May I have your leave to sit, sire?" Dulan asked gently.

"What? Oh, certainly. Good idea." He took his chair. "So, you can send eight hundred, eh?"

"Yes, sire," Dulan said, lowering himself slowly into a chair. "We began picking the men last month. After all, you did tell me we'd have peace with Cotswold," he added with a slight smile.

Arthur nodded vigorously. "That's right." He drained his tea suddenly and reached for the pot before Dulan could move. "No, no. Don't move. I'll pour."

Dulan settled back and eased his left leg out straight.

Arthur managed to fill both cups without spilling too much tea. "So, are you going to send the Falcons or the Lances?"

"Neither, sire."

"Oh, a mixed contingent, eh? Some of both?"

Dulan shook his head. "No, sire. We've formed a new unit."

"Who will command?"

"I'm not quite sure," Dulan lied. "It will be one of my sons."

Arthur blinked. "Well. Can't ask more than that, can I?"

Dulan smiled and raised his cup in a small toast. *I certainly hope not.*

The paper in front of Captain Koss read "Personnel File: Myron Gahnfeld." He skimmed it, to see if his memory matched the facts recorded. They did. He sighed, then said in normal voice, "Orderly!"

A soldier stepped through the open door into his office. "Sir!"

"Is Coronet Gahnfeld out there yet?"

"Yes, sir."

"Send him in." Koss leaned back and waited.

Gahnfeld walked quietly into the room, stopped before Koss's desk, and saluted. "Reporting as ordered, sir." His feet were together, his back was straight, and his hands were at his sides. In short, he stood at attention, but not in the way that most people stood at attention. He stood there looking *comfortable.* Something about his way of standing looked as if he would fall asleep in that position in the next few moments.

*Damn it! People at attention are not supposed to look comfortable.* Koss tried not let the irritation touch his face. He stared at Gahnfeld for another minute, looking for a hint of nervousness, but the coronet looked far from uneasy. In fact, he looked as if he could stand there under the captain's gaze until moss started growing on him.

"How long have you been a Falcon, Coronet Gahnfeld?" The tone of his voice was conversational.

"Ten and a half years, sir."

Captain Koss nodded. "And how many times have you been a halvidar?"

"Three times."

"Yes." Captain Koss looked at the ceiling. "What the hell am I going to do with you, Gahnfeld? Maybe old Captain Martin made you halvidar too soon. And you did a good job, too. Decorated for that piece of action at Meldon Ford." He paused, staring hard at Gahnfeld. "But on leave at Pottsville what happens? Two months in the guard house. Then back in the ranks as a basic foot soldier. For how long?"

Gahnfeld's eyes narrowed slightly. "Two years."

"Right. Then the Anvil Bandits. Promoted in the field when Marshall and Beckett died. You came out of that decorated, too."

Gahnfeld nodded slightly.

"But you found a way to foul that up, too, didn't you? What's wrong with you boy? Maybe you don't like being a halvidar?"

He looked hard a Gahnfeld. "Well?"

"I don't know, sir."

"You don't know? You don't know!" He slammed his fist down on the desk.

Gahnfeld blinked.

"What's the matter with your head? Isn't it attached? Against my advice, Dulan promoted you last summer and decorated you again!

"And then? Why did you do it?"

He stared hard at Gahnfeld. When the coronet didn't speak, Captain Koss said, "I am ordering you to tell me why you struck Captain de Laal last summer."

Gahnfeld closed his eyes for a moment. "Sir. I do not remember."

"Still? The harvest wine, no doubt." Koss paused. "Last night you spent the banquet gorging yourself and drinking like a horse! Is that what you call bodyguarding? By rendering yourself unfit for duty?"

Gahnfeld's eyes widened. "Surely the captain is jesting?"

"What do you mean?" snapped Koss.

"I mean that I could have eaten twice as much and drunk four times as much before I was unfit. I may have had my past lapses, but never in the actual performance of my duties."

*No, there's always that,* Koss thought as he glowered angrily. *When you hit Ricard it was in a bar.* "Maybe you should leave the service, Gahnfeld. You seem happiest when pursuing civilian activities."

"Sir! I am happy with the service."

"Oh? Even if I were to transfer you to the Pikes?"

Gahnfeld said nothing.

"I have the feeling that you find the thought of being under Captain de Laal less than appealing. Never forget that it's in my power to do so."

"Yes, sir."

Captain Koss bent forward then and wrote something in the folder before him. "I am transferring you, though, but not to the Pikes. You better not screw this one up," he said, still writing. He looked up. "Coronet Jeston will relieve you of the bodyguard duty shortly. You will take charge of the headquarters detachment of the new unit. You have a staff meeting to run immediately after dinner. The halvidars and coronets will meet with you in the staff lounge. As senior halvidar, I suggest you take charge early. You've got one reputation to disprove and another to live up to."

Gahnfeld stood there for a moment, blinking. "Yes, sir," he finally said, and turned to go.

Captain Koss spoke, and Gahnfeld paused to listen.

"This is important, Myron."

Without turning, Gahnfeld said, "I understand, Uncle."

And then he walked on.

Leland rode out at dawn escorted by four bodyguards. Two of the guards went ahead, their horses' hooves kicking up faint traceries of dust to mix with the steam of exhaled breath. The wind was from the north—chill, giving a mild preview of the icy gales due in two months. Leland gathered the reins a little tighter as his horse danced sideways around a weed in the road.

*Malnutrition!* He paid more attention to his riding. He'd ridden all his life, but nine months of manual labor, beatings, and the exercise in Red Rock had altered the way he sat in the saddle. It didn't help that he'd grown five centimeters and gained fifteen kilograms in that period. On his own two feet he felt somewhat graceful. In the saddle, his new mass and height felt *awkward.*

THINK OF IT LIKE UKEMI. STAY CONNECTED AND CONCENTRATE ON YOUR CENTER.

That helped.

They slowed to a trot at the town and then to a walk when they crossed the central market square. There were lots of people out, setting up their stalls. A few early shoppers were there, to pick the fruits and vegetables they wanted as they came off the carts. Several people nodded and raised a hand as Leland and the bodyguards rode past.

The dojo was an outbuilding behind the bindery, but, because of the fine weather, the tatami mats had been moved out onto the courtyard formed by the bindery, the dojo, the Druza household, and the print shop.

Jeston, the coronet now in charge of the bodyguard, put one of his men at the stables and the other two men on the street. He accompanied Leland into the courtyard. "Let me carry that bag," he offered.

Leland shook his head. "That's all right."

One of the Druza daughters, dressed in a gi and *hakama,* led them to the changing room. Jeston preceded Leland in, one hand on his sword.

Leland rolled his eyes at the ceiling. "Jeston, I don't want any talk of this. Period." Leland started changing into his gi and *hakama. "You* can come inside, but leave the others on the perimeter and what happens in here is *my* business—understood?"

Jeston hesitated. He hadn't been told what they were doing here, and Leland could see his imagination run riot. "Yes, Warden. Your business."

HE PROBABLY THINKS YOU'RE HAVING AN AFFAIR.

*Ha!*

He found Jeston a bench at the back of the bindery, then bowed on to the mat and began stretching with the dozen people already there.

Charly taught the class using Leland as *uke.* They started with *kotegaeshi,* a wrist immobilization and throw requiring a break-fall. As Charly was applying the pin, Leland could see Jeston on his feet, his hand on the hilt of his sword and his eyes very wide.

Leland raised his free hand and Jeston subsided, licking his lips. HE THOUGHT SHE WAS KILLING YOU.

Charly threw him again—hard.

*And she's not?*

Jeston was a nervous wreck by the end of the class. Leland felt tired but invigorated.

"Buy you breakfast, Charly?"

*"Hai."*

The changing room was full and, to spare Jeston's feelings of paranoia, Leland waited in the courtyard. "I'm going to take Guide Charlina to breakfast. The Blue Whale. Perhaps you could send one of your men over and get us a table."

Jeston frowned. "You're going to *eat* in a public place, Warden?"

"It happens all the time. Your man doesn't have to say who the table is for." The last person left the changing room and Leland turned to enter it. "Please ask the Druzas if you can leave the horses here."

"Warden, I really wish you'd reconsid—"

"Coronet! Your job is to guard my body, not hide it." He wished Coronet—no, Halvidar—Gahnfeld still had this detail. Or better yet, he wished the guard was dismissed, but when he'd tried to suggest as much to Captain Koss the night before, he'd been adamant. The guard would stay until his father deemed otherwise.

On the short walk to the inn, Leland did his best to ignore them.

Charly teased him about the guard. "So, what's it like to have an entourage? I wonder if they can card wool?"

"You want them? I'd give them to you in a second, if I could."

At the inn there was another argument and a delay while Jeston checked out the interior and the selected table. Leland swore under his breath. "I wanted to eat outside."

Charly laughed. "So does everybody else." The long winters of Laal gave the locals an appreciation for sunshine. The outside tables of the inn were crowded.

The landlord, a smiling man with thick forearms gnarled like tree branches, welcomed them warmly at the door. "You honor us, Warden."

"Honor? It's simple greed. Do you still have migas on the menu?"

"Certainly."

The interior was half full and Jeston's head was swiveling back and forth like a weathervane.

The landlord led them to a table in an alcove where one of the squad already stood. "Migas, then. And for you, my lady?"

"I'll try the migas. And I'm thirsty. Water would be welcome."

"Yes, water, please, and some tea?" Leland looked at Charly and she nodded. "Yes, tea." He indicated Jeston and the other soldier with a tilt of his head. "For them, as well. Have you and your squad eaten yet, Jeston?"

Jeston answered without taking his eyes off the crowd. "Yes, Warden, at dawn."

"Bring them tea, then, please. And if they get in the way of your staff, just beat them about the head and shoulders."

The landlord smiled and left. Jeston glared at Leland.

Breakfast came with the flat bread called none. He took a bite and felt an odd overlay of recognition. NAAN, NOT 'NONE.' IT'S INDIAN.

*None. The child asked if there was any bread and his mother said "none." When they looked, the fairies left this. It's the kid's story—my mother told it to me.*

OKAY—NONE AND NAAN.

"What's the matter?" Charly asked.

"Do you ever talk to yourself?"

"Sure," she said, pouring tea.

"Do you ever have arguments with yourself?"

Charly stopped pouring and looked at him over the pot. "There are times I'm conflicted—is that what you mean?"

"I suppose." *In a really extreme way.* He changed the subject. "Do you suppose Druza Sensei would mind if I practiced with them after you've gone back to the city?"

She put the teapot down and gave him an odd look. "She would be delighted—it's been a long time since there's been a *shidoin* here on a regular basis."

"Isn't she?"

"*Fukushidoin*—assistant instructor. We can't all take nine months off to work with a *shihan* like Denesse Sensei."

MASTER.

"How many *shihans* are there?"

"Three. Denesse, here in Laal—eighth dan. Raloff, in Montrouge—eighth dan. Prokopczyk in Rio—seventh dan. Kroodsma, my old master in Noram, died two years ago. She was *Doshu.*"

MASTER OF THE WAY.

Charly looked sad for a moment and Leland asked softly, "What was her rank? Kroodsma's?"

"The Doshu is not ranked. She was eighth dan when she succeeded her father."

"So, who's *Doshu* now?"

"There isn't one. Kroodsma's two children died before her. I'm dojo cho-head of dojo in Noram, but that's mostly an administrative thing. Eventually one of the *shihan*s will become *doshu.* Kroodsma's death was unexpected—she hadn't selected a successor. None of the *shihan*s felt ready. They'll be meeting next year to discuss it again."

Leland heard the town bells ringing the quarter hour. "Damn. I've got to get going—my father wants me at his ten o'clock staff meeting." He told Jeston to send one of his men for the horses, then signaled to the landlord.

"Give him my regards," said Charly.

"My father? You've met him?"

Charly laughed. "Yes. Many times."

Leland wanted to ask for more details, but the landlord arrived at their table. "Something else, Warden?"

"Uh, I need to settle the bill."

"Certainly. Consider it settled." He bent slightly at the waist.

"No, really—what's the reckoning?"

The landlord straightened, seeming suddenly much taller. "I came here from Cotswold, lord, when I was seventeen. My father ran a restaurant in Montrouge, and if a member of the guardianship stopped to eat at his table, the guide expected to eat for free. And this was on top of the taxes. My father was a good cook—guides stopped there often. His restaurant and our home was confiscated to pay his back taxes. My father was hung."

Leland, a sober expression on his face, said, "This is not Cotswold."

"No, it's not. If a patron, guide or otherwise, doesn't pay his bill, I have many avenues to recover the damages. But mostly they pay promptly.

"So, here in Laal, it's *my* choice. And today my choice is that you eat free."

Leland was flustered. "I don't know what to say, besides . . . thanks." He stood and shook the man's hand.

When they were outside, Charly said, "What did you put under the plate?"

Leland looked around for the horses and spotted them being led up the street from the Druzas'. "The price of our meal and a good tip. My father would be furious if he found any of his sons trading on our name."

"What about the landlord's feelings?"

"Then he can give the money away. Gotta run. Don't want to be late for the meeting, and I want to get out of here before they clear the table."

He gave her a quick hug.

"Class tomorrow morning? You can teach?"

"I'll try."

* * *

"Sit," Guide Dulan said as he entered the room.

The assembled council obeyed. Martin and Bartholomew sat to the right of Guide Dulan's chair. On the left sat Captain Koss and Captain Ricard de Laal. Farther down from the captains sat Anthony and Dexter with Dillan seated at the foot of the table. Leland took the remaining seat at Dillan's left.

For a moment, Dulan stood there his eyes looking past them, his hands resting on the back of his chair. Leland watched his father impassively, ignoring the stares from Anthony across the table. *He's old,* Leland thought, surprised. The mental image he held of his father was different than this man with the lined face and the gray hair. Then Guide Dulan spoke and Leland felt oddly comforted. The iron was still there, in the voice.

"Facts and figures, gentlemen. It's time for facts and figures." He swung to the map on the wall, a chart of the occupied lands of Agatsu. "Fact number one: We have signed a nonaggression pact with Cotswold. Fact number two: Cotswold has ten thousand men-at-arms trained or in training. Fact number three: Our intelligence reports extensive stocking of Cotswold depot points here, here, and here." He pointed at three towns within a day's ride of the Cotswold/Laal border. "Fact number four: We are supporting at this time less than four thousand trained men with militia reserves of another three thousand."

He stopped then and pointed toward the right of the map, at the plains nation of Nullarbor and the Plain of the Founders. "High Steward de Noram has called on us to support him in his annual battle for the First Landing Site. We are sending him one-fifth of our active forces—eight hundred men. This reduces our active forces correspondingly, which means that Cotswold will outnumber us in this theater by almost four thousand men."

He paused, then said, "Comments?"

Ricard de Laal spoke. "What of the treaty? Does Siegfried dare ignore the combined forces of Noramland? By arranging this agreement, High Steward de Noram has committed all of the Stewardships of Noram to our defense."

Guide Dulan nodded. "True in principle, if not in fact. It all depends how extensively Arthur commits himself against the Rootless. If his forces are tied up at the Plain of the Founders, Siegfried may have time to attack, eliminate all mobile resistance, isolate strong points in

Laal proper, and race for the passes." He pointed to the Cloud Scrapers and tapped the three passes that could be crossed in the fall and winter. "Here he can hold the might of Noramland with relatively small forces, leaving Arthur no option but to wait for spring and cross the high passes or fight his way around the east end of the Cloud Scrapers through this corner of Cotswold." He pointed to where the Black River cut through the tip of the Cloud Scrapers in the Bauer Rent, an impassable canyon filled with thirty kilometers of rapids, then traced the route through Cotswold necessary to reach Laal.

"Getting to Laal this way would take almost as long as waiting for the high passes to clear, and the fighting would cut his army to ribbons. In any case, Siegfried would have four months to finish the resistance in Laal, reinforce his army, and strip Laal bare. What is Arthur going to do with Siegfried then? Spend the entire summer digging him out of Laal while Roland of Nullarbor threatens his western border?"

Ricard nodded. "Yet this *is* conjecture?"

"Of course. But it's conjecture we cannot ignore." Dulan came back to the table and sat heavily. "Does anybody think we should?" He looked around. "I thought not. So, we will take the following precautions."

He looked at Captain Koss. "Leonid, you will move the Falcons to full field status and establish strong points at all fords of the Black east of Jaren's Ford. In addition, you will step up intelligence-gathering activities. I want to know what is really happening in Cotswold. Ricard—you'll move the Lances to strengthen all fords west of there, and I want you to step up counterintelligence activities. I don't want any spies reporting our troop dispositions to Siegfried. In addition, you'll detach a hundred of your men to form a body of signalmen and couriers working out of here. I want the best communications possible. Anthony will command this signal unit. I'll keep the militia in reserve, ready to reinforce wherever. Dillan will command the reserve units west of the trunk road. Dexter will command those east of the road. I will not mobilize the militia until Captain Koss's intelligence crew gives me information that warrants it, but once-a-month militia drills are changed to once a week. Dexter and Dillan will inspect and improve training as necessary."

Dulan turned to face Martin and Bartholomew. "Provisioning of the forces in the field will be direct from the harvest. Existing reserves will stay in the storage bins. Distributed storage points must be found to supplement extended fighting. Whenever possible, these points must be hidden, keeping supplies safe even if we are occupied."

He looked around. "Clear so far?"

Anthony spoke. "Is the signal unit under your direction or Ricard's?"

Dulan sighed. "They're to be an independent command. They are under your direction, Anthony. You, however, are under *my* direction."

"Of course, sir."

Dulan stood and walked to his desk. He returned with four sheets of paper. Standing by the window he said, "Dillan, come here." Dillan did so. Dulan handed him the first sheet. "This is your commission as commander of the Southern Reserves." He put it on the windowsill facing Dillan. "Give Oath."

Dillan drew his dagger and cut into his right thumb with the tip, wincing as the blade bit. He pressed the bloody finger onto the bottom of the paper and said, "I give Oath, fully understanding what I do and what it means to do so. For Laal." He picked the paper up and handed it back to his father. *"Littera scripta manet."*

Dulan nodded. Dillan stepped back and Dexter stood. When he too had given Oath, Anthony came forward and repeated the process. Dulan turned from the window and faced the table. "Leland, come here."

Leland stood and walked over to his father. For a moment he trembled, but he was able to quell it almost as soon as the tremor began. He calmed himself, feeling for his center, picturing a wellspring of energy flowing out into all his limbs.

His father held up the fourth piece of paper. "This is your commission as commander of the eight hundred we are sending to Arthur."

Behind them, Anthony gasped.

Leland recoiled and took a step back. *He can't mean it!*

Dulan eyed Leland for a moment, then put the paper on the window sill. "Give Oath."

*He does mean it.* "I don't have a knife," he found himself saying in a hoarse whisper. "I'll have to borrow one."

Dulan started to draw his own when Bartholomew stood. "I have a dagger for the warden." He reached into his boot top and brought forth a small, slightly curved, wooden-sheathed knife and carried it forward. "I carried it against the Rootless myself once."

"Thank you, Bartholomew," Leland said. He drew the knife from the sheath. The Laal crest was worked in silver on the handle. It gleamed in the sunlight, the candle flame over the book seeming for an instant to twist like real fire. He jabbed the tip firmly into his thumb tip without wincing. He pressed his thumb against the paper. "I give Oath, fully understanding what I do and what it means to do so. For Laal." He picked the paper up and handed it back to his father. *"Littera scripta manet,"* he said. "The written word remains."

# EIGHT

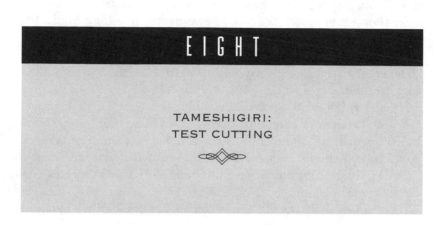

## TAMESHIGIRI: TEST CUTTING

"Push the front wings a little wider," Gahnfeld ordered. "No point in getting dust in the high steward's eyes."

The coronet he was addressing kicked heels to his horse and moved forward past Siegfried Montrose and his party. On the road ahead, two columns, each holding a hundred mounted archers, moved to each side of the road, onto the wild grass on the plain leading down to the Black.

Leland, riding silent beside Gahnfeld, watched coronets riding up and down the line, dressing the column, shouting new soldiers into line.

"Well, at least they can ride," Gahnfeld said. "Even if it isn't in a straight line."

Leland nodded and reined up to look behind him.

Down the road marched four hundred foot soldiers, half armed with long pikes, the other half with bows. Behind them rode two hundred men armed with lances. "They need a name," Gahnfeld said, also stopping.

"A name?" Leland said absently.

"Yes. After all, there's the Falcons and the Mounted Pikes, not to mention the name every militia unit takes."

Leland started riding again. "All right. They're the Eight Hundred.

And since we have eight units, they'll be called in order. The First Hundred, the Second Hundred, the Third . . ."

Gahnfeld shrugged. "There's the question of morale. A name of an animal or a type of warrior would give them something to identify with."

Leland lifted a hand to his head and frowned. PRIMITIVE ANIMISM. "The Eight Hundred will have to earn it. And if they do earn it, they won't need it."

Gahnfeld nodded slowly. "Yes, Guide."

"See to assigning the unit designations. The unit banners will be white with the numbers in black. Make sure the numbers are Arabic—roman numerals are too hard to read at a distance."

"Yes, Guide. And what about your banner? Will you carry the Laal family crest?"

Leland shook his head. "No. In fact, no banner. The headquarters unit will take the stewardship's flag with an Arabic eight hundred over the flame."

"Yes, Guide."

Leland blinked as a gust of wind caught him by surprise. *What am I forgetting?*

IT'S ALL VERY GRAND TO PLAY SOLDIER, BUT I'LL BET YOU WON'T THINK SO WHEN THESE CHILDREN START DYING.

Leland winced. "What am I forgetting, Gahnfeld?"

Gahnfeld was silent.

Leland smiled. "I mean it, Halvidar. I'm not just being polite. You'll hurt all of us if you say less than what you think."

"Actually, you seem to be doing well, Guide. Sometimes you try too hard. You've got to remember that we can take care of all the ordinary things. Your halvidars and coronets know how to set up camp and know marching order for friendly and hostile country. We can take care of the little things. You have to worry about the big things. When we fight and where."

Leland stared at the dust kicked into the air by the marching and riding troops. Another image popped into his mind, unbidden, unwanted. It was a planet hanging in the sky, completely shrouded in white.

Under his breath he said, "Or whether we fight at all."

* * *

Siegfried touched his breast pocket and frowned. He could feel the parchment inside, stiffer than the fabric. He didn't know whether to burn it or keep it.

*May his teeth fall out and he suffer from shingles.* He fought to contain his irritation. The note was from the traitor. He was sure because it contained verifying information from past exchanges. But he was no closer to knowing who the traitor was than he'd been two years before, when the first note was delivered to his spy in Brandon-on-the-Falls. This last note made six in all, each containing information on Laal's troop dispositions before they were made. He'd used the first three notes to check on the accuracy of the information. The fourth note he'd used to wipe out two Laal patrols and steal the grain reserves of a Laal village near the Black.

This last note had been in his shirt pocket before he dressed that morning. He'd taken it out upon feeling the unnatural stiffness, thinking it was something Niels had missed from a previous wearing. Sylvan was there, briefing him on the Warden Leland de Laal. Siegfried read three lines before realizing what the note was, then casually put it back in his pocket. He'd been unable to concentrate on the rest of Sylvan's report.

This last note contained more than troop movements. Oh, troop movements were there, but there was also an offer—a tangible act of aid. At an agreed-upon time, the Floating Stone would drop to the ground while still open and he could storm Laal Station—provided he could get men close enough undetected.

*But what if it's a trap?*

He just couldn't see Dulan de Laal sacrificing men to give a false traitor credibility. Siegfried thought Dulan too soft for such a move. *But what if he's not?*

Taking Laal Station without siege would give him an enormous edge. And most important, he could take the Glass Helm intact. *Ah, the Helm! I know about the Helm, Dulan. Much more than most.* His lips drew back from his teeth in an unconscious rictus.

The note contained something else, too. For the first time a price was mentioned. And the price was surprisingly reasonable—so reasonable that Siegfried considered not killing the traitor after his usefulness was finished. Siegfried considered this at length . . . but not very seriously.

* * *

At the Black, Siegfried paused to thank Leland for his escort. Gahnfeld reined his horse forward and let it drink so he could overhear what was said.

"Please give your father my thanks for this escort."

"Yes, Steward," Leland said. "I hope you have a safe journey the remainder of the way to Montrouge. I understand it's a dry journey across the Anvil."

Gahnfeld winced at that. He'd nearly died in that blasted rock waste.

Siegfried nodded. "We only cross a bit of it on our route. I'm sorry you can't come with us. Talking to a scholar would break the monotony of the trip."

Leland nodded. "Kind of you. Still, as you know, I've got a journey in the opposite direction."

"Yes. Congratulations on your command. I hope you have luck against the Rootless—I've had my share of trouble with them." Siegfried saluted casually and spurred his horse into the water.

Gahnfeld and Leland watched him catch up with his party and splash on across to the waiting Cotswold troops.

"Halvidar."

"Guide," said Gahnfeld.

"How long will it take us to get back to Brandon-on-the-Falls, now that we don't have the high steward's party to slow us down?"

Gahnfeld frowned. "At the double with ten-minute rests on the hour, experienced troops could make it in ten hours. These troops would probably take longer, perhaps twelve or thirteen hours. The cavalry, of course, can do it in four hours."

"In other words, we'd camp tonight."

"Yes, Guide."

"That would put us back at the Station tomorrow around noon."

"Yes, Guide."

"I want to be in Brandon-on-the-Falls by midnight."

"Yes, sir. The Third can escort you in by horse. I'll bring up the other seven hundred tomorrow."

Leland shook his head. "You misunderstand me. The Eight Hundred will be in Brandon-on-the-Falls by midnight."

Gahnfeld frowned, started to say something, then closed his mouth abruptly. *Damn your hide!* he thought. "Yes, Guide. May I ask a question?"

Leland grinned suddenly. "Certainly, Halvidar."

"How?"

"Wait and listen. Assemble the men."

Gahnfeld jerked erect in his saddle, then saluted formally. "Yes, *Warden.*" He faced the long column of troops and semaphored "assembly" with his extended fist. Coronets and halvidars caught the sign and began shouting the men into order on the bank.

Leland rode through this chaos until his horse stood halfway up the rise of the bank. The halvidars faced the men toward him.

Gahnfeld rode a quick inspection down the ranks before riding up beside Leland. "The men are assembled, Warden."

Leland chuckled. "Thank you." He stood in the stirrups and raised his arms. "Gentlemen! The day after tomorrow we march for Noram City with Arthur High Steward de Noram. From there we march to the Plain of the Founders to fight the Rootless. We do this because my father orders it."

He paused then, wondering if this was the right tack to take. Something inside felt right, but he wasn't sure.

"Tonight is the second night of the Harvest Festival. How many of you have families to say good-bye to? Sweethearts? Friends?"

Nearly every soldier lifted his arm.

"If we march at regular pace, camping tonight, we'll be in Brandon-on-the-Falls tomorrow afternoon. That will leave you the evening and the night to say farewell." He paused. "Personally, I don't think that's near enough time. Do you agree with me?"

There was a low growl of assent.

"Halvidar Gahnfeld tells me it will take green troops like you twelve to thirteen hours to get to Brandon." He paused. "I think we can make it by midnight.

"You have thirty minutes to water your horses and yourselves. At the end of that time, all mounted troops will move at a gallop five kilometers up the road. Horses will be picketed at that point under minimal attendance. Mounted troops will proceed *on foot* for another five kilometers. Infantry will leave at the same time, on the double. At the end of five kilometers, infantry will ride. This procedure will be continued until we get to Brandon. Carry on."

Halvidars and coronets moved their men to the river. Leland turned his horse and spoke to Gahnfeld. "That's how, Halvidar. As to why, I want to see if it can be done. Do you have any other questions?"

Gahnfeld shook his head, speechless.

"I'll want flanking scouts a half kilometer to each side. If there are any injured men or mounts, give them a full mounted squad as escort and let them come in slow." He dismounted and started walking his horse down the bank to drink. Gahnfeld followed his example.

The actions still felt right deep inside Leland. It suddenly occurred to him that he'd never spoken before a group larger than twenty people in his life. And the thought scared him. *Stupid—I should have gotten the shakes before I talked to them.*

"Do you think it will work, Halvidar?"

"I don't know, *Warden.*"

Leland winced. "You're still mad at me, aren't you, Myron?"

Gahnfeld breathed in sharply. "Such familiarity is bad for discipline."

"And *you're* avoiding the question. Never mind. I know about discipline. And I even know about punishment."

Twenty-five minutes later the troops assembled along the road. Leland called the halvidars together. "Including officers, we have more mounted than foot. I want you to mount your cooks and send them ahead with the packhorses to Lingshill." Lingshill was halfway to Brandon from the Black. "They're to expect the unit at eight for a hot supper." He looked around at the halvidars, his eyebrows raised. "Are your troops arranged?"

"Yes, Warden, except for the cooks."

"Get to it. We leave in five minutes." He took the reins of his horse from the soldier holding it.

Behind him, the halvidars mounted and rode to their men, shouting out orders as they went.

He started to mount and the soldier moved forward and held the horse's cheek strap. Leland stopped halfway up when he saw the man stroke the horse's nose gently. He stepped back down and out of the stirrup.

"What's your name?" he asked.

The soldier blinked. "Warren, sir, Warden, uhr."

Leland repressed a smile. The soldier was older than he was by at least five years. "Can you ride, Warren?"

"Yes, sir."

"Come with me."

"Sir? I mean, yessir!"

Leland handed him back the reins and walked to the front ranks.

Gahnfeld met him there, mounted. "Ready when you are, Warden."

"Thank you. Warren, get on this horse."

Warren stared for a moment and blinked.

"That's an order, Warren."

The soldier shut his mouth and scrambled into the saddle.

Leland held the bridle until he was settled. "I expect him to be waiting in five kilometers. Join the cavalry."

Gahnfeld was frowning when Leland turned back to face him. "Cavalry away, Halvidar."

Gahnfeld raised his signal fan and drew it down sharply. The mounted troops moved out onto the road and started off, first moving at a walk, then a trot, finally a gallop. After they'd cleared the top of the bank, Leland said, "Cooks away."

The cooks, some of them unused to riding, moved out at a brisk trot, the packhorses trailing behind. Leland walked out into the road and said loudly, "We get to ride for five kilometers when we catch up with them. What are we waiting for?"

He began walking up the road. When the troops were on the road behind him and moving at a brisk march, he started to run.

Sylvan delivered the gift to Guide Marilyn after dinner, as she, Lillian de Laal, and Carmen Cantle de Laal were watching the preparations for the evening's festivities from the west wall.

"A trifle, Gentle Guide, for your pleasure." He gave her the cloth-wrapped package with a sweeping bow.

Marilyn smiled and thanked him.

"Well, open it," little Lillian commanded. "I mean, don't you want to know what's in it?"

"Hush, Lillian," said Carmen. "It's her gift. She can open it in her own sweet time." She looked over Marilyn's shoulder. "As long as that time is *now.*"

Marilyn laughed and pulled the ribbon and cloth from a small wooden box. In it was a brass and silver tube, with a steel pen nib sticking from one end.

"Oh, a new pen. Brass with electroplated silver—very pretty. We saw the plating works yesterday. All my nib handles are wooden."

"Ah, Gentle Guide. This isn't just any pen." Sylvan took it from the box and produced a sheet of parchment. "Watch." He drew the nib across the parchment and ink flowed out onto the paper.

"You must have dipped the nib just before you joined us."

"No, Gentle Guide. I didn't. This is a re-creation of a pre-

Founding device called a fountain pen." He pointed the tip of pen down and removed the end piece on the brass cylinder. "You put the ink inside this pen and it flows down into the nib."

Marilyn tried the pen herself, writing ten consecutive lines on the page without running out of ink. "This is perfect!" She hugged Sylvan impulsively. "How did you know I'd like this?"

"Insight, Marilyn." He smiled. *My father's. Left to myself, I would have tried jewels.* "That you like it gives me great pleasure."

Marilyn turned to show Lillian and Carmen.

Lillian shrugged. "I've played with Father's. I was hoping it was something more romantic." Carmen laughed out loud and Marilyn blushed.

Carmen took Lillian by her shoulders. "Well, little one, it's time to go dress for the dance."

"Ah, Aunt Carmen."

"No protests, little one. Even if you don't care, I want to look my best tonight!" she said firmly. "See you both later, Guides."

After they'd left, Sylvan and Marilyn walked along the top of the wall as the sun went down and the stars came out.

The Eight Hundred regrouped three kilometers from Brandon-on-the-Falls an hour before midnight. They were tired but in good spirits.

"I'd not have believed it," said Gahnfeld.

Leland smiled before taking a deep pull from a canvas water bag. He passed it to Gahnfeld. "Have the men take their time. We want to look pretty when we get to town."

"Yes, Guide."

*Well, at least he's stopped calling me Warden,* thought Leland. He rubbed his eyes tiredly and watched the men straighten their clothing and weapons. *What about uniforms?* He mulled the pros and cons. The Falcons did very well without and the Mounted Pikes did pretty good with uniforms.

MASKAROVKA. THE UNIFORMS SHOULD SERVE A PURPOSE.

Leland blinked and felt a soundless thunderclap from the dark knot in his head. When it had passed he was left with a connected network of ideas. The word was foreign to him, and though its exact meaning wasn't clear, its implications were tremendous.

The second night of the Harvest Festival was in full swing with a large dance and bonfire in the town center. Sylvan was teaching Marilyn a dance step from Cotswold when the music stopped at the end of the song. That's when everyone heard the singing.

"What's this, a chorus?" asked Marilyn. "It sure seems far away. What are they singing?"

Sylvan held a hand to his ear. "Sounds like a marching song. 'She Wore a Yellow Ribbon.' "

Guide Dulan was sitting with Captain Koss and High Steward Arthur de Noram when he heard the singing. "Who the hell is that? What time was Leland's unit supposed to rendezvous with the Cotswold escort?"

"Midafternoon," Captain Koss told him.

"They couldn't be back so soon then."

Captain Koss watched a small group of approaching riders. "I'm not so sure. Unless I'm mistaken, that's the warden there."

Leland trotted up and dismounted. Bowing, he said, "The High Steward Montrose is safely into Cotswold, sir."

"Where are the rest of your men? Did you leave them to camp and ride ahead?"

"No, sir. I brought them with me. They should be here shortly."

"The *entire* unit?"

"Yes, sir."

"Oh," said Dulan. With the ghost of a smile he added, "Good time."

"Thank you, sir."

The first section of cavalry rode into sight, singing. Behind them came a section of foot. It took five minutes for the entire Eight Hundred to come to a halt in passable formation. Gahnfeld dressed them before riding up. "Permission to dismiss the men, *Warden?*"

Leland winced, then turned back to his father. "Sir?"

Dulan waved his hand. "Let them enjoy themselves."

Gahnfeld still looked expectantly at Leland and he blinked. "Oh. Turn them loose, Halvidar."

The dance was a little livelier after that.

A little later Captain Koss pulled Halvidar Gahnfeld aside and handed him a drink. "How'd you do it, Myron? How'd you get these green troops back here so quick?"

Gahnfeld swallowed half the mug of dark beer, then wiped his lips. "*I* didn't do it. *He* did." He jerked his thumb over to where Leland was standing alone and told Captain Koss about the leapfrog run/ride trip. "I don't know if I'd do it in hostile country, but you should have seen the troops take after him when he started running."

Captain Koss whistled.

"You said it," said Gahnfeld. He looked over at Leland and saw him edging farther back from the crowd. Leland seemed to be looking up at the Needle. "Oh."

"What?" asked Captain Koss.

"It was last Harvest Festival that he climbed the Needle and put on the Helm."

"Right." Koss looked over at Leland. "So it was."

Just looking at it made his hands hurt.

Leland looked down at his scarred fingertips, then back at the Needle. He reached those same fingertips up to his scarred temples.

He stared vaguely out at the dancing couples, then blinked when he saw Sylvan and Marilyn go whirling by. She was laughing out loud, her teeth flashing in the light.

Unbidden, his hand reached out in their direction and half closed. Then he dropped it back to his side.

One of the coronets from the Eight Hundred passed close by bearing a tray of ale-filled tankards to his fellows. He stopped when he saw Leland there and offered him one.

Leland was still watching Sylvan and Marilyn dancing and, for a minute, didn't notice the soldier standing there. He finally realized the man was there when the dancing couple disappeared behind the fire. He blinked and accepted a tankard with thanks and a sorry attempt at a smile. The coronet beamed back and moved on.

Leland drank the beer slowly. He saw his brother Anthony dancing across the ground with Clarissa de Koss. Dillan was over by Guide Dulan talking with Ricard de Laal and Margaret de Jinith. Dexter swept by among the dancers, two girls in arm.

Suddenly Leland was very tired. He put the tankard on a table and started walking back to the castle. He noticed his bodyguard fall into step around him but, mercifully, they didn't say anything.

Neither did he.

His lovemaking was not artistic, though her reactions convinced him he was expert. They lay back in the bed afterward, the covers thrown back, touching at hand and shoulder. His breathing was hard, almost labored, his pleasure great. Her breathing was quiet, her pleasure minimal. She used her free hand to fan herself lightly, quietly, trying to dry the sweat he'd left on her breasts and stomach.

"Oh, girl. That was something."

She smiled to herself, being called a *girl,* and kissed his shoulder. "The best ever," she said quietly. She scooted minutely toward the foot of the bed to further the illusion that he was taller than she. A languorous stretch covered the motion.

"You're wasted here, Carmen. Come back to Noram City with us."

She thought about it. "How could I, Arthur? My place is here. Besides, here I'm special. There I'd just be another hanger-on at Noram House." *And there are things I have to do.*

Arthur de Noram shrugged.

She waited for him to say something. Plead with her, perhaps. If it really meant something to him, it could be worth her while to go—worth Ricard's future.

His breathing deepened, slowed, and he slept.

She clenched her teeth together. No, he didn't really want her to go back to Noram City with him. She waited until he was deeply asleep before slipping from the bed.

*All men are bastards!*

High Steward Arthur de Noram had breakfast with his daughter and his sister in a room that overlooked the south garden. There was a charcoal brazier set near the window to take some of the bite out of the early-morning air. As usual, Arthur and Marilyn found it restful to have breakfast with Aunt Margaret. She was able to hold a perfectly satisfactory conversation without the slightest contribution from either of them.

Marilyn stifled a yawn that was more from lack of sleep than boredom and tried to smile at something her aunt said. Her thoughts were on last night's dance and the fire that had not only reached into the starry sky but had also raced through her as she danced with Sylvan.

*He's so strong,* she thought. *The way he threw me into the air . . .* She blinked as she remembered the arrival of Leland and his soldiers. She tried comparing the two of them, Sylvan and Leland, in her mind, but they blurred. She thought of Sylvan in terms of power and courtliness. She thought of Leland in terms of . . . anger! Yes, anger. His words from two months ago and those from just the other day in the library still burned her. *The insufferable little . . . little . . . scholar?* Another aspect of Leland, the only other side she had met, haunted her just as much. The scholar, *damn him!* She remembered the scholar with the gentle mouth and the tragic eyes.

"What's the matter, dear?" asked her aunt. "Aren't you hungry?"

Marilyn shrugged. "I guess not."

Arthur was quite hungry and in good spirits. "It's this place. You'll be glad to get back to Noram City, the court, and the university."

Marilyn said, "I certainly will!"

Arthur looked up from his omelet, surprised at the vehemence in her voice.

"This time next week, child," said Aunt Margaret. "Arthur, we should have a formal ball." She turned back to Marilyn. "I know you don't like those things normally, dear, but we have to introduce Sylvan to the social life in the city, don't we?" She sipped her tea. "Besides, the warden will be there for a couple of weeks. There are quite a few young ladies at the court who would love to devour him."

She glanced up at her brother and niece, and almost choked. "What did I say? You two both look like you have a toothache. Don't you want to have a ball?"

Arthur opened and closed his mouth a few times. "A ball is a fine idea. I'm not sure young Leland will show so well, though, at the court. After all, Laal isn't exactly Noram City."

Margaret put her tea down. "Oh, I don't know. I think he'll compare pretty well. If for no other reason than he knows how to *listen.* Most young men I know live to hear themselves talk. What do you think, Marilyn?"

Marilyn stood up suddenly, her napkin falling to the floor. "I think I'd like to be excused from the table. There's a million details to take care of before we leave tomorrow." She left quickly.

Margaret watched her exit, eyes wide, mouth parted. "Well! What do you suppose that's about?"

"I don't know," Arthur said abruptly, a scowl on his face. "I don't care." He stood. "Have a good morning!" His exit was, if anything, more sudden than Marilyn's.

Margaret stared at the empty chairs and shook her head. Then she pulled his plate over and started finishing off his omelet. After a minute she called her secretary and began dictating heliograms. If there was to be a ball, the staff of Noram House would need plenty of time to prepare.

* * *

Leland rose before dawn, riding with difficulty into town to teach the morning aikido class.

"Why are you so stiff?" Charly asked privately.

"You'd be stiff, too, if you'd run twenty kilometers yesterday and rode another thirty." He peered sideways at her. "Well, perhaps *you* wouldn't. Did you get my message?"

"Yes. Love to travel with your group. I hope you'll be able to train at the dojo?"

"I'll make time."

He dashed back to the station to breakfast with Martin, Myron Gahnfeld, and Captain de Koss in one of the military wardrooms. Captain Koss was briefing Leland and Myron about the tactics of the Rootless. Martin was there to brief them about their supply situation.

"Nothing really new about the Rootless," Captain Koss was saying. "Just never get in a running battle with them because they understand hit-and-run. They'll ride into extreme firing range and loose arrows. If you try to close with them, they'll fade out and hit you elsewhere. On flat terrain they're deadly. When you have a fixed front, like along the Black or the Silver, they're not so terrible. Give them room to maneuver and you can kiss your ass good-bye.

"*Never* try to chase them down. They keep six horses in reserve for each man. And that doesn't count the packhorses with extra arrows. We try to keep at least three horses in reserve for our cavalry, but your unit—the Eight Hundred, eh?" He nodded as he remembered. "Your unit is going more as mounted infantry. We're providing horses enough to mount the entire unit, but that's just transport. Along the Black your objective is to take and hold real estate. There will be other cavalry at the Black from other Noram stewardships. I think Malcom de Toshiko is sending almost all cavalry.

"Besides that, take your cues from Gahnfeld here. He's gone against the Rootless three times now. So have all your other halvidars."

Myron said nothing, just kept eating.

Captain de Koss leaned back. "Well, that's my piece. There's a lot more but there's not enough time." He looked at Leland. *I'm hoping those scars on your temples are more than just decoration.*

Martin put a leather dispatch case on the table and opened it. "We're not supplying you directly, other than marching rations to Noram City. Here is a letter of credit drawn on our surplus with Grissom & Sons of Noram City. It is redeemable in cash, but I recommend you let them provide the bulk of the supplies directly. This will save them and us money. We are also giving you cash for payroll and other supplies as needed. Your personal expense money is fifteen hundred soys, but of course you can draw from Grissom & Sons for anything extra you need."

Leland nodded, slightly dazed. The value of a soy was tied to the buying power of one bushel of soybeans. Fifteen hundred of them was a large sum of money.

Martin smiled. "Should you draw more, your father will want to know why."

"By the founders, Martin, what would I spend it on?"

Captain de Koss laughed. "You haven't been to Noram City since you were seven. A young man can find plenty of things to spend money on there."

Martin went on. "I sent notice to air out Laal House and for Phillip to buy fodder." Laal House was Guide Dulan's estate on the outskirts of Noram City. Phillip was Laal's factor in Noram. "They've just finished harvesting the peanuts so you can billet the troops in those fields. By the time you get there, things should be in order. They better be."

Leland and Captain de Koss laughed. "I'd think you'd have more confidence in your own son, Martin," said de Koss. "You know things will be perfect."

Martin sighed and tried not to smile.

"You'll need to keep the troops polite in Noram City," de Koss added. "There will be soldiers from all over Greater Noram gathering there for the march to the plain. If you don't keep them under iron control, you'll have enough brawls to wreck the city."

Leland nodded. "We're only supposed to be there a few weeks. I'll keep them on the estate."

de Koss and Gahnfeld exchanged glances. "You'll *try.* Good luck to you."

"I'll find something to keep them busy," Leland said.

# NINE

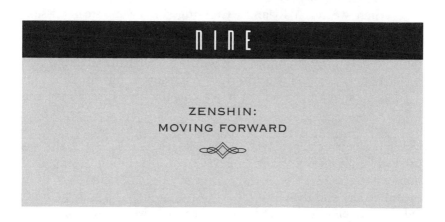

## ZENSHIN: MOVING FORWARD

By changing horses at the high steward's post stations, a hardy man can ride from Brandon-on-the-Falls to Noram City in about twenty-four hours. To travel the same route at a rate suitable for the backsides of guardianship took a week.

Halvidar Gahnfeld was steaming. "How in the hell am I supposed to teach these clowns to march like soldiers if we continue at this snail's pace?" As an afterthought he added, "Sir."

Leland suppressed a smile. "By tonight we'll be through the Cloud Scrapers and we'll have some options." He pulled his horse to the side of the mountain trail in one of the few places that was possible. Gahnfeld followed. "Get out that map, please."

Gahnfeld pulled a rolled map from his saddle map tube and spread it across his lap.

Leland pointed at the northern foothills of the Cloud Scrapers, just over the border into Acoma, one of the stewardships that, like Laal, made up Greater Noramland. "Look, here we can leave half the Eight Hundred with the high steward and take the other half on forced marches, covering as much mileage as you deem necessary and then rejoining the party by nightfall at the next inn. Or, if you want, the next day. You'll know best about how you want to do this, but you can break them up into individual hundreds, as well." He waited for a gap in the troops riding past at a walk, then edged his horse back into line.

"Just be sure you don't damage anybody's fields. I don't want the reputation that Arthur's own troops have."

Gahnfeld nodded. "Right."

"When we reach Ryland's Crossing, I'll have a real mission for you."

"Sir?" Ryland's Crossing was on the border between Acoma and the stewardship of Noram. Deep within Great Noramland, it was nowhere near any enemy territories. "What sort of mission?"

Leland shook his head. "Worry about the men first. I'll tell you later."

Marilyn was as sick of this snail's pace as Halvidar Gahnfeld. She was tired of being on horseback. She was tired of residing in strangers' homes and strange inns. She was especially tired of being away from the university and the Great Library. And, though she hadn't admitted it to herself, she was getting tired of Sylvan Montrose.

"Father, be reasonable. I could leave now and be home in two days."

"Oh? And who will escort you? Do you expect your Aunt Margaret to gallop all day for two days?"

"Aunt Margaret needn't come. You can have some of your troops escort me . . . and I'll have my maid, Dora."

Arthur shook his head firmly. "Those troops stay with *me* until I'm back in Noram City."

She knew better than to argue with him when he used that tone. "Well, then, I'm sure the warden would give me an escort from his men."

"Absolutely not!" he responded angrily. He attempted to calm himself down. "If I had another troop of our men here or some of Cotswold's troops, I'd send you in an instant. But it isn't possible, so don't bother me about it again."

She demurred. "Yes, Father."

It wasn't until her horse had traveled another twenty meters that the shock hit her. *Oh, my stars! He trusts Cotswold more than Laal. Why?*

They stopped that night at an inn in the foothills, the Eight Hundred camping in a recently harvested field of wheat nearby. As in the previous two nights, Leland called on the high steward for the next night's destination before eating with his halvidars.

"Oh, say, this inn here at Louisberg should do, I think. That's about thirty kilometers if I remember."

"Certainly, High Steward," Leland said, rolling up the deerskin.

They were in the common room of the inn, Arthur sitting in one of his own chairs, a wooden camp chair with leather back and seat. Also in the room were the Guides Marilyn and Margaret, as well as two of Arthur's own guards.

Leland made to leave but was stopped by Gentle Guide Margaret. "What's your hurry, Warden? Please join us in a glass of wine."

Leland glanced at Marilyn. She was looking at the fire, her expression featureless. He bowed. "I'd be honored, Gentle Guide. I'm surprised to find you so ill-attended."

"It's a secret, I suppose," said Marilyn's aunt. "But Sylvan Montrose has apparently lured all my brother's officers out into the barn to dice." She leaned forward and winked. "If they want to do this sort of thing in private, they shouldn't talk about it under my window."

Marilyn looked at her aunt, surprised. "Sylvan is not! He's resting before dinner."

Margaret chuckled. "Is that what he told you?"

"Yes!"

Margaret poured wine into a goblet and set it at the place across from her. She gestured at Leland to sit. "Well, then, that must be what he's doing. Perhaps I mistook someone else for him going across the yard and into the barn with the rest of Arthur's officers. Surely that's what happened." Then, arrow loosed, she shut her mouth.

Marilyn blushed but remained calm, seemingly unconcerned.

Leland sat and picked up his wine. It was *Eiswein*, from Laal, sweet and potent. He took a sip, then another. The stuff slid down into his empty stomach and started a glow there.

He looked around the room and couldn't help but notice how much cleaner and brighter the Blue Whale Inn was than this place.

Marilyn looked up at he set the goblet back down.

When Leland looked into her eyes she frowned suddenly and dropped her eyes to a book she held in her lap, one finger marking a place. Leland took a sudden gulp of wine, then ventured, "What are you reading, Gentle Guide? One of the medical books you found on your trip?" *If I get her talking, all I'll have to do is listen.* And he wanted very much to listen to her voice.

She nodded slowly. "Yes. It's a book on *pathognomy.*" She took extra care with the pronunciation. "We located it in Siegfried's private library. We don't have anything quite like it. I'm only vaguely sure what it means."

Leland spoke reflexively. "From the Greek, *pathognomonikos,* one who is skilled in the diagnosis of disease." He paused. He hadn't intended to speak at all. Worse, he didn't know where he'd learned that piece of information. He drank again to cover his bewilderment. Marilyn and her aunt Margaret were both staring at him, faintly surprised. Leland went on. "Ultimately from the Greek words *pathos,* meaning disease, suffering, or emotion, and *gnomon,* meaning judge."

Arthur, over by the fire, muttered something under his breath. Marilyn frowned, as if annoyed by something.

Aunt Margaret poured more wine in Leland's cup. "Well, go on, *Warden.*" She accented the title, speaking it just a little louder than necessary. Arthur stood abruptly and walked from the room.

A feeling of unreality overcame Leland as he began talking again. "Essentially then, it would be the study of the *symptoms* of disease, just as pathology is the study of disease in general."

"You're very well informed on medical terminology," Marilyn said grudgingly.

Leland shrugged. "Look for the roots, the beginnings. We speak only a few languages on this planet. On Earth they spoke thousands. Cultures borrow terms for things new to them from cultures already experienced with that thing. Have you ever wondered why the Founders included Latin and Greek dictionaries in the books?"

Marilyn nodded. "I suppose you're right. And here I'd thought you had some supernatural source for your knowledge."

It was Leland's turn to blush, but Marilyn didn't notice in the dark room.

"We can talk about it at dinner, can't we?" said Aunt Margaret. "You'll join us, of course?"

"I can't, Gentle Guide." Leland stood and bowed. "I'm afraid my officers and our guest are expecting me back for dinner. I enjoyed talking with you both, though, very much. Good evening."

Margaret pursed her lips mischievously. "Your guest? I'd heard you had a woman traveling with you. Some *close* friend?" She glanced sideways at Marilyn.

Leland ears turned a deeper shade of red. "The Guide Charlina is indeed a good friend, but it's not romantic. She's twice my age." He paused. "Did I say something wrong?"

Both women were staring at him. All trace of humor had left Margaret's face. "Charlina *de Rosen?*"

"Yes. Is there a problem?"

Marilyn and Margaret were looking at each other. Margaret turned back to Leland and smiled brightly. "No problem. We'll let you get back to your dinner plans. Please give Charly my regards."

"And mine," said Marilyn in an oddly intent voice.

Leland bowed. "I hear and obey."

Leland left the inn both relieved and frustrated. He wanted to stay and spend more time with Marilyn, but he was pretty sure she was still angry with him for his behavior in Laal. In addition, the high steward was only coldly polite toward Leland, giving him the impression that they'd both be much happier out of each other's presence. And then there was Sylvan Montrose. Leland didn't know whether it was jealousy, ancient hostility, or plain dislike, but he couldn't stand to be around the man.

As he walked out onto the road, followed by the two men Gahnfeld had assigned as escort, Leland heard laughing, shouts, and the occasional curse from the direction of the barn. He was also sure that one of the voices was Sylvan's.

*Score one for Guide Margaret,* he thought. *I shouldn't think Marilyn would care if he played at dice. But I'll sure as hell bet she doesn't like him lying to her.*

He took some pleasure in this thought.

The sun was one diameter above the horizon, and some of Leland's unit were playing soccer at the far end of the encampment. He watched the distant players for a moment, then walked on thoughtfully.

"How many soccer balls do we have?" Leland asked Halvidar Gahnfeld upon entering the area set up for the officer's mess.

The assembled halvidars, seated on camp stools, stood abruptly. "Oh, sit down," Leland said. "Well, how many?"

Gahnfeld sat back slowly. "I don't know, sir. One moment." He turned back toward the halvidars. "Report, by unit."

Halvidar of the First Hundred said, "The First has four, I think."

Halvidar of the Second Hundred said, "I don't know how many the Second has, sir."

"The Third has eleven."

Leland raised his hand. "Enough. Is soccer as popular among our men as it is in Laal proper?"

"Probably more so," said Gahnfeld. "What we have here are mostly boys who've just finished mandatory schooling."

"All right. When we get to Noram City we'll buy enough balls to give units at least ten each. Organize teams. They can play for an hour after evening mess. Dominant teams within units can begin playing each other." He sat. "Clear?"

Gahnfeld nodded slowly. "Yes sir."

"Reservations, Chief Halvidar? What are they?"

"Sir, these are green troops. In order to train them to face the Rootless, we'll need every spare moment until battle."

Leland smiled. "It's my intention that this competition be expanded from soccer into all phases of training. We'll create standings among the units." He turned to the halvidar of the First. "From now on units will pass in review in order by standing. There will also be a pennant to fly from the top unit's banner."

Gahnfeld was nodding now. "Yes, sir. That should work."

"I hope so. Let's try it, anyway. We'll start with performance on the line of march. Perhaps unit standing will also determine order of march?"

He smiled then and said, "I better wash before supper. Has anybody seen Guide Charlina?"

"Yes, Warden—she's refereeing the soccer game."

"Oh. Well, good. Hope they play clean." *For their sake.*

Later, at dinner, Leland passed on Margaret's and Marilyn's greetings to Charly.

She smiled. "That was nice of them. I'm going to guess that the high steward wasn't in the room at the time."

"How did you know?"

"I'm not exactly one of Arthur's favorite people. My name is usually not mentioned in his presence." She looked a little guilty. "Perhaps I should've mentioned this before accepting your offer of transportation. It might even get you in trouble."

"Are you a criminal or something?"

Charly laughed.

Leland shrugged. "I don't care. He's barely civil with me as it is. Let it spoil his digestion."

"Marilyn will probably come to see me tonight."

Leland raised his eyebrows. "Why?"

"She's one of my students and she hasn't seen me for over nine months. Her sister is, too."

"Zanna de Noram."

Charly smiled at the name and her voice softened. "Yes, Zanna."

"Is that why Arthur dislikes you? Because you teach his daughters aikido?

"No. It has more to do with his grandchildren."

"Grandchildren? I didn't think he had any."

"Right. And, from Zanna, he's not likely to get any."

Leland frowned. "I must be stupid. What do you have to do with Zanna's children?"

"Oh, it's simple enough. For the past five years Zanna and I have been lovers."

At sunrise the next morning, hours before the High Steward of Noram got out of bed, the First, Third, Fifth, and Seventh hundreds had marched, dismounted, on a side road that would take them a roundabout forty kilometers to reach that night's stop at Louisberg. Their mounts went with the main party.

"Will you make it in by sunset?" asked Leland of Halvidar Gahnfeld.

"Probably. But send scouts only if we're not in by midnight."

"As you will, Halvidar. I hope you plan to train them how to do something other than march eventually."

Gahnfeld stiffened. "Sir. I've prepared a schedule of training for our stay in Noram City. Would the Warden care to see it?"

Leland winced. "No need to get huffy, Myron. It's not as if you've never questioned *my* actions."

"Sorry, Guide Leland." He paused, then said, "Captain de Koss made it perfectly clear that if I took these men into battle inadequately trained, I needn't bother returning to Laal."

"Ah. Apology accepted. I don't want to see the training schedule, but I'm going to need at least an hour per day of the officers' time the second week. Please work it into the rotation—halvidars and coronets."

Gahnfeld opened his mouth as if to ask something but only said, "Yes, Guide Leland. Any other instructions?"

"Yes, keep them quiet for the first kilometer. I don't want to wake the high steward." He smiled then and said, "Get them going."

Gahnfeld saluted and started the four hundred men out with a wave of his hand.

It was Sylvan Montrose, not Arthur de Noram, who noticed the men were gone. At midmorning he came riding up the road at a gallop, careless of the horses he spooked, to rein in before Leland.

Leland said, "Good morning, Guide," and started to steer his horse around Sylvan's mount without stopping.

Sylvan frowned, then jerked the reins around hard. His mount whinnied in protest but turned quickly enough to block Leland's mount.

Leland turned his horse to the other side.

Sylvan tried to duplicate the jerking maneuver and his horse began bucking. He was forced to bring his horse to a walk along side of Leland's mount.

Leland repressed a smile and said, "A difficult horse, Guide?"

Sylvan ignored this and said, "Half your saddles are empty, Warden. How do you account for it?"

Leland raised his eyebrows. "I don't. I don't have to."

"What do you mean?" Sylvan asked, raising his voice.

"What, pray tell, do *you* mean, Guide? Are you under the impression that I must account for my actions to you? Or are you implying that I've done something improper or wrong?" Leland was the soul of politeness and reason, his voice quiet and even. "Perhaps if you could tell me what's bothering you, I'll be able to help you." *Let's see if that doesn't make you fly off the handle.* He watched Sylvan's reaction carefully.

Sylvan's mouth widened for a moment and Leland saw a dark flush begin to rise up his neck. Then Sylvan did the unexpected. He closed his mouth, took a deep breath, and exhaled. Then he grinned.

"I seem to have gotten off on the wrong foot with you, Warden. Please forgive me for my manner—I haven't been out of Cotswold very often. I'm accustomed to outranking every military officer in my vicinity. I spoke out of habit, perhaps even a bad habit." He smiled again.

Leland was impressed. Not with the charm or the apparent goodwill but by the discipline that brought such a change of tack when Sylvan clearly felt just the opposite. *What does he want from me?*

"Don't worry about it," Leland said, apparently dismissing the affair. "Since you're interested, my men are off on a training march.

They'll rejoin us this evening. It's certainly no secret; I informed the high steward's Captain of the March about it last night."

"Ah, Marshall de Gant."

Leland nodded. "That's right. Apparently the good marshall will be commanding the combined forces against Nullarbor. He expects me to conduct all future training without disturbing him."

"The marshall is getting on in years, isn't he?" Sylvan said. "I imagined you disturbed his plans for bed?"

"No," Leland said neutrally. "I disturbed his swordplay. He was instructing his halvidars in *Batto Ho.* As for his age, well, that means he's gone against the Rootless more than ten times. I shouldn't be surprised to find that experience useful."

Sylvan half nodded. "Well, hopefully you'll see lots of action. I've fought the Rootless myself, on our eastern border. They're nothing much against a fortified position, but watch out for their archers. They're deadly accurate. You'll need to keep your head down."

"I'll take that advice." *And not just with the Rootless.*

For the remaining days of the trip, Gahnfeld continued to train the men with a series of marches, mounted side trips, and unit races. The men dragged in each night, exhausted, but, as far as Leland could tell, their morale was good.

When they reached Ryland's Crossing, on the border between Acoma and Lesser Noram, Leland dispatched Halvidar Gahnfeld's staff assistant, Coronet Sanchez, to the northwest. He left before dawn, silent and unnoticed. The coronet's destination was the Land-of-Lakes region in western Acoma, and he took with him six men and twenty unladen pack mules. They were to rejoin the Eight Hundred at Noram City.

They were now on the rolling plains of Noram, some of the richest farmland on the planet. Farms were spotted across the land as densely as the customs allowed, with wild wood and prairie spread between. The towns and villages occurred some forty kilometers apart, and the inns upon the highway were numerous.

Harvest was still in motion and the grass was beginning to brown. Trees that changed color with the season were just beginning to darken. Mornings were nippy though, unlike mountainous Laal, there hadn't been frost yet.

Charly stayed back with Leland's troops, occasionally on horseback, but usually in one of the commissary wagons making one of the infatuated foot soldiers card wool while she spun it. When Leland had offered to include her in his transactions with the high steward's party, she'd refused gently.

Sylvan continued to talk with Leland occasionally on the road, sometimes including him in conversations with Marilyn. Leland remained polite but distant to both of them, though he would ride with the Guide Margaret for hours at a time. She talked of the court at Noram, of the city's many attractions, and of the Great Library, where she would go to "smell the books and try to soak up some knowledge by touch."

Occasionally the conversation would touch on Margaret de Jinith's childhood and her memories of her father, the famous William de Noram, and, to Leland's surprise, the Privy Consul of Noram, Dulan de Laal.

"Oh, your father was important to William, you can be sure! He wouldn't make a major move without consulting him. There were times when it seemed like the guardianship was centered in Laal rather than Noram. I'm afraid my brother didn't care for that very much."

Leland nodded. "I remember your father. I was three or four on his last visit. He sat me in his lap and told me to call him Uncle Willi."

"That sounds like Father. I still miss him." She shifted her ample posterior to a better seat on the padded saddle. "I remember the time your father met your mother."

"Oh? My father doesn't talk about her, but my brother Dillan has told me something about her. I'd appreciate hearing about it."

"Well, I was fourteen, and lucky, because I wouldn't have been allowed to attend the ball if I'd been anything but the granddaughter of the high steward. You're father was there with your grandfather, of course. He should of have been, oh, twenty-two years old? That's right, twenty-two years old and not particularly handsome, but striking in a stern way. Your brother Dillan takes after him, I'd say, but you, Warden, take after your mother.

"She was the most beautiful creature in the stewardship. She was twenty then and had every unmarried guide in Noram after her hand. At that ball there were two fistfights over who would be next to *dance* with her. Imagine! Fistfights at the high steward's ball. It was unheard of." Margaret repositioned her hat to better unlock the afternoon sun.

"Well, your father didn't even try to dance with her. He's smarter than that. No, he asked the Guide Alethea to dance instead. Do you know who she was?"

Leland nodded. "My grandmother."

"That's right." Margaret chuckled. "Your mother's mother. When they finished dancing, the Gentle Guide Alethea took him over to where all those knuckleheads were arguing over who had the next dance with your mother and said, 'Lillian, I want you to meet this young guide, Dulan de Laal.' Well, your mother smiled at him but he just bowed, no expression whatsoever on his face, like granite. 'Honored,' I think he said. Then, almost as an afterthought, he asked, 'Do you dance as well as your mother, Gentle Guide?' And she said, 'There's only one way to find out.' And before any of those idiots with the loud voices could say a word, she was out on the floor with him.

"They announced the engagement the next month. Father was relieved. He wanted your mother married before some idiot killed another over her."

Leland shook his head, unused to thinking of his father that way. "I wish I'd known her better."

Marilyn and Sylvan, accompanied by four of the High Steward's officers, came galloping back to the road just then. Marilyn had been using some of her stifled energy to gallop across a stretch of wild prairie. While they were still some distance away, Leland half bowed in his saddle and said, "Thank you so much for the story, Gentle Guide. It means a great deal to me to hear about my mother. Perhaps later we can talk again?"

Margaret eyed the approaching riders and grimaced. "So, you're going to do your disappearing act on us again, eh? Well, go. To tell the truth, I can't stand to be around Guide Sylvan, either, but one must go through the proper motions." She shooed him off with a wave of her hand.

Leland smiled and rode forward to his men at the head of the column.

Marilyn reined in beside her aunt Margaret. "Talking with the warden again? I imagine he has a great deal to say on many subjects."

Margaret sniffed. "That may well be, child, but he keeps his council on them. As I've said before, he knows how and when to listen." She glanced sideways at Guide Sylvan. "Such courtesy is not very common."

Almost as if on cue, Sylvan Montrose broke in to talk about their gallop. Margaret, still facing Marilyn, rolled her eyes to the heavens. Then she composed her face into a smiling mask and turned to listen.

Later, after Sylvan and the officers had left them in peace, Marilyn asked, "Well, Aunt Margaret, I'm still curious. What did you and the warden discuss?"

Margaret massaged the bridge of her nose. "Well, if you must know, we talked about young love." And, though Marilyn pressed her, she wouldn't say another word on the subject.

Noram City, seat of the Stewardship of Noram, Jewel of Noramland, the City Without Walls, sits on a mountain, albeit a small one, surrounded by the high veldt of Noramland. The travelers saw it rise steadily from the plain as they traveled closer and closer.

In fact, the large hill was an outcropping of granite, not unlike the Needle, though much wider. The city on top was blessed with security, climate, a magnificent view, and artesian springs that bubbled forth from the rock itself. The one wide road up into the city consisted of a series of switchbacks cut out of the least precipitous face. At three places gaps in the road were spanned by wooden drawbridges. The raising of any one of these rendered the road impassable, but there had never been an occasion for their use, though they were repaired and tested regularly.

Twenty years previously, Leland's father had been given an estate by William, for his service to the stewardship. It lay some two kilometers from the city, off the trunk road from Laal. Leland and the Eight Hundred parted company with the high steward at the turnoff.

Arthur nodded curtly at the leavetaking, Marilyn gave him an uncertain smile, Sylvan took his hand with synthetic goodwill, and Margaret hugged him impulsively. "You've been good company, Leland. Come see me up at Noram House."

Leland blushed at the attention. "Of course I will, Gentle Guide. Count on it."

The Eight Hundred rode onto the estate in parade formation. Gahnfeld told the unit halvidars, "Laal's factor will be in attendance. The formation *will* be perfect." That was all he'd said, but such was his tone of voice that more than one of the unit leaders had broken into a sweat.

They managed it, too, except at the end when one of the Seventh rode off the road into a ditch, but he was out of it so quickly that Gahnfeld chose not to notice.

Leland and Gahnfeld reined up outside of the large, three-story house and watched all of them parade past and into the freshly harvested peanut fields. Then they dismounted and shook hands with Phillip Spruill.

"Leland, Halvidar Gahnfeld. Welcome to Lillian House." Phillip was a tall, thin, and serious-looking man around thirty. He was a good friend of Leland's oldest brother, Dillan. He wore a formal suit with the crest of Laal on a tablet hung from his neck on a chain.

Leland smiled as he greeted him. "Thank you, Phillip. Your father and mine send their respects. I hope things are well with you?"

"Very well." He gestured and a servant came forward to take their horses. He led them into the house. "You've grown."

Leland laughed. "It's been four years!"

"Father suggested I put you in the family's rooms on the top floor, which leaves the guest rooms for your halvidars. Will you be needing servants for the house? When your father stays he usually brings the personnel he needs. We can, of course, call on the farmhands and their families if needed."

Leland shook his head. "No, that won't be necessary. We will continue to operate as a military unit for the duration of our stay here." He turned his head toward Gahnfeld. "This includes sentries. Do you have any special needs, Senior Halvidar?"

Gahnfeld nodded. "Yes, sir. Fodder for the horses, plus hay for a target range. About two hundred bales. And of course provisions for the men. We've enough, the supply officer tells me, for two more days."

Phillip nodded. "Give me a list and I'll convey it to Grissom & Sons."

"If you'll excuse me, gentlemen, I'll see to that chore, then," Gahnfeld said.

Leland nodded. "Certainly."

Gahnfeld left and Leland followed Phillip up the stairs. "I remember sliding down these stairs on a kitchen tray," Leland said. "I was only seven the last time I was here. Is there still a diving platform at the pond?"

"I've no idea. I stay in your father's townhouse, to be near the council." He took an envelope from his shirt. "Speaking of things 'official,' this arrived at the house this morning." He handed it to Leland.

"It's your invitation to a ball, to be held in honor of the betrothal of Guide Sylvan Montrose and the Gentle Guide Marilyn de Noram. It takes place a week and a half from today. There was one for myself, as well."

Leland fingered the paper silently, staring sightlessly at the wall. "Well, won't that be interesting," he finally said.

They resumed climbing the stairs and came out on the third-floor landing. The master bedroom was huge, much larger than the cubby-hole Leland had shared with Anthony the last time they were here. He went to the window and stared up at Noram City rising above a line of trees on its column of granite. "Won't that be interesting, indeed."

# TEN

## HITORI WAZA: INVISIBLE PARTNER PRACTICE

Guide Cornelius de Moran was trying to look at the mountains when the disturbance came.

From the office window, provided the weather was clear enough, you could see the dark smudge of the Preean Alps, or at least a tiny portion of those mountains. You had to crane your neck to one side and stand on tiptoe to see through the gap between the bell tower and the barracks of the city guard. The gap was framed below by the guard's stable, effectively blocking any view of the high plains that stretched between Noram City and the mountains.

But you could say that the office had a mountain view.

Guide Cornelius was having trouble stretching his neck as he aged. He wished to see the mountains through that window while he still could.

From outside the office Cornelius heard running footsteps echoing up the stairwell. He straightened his neck and thumped down onto his heels from tiptoe. He just managed to open the door before the running footsteps reached it.

Senior Librarian Potter, bent over, lungs heaving from his run up the stairway, leaned against the door frame, reached out, and knocked on Cornelius's face.

"Dammit, man! Watch what you're doing!" He put a hand to his forehead and winced.

Potter turned bright red. "Sorry! Oh, malnutrition! I didn't see you open the door."

"Idiot!" Cornelius said. "Did you think I wouldn't hear you pounding up the steps?" He backed into his office, a hand still to his face. "Well, what is it? Has someone torn a page in one of your copies?"

Potter, still gasping half in embarrassment, half in exhaustion, shook his head. "No, Chancellor. Someone is reading from the shelf."

Cornelius whirled, his head forgotten. "*The* shelf? The marked one?"

"Yes, Guide."

"You're sure he's not just browsing, flipping through the pages?"

"Positive. He's been reading the text on particle physics for the last hour and a half. He's been scribbling many equations down on paper. I walked behind him to shelve a book and couldn't make sense of them. There were several integral signs and some summations but I couldn't comprehend the steps."

Cornelius sat down in his desk chair and stared for a moment at the wall. "Well," he finally said. "Who made the leap? Was it one of our professors or a student?"

"Neither," Potter said, eyes wide. "It's a stranger!"

"Calm yourself. Describe him."

"He arrived this morning attended by four armed guards. He paid the fee to have their horses kept in the school's stable during the day. He's young, perhaps twenty-one, and very quiet. Lorenzo said he asked a few polite questions about the organization of the library, then spent the remainder of the time going from advanced text to advanced text."

Cornelius shook his head and hobbled over to his cane, leaning against his desk. "Must I do everything? Potter, you're a fine librarian and as fine a hand at calculus as I've ever seen, but sometimes you distress me."

Potter looked at the floor. "Yes, Guide."

"Don't look so pitiful. Send one of your assistants to ask the guards who our scholar is. When you know, come back and meet me at the bottom of the stairs. I want to meet this young man."

Leland didn't exist.

The books didn't exist.

He was a fish immersed in water. He flowed, he glided, he twisted sinuously through concepts, ideas, formulas, and words. At midday rites he surfaced enough to send the guards out to feed themselves before he sank back into the current without a ripple.

In the middle of the afternoon he closed a book and, in the midst of rising to get another, found himself facing an old man, standing with the aid of a cane. He blinked, fought down sudden irrational annoyance at this intrusion. The feeling brought him further out of his immersion. He became Leland again and all the associated concerns of that person returned.

"Good morning," he said, then remembered sending the guards out at midday. "I mean good afternoon."

The old man smiled and stepped closer. "Good afternoon to you, Warden." He half bowed. "I am Cornelius de Moran, Chancellor and Chief Archivist of the library."

Leland bowed low. "I am honored beyond speech."

"Oh, come now. Get up. I'm not the high steward."

"No, Chancellor, to my mind you're more important."

Cornelius looked around to see if anyone was within hearing. "Don't mouth nonsense, Warden. Besides, regardless of any truth or falsehood such a statement contains, speaking it can get you in serious trouble in this city."

Leland frowned. "Surely the high steward realizes the importance of the Great Library?"

Cornelius shrugged. "The high steward is greatly concerned with, how should I put this . . . place and position. There are many here in the capital who use this preoccupation. Your statement would mutate in the retelling. It's meaning would shift from respect for learning and the customs to high treason."

Leland shrugged. "I suppose, then, that I should keep my tongue still around here. The steward certainly doesn't seem to care much for me as it is. No sense in causing more harm." He motioned to the side. "May I fetch a chair for you, Chancellor?"

"Actually, Warden, I was about to take tea. I was hoping you would join me if you're at a stopping point."

"Gladly."

Cornelius led Leland into another room where a tea service had been set up. When Leland saw the nutcakes on the side, his stomach growled.

Cornelius lowered himself into a chair and waved Leland to another. He smiled and said, "Perhaps you could pour, Warden. My hands shake and tend to spill things."

Leland poured two cups and offered the nutcakes. "I notice there are three cups. Are we expecting someone else?"

"Hopefully," said Cornelius. "One of my favorite students has been gone from the city and has just returned. We usually have tea together when she's in residence."

Leland had just taken his first bite when he realized who Cornelius must be talking about. He continued chewing mechanically, the cake suddenly tasteless in his mouth. He took a swallow of the tea to wash it down. "That would be the Gentle Guide Marilyn de Noram?"

"Yes. I take it you had occasion to speak with her during her travels?"

Leland nodded. "Yes. She and her father spent time with us in Laal before and after the trip to Cotswold. She was collecting medical texts. My troops and I had the honor to escort the high steward's party from Laal to here."

Cornelius beamed. "Ah. We're very pleased with the Gentle Guide Marilyn."

Leland nodded and drained his cup. He heard light footsteps in the distance that were heartrendingly familiar. "I'm afraid I must leave now, Chancellor. I promised our factor I would be at his office before midafternoon." He stood. "I'm already late."

Cornelius spoke quickly. "Surely you can send a message to your factor and spare an old man a few more minutes."

Leland bowed low. "I'm sorry. If it were my own business I would gladly to it, but it is my father's and hence Laal's."

Cornelius raised his eyebrows. "If you must, Warden." He waved a hand in dismissal. As Leland walked out the door that led away from the footsteps, Cornelius called out softly, "She's never here in the mornings."

Leland nodded without turning, then went on.

It hadn't been a lie—Phillip really had been expecting Leland at Dulan de Laal's townhouse. The urgency was a matter of interpretation.

"I'm sorry to have kept you waiting," Leland said when ushered into the main salon.

Phillip and another man stood when he entered. "That's all right, Leland. Andre spent the time getting my measurements. We'd only just sat down."

Leland spent the next half hour being thoroughly measured by the tailor.

"And what are we looking for in the way of fabrics, Guide?" Andre asked. He pointed to the samples strewn across a desk. "Something ornate, or do you prefer a more classical cut?"

Leland looked helplessly at Phillip. "I don't know. Something comfortable, I hope."

Phillip looked at Leland studiously. "Well, he's got the figure to wear something simple. Slim hips, broad shoulders. Something dark, perhaps, with just a touch of gray trim at the collar and sleeves."

Leland ran his fingers through the samples, musing. Something occurred to him and he began looking in earnest. "Andre," he said.

"Yes, Warden."

"Could I have these two samples, do you think?" He held up two small scraps of cloth—one sandy brown and the other a drab green.

"Surely you aren't considering those colors for the ball?"

Leland laughed. "Oh, no. Just a small project of my own."

"Keep them, by all means," said the tailor. He picked out a pair of cloth pieces in black and silver. "Perhaps this for the ball? It's silk from Nueve France."

When Leland didn't say anything, Phillip nodded. "Yes, and maybe something stiff for the collar?"

"I know just what you mean, Guide. I'll have both suits ready for fitting by Saturday."

"Good," said Phillip, and escorted the man out.

Leland stared out the window until Phillip returned. The view from the study was unobstructed by higher buildings. Leland saw a thunderstorm far out on the plain dropping rain kilometers away. Lightning played about its dark belly, barely visible through the bright afternoon sunlight. Still, he could imagine the force of the storm and its local winds.

He shivered, unable to draw away from the overt symbolism, the image of a dark portent, a literal storm on his horizon. *Damn, it's hard! What do they expect from me? I'm only seventeen!* Suddenly he felt unbelievably weary.

Phillip came back into the room. "By the way, while you were at the library a rider brought a message from Halvidar Gahnfeld." He moved over to the sideboard and poured two glasses of wine. "You've been asked to attend a briefing this evening at Marshall de Gant's.

Also, he said something about Coronet Sanchez getting in with his 'cargo.' Does that make sense to you?"

Leland nodded. "Yes, it does. What time is this briefing supposed to be?"

"Half-past seven."

"May I eat with you here?"

Phillip nodded. "A pleasure."

"Well, I'll send one of my guards to tell Gahnfeld to join me here by seven. Then we'll go on to the meeting."

"Certainly, Guide."

It was dark when Leland and Gahnfeld arrived at the quarters of Marshall de Gant. The Noram officer had a townhouse on the edge of the City Guard's compound. Unlike most of the houses around, its exterior was well lit and the posted sentries wore armor.

An officer Leland recognized from the trip from Laal was seated just inside the building, checking people off as they arrived. He nodded gravely to Leland and Gahnfeld and made another check on the list.

It was moderately crowded inside the briefing room. Chairs had been arranged in rows and a bar set up to one side. Leland noted Sylvan Montrose by it, holding forth on some subject or another before a small group of younger male and female officers. Several other officers stood or sat in small groups across the room. More than one of them, Leland noted, were looking across at Sylvan with a sour expression.

Marshall de Gant was standing over by a wall map talking to one of his aides. He nodded briefly in Leland's direction when Leland entered the room.

Leland bowed back.

"Do you want something from the bar, Warden?" Gahnfeld asked.

Leland frowned, then said quietly, "What's the protocol on something like this, Gahnfeld? Is it social or serious? Or somewhere between?"

Gahnfeld stared at Leland, the corners of his mouth twitching for a moment before he said, "Somewhat in the middle. I suggest you have a cup in your hand, though. The marshall is a great one for toasts."

"Oh." Leland thought for a moment. "Cider then, or tea. If there's nothing free of alcohol, then wine."

Gahnfeld nodded and moved over to the bar.

A voice, heartrendingly familiar, came from behind Leland. "Climbed any good rocks lately?"

An expression of anguish passed across Leland's face as feelings, bottled up for months, threatened to pour out. He took a deep breath, then turned around. Almost whispering, he said, "It's good to see you, Uncle Malcom."

Malcom de Toshiko stood there, smaller than Leland remembered him. Leland never remembered looking *down* on Malcom before. The steward's hair was silver and the skin around his eyes was etched deep with lines. He glared at Leland almost challengingly, then, in a motion that could easily have been a twitch, he winked. Quietly he said, "No use giving these jackals more arrows than they already have. We'll talk later at the estate." Then he turned and walked away, greeting others with considerably more warmth than he'd shown Leland.

Leland fought down a smile and did his poor best to look dejected. He was spared further effort in this by the arrival of Gahnfeld and a request to be seated by Marshall de Gant's aide.

As they sat, Leland cautiously sipped from the tankard Gahnfeld had given him. It turned out to be carbonated spring water flavored with pear juice.

"Gentlemen," Marshall de Gant started. "Thank you for coming. Not that you had any choice, of course." He paused for a moment and a small chuckle swept the room. "Although I have your units' sizes and strengths on paper, I'd like a chance to review those before we march. Especially those new units and captains I may not have served with. To that end, I'd like unit leaders to introduce themselves in turn and describe the forces they command." He pointed to a man on the back row and said, "Suppose we start with you, Mildred."

A middle aged woman, thick waisted and stern, stood. "I'm Mildred de Fax of Scotia and I've two hundred pikes and two hundred archers for the dance."

One by one, skipping seconds, subalterns, and halvidars accompanying them, the unit leaders stood, gave their names and titles, and described what they were bringing to the campaign.

Spring artillery from New New York, light cavalry from Nuevo Tejas, archers from Napa, crossbow men from Acoma, and armored foot from Noram. When it was Uncle Malcolm's turn he only said, "Malcom de Toshiko bringing the Claw of Newland, four hundred heavy cavalry."

Leland's turn came a minute later. He stood, cleared his throat, and said, "Leland de Laal. With me are eight hundred mounted infantry."

de Gant frowned. "What do you mean, mounted infantry? Don't you just mean cavalry?"

Leland shook his head. "No, Marshall. We are mounted to reach where we're needed quickly, but once there my men are trained to fight afoot."

From the side of the room Sylvan Montrose's voice raised. "That's because Laal's troops are green. They can barely ride."

Beside Leland, Gahnfeld stirred in his seat and started to rise. Leland put his hand on Gahnfeld's shoulder and pushed down. In a calm but firm voice he said, "I ask anybody to name a time when Laal has failed Noram."

There was a murmur of approval at this statement.

de Gant frowned at Sylvan. "Guide Sylvan, you are here at the high steward's request, but he said nothing about letting you speak. He only asked that you be allowed to watch and listen. And he only asked—he did not command this. I'll thank you to let me determine the fitness of my forces."

Sylvan shrugged and sketched a derisive salute, but Leland thought he could detect a flush working up the man's neck.

de Gant went into a general discussion of the forces they could expect to meet and the general terrain of the Plain of the Founders. "The daily weather report from the Hearth Mountains says the snow is falling thick and the daytime temperatures are rarely exceeding freezing. It's already snowing in southern Kun Lun. That means we've got about a month before the water levels of the Black drop enough to begin the campaign. So, I want the last unit on the road two weeks from today. Any questions about the general scheme of things? I'll be going into detail later."

There were none. "Well, then, I offer you the health of High Steward Arthur de Noram. And Zanna!" He raised his glass and all stood.

Leland found his mouth dry, so he drank half of the tankard in the toast. The next toast, to victory, finished off the water.

"Well, as we've accomplished what *I* set out to do," said de Gant, "I suggest we adjourn to the bar and accomplish what the rest of you have already set out to do."

The men surged toward the bar, groups forming here and there to talk as the wave receded. The noise level rose correspondingly. Leland stood and stretched. When he turned to look at Gahnfeld, he saw him glaring across the room at Sylvan.

"Stop it, Halvidar! You're not here to get in a brawl." He pulled Gahnfeld around so he wasn't facing Sylvan. "Besides, you could probably get executed for bruising the high steward's prospective son-in-law." Leland rubbed his stomach unconsciously. The carbonated water was not agreeing with him.

Gahnfeld glared at the wall. "He'd no right to talk about the Eight Hundred that way. Sir."

"Perhaps. But, Halvidar, *we* don't care what *he* thinks."

Gahnfeld shook his head angrily. "But, Guide—"

Leland held up his finger in warning. "You're not listening, Myron. What did I say?"

Gahnfeld slumped. "Right, sir. *We* don't care what *he* thinks."

Leland grinned. "That's the ticket. Let's get out of here."

He started threading his way through the crowd, nodding politely to people as he passed. As he reached the door he looked back to make sure Gahnfeld was still with him and found Sylvan blocking Gahnfeld's way.

"You had something to say to me?" Sylvan was saying, one hand resting on the hilt of his dagger. "You seemed anxious to catch my eye a moment ago."

Leland took a quick step back toward them and spoke just as Gahnfeld opened his mouth. "Halvidar! Are you going to keep me waiting all night?"

Gahnfeld stiffened, then closed his mouth and slowly turned. "Coming, Guide." He stepped around Leland and walked toward the door. Sylvan started to step after him and bumped into Leland.

"Oh. Excuse me, Guide Sylvan. Most clumsy of me." Leland stepped back, as if to give Sylvan more room. In doing so he completely blocked Sylvan's advance.

Sylvan stopped then and focused on Leland. He moved closer. His breath smelled of Apple Jack and he was swaying slightly. He was frowning, angry.

"Ah, it's the child from Laal. A green leader of green troops."

Leland smiled. "Green wood is flexible. It has the capacity to absorb punishment without damage." He bobbed his head preparatory to leaving and, quite unintentionally, burped loudly in Sylvan's face.

Those people in the immediate vicinity, who'd been watching the proceedings with interest, laughed.

Sylvan flushed bright red. His hand flashed out to grab Leland's throat, but Leland, veteran of the singing bamboo, slid to the side. As a result, Sylvan grabbed the shirt of the man who'd been standing behind Leland and started pummeling him, so angry and drunk that it took him several blows to notice it wasn't Leland.

Several officers ended up holding Sylvan down long enough for him to stop thrashing around. By the time some measure of decorum had been restored, Leland and Gahnfeld were long gone.

Early the next morning Leland examined Coronet Sanchez's cargo in the privacy of the barn. The coronet, a stocky man with red hair and a perpetually sunburned noise, stood by nervously.

Finally Leland nodded. "Excellent, Sanchez. These will do the trick nicely."

Sanchez frowned, then asked, "Pardon me, Guide, but *what* trick are they going to do? They're just fish nets."

Leland ignored the question. "Was there any problem?"

"No, sir. We did just what you said and bundled our weapons on the packhorses. I made out that we were merchants from Napa, thinking of selling nets to people living near the mountain lakes."

"Good." Leland straightened. "I've got another job for you." He stepped closer to Sanchez and pulled two scraps of cloth from his pocket.

"I want you to go to Grissom & Sons and talk with Abel Grissom. Halvidar Gahnfeld will write you a letter of introduction. They're to commission the manufacture of eight hundred twenty cloth ponchos, hooded. The ponchos are to be this color on one side and this color on the other." He handed Sanchez the scraps. One was tan and the other dark green. "They must be completely reversible and warm. They should also be treated with oil and beeswax to make them as waterproof as possible."

Sanchez nodded. "Like uniforms."

Leland smiled. "Yes. But make sure that they're at least knee length on our tallest men. We'll need them in two weeks."

"Isn't that pushing it, sir?"

Leland nodded. "Yes, it is, but the price we're paying reflects that delivery."

"Yes, sir."

"Right, then. Hop to it. I've already told Gahnfeld about the letter."

Sanchez saluted, started to leave, then turned back. "Begging your pardon, sir, but should I post a guard on the nets?"

Leland shook his head. "No. Why should we? They're just fish nets, after all."

Sanchez shook his head. "Uh, right sir." He left.

Leland spent the rest of the morning moving about the estate. He watched the Third and Fourth hundreds engaged in spear, sword, and shield work. He saw the Fifth and Sixth hundreds in archery practice. He watched the Seventh and Eighth hundreds practicing unit maneuvers at the walk, trot, and run. The First Hundred was standing sentry duty around the estate while the Second tried to sneak past them.

Shortly before noon he returned to the house to find Gahnfeld reviewing training schedules.

"Well, Halvidar? What do you think?"

Gahnfeld looked up from the sheets of paper. "It's hard to say. If we truly have the two weeks that Marshall de Gant has promised, we might have something that doesn't fall apart at first contact with the enemy. These boys may be green but they went through complete militia training under Captain Koss. By now they won't kill their horses through ignorance, and I *know* they have stamina. Not that this will help them much at the plain. These things have always been fixed-front affairs in the past."

Leland nodded slowly. "I know. Do they know how to dig?"

"Like rabbits, Guide."

"Have you scheduled any training on indirect fire?"

Gahnfeld looked hurt. "Of course."

Leland smiled. "Very good. I just want you to add one thing to the schedule."

Gahnfeld frowned. "Yes?"

"Teach them to be still on command."

"I don't understand, sir."

Leland paused. "I want them able to freeze in one position for long periods of time. I don't want them to scratch, sneeze, yawn, stretch. I want them to be as rocks."

Gahnfeld nodded slowly. "Yes, Guide."

"Any messages for me while I was out?"

"Yes, sir. I had the orderly put them on your desk."

"Thanks." Leland nodded and stepped into his office.

The office was his father's, of course, but Gahnfeld hadn't hesitated a second in setting up his own office in the anteroom outside and moving Leland's few papers and books into the big desk.

Leland tried not to think of his father as he sat in the chair, but found this impossible. The chair alone, built for his father's more heroic proportions, made him feel like a child in a grown-up's seat. He shook his head and picked up the messages.

There were five of them. The first one was from Chancellor Cornelius de Moran, inviting Leland to join him and a few of the university faculty for supper that night.

The second was from Marshall de Gant, confirming in writing the Order of March he'd outlined the night before. In addition there was the statement that Cotswold was *not* expected to have observers in the coming enterprise. Leland smiled at this. *I wonder what de Gant would do if Sylvan became steward of Noram?*

The third was from Sylvan Montrose's secretary saying that "Strong drink does strange things" and Sylvan truly regretted any offense he might have given the night before. Leland merely noted that Sylvan had not regretted it enough to write the note himself before putting it aside.

The fourth note was from Guide Margaret de Jinith, requesting Leland to call on her at his earliest convenience. It closed with the phrase "and no excuses!"

Leland smiled at that.

The last note said "*Keiko.* Four P.M." *Keiko*—practice.

"Orderly!" he called.

One of Gahnfeld's hand-picked headquarters staff appeared in the door. "I'll be riding into the city after lunch. Please have my horse ready."

"Yes, sir. And your guards, sir?"

Leland frowned and thought of Gahnfeld's reaction if he tried to go without at least two men. "I suppose so. But no banners!"

The Gentle Guide Margaret received Leland, appropriately, in the reception room of her apartments. She was attended by several young daughters of the Noram guardianship whom she insisted on introducing to Leland.

Leland kept himself from fleeing, but just barely. He responded to the introductions with a glassy-eyed smile and "Honored, Gentle Guide," over and over again. When the introductions were through,

Leland turned to Margaret and said, flat-voiced, "What an unexpected pleasure."

Margaret eye's sparkled. "Here. Sit by me and tell me what you've been doing since you've arrived." She looked up. "Somebody bring the warden a cup of that tea."

Almost immediately Leland found himself holding a cup of tea, a scone, and muffins presented by three of the women. Another brought him a napkin, and still another moved a small table nearer for him to set his bounty down. Several chairs sidled closer.

Leland began to sweat.

"So, what have you been doing?" Margaret repeated politely.

"I've been attending to small chores, nothing very exciting. We're training our men, seeing to provisions. Things like that. I did get to visit the Great Library, though." He sipped his tea. He started to ask what sort of things he should see in Noram, but reflected that he couldn't cope with the tour "guides" that might suddenly rise up. "I'm afraid that in Laal our dances run to outdoor affairs, country style. I've never attended a formal ball. Perhaps you could tell me what they're like."

The question was inspired. For the next thirty minutes Leland's part of the conversation consisted of an occasional question and polite noises of surprise. He drank three cups of tea and ate two scones and four muffins. In addition, he learned things about the social side of Noram that he'd never suspected, much less wanted to know even after learning them.

Finally Guide Margaret said, "Well, dears, I want to talk to the warden alone for a while. Thank you so much for coming."

When they'd left, Margaret laughed. "I thought your eyes were starting to glaze over, toward the end. I won't do that to you again, but at least you'll have someone to dance with at the ball."

Leland glared at her, then laughed as well. "I've heard more about clothing in the last half hour than the last year. Is that all they talk about?"

"Well, not really. Advantageous matches are a popular subject. What do you think the match between Marilyn and Sylvan is about? True love?"

Leland stood and walked to the window. "But Marilyn doesn't talk about dresses and hairstyles and dancing. She talks about medicine, physics, chemistry, and engineering."

Margaret said dryly, "Yes. She and her sister have always been a disappointment to me."

Leland spun around, shocked, before he saw the laughter in the woman's eyes.

She laughed at his outraged expression. "It's not always the women who talk about style and fashion. You should hear Sylvan on the subject of raised collars. He's quite eloquent."

Leland relaxed his face, almost smiled. "I should imagine his betrothed listens to him for hours."

Margaret shook her head. "She's good for about thirty minutes, I'd say. Then her eyes glaze over like yours and she develops a headache. Poor girl. The last week she's had over a dozen sudden migraines."

Leland grinned.

"By the way, Warden. I heard the most astounding story this morning from one of the guards. It seems the scion of Cotswold drank too much at Marshall de Gant's staff reception and started beating up Mildred de Fax's aide. They say they had to sit on him for ten minutes before he quit thrashing. Weren't you at the reception?"

Leland felt his ears go warm. "I was, Gentle Guide, but this must have happened after I left. Surely it's just a wild rumor. I'm sure Guide Sylvan would never do anything so rude."

Margaret looked at him strangely. "Well, I'm not quite sure of *that,* but you never know." She paused, then said casually, "You can't avoid Marilyn forever, you know."

"What?"

Margaret lowered her eyelids. "Don't try to pretend. I visited my old friend Cornelius this morning. He said you practically left a hole in the air when you realized Marilyn was also attending tea."

Leland gulped. "I had an appointment. Besides—I feel awkward around her," he stammered.

"Hah! Awkward! You act like an idiot!"

Leland glared, confused.

Margaret continued. "Don't you see it? It's plain as rocks to anyone else. You both sit in the same room trying so hard to ignore the other's presence that it's obvious that you both want—no, *need* to talk to each other. You each have things to say, ideas to express, images of such complexity that the only persons in the world who'll understand them are the two of you. At least that's how it looks to me." She sat back in her chair. "But what do I know?" she finished with a smile. "I'm just a scatterbrained, loose-tongued old woman."

Leland stared at the wall, a sunken feeling in his stomach. "Have you said as much to Marilyn?"

Margaret frowned. "No. She's even more of an idiot than you. She'll spend all day putting Sylvan down until I bring up your name. Then it's off to go riding with him. Or off to look at the moon with him. Or off to show him the view from the south rim. Then she comes back with another one of her headaches."

Leland looked, if possible, even more dejected.

Margaret nodded slowly. "It's more than ideas you want to express, isn't it?" she said.

Leland put his face in his hands. "I don't *know.* Gentle Guide, I turn eighteen next month. I never played those games. And what does it matter? She's betrothed to Sylvan."

Margaret frowned. "Only seventeen? I could have sworn you were years older. Poor boy. An old man at seventeen." She straightened. "Oh, well. After your father, you're probably the smartest person I know, but you're still an idiot."

She reached out and grasped his jaw, turning his head toward her. "Listen to me, idiot. Marilyn isn't married yet. Betrothals aren't always fixed, especially this one. I don't know what's got into my brother's head, but don't think things are set in stone. The only thing that stays the same is that things change.

"If you and Marilyn don't start talking to each other, I'm going to break both your skulls. Even if Marilyn does marry Sylvan, she'll still need someone to talk to—someone as smart as she."

She released Leland's face. "I leave it in your hands, idiot. If you drop things, don't expect me to pick up the pieces."

Leland left his guards in Charlina's front parlor, then followed Charly through a passageway in the back of the building that connected her residence with the dojo on the street behind.

"This is only known to a handful of people," she said, indicating the passage walls. "It's about the only way Zanna and I can spend time together without half the Portal Guards camping in the front room."

"Have you seen her since you returned?"

Charly smiled serenely. "Oh, yes."

"Nine months hasn't . . . well, cooled your relationship?"

"You don't know Zanna."

He slipped out of her office at the back of the dojo and, following her directions, found the men's changing room. It was almost as large as the practice floor at Red Rock Station, and even so, it was crowded.

"de Laal, isn't it?"

He looked over to see a man tying on a *hakama.* "Yes. You look familiar, but I'm afraid I don't place you . . ."

"Ah, well, I saw you at Marshall de Gant's briefing last night." He bowed. "I'm Kuart, captain of the Pottsdam Engineers." Pottsdam was the second largest city in New New York.

"I remember now. Please forgive me."

"Nothing to forgive. Didn't know you did aikido. There's not that many of us in the military, and I thought I knew them all." He gave another half bow and said, "See you on the mat."

One of Charly's *uchideshi* was waiting for him outside the changing room. "Sensei is in her office. She asks that I bring you to her."

"Certainly."

They passed the entrance to the practice mat. It was a huge space, as large as the main hall back at Laal Station. Leland asked the *uchideshi,* "How big do your classes tend to be?"

She bobbed her head. "We often have sixty or seventy people on the mat, especially since Sensei returned from Red Rock."

They came to a small room adjoining the practice mat. Inside Charly was sitting *seiza,* dressed for practice. Across a low table from her another woman, also in *hakama,* sat smiling.

Leland bowed at the entrance to the room.

"Please come in, Leland. Thank you, Kabeca, get to class."

Leland sat and looked at Charly's guest and a shock hit him in the pit of his stomach. *Marilyn?* But it wasn't her. The woman was older and her hair was lighter.

"I would like you to meet Zanna, Leland."

Leland bowed low. "Honored, Guide." This woman was likely to be the next ruler of Noramland.

Zanna frowned. "We leave those titles outside these doors. I'm pleased to meet you, Sensei. My aunt has told me a great deal about you, but she didn't mention aikido as one of your accomplishments. But then, she characterized you as a listener, not a talker."

"I enjoyed my conversations with her," said Leland.

"My sister know of your involvement with aikido?"

Leland felt his face close. "When I first met your sister, I"—*didn't really have any involvement*—"well, it didn't come up. I haven't told her. I don't know if anyone else has." He looked at Charly.

"I didn't. When she visited me during the trip, we mostly talked about Zanna and what's been happening at the dojo here."

Zanna said, "I didn't know until today. Do you want her to know? She does study here, you know."

"Today?"

Charly and Zanna laughed. "No," said Zanna. "She's entertaining Sylvan this afternoon."

Leland shook his head. "I won't hide from her, but unless the subject comes up or I run into her on the practice mat, I'd just as soon leave things as they are."

Zanna and Charly exchanged glances and Charly said, "Would you teach class, Leland?"

*No!* "I'm reluctant, Sensei. I've never even been on this mat. It strikes me as presumptuous."

Zanna nodded. "He's very young, Sensei." She seemed surprised at the offer.

"Age, *Kohai?*" The phrasing was a mild rebuke, but the tone of Charly's voice was a caress. "What of ability?" She turned back toward Leland. "I ask again, humbly."

DO IT.

*I'm afraid.*

FACE YOUR FEAR.

"I would be honored, Sensei."

Charly nodded. "Strike the clapper, Zanna."

*"Hai."* Zanna bowed and left the room.

"Is there an *uke* I should use?"

"Anyone wearing a *hakama*—but Zanna is good."

"If I break the future ruler of Noramland, I could be in a bit of trouble."

"Try her."

After a moment Leland heard the loud clear sound of a wooden mallet striking a suspended wooden block. Three times the clapper sounded. The background noise—the muted talking and the rustling sound of people stretching and moving—ceased.

Charly stood, but instead of going to the door, the one that led to the hallway, she pulled aside what Leland had thought to be a wall hanging and revealed a doorway that opened directly into the practice area.

They both bowed onto the mat, then Charly stayed at the edge of the mat and looked at Leland.

He swallowed and stood, walking out into the area before the *kamiza.* He crossed over until he was just to the left of the center line, the "junior" side of the mat, and sat facing the altar. Again, there were the two pictures. Again, something inside him rejected the picture of the woman. He waited, his eyes on the Founder's picture, *O-Sensei*—great teacher Morihei Ueshiba, dead for over five hundred years.

*Help me find my center.*

After a minute of measured breathing he bowed. Behind him, he heard the creaking and rustling as the rest of the class bowed. He turned to face Charly on his knees. They exchanged bows. Then he turned to face the class, two neat rows of dark blue or black *hakama* and white *keiko* gi jackets. He bowed and said, " '*gashimas.*' " The class called this back to him as they bowed, a rolling echo in the large room.

He led them through warm-ups, then called for *ukemi.* He sat to one side of the *kamiza* and watched, thinking about what he should teach.

After five minutes he clapped his hands and they lined up.

*Face what I fear?* He gestured with his hand and said, "Zanna."

She jumped up and they bowed to each other. Then he pointed at his right temple. She nodded.

He leaned slightly forward and she attacked with *yokomenuchi,* a hand blade diagonal strike to the side of his head.

Leland entered deeply, *irimi tenkan,* stepping in as he met her wrist with his hand, then turned hard, striking at her face with his free hand.

Her eyes went wide but she moved with it, her entire body flipping over to get her head out of the way, her back arching and her feet flying up in the air. She landed, slapping hard with her free hand, her other arm still captured by Leland.

He released her and they repeated it on the left side. Then twice more.

"Strike with *kokyu. Uke* has to believe they'll be hit if they don't move. But be careful!" Leland told the class. He bowed to Zanna. "Thank you."

She bowed back and grinned, then paused for a second as if she wanted to say something, but an older student stepped forward and tapped her on her back. "*Oneigashimasu.*"

"*Hai,*" said Zanna, and they moved off together to practice.

Leland looked over at Charly. She was still sitting at the edge of the mat, looking at him with a smile on her face. He wrinkled his nose and bowed.

Leland used Zanna as *uke* throughout the class, concentrating on *irimi* variations against *yokomenuchi.* Her ukemi was good, though she was clearly stiff in the shoulder during *shihonage,* a throw and immobilization that takes the wrist over the shoulder of the same arm and down to the ground. "So stiff," he said quietly. "Relax."

"*Hai,*" she said.

He threw her down again. She got right back up.

TAKES A LICKING AND KEEPS ON TICKING.

*What rank, do you think?*

A RECENT SANDAN, PERHAPS. Third-degree black belt.

Later, over tea in Charly's office, he asked the same question and was told "She would've tested for *sandan* at the Noram summer camp two months ago, but I was in Red Rock and she wanted to test before me. How was she?"

"Very good—a little stiff in the right shoulder."

"Yes—that's an old injury and another reason why Arthur distrusts me."

"You broke her shoulder?"

"Dislocated it. She contracted during *koshinage* and fell on it right before her *shodan* test. It pops out occasionally unless she's careful." She changed the subject. "How much longer will you be in the city?"

"Ten days, perhaps. We're late in the marching order."

"How often can you teach?"

Leland shook his head. "More? You want more?"

"Well, why not? Is there something wrong with what you have to teach?"

*Yes.*

YES . . . AND NO. HOW YOU TEACH, PERHAPS.

*You're never satisfied.*

HAI. KEIKO, KEIKO, KEIKO.

*Face my fear?*

HAI.

"I'd like to practice *every* day, but that's difficult. Do you have a dawn class?"

Charly paused for a second. "Every other day, but this would be a good time for a week of dawn *misogi.*"

RITUAL PURIFICATION THROUGH PRACTICE.

"I could certainly use *that.*" Leland exhaled. "Dawn works for me—it leaves the entire day free for my other duties."

"I'll announce it in my classes tomorrow. We'll start Sunday morning?"

"Your choice."

"Sunday morning."

Like most cities, the capital of Noram had what would be called a bad neighborhood, an area of town that fed the darker appetites of Noram City's inhabitants. Unlike most cities, the barriers between the good and bad neighborhoods were clearly and rigidly defined.

The Lower City was not on the rock mesa that the Upper City was. It was below, butted against the north side of the rock cliff in an area of the plain that made poor farmland because of the small amount of sunshine it received. It was a twisty warren of buildings and streets made even more claustrophobic by the perpetual gloom and the overbearing presence of the rock tower above. Naturally it was most alive at night.

Sylvan Montrose rode into the Lower City after the twenty-minute torch-lit ride down the switchbacks. He wore a cloak, hood pulled far forward to hide his features. His two companions, one riding in front and one behind, were equally anonymous.

The streets were crowded at this time. There were patrons moving from tavern to bar to gambling house to whorehouse. There were shills trying to drum up trade for their respective businesses. The poor were out, as well, simply taking in the free spectacle of the streets. More than once, Sylvan fought down the urge to ride over some of the clods in his way, but the agent-in-place had been clear on this. *Do nothing to attract attention. Reveal our identity,* he'd said, *and I'll abandon you immediately. Your father gets far too much value from my services for you to jeopardize them.*

Sylvan thought this might change soon.

They reached an inn and the guide turned into its stable yard. A boy came forward to take their horses. Money changed hands to keep the horses out of sight but ready. Then the three of them walked to the side entrance of the inn. They were met at the door by a small man who led them not down the hall to the common room but up a narrow stairway to the second floor. He knocked quietly on a door in what was clearly a coded signal, then he squeezed back past them to return to the floor below.

The door opened and they entered.

The agent closed the door firmly before pushing the hood back from his face. A man, seated in the corner where the lantern threw a shadow, stood and came forward into the light. Sylvan recognized the man as an officer of his father's bodyguard.

"What news?" Sylvan asked.

The man's eyebrows rose. "News? That's as good as any a word to use for instructions."

Sylvan's eyes narrowed. "Little man, I'm not in a particularly good mood. Stop wasting my time."

The man shrugged. "As you wish. Your father refuses you permission to kill the warden. His specific words were 'Tell Sylvan that his life is less important than Leland de Laal's. I have specific plans for that young man.' " The messenger smirked, clearly enjoying this. "Our steward instead wishes the warden kidnapped, but only if this can be accomplished without risk to the warden or our relations with Noram."

Sylvan swore so loudly that the agent raised his hand and said, "You want to be discovered? Keep quiet!" The agent turned to the messenger and said, "Was there anything else?"

"Yes. The high steward wants to know if Leland travels with the Helm. Also if our young guide has bedded the gentle guide yet."

The agent turned expectantly to Sylvan.

"There's been no sign of the Helm." Sylvan growled. "And no! I've never been able to get her alone long enough."

The messenger hid a grin behind his hand, but not very well. Beneath his cloak, Sylvan's hand closed on his dagger. The messenger said, "Your father said to remind you that he isn't that sure of Arthur's commitment. Get the girl totally committed to you as quickly as possible. These Noram are sentimental. If she's pregnant with your child, Arthur is less likely to back out."

"I'm working on it, little man! You may rest assured that it's only a matter of time."

The messenger smirked again. "Years or decades?"

Sylvan wiped the rage from his face. He smiled slightly. "Do you have any more *instructions* from my father?"

"No," said the messenger, suddenly less cocky.

Sylvan turned away from him, toward the agent. "Are you ready to leave?" he asked.

The agent nodded. "Yes, Guide."

Sylvan shrugged and lifted one hand to pull his hood up. Under cover of that motion he spun suddenly, steel flashing in the lamplight. The dagger went in under the messenger's jaw and up into the brain. The man arched back, his arms convulsing. He gave a bubbling, muted cry, barely heard as it was literally pinned within his throat. Blood poured out of the man's nose and mouth. More blood gushed down the dagger and onto Sylvan's glove. One-handed, Sylvan held the man up on his toes until the spasming stopped, then he took a step forward, yanked the dagger free with a jerk, and let the corpse fall into the dark corner.

There was no outcry from the inn. The distant noises of revelry continued unabated.

Sylvan wiped his dagger on the clothes of the dead man, then took his gloves off, carefully holding the bloody one by an unsoiled edge. Almost casually, he dropped them on the corpse's face. He turned and locked eyes with the agent.

After a moment the guide lowered his eyes, turned to the other man in the room and said, "Dispose of the body. Remove all traces of identity—disfigure the face."

Then he turned and led Sylvan from the room.

# ELEVEN

## SETSUZOKU: CONNECTION

The chancellor looked distracted when he met Leland in the hallway to the Great Library. After a minute he said, "Although I'm delighted you could come, Warden, I would be doing us both a disservice if I did not warn you of some changes." The old man paused then as if unsure how to continue. "I was visited this morning by the Gentle Guide Margaret de Jinith, an old friend of mine and, she tells me, a new friend of yours."

Leland nodded, "The gentle guide has been very kind to me."

Cornelius nodded back. "To come directly to the point, she told me to invite the Gentle Guide Marilyn to dinner, as well. I hope you'll understand when I tell you that her requests, both as an old friend and the sister of the high steward, hold some measure of weight with me."

"As they should," Leland said quietly. His stomach felt odd.

"Despite this, I have not told the gentle guide that you are here yet. If, at this time, you wish to decline my invitation, I would if not understand at least respect your wishes. I could then tell Marilyn that a last-minute duty kept you from coming."

Leland was moved. "I hardly know what to say, Guide Cornelius. Your willingness to bow to my mindless and aberrant behavior is the heart of tolerance itself. If you and the gentle guide can be so tolerant, I can hardly avoid an attempt at the same." He took the man by his arm and said, "If you'll lend me some of your courage, I'll brave the gentle guide."

"Of course, Warden."

They walked slowly through the Great Library. The books, dimly seen things in the evening dusk, comforted Leland with every step. The chancellor, sensing some of Leland's unease, began talking about inconsequential things. "I remember, back when I was your age, sitting at the table and trying to calculate the number of words this library holds. A silly thing. The figure I eventually arrived at was nine billion plus or minus fifty million. Not exactly a precise number."

Leland said, "Interesting to think on, though. What a structure we could build with nine billion bricks."

"Yes, but it would collapse under its own weight. I sometimes wonder if knowledge is like that. Oh, well. A word is a great deal lighter than a brick. And then again, sometimes the right word is heavier than the world." He shrugged expressively.

Cornelius and Leland entered the faculty dining room a few minutes later, arm in arm, laughing. Cornelius looked up to see a half smile fight a frown on Marilyn's face. Both men made the mistake of stifling their laughter immediately, making the elderly chancellor and youthful Leland look like schoolchildren caught in some prank.

The frown became predominant. "Talking about me behind my back?" she asked severely.

Guide Cornelius, who'd known Marilyn all her life, saw the corners of her eyes crinkle, not in eye-narrowing anger but with repressed laughter. He covered his mouth to keep from laughing again.

Leland, though, bowed and spoke quickly. "Forgive us, Gentle Guide. It's true that the chancellor was talking about you, but it was in no way derogatory. He was telling me the text you chose for your Rites of Thirteen reading."

Marilyn rolled her eyes to the ceiling. "Not that again? Really, Cornelius. You might as well have told him about the time I wet your lap as a baby. I don't see what the big fuss was. It's not as if the thing had been in the original Ger . . . man?" She stumbled over the pronunciation, using a hard G.

Leland said, almost automatically, "Juh, Gentle Guide, like 'germ.' "

This earned him an immediate glare.

Cornelius laughed out loud. "You have to admit that the *Tracta-*

*tus Logico-Philosophicus* might as well have been in the original for all your audience understood it. I'm always surprised at the books included by the Founders and the books not included."

Leland nodded. "I would have liked to see their faces when you read the first line, Gentle Guide. Taken literally, they probably thought it was an attack on the Founders."

Marilyn stared at Leland. "Where did you read the *Tractatus,* Warden? I didn't see a copy in Laal's library and I looked."

"Uh, I'm not exactly sure." He frowned in thought.

"You're not sure? You must have read it somewhere. You're certainly right about the first line."

Leland scratched his head. "Maybe I'm thinking about a different work. The piece I'm thinking about begins, '*Die Welt ist alles, was der Fall ist.*' "

Cornelius raised his eyebrows. "What did you say, Warden? What language is that?"

Leland played the words back in his head. "I'm sorry. I meant to say 'The world is everything and that's all there is.' "

Marilyn narrowed her eyes. "Was that German, Warden? Was that the original text?"

Leland blushed. "I suppose it is."

"Do you speak German, Leland?" asked the chancellor.

"No, sir," Leland said. "I must have memorized the phrase."

Marilyn stared at Leland hard. "The only copy of the *Tractatus* I've ever seen is in English. Is there another copy somewhere? One with both languages perhaps?"

Leland blinked, opened his mouth to speak, and then shut it again. Finally he said, "I don't remember."

He was saved further discomfort by the arrival of dinner and the other guests.

Cornelius did his best to put Leland at his ease, but during the first part of dinner, Leland didn't say much, fidgeting in his chair and only toying with his food.

Later, though, he seemed to relax a bit, although he confined himself to asking questions instead of answering them, drawing the others out about their work and fields of interest. By the time dessert was served, his anxiety seemed to have left him. He was relaxed and smiling, clearly enjoying himself, even offering a small joke here and there.

Marilyn, Cornelius observed, seemed constantly on her guard, treating Leland with an odd mixture of attention and reserve.

The other faculty, charmed by this intelligent and ready listener, talked freely, even passionately, about everything from engineering to education. Cornelius, sitting quietly at the head of the table, wondered if the rest of the faculty were noticing what he was.

Leland's questions revealed almost as much as his earlier, unguarded statements. There was a broad spectrum of interests, displayed by those gathered at the table and Leland was able to ask questions that showed more than passing familiarity with every field discussed.

When the table had been cleared and wine and tea distributed, Cornelius moved the conversation to less elevated planes. "Have you been enjoying our city, Warden? I hope you've seen more of it than the Laal estate and the library."

Leland smiled. "The Great Library alone would be worth any journey. However, I've seen the palace briefly during a visit to Gentle Guide Margaret, and Laal's factor here has shown me a few of your justly famous restaurants."

"What of the cliff gardens, Warden?" Marilyn asked. "Have you seen them?"

"I haven't even *heard* of them."

"Well, then, you should be enlightened. If you've time tomorrow I'll make it my business."

Leland looked down at his wine. His voice was almost hoarse when he answered, "I would be honored, Gentle Guide."

"One o'clock, then. If you've time afterward, perhaps you can join the chancellor and me for tea?" She paused and sipped from her wineglass. "I understand that I've missed the honor of your company at tea once already."

Leland, Cornelius observed, was not too old to blush.

Halvidar Gahnfeld gave instructions to the orderly not to wake Leland for breakfast. "He didn't come back from the university until three in the morning. Don't disturb him."

"Yes, sir."

Leland, lying wide awake in bed, heard this quiet exchange and smiled. He'd slept four hours and then woken, preternaturally alert, his brain swimming with ideas, concepts, and questions. And then there were feelings and desires, too.

Besides solitary excursions better characterized as sexual scratching, Leland's only sexual experiences had been with a servant girl, several years older than him, when he was fifteen. There had been three encounters in dark storerooms behind the kitchen that had scared him more than anything. She'd left shortly thereafter to marry a soldier. Though Leland tried hard to be heartbroken, he had to admit, after kicking around Laal Station for a few days, that he was mostly relieved.

Now, though, he found himself wishing he'd studied this boy/girl thing more closely. Like all people raised with a reverence for the customs, he was familiar with the human reproductive cycle and those methods available to avoid or achieve conception. But he wasn't at all sure what sort of things a man says to a woman that might lead to needing this knowledge.

Besides, *he* wasn't the one betrothed to Marilyn.

He got out of bed, robed himself, and marched down to the baths. There was hot water available, but he didn't use it.

Dressed, but still shivering slightly, he walked into his father's office and began reviewing the reports Gahnfeld had left him on such matters as supplies, training, and punishment detail. Unsure of what was normal and what wasn't, he called out, "Orderly!"

The trooper on duty stepped in and bowed, "Yes, Warden?"

"Where is the staff halvidar?"

"Teaching sword work, sir, to the Third Hundred."

"Please ask him to join me here for lunch at half-past eleven. Then find Coronet Sanchez and have him report to me now. When you've done that tell the cook about my lunch plans."

"Yes, Warden." He left the room quietly, but Leland heard his steps pound down the stairs at a run. He smiled briefly.

Sanchez arrived ten minutes later, a bundle under one arm. "You must've read my mind, sir."

Leland raised his eyebrows. "What do you mean?"

"This prototype of the poncho just arrived from Grissom & Sons. They must have had someone working around the clock."

They examined the garment carefully. Leland had Sanchez wear it, first green side out, then light brown side. They tested the waterproofing with a splash of tea. He examined its length and width. Then he had Sanchez walk around to see how much noise it made.

"Good," he said. "Is their messenger still here?"

"Yes, Warden."

"Tell them to proceed as is. If they need the poncho back, send it. Otherwise bring it back here."

Sanchez bowed on his way out. "Yes, Warden."

When Gahnfeld arrived and the lunch was laid out, Leland dismissed the orderly and the waiter, having them shut the door behind them.

They sat and Leland said, "I hope, Myron, that I didn't pull you away from anything important."

Gahnfeld looked around at the closed door, then relaxed visibly. "To tell you the truth, Guide, I needed the exercise. We've competent instructors but I've been sitting behind that desk too much."

Leland smiled. "I'm sure it does the men good to see you show a personal interest. I asked you to eat with me, though, because I will be in the city this afternoon and I wanted to go over these reports with you."

"Is there something wrong with the reports?" Gahnfeld asked, frowning.

Leland raised his hands. "How would I know? That's the point. I'd like you to tell me what, in these reports, is normal, what isn't, and even if there are things not covered here that should be." He pointed at the stack of papers. "You've been doing this sort of thing for years. I've been doing it for weeks. I know you said to leave the routine to you, and I intend to do that. I just want to know what the routine *is*."

Gahnfeld nodded. "Okay. Forgive me for being frank, Guide, but there are other areas of your education that are equally lacking."

"What do you mean?"

"Sword work, sir. Should the enemy break through, what chance do you have of defending yourself? Your brothers have been studying the sword for years; what about you?" Gahnfeld paused. "I am not without some experience in this. If you wished, I could tutor you privately."

Leland stared at him for a moment, then said, "Thank you, Myron. I appreciate your offer, but I'm not one of my brothers. The time to fit me to that mold was years in the past, and it wasn't done. You'll just have to make sure the enemy doesn't break through." He toyed with his fork. "What other areas of my education are deficient?"

Gahnfeld looked down at his plate. "Well, you'd better learn the battle fan, so you can give commands at a distance. And you should learn what your troops are capable of and, more important, what they're not able to do."

"All too true. That's part of what we're doing right now. I've actually read the Laal signal manual. I promise to practice them, as well."

Gahnfeld nodded. "Yes, Guide."

"How are the soccer games? Are they screwing up your training?"

"No. Except for the occasional injury, I think it's enhancing the unit competition. We should make a weekly judgment, don't you think?"

"Yes. Perhaps tonight?"

"Certainly, Guide."

"I'll design a pennant for the top unit. Oh, by the way, I've ordered eight hundred and thirty of these." He got up and showed Gahnfeld the poncho. "They'll help keep our lads warm and dry. They might also help in a scheme I have in mind."

The halvidar fingered the cloth then tried it on. He pulled the hood back and drew his sword from its back scabbard up through the neck hole. "They'll need some practice drawing." He tried a few cuts and thrusts. "And if they're not careful it will get in their way." He twisted suddenly, bringing the edge of the poncho swirling up. "It could come in handy, though, to snare the enemy's blade, maybe even blind him."

Gahnfeld scowled for a brief minute, then suddenly grinned. "I'll confess, Guide, that my conservative mind is leery of new innovations, but then I remember you moving the Eight Hundred to Laal Station from the Black River in under ten hours. Even if they don't work in your scheme, these things will keep the men warm."

"I don't care if he wants to go riding, I've a previous appointment," Marilyn said calmly to the servant who'd carried Sylvan's invitation. "Perhaps if he'd care to find out what my plans are *ahead* of time, we'll be able to arrange something." In a less serious tone of voice she added, "Make it sound good, though. You know, 'Heartbroken regrets, but duties makes it impossible to accept your invitation. Inescapable duties.' That sort of thing."

"Yes, Gentle Guide. I'm sure he'll understand."

As the servant left Marilyn muttered to herself, "I doubt it."

*Inescapable duties. Where did I hear that before?*

She checked the pendulum clock on the wall. It would be time for Leland to arrive soon.

She went to the mirror and examined herself carefully. She frowned. *Why am I primping?* The thought didn't stop her from unbuttoning the top of her dress two stops, just enough to show a hint of cleavage. She blushed at the image in the mirror but didn't refasten the buttons. She found the bottle of scent given to her by Aunt Margaret the season before. It was still sealed, never before used. She opened it carefully and applied just a touch behind her ears.

She felt strangely nervous, her hands flying this way and that as there was suddenly no proper way to hold them.

*Center yourself!*

She picked up a book but couldn't concentrate. The words seemed to crawl across the paper like bugs. She snapped it shut with a curse, but continued holding it to give her hands something to do and sat, *seiza,* and tried to concentrate on her breathing.

*Why did I invite him? Was I just being polite?* She paced to the window and stared blindly out at the mountains.

"Gentle Guide," Dora, her maid, called from the door. "The Warden de Laal is in the reception hall."

She dropped the book on a table, scooped up her light cloak, and ran down the hall. Had she noticed, Dora's look would have told her volumes. She had the sense to slow to a walk before entering the reception hall, but she was still flushed from the dash down the stairs.

Leland had trouble taking his eyes from her.

"Oh," said Marilyn, affecting a poise of indifference. "There you are. Ready?"

Leland bowed. "Certainly, Gentle Guide. Do we ride to this marvel or walk?"

Marilyn indicated a door. "Walk."

She led him down a hall to the back of the building, through a small landscaped courtyard with high walls, and out the back gate of the palace. The guards there bowed low when they saw her. She smiled and called them by name.

"Does your father know every guard's name, as well?"

"My father is a busy man."

The gate opened onto a street, narrow, but lined with the rich homes of the Noram guardianship. Several persons sketched half bows as they passed or called out respectful greetings. A short walk later the street ended at the western edge of the plateau. A waist-high balustrade terminated the cobbled avenue. Benches were placed so a person could sit and admire the view. To one side a gap in the stone led to a descending stone stairway carved out of the cliff itself.

Marilyn paused here. "When Noram became truly populous,

space here in the High City grew very dear. An enterprising merchant came up with the idea of carving these steps down to some natural ledges a ways down the cliff. His goal was not the gardens that are there now but houses that he could sell for a fortune. Well, one of my ancestors let him finish the steps, then decreed that houses on those ledges would be in danger of siege weapons from the plain below. Hence, no houses. But, as he wasn't a bad high steward, he paid the fellow a small fortune to create the gardens instead."

She led the way down the stairs. The side away from the face had been securely railed with wrought iron. Even so, the drop seemed dizzying to Leland and brought back unpleasant memories of the Needle. He concentrated, instead, on the nape of Marilyn's neck, bare to his vision since she was wearing her hair up.

As they continued down the steps, Marilyn told him some of the problems the original inhabitants of the High City had. "Lightning, for instance. Until someone did some serious reading and research on lightning rods, houses were burning and people were being struck dead in the streets. Moving the construction materials up from below was a problem, too."

The stair took a turn and Leland saw a splash of color against the gray rock below. A few more minutes and they were standing on a ledge perhaps ten meters deep and a hundred meters long.

City compost had been used to form a meter of loam. Stone and iron walls with gravel-filtered drains kept the dirt in place. Another stairway led the way down to two other smaller ledges.

Halfway across the top terrace a stream emerged from the cliff face, ran through a series of ornamental ponds and falls, then cascaded down the rock face to a similar arrangement on the terraces below. Marilyn stopped on the curved wooden bridge that spanned this little brook and leaned back on the railing.

"I have an apology to make, Leland." She stared past his shoulder, at a bush covered with bright yellow flowers. "I've been rude to you several times in our interactions. I'm not usually like this—I know better behavior."

Leland shook his head, "Gentle Guide, it's I who must beg forgiveness. You've treated me most kindly. In fact, when you interceded for me at Laal, it was the first kind act I'd received in a great deal of time. I reacted very badly."

Marilyn frowned at the memory. "Well, now that you mention

it," she said, a wicked gleam in her eye. Then she smiled. "No, I didn't understand the situation. I shouldn't have interfered." She tilted her head to one side. "Come to think about it, I still don't understand the situation."

Leland flinched away from thoughts of his father. "For what it's worth, I don't, either. Do I have your forgiveness?"

"Perhaps we can exchange them?"

"You've done nothing to forgive," Leland said.

Marilyn put her fists on her hips. "Are you trying to start a fight?"

He held up his hands, placating. "Forgiven, now and forever!"

She reached out and placed one of her palms against his. "Forgiven."

"There, Guide, you can see them from here."

The servant leaned over the stone railing and pointed. Sylvan Montrose, careful to keep an eye on this man, leaned over and saw the distant figures of Leland and Marilyn standing in the garden below. He watched their hands touch as they stood on the bridge.

The servant was a palace functionary whose primary duty was to keep a protective eye on Marilyn, no matter where she roamed, without being obtrusive about it. Marilyn knew of his existence but ignored him. The man had been approached by Sylvan early in the Cotswoldian's stay. A purse had changed hands. A "favor" had been asked. After all, was it reason to let the gentle guide's betrothed know where his beloved was?

Sylvan's face was blank as he turned back from the cliff. Casually he asked, "So, has she been spending a great deal of time with him?"

The servant answered carefully. "There was a small dinner party at the Great Library last night. She didn't get home until three. Also, the warden has been spending a great deal of time in the library. The gentle guide has, also, but this is normal for her. I cannot say whether they've seen each other there."

Sylvan nodded slowly, staring over the servant's shoulder at nothing. To his mind, a "small" dinner party instantly translated to "intimate" and the library "visits" became "trysts." He handed the man a coin and said, "Keep me informed." Then he walked back up the street to where one of his own servants held his horse's reins.

*May his teeth rot out of his head and the sores of scurvy fester his gums!* Sylvan stroked the handle of his dagger and clenched his other fist.

He very much wanted to kill Leland. *Damn, Father, why won't you let me gut him?*

He thought of other ways to punish Leland. Duels were illegal in Noram, but "training" bouts with wooden swords were common, and even fistfights weren't unheard of. Sylvan wondered how much damage he could do Leland and still satisfy his father's instructions.

"Send a message to our friend in the Lower City," he told the servant. "I want the Warden de Laal watched. I want to know where he goes and when. All his regular haunts."

"Yes, Guide."

Sylvan mounted quickly and sawed at the reins, twisting his horse's head roughly around. *When he's in my hands,* he thought, *who knows what might happen?*

The morning of the banquet saw Leland up before sunrise to ride into the city for the last day of the dawn *misogi.* Every morning he started class wondering if this would be the day that Marilyn attended, but she hadn't yet. He asked Charly about it at breakfast after class.

"She been coming to the early afternoon class—the one I teach for the *uchideshi,*" Charly said. "I believe she spends her mornings entertaining Sylvan Montrose or, as Zanna refers to him, 'Daddy's latest mistake.' "

"Does Zanna talk like that in public?"

"No, of course not. She says it to his face, though."

Leland raised his eyebrows. "That can't be very popular."

"He's used to it. He blames me, of course, though every contrary opinion Zanna expresses has been her own."

"Is Marilyn more agreeable?"

Charly laughed. "Well, yes and no. Her opinions are her own, too, but she's more 'politic' in her expression. When Zanna *really* doesn't like something her father has decided, she gets Marilyn to talk to him about it. Marilyn has a way of pointing out the problems with a position without making him feel like an idiot. Zanna can do this, but their past disagreements have been so stormy that it's much harder for her to accomplish."

Leland rode back to the estate in time to preside over a morning parade culminating in the presentation of the unit pennant to the Seventh Hundred. The remaining Hundreds saluted while the Seventh paraded before them carrying the flag of Laal and their unit banner with the bright blue award pennant streaming from its tip.

Watching the ritual, Leland wondered if they should have a band like Noram's palace guard. He shook his head. *No, far better to keep some mobility. They can always . . .*

"Halvidar," he said quietly as the Seventh swung into place.

"Guide."

"I would speak to the men."

"Yes, Guide." The halvidar stepped forward quickly and raised his voice. "The Guide Leland de Laal, Captain of the Eight Hundred and Warden of the Needle, will speak. All attend."

Leland resisted an urge to stick his tongue out at Gahnfeld. *A simple "Listen up" would have sufficed!* He stepped forward, passing Gahnfeld. He paused for a moment, then said loudly, "We've just finished honoring the Seventh Hundred for their outstanding progress in overall training. Some of you are thinking 'So what?' Is this little strip of cloth worth the extra sweat and effort? My answer for that question is in two parts.

"First, what is the effect of being better at these skills than the next person? I think the answer is you are more likely to survive the coming conflict. I don't know what you think, but there are too many women I haven't kissed for me to want to die now."

There was laughter from the troops at this statement.

Leland continued, "Whatever the right or wrong of the coming fight, its cause is about symbols. We seek to control the place man first stepped on this planet for symbolic and economic reasons. It's the richest farmland on Agatsu. The Rootless want the plain for similar reasons. Symbols and food. At least if we win, there's a tangible result—something more than the pennant that hangs over there." He paused. "So, to give that pennant some tangible meaning, the Seventh Hundred has a six-hour pass tonight, starting at six."

There was a spontaneous cheer from the Seventh.

Leland then said, "It is noteworthy that the Seventh won this week's pennant without expecting a tangible reward. I will not tempt your virtue by promising such a prize every time the pennant is awarded, but, as long as you are alive, the possibilities are endless."

He turned to Gahnfeld. "I'm done, Halvidar. Perhaps a song to finish?"

"Right, sir." The Halvidar barked out, "Unit halvidars to your training assignments. And," he added, "a song. Something to wake up those late sleepers in the High City. So sing *loud!*" Then he started them off in "The Girl I Left Behind Me."

While they probably did not wake anybody, those in the High City who were already awake heard the distant singing as it drifted down cobbled streets through the early-morning sunlight. Many of them smiled.

# TWELVE

## TANINSUGAKE:
## TRAINING AGAINST MULTIPLE ATTACKERS

Leland was not allowed to go to the ball on horseback.

He hadn't slept well the night before, a combination of frustrated desire and nightmares. The cause of his frustrated desire was obvious. His was a problem wrestled with by most young men, but when he finally dropped off to sleep the bad dreams were waiting.

The dream started innocently enough. He was walking through an endless maze whose walls were bookshelves. Every so often he'd pull a book from the shelves, but, no matter how many he tried, he was unable to open them. Each book was closed with a locked clasp and Leland didn't have the key. It was somehow vital that he find that key.

He woke covered in sweat with the bedclothes twisted around him. Fully awake, the dream seemed silly, without the feeling of terrible significance and meaning it had when he was asleep. He straightened his blankets and lay back, ready to go to sleep again, but then Marilyn invaded his thoughts and the other problem was back. When he'd finally dropped off to sleep, the locked books had been waiting.

So this morning he was grumpy, irritable, and unreasonable. "What do you mean I can't go to the ball on horseback?"

They were in the big office of the estate. Leland leaned on the edge of the big desk while Phillip and Gahnfeld presented their reasons.

"If, *Warden,* you were just the Captain of the Eight Hundred, you could go mounted to the ball." Phillip paced as he talked. "Provided, of course, you had an escort of at least four outriders. But if you were just the captain, you wouldn't be invited to the ball in the first place." He paused. "As the son of your father, you represent the person, family, and Stewardship of Laal. Certain standards must be maintained."

"This is ridiculous," Leland said. "My father doesn't sit still for this nonsense in Laal."

Phillip nodded. "In Laal, no. Here, where the perceived importance of the Stewardship hinges on appearance, he plays every bit of pomp to its fullest." He stopped pacing and shrugged. "While William de Noram was still alive, your father could have come to a court function dressed in rags and his advice would still be sought and respected. But Arthur is a different fish. To put it bluntly, since his reputation rests not on what he's done but on who his father was, he puts a great deal of importance on appearances."

Leland thought about it. "Yes, he certainly does seem to care about place and position. Very well, we'll do it your way." He then asked, "What way is *your* way?"

Phillip smiled. "Come to the townhouse this afternoon. Bring a presentable escort of, well, eight men. We'd have twelve for your father, but that would be overdoing it for you."

Gahnfeld nodded. "I've already picked out the men, Guide."

"Why doesn't this surprise me?" Leland said. "On what basis has my escort been chosen?"

"Well, the soccer team from the Second leads the league. I would have used some men from the Seventh, but you gave them that pass."

Phillip creased his forehead. "It's important that they have suitable clothing."

Gahnfeld nodded again. "Of course. Coronet Sanchez is scouring the entire Eight Hundred for suitable dress. The escort will be better dressed than many of the guardianship attending the ball."

Phillip grinned. "Well, just so they don't look better than me." He turned back to Leland. "Your father's carriage is stored at the townhouse. My stableman has spent most of the morning polishing it. You'll take the carriage. I'll ride with your escort."

Leland pushed away from the desk and stood up straight. "Now that is going a touch far, Phillip. Surely that thing will hold the two of us without crowding? Will it do Laal any harm if I'm not lonely in the carriage?"

"None, Warden. I would be honored to join you."

* * *

It was seven when Phillip and Leland finished dressing. Phillip made minute adjustments to Leland's high collar, shifting the silver frogs that closed it.

"We should have done something with your hair earlier, Warden. The style these days is shorter. Well, too late now. Let's see what I can do." Phillip rummaged through a drawer. "Ah, here we are." He had Leland brush his hair straight back, then tied it in a short tail with black and silver ribbons.

Leland looked at his reflected image and was surprised. With his hair pulled tightly back, his hairline seemed higher, making him look older. The high black collar made his face seem whiter than it was and accented the faint dark circles under his eyes, left from his troubled night's rest.

The hair pulled back also showed the crescent scars on Leland's head. They had faded with time, but to Leland they were obvious as antlers. Briefly he considered putting the hair back over his temples, but decided to brave them. *After all,* he thought, *I came by them honorably enough.*

Phillip cleared his throat and Leland realized he'd been staring blindly at the mirror for some time. "Excuse me, Phillip. I was daydreaming. Are we ready to conquer Noram society?"

Phillip gave a half bow. "They don't stand a chance."

There were bigger carriages among the guardianship than the carriage of Dulan de Laal.

The High Steward de Noram's, for instance, was a huge six-wheeled affair with stations for footmen, butler, and maid. It had a wine rack, insulated compartments for keeping food warm or cold, and a curtained closet for two musicians. It was sometimes drawn by eight horses and other times by an ornately decorated steam tractor.

Most of the guardianship's carriages were four-wheeled, some covered, some not. Most were pulled by four to six horses.

Dulan de Laal's carriage was pulled by only two horses. It had two oversized wheels, padded on the rims with layers of gum rubber. Unlike other carriages, Dulan's was sprung with steel leaf springs. It would seat four, besides the driver, and had the Device of Laal emblazoned on its back and doors.

"Squad, attention!" Gahnfeld barked as Leland and Phillip came out the door. The escort, lined up at their mount's heads, straightened.

Leland noted that two men on the end held standards, Laal's and one Leland didn't recognize. He looked closer and saw a section of bamboo with sprouting leaves done in yellow and green on a field of black.

*"What the hell is that and where did it come from?"*

Gahnfeld blinked. "Sir?" He looked shocked and Leland realized that he'd shouted, something he hadn't done before now.

"That standard, the one with the bamboo—where did you get it?"

Gahnfeld actually flinched. He snapped to attention and said, "Sir! Your personal standard was put in my hands by the steward."

Leland sputtered. "The steward? You mean . . ."

"Your father, Warden."

Leland dropped back on his heels. *What does this mean? That devious old . . .* He noticed that both Gahnfeld and Phillip were staring at him. He took a deep breath. "As you might have guessed from my reaction, this is the first I've seen of it." He sat down abruptly on the steps of the townhouse and stared at the black piece of cloth.

Gahnfeld looked distressed. He shifted to a parade rest, then back to attention.

Phillip said quietly, "If I'd known you were going to sit on the steps, I would have had a cushion brought."

Leland realized this was reminder that he was wearing his new clothes. He stood hastily, brushing off the seat of his pants.

Gahnfeld spoke. "The steward didn't give me any instructions about displaying your device, Guide. Shall I have it put away?"

Leland shook his head abruptly. "No, Halvidar. Let it fly. My father knew exactly what he was doing when he gave it to you." He turned back to Phillip. "Shall we go?"

Of course one doesn't go directly to the ball when one is riding in a carriage. As Leland had said originally, "I could walk to the palace from the townhouse in five minutes. Why do we have to ride?"

Phillips answer had been "The point of having a carriage has nothing to do with transportation. What's the point of having a carriage if one isn't seen in it? As you noted, one can walk from one end of the High City to the other in fifteen minutes. Distance has nothing to do with it. You'll see."

And Leland did. As the carriage and outriders pulled out onto the first major avenue, he saw other carriages, all going away from the palace with their full complement of passengers.

"It's the grand circuit," said Phillip. "Even the guides who live in the High City spend at least thirty minutes riding around the city. It's a pageant. The point is to show off to each other and to the settled."

Leland found himself being nodded at or waved to from the other carriages. He did his best to return the greetings as Phillip pointed out the more notable guardianship. "I suppose jumping up and down on the seat and waving wildly is frowned upon?"

Phillip chuckled.

"Well, there at least is someone I know. Who's that with the chancellor?"

Guide Cornelius de Moran was approaching from the opposite direction in a plain carriage with a middle-age couple across from him.

"Ah, yes," said Phillip. "That's his daughter and son-in-law. They hold the de Moran family lands, I believe, north of here."

As the two carriages neared each other, Guide Cornelius smiled quietly and bowed slightly from his seated position. Leland rose to his feet and bowed from the waist. He saw Cornelius's daughter straighten in her seat when he did this, then the two carriages were past each other.

Phillip saw people in other carriages whispering to each other and pointing. He frowned.

Leland said, "What's wrong, Phillip? I didn't jump up and down on the seat."

Phillip shook his head distractedly. "I don't think you've done any harm. The chancellor was greatly respected here in Noram but has lately fallen out of favor with Arthur. You would have started as much gossip if you'd just nodded to him, but a warden standing and bowing to a mere landed guide is going to keep the tongues wagging for weeks."

"If he's so out of favor, why was he invited to the ball?"

"Most likely because he's definitely *not* out of favor with the high steward's sister and daughters."

Leland leaned back. "Should I have ignored the man?"

Phillip shrugged. "You've got to answer that sort of question for yourself. It might have been more politic to keep your response down to a mere nod. Who knows what the high steward will think?"

Under his breath, Leland muttered, "And who cares?"

Finally, after the palace had been circled at least twice, the carriage joined the queue of vehicles and horses waiting to unload at the steps of Noram House. When their turn came, they found themselves joining another line inside the mansion, just outside the ballroom.

"Is there a reception line?" Leland asked.

Phillip shook his head. "No. These people are waiting to be announced."

"Well, then," Leland said. "Why don't we sneak around to the side and go straight to the punch bowl? If I'd known we were going to ride around for three-quarters of an hour I would have brought a canteen."

Phillip shook his head. "You agreed to do it my way, Warden. Your father would have arrived an hour late so there'd be more people to watch him walk down the grand staircase. We're practically on time so they'll only be a small crowd to watch you trip on the stairs."

Finally Phillip handed their invitations to the majordomo and Leland had to hear his title read in heraldic tones to the ballroom at large.

"Guide Leland de Laal of Laal, Warden of the Needle and Captain of the Eight Hundred." He started to wait for Phillip but the factor made abbreviated shooing motions, so Leland walked down the center of the stairway alone. He concentrated on the far end of the hall, where four chairs had been set on a dais, and ignored the faces looking up at him.

Only when he reached the floor was Phillip announced. Leland walked to one side and waited for him.

The hall was the largest room Leland had ever been in, dwarfing the Great Hall at Laal Station. The ceiling rose three stories and balconies and windows opened onto the hall from the floors above. Biogenerated methane flowed through nearly a hundred white-hot mantles in crystal-chimneyed lanterns, casting a warm yellow light throughout the hall. Fifty or so early arrivals barely made a dent in its expanse. Tables set up to one side offered beverages and small foods.

Leland looked up at Phillip descending the stairs and thought, *Why isn't he captain of the Eight Hundred? He has the bearing, the experience.* Like Leland's brothers, Phillip had served in Captain Koss's Falcons and had seen action against Cotswold border raiders.

Leland glanced around and saw more than a few people watching Phillip descend. It disturbed him, however, to find that even more of them were watching him.

He turned and walked briskly over to the refreshment tables, where he asked for two glasses of the punch. When Phillip joined him, he gave him one and drained half of his own glass.

"Why are they staring at me?"

Phillip laughed. "Surely they wouldn't be so rude."

"Well, they are. Especially those older women." Leland finished his punch and asked for another.

Phillip frowned. "The punch is alcoholic, *Warden.*"

Leland looked at him, surprised. "It is?" Then he felt it hit his stomach. "I didn't realize. I'll be sure and take the next one more slowly." He accepted the new glass from the servant and turned back to Phillip. "So what's with these women?"

Phillip grinned. "All those women have daughters, Leland. I hate to say it, but you're the son of a Principal of the Council of Noramland. This makes you one of the more eligible bachelors in the city. Do you get my point?"

Leland felt his face go numb. He nodded stiffly. "How soon before we can leave?"

Phillip's sudden and loud laughter caused several people to look around.

Leland glared at him. "It's not funny."

"Of course not," said Phillip, still laughing. "Not even the slightest bit."

Leland glared at him. "How would you like to wear my hat? You wouldn't find it so funny, I'll bet." He took another swallow of the punch. "Look at them. It's like I was a prize goose."

"No, Leland. It's more like you're the biggest fish in the stock pond and there's a fishing contest about to start. And if you drink much more of that punch, you're going to swallow the first hook that comes your way."

Leland vividly imagined a large fishhook piercing his cheek and shivered. He put the half-full glass back on the refreshments table, where a servant scooped it up.

"More punch, Guide?"

"Something with less *punch.*"

After some deliberation he accepted a glass of pear nectar in a wineglass. The servant seemed surprised when Leland thanked him.

"Look, there's Cornelius and his daughter. What are they doing off by themselves? Where's her husband?"

Phillip shrugged. "It's as I said in the carriage. Cornelius is out of favor so he doesn't embarrass old friends and students by approaching them. Even his son-in-law roams the hall rather than be seen with him. I like the man, and your father respects him, but even I've been circumspect in my association. Arthur has not been exactly respectful of Laal lately. I didn't want to muddy things more than they were."

Leland frowned. "When we can't see who our friends are, the waters are muddy indeed. I'm very young, Phillip, and susceptible to the attention of great men. I'm ashamed to say it, but if Arthur had been the least bit kind to me in our trip from Laal, I would probably feel different. As it is, I don't care who is in or out of his favor." He paused. "Maybe it's the punch."

Phillip wasn't smiling anymore. He regarded Leland seriously. "Maybe it's a fresh viewpoint. I've been watching these stupid status games for so long, maybe I've lost sight of what has value and what's dross."

Leland shrugged. "I don't know, Phillip. Your job is to represent Laal's interests here in Noram. You can hardly do that by offending his nibs."

"Is it in Laal's interests to involve myself in Arthur's petty likes and dislikes? To let all of Noram think that old friendships are subject to childish whims?"

Leland smiled. "I don't know. Tonight I don't care. Would you take my arm, sir?"

"Honored, sir."

They walked across the floor to the chancellor.

The high steward and his sister sat in a shadowed balcony, high above the hall, eating a late supper while they watched the arrivals.

"What is that de Falon woman wearing?" Arthur said. "Makes her look like a piece of rotten fruit."

"I rather like it," Margaret said. "It's the perspective. From this angle, any gown looks different. You're just upset because it's high necked."

Arthur ignored her. "There's the Laal boy. His tailor should be *whipped*. That cut is ridiculous. Looks like a bloody servant. I thought Phillip had better taste."

Margaret smiled. "You really think so? I rather like it. And in this crowd he stands out like a hawk among peacocks."

"Really, Margaret. I thought you had *some* taste. I've known it from the moment I set eyes on him. The boy has no class, no style."

"Whatever you say, Arthur. When are Sylvan and Marilyn going to make their entrance? I wish they'd hurry. Everybody seems to have arrived."

He shrugged. "Soon, I should think. After all—I don't believe it. Those stupid clods!"

"What? Oh, it's Cornelius and his girl. Why are you so angry?"

"Did you see the bow Phillip and Leland gave them? They have no sense of place or propriety. I don't know what his father was thinking of when he made him a warden. He isn't acting the part. A bow that deep is due *him* from a mere landed guide. What did I say—no style. And that pompous fool Cornelius is lapping it up."

"Arthur!"

The high steward cringed suddenly at the edge in his sister's voice. Then he straightened suddenly. "What are you snapping about!"

She stood suddenly, towering over him. "You petty little man! You have no respect for the customs, for simple decency, for learning and scholarship, for one of our father's dearest friends, *for the man who taught us to read.* You make me ashamed to be your sister."

He opened his mouth to answer, but she was gone, the curtain to the alcove swinging in her wake. He felt his ears burning furiously, felt the urge to run after her, to scream into her face, *Father never showed me the smallest piece of the respect he showed that man. I'll be damned if I'll treat him better than the servant he is!*

He drank from his wineglass, gulping convulsively. *Soon it won't matter. Things are going to change, sister—wait and see.*

Leland, Cornelius, and his daughter, the Gentle Guide Amalia, were laughing at something Phillip said when the fanfare sounded. Sylvan and Marilyn, being the guests of honor, were not announced. Instead strings, flutes, guitars, and a drum heralded their descent.

Sylvan was dressed in scarlet and green, with a belt worked in gold. Marilyn wore white, with underdresses in shades of cream and ivory. They walked down the stairway slowly, Sylvan carrying his shoulders back, his chin raised quite high.

GREAT ADAM'S APPLE.

Marilyn's eyes were on the crowd, a quiet smile on her face. She floated on the stairs, her feet invisible, hidden beneath the slips. Her skin was so pale that her dress seemed to blend with her bare shoulders.

They reached the bottom and the music stopped. From his position at the top of the stairs, the majordomo's voice echoed through the hall. "A toast to Guide Sylvan Montrose and the Gentle Guide Marilyn de Noram. Long, clean, wise life."

When the response from the assembly had rolled off the walls he announced the next couple. "The Gentle Guides Zanna de Noram and Charlina de Rosen."

Charly was wearing a long, loose gown in blue—something with a complex weave that included bits of metallic gold and silver. Leland was willing to bet that she'd woven it herself.

Zanna was dressed in dark pants and a matching cutaway jacket over a blouse of scarlet silk. Her hair was tied back much like Leland's, and the heels of her polished boots made her seem slightly taller than Charly, though Leland knew Charly was actually the taller of the two. He checked as they walked down the stairs and saw that Charly was wearing flat slippers.

As the couple neared the bottom of the stairs the majordomo spoke again. "The first dance will be 'The Balanced Diet.' "

Sylvan and Marilyn took the head of the set. Leland turned to Cornelius's daughter and bowed. "Guide Amalia, would you honor me?"

Her eyes grew very large. "Certainly."

Leland led her onto the floor. They ended up the second couple down, Leland as vegetables, Amalia as fruits, to Sylvan's legumes and Marilyn's whole grains. The pattern repeated every third couple, down the length of the set.

"The Balanced Meal" was the one dance Leland knew well. He'd learned it as a child, as did all children in Greater Noram, to supplement instruction in the categories. He went through the steps automatically, smiling at his partner or his temporary partners, as the dance progressed. He didn't realize that this unconscious competence lent a great deal of grace to his simple, clean movements.

Sylvan, on the other hand, did not know this dance. His expertise lay in partner dances. The instruction of the categories in Cotswold was not universal, and line dances, calling for the mixing of ranks, were not fashionable. He managed to complete the first steps without any great disasters, but he was scowling by the end of the first cycle.

Leland wove around Sylvan during one of the extended figure-eights and nodded pleasantly. Sylvan glared back and nearly collided with the next couple down. Leland suppressed a smile and returned to his partner.

Then they did the mixed stew, all four categories coming together to form a four-spoked wheel, then doing a linked-arm turn with a temporary partner. Leland ended up with Marilyn.

"Some zucchini in your rice?" he asked.

"Avocado on my bread," she answered. Sylvan reclaimed her, taking her arm with unnecessary firmness.

Later, after Leland and his partner had reached the top of the set, converting to legumes and grain, they encountered Marilyn and Sylvan, working their way back up the set as vegetables and fruits. Again, after the mixed stew, Marilyn ended up with Leland.

"Some onions with your beans?" she offered.

"Gives me gas."

They laughed out loud.

Sylvan turned a beat early and snatched at Marilyn's arm. She avoided it and Leland heard her whisper, "I am not a valise! You've already bruised me once tonight, keep your hands to yourself!" Then she pushed him away from her, to his next position in the dance.

Leland clenched his teeth together and hurried to keep from messing up the next turn. Safely in step again, he noticed Sylvan's ears were a bright red.

Leland and his partner reached the end of the set and stood out for the necessary cycle.

"You seem troubled, Warden."

Leland smiled briefly. "I worry about things that are not my business. It serves me right. Ah, time to reenter the set?"

"Yes, Guide."

After the dance, Leland escorted Amalia back to her father.

Phillip did his own share of dancing, but when he and Leland weren't, he did his best to introduce Leland to as many of the guests as he could. He was surprised when, in the midst of several introductions, Leland or the other person being introduced would say "We've met." Then they would bow to each other—not the nod or casual bow of greeting, but a formal bow, from the waist.

"For someone who hasn't been in the city in over a decade, you know a lot of people. Have they visited Laal?"

Leland smiled and said, "No. I met them at Guide Charlina's place."

Phillip nodded. He and Gahnfeld had discussed Leland's morning trips to the townhouse. Gahnfeld had said, "I think he's having an affair with the woman. I wouldn't blame him. I'd like to have an affair with her myself."

Phillip had been surprised. "Preposterous. He may be having an affair and using her house for the purpose, but it's highly unlikely that it's with the de Rosen woman. She's Zanna de Noram's chosen companion."

"Oh. *She's* the one. I thought they were going to marry?"

Phillip shook his head. "The high steward's against it. Says he'll disinherit Zanna if they make it official. But he hasn't been able to get her to give de Rosen up."

Gahnfeld said, "Well, my men have told me nobody arrives after Leland. Maybe she's bisexual?"

Phillips shook his head again. "I'm pretty sure she's monogamous, whatever her orientation."

Gahnfeld shrugged. "I just hope he's careful, whoever he's screwing."

When Leland danced with the Gentle Guide Charlina, Phillip wondered anew about Gahnfeld's suspicion. But when he saw Zanna watching the dancers with a smile on her face, he dismissed the notion.

Sylvan avoided the line dances after the first but tried to monopolize his betrothed for all the partner dancing. She put up with this for a while, but then, as the evening wore on and Sylvan drank more and more, she started accepting the petitions of other admirers. Sylvan accepted this with seeming good grace, using the opportunity to dance with some of the more attractive and forward women. Later, though, when Marilyn refused several supplicants and pulled Leland from a conversation with Marshall de Gant, Sylvan was clearly distracted, dancing poorly with his current partner and glaring across the room at Marilyn and Leland.

More than one onlooker's hand was raised to cover smiles as they watched Sylvan's reaction. Cotswold had been at conflict with Noram too long for Arthur's recent treaty to smother accumulated ill feeling, and Sylvan had not helped things with his behavior since his arrival in the city.

Phillip didn't know whether to be pleased or worried about the Cotswoldian's reaction. After watching Sylvan's expression worsen over the course of the dance, he decided.

*Worried—I should be worried.*

* * *

When their escort and the carriage had been fetched, Gahnfeld and two of the other soldiers were missing. The coronet left in charge said, "A man came, sir, from an inn. Some soldiers from the Seventh got in a fight with some other unit down in the Lower City and are under siege in some tavern. The halvidar said he'd meet you at the estate when he'd straightened it out."

When they'd returned the carriage and Phillip to the townhouse, Leland left, mounted, with the escort. He still wore his dress clothes. "I can change at the estate," he'd told Phillip. "If I splash mud on them now, it won't matter. It's pumpkin time."

"You're welcome to stay the night. No reason to ride back in the dark."

Leland considered it. His head was still muddled from the drink and food. "No. The night air is what I need. Besides, I have a staff meeting at breakfast."

By the time they'd reached the bottom bridge his head was clearing nicely, but he was yawning and thinking of bed. A rider hailed them on the other side of the bridge.

"Warden de Laal? Captain of the Eight Hundred?"

*Now, how in the hell did he know that?* The pennons were furled.

MAYBE IT'S YOUR MONKEY SUIT.

"Yes? What is it?"

The man was dressed well, riding a good horse. He had an educated voice. "Halvidar Gahnfeld and several of your men are injured and the landlord of the inn your men demolished won't let the a doctor attend them until he's received recompense for the damages."

*Great! Just what I need. I hope the high steward doesn't hear of this.* "Well, we'd better go and see what's what."

They followed the messenger onto the Great Circle—the road that circumnavigated the plateau of the Upper City. After a quarter hour at a slow gallop, they came to the Lower City and, as there was still quite a bit of traffic, they slowed their horses to a walk. Five more minutes of twisting through narrow dirt streets and the messenger turned into the enclosed yard of the Good Landing. A wedge-shape shuttle, standing on multiple pillars of fire, was painted in faded colors on the sign above the inn's name.

Leland narrowed his eyes. The inn had several windows made of multipaned rough yellow glass. They were all intact.

The messenger dismounted and tied his horse at the public rails near the stable end of the yard. He gestured. "If the warden would follow me?"

Leland turned to the soldier left in charge of the escort and said quietly, "Have you ever been in a barroom brawl, Coronet?"

"Uh, well, yes sir, I have."

"Do the windows get broken?"

"Often." The coronet looked at the front of the inn and frowned.

Leland nodded. "Something isn't right. Combat status—quietly."

The coronet lifted his right hand and clenched his fist. The soldier behind the coronet snapped his jaw shut in midyawn and his eyes widened. The rest of the soldiers went from sleepy to wide awake.

Leland said softly, "I may say some crazy things shortly. Pretend I mean them, all right?"

The soldiers nodded, then, following Leland's lead, they all dismounted.

Leland called across the yard. "One second, friend." He beckoned to the man waiting before the unopened door. The man hesitated, then walked casually across. "Yes, Warden?"

"Would you be so kind as to wait here with these two soldiers?" He gestured to two of his escort. The two men stepped forward to stand at each side of the messenger. Before the man could answer, Leland said to the soldiers, "If this turns out to be a trap, cut off his head."

"What! Are you mad?" the man said.

Leland turned back to him as all of the soldiers reached over their shoulders and drew the slightly curved swords from their sheaths. "Well," he said, "is it a trap?"

He snapped, "Of course it isn't a trap!" He started to edge away from the soldiers, but the bigger of the two reached out and closed one hand across the back of the man's neck.

Leland smiled slightly. "Then you have nothing to worry about, do you?" He turned, as if to go.

"No, wait!"

"Yes?"

In a low, intense voice, the man said quickly, "I don't know if it's a trap or not. I was paid to take you the message. It's not my fault if the person who hired me was lying!" He was sweating more than the temperature warranted.

"And who might that be?"

The man hesitated, then shook his head. "I never saw him before."

HE'S LYING.

Leland looked back at the inn. He thought he saw movement at one of the upper windows. "Let's tie the horses to the hitching rail," he whispered. Then he pointed his thumb at the messenger. "Him, too."

They moved, en masse, across the yard. The hitching rails were hidden from the inn's upper windows by the eaves of the lower roof. The two soldiers tied the messenger's wrists securely to the post. Leland took a bandanna out of his saddlebags and pointed at his mouth. One of the soldiers nodded and gagged the man, as well.

Visible between the stables and the inn proper was a passage, barred by a high wooden gate, leading toward the back of the inn. The coronet gestured at it and Leland nodded. "By all means—if it's not locked."

It wasn't, but it was occupied.

The men waiting in the dark passage were armed with clubs, staffs, and daggers. They seemed surprised when the door was opened, but charged out. More by accident than intent, the first one spitted himself on the coronet's sword, but the next man struck the coronet down before he could untangle his sword.

"There he is!" someone shouted, and Leland realized that they were talking about him. A man with a short staff thrust at Leland's belly and he pulled his hip automatically, letting it slide past his stomach. He grabbed the staff, putting one hand near the middle and the other at the free end, then twisted, pivoting the attacker's hands up and across the man's face. He thrust down then quickly, throwing the man to tangle in the feet of his compatriots.

Leland held onto the staff and blocked an overhand blow with a club, then dropped, making a circle with the ends of the staff, which slid down the club into the attacker's hand. The club fell, but before it hit the ground, Leland thrust hard into the man's belly, doubling him over.

Then he found himself crowded back as his escorts threw themselves forward slashing fast and furious. The men from the passage pulled back, but others came in through the gate to the yard *and* from the entrance to the inn. To make matters worse, the upper windows opened and two archers leaned out, though they held their fire.

Leland shouted, "Into the passage!"

He charged past his escort, the staff held at the ready, screaming "*LAAL!*" at the top of his lungs. Behind him, his men took up the cry.

One of the two men blocking the passage flinched back but the other thrust his staff out. Leland counterthrust, sliding off the line. Leland's *chokutsuki* took the man in the throat and he went over backward, choking. The other man stepped forward, striking overhand with a club. Leland dropped his staff and went under the descending blow, striking the man's stomach with his shoulder and lifting him off his feet. The air rushed out of the man's lungs with a *whoosh* and Leland thrust hard with his own legs, pushing the body into the men behind him, fighting to clear enough space in the passage for his men.

A club blow glanced off the body in his arms and across his upper arm. He extended his arms, thrusting the body even higher, then stepped back, just in time to avoid another thrusting staff, coming at his groin. The body fell on the thruster's arms, knocking the staff out of his hands and tangling his feet.

A man with a club jumped over the prone body and Leland leaned forward, as if to reach for the staff. The club man took the bait and struck down at Leland's head. Leland slid off the line while meeting the other man's club arm with his own. He blended with it, guiding it down and past him, then cut back up, turning the man's arm over. He slipped his hand down to the outside edge of the man's club hand and lifted while he twisted the hand and wrist back into the body. The club man gasped from the excruciating pain and flung himself to the side, trying to relieve the pressure on his wrist. Leland followed, pivoting around his center, throwing the club man across the passage to slam, back first, into the inn's wall.

The next man jumped forward with a staff, thrusting. Leland twisted the other direction, this time putting pressure on the club man's forearm, as if it was a sword, and cut out at the other side of the passage. The club man flew forward, tangling the staff as it thrust and slamming into the side of the stable hard enough to crack boards.

Leland reversed again, back into the *sankyo* wrist pin, and cranked the man across the passage again. The man wasn't able to follow as swiftly this time, and he screamed as tendons tore in his wrist. When he'd bounced off the inn wall yet again Leland shoved him forward, to tangle with the attackers at the end of the passage.

Leland glanced behind him. His escort was completely within the passage and had even managed to drag the coronet's inert form with them. Four of them blocked the passage and the fifth was standing behind Leland, his sword ready, his eyes very wide.

Leland scooped up the staff at his feet and gestured for the swordsmen to join him.

"I would've been here before," the soldier said, "but I was afraid I'd get in your way."

Leland laughed.

There were three men left at his end of the passage, two with clubs and one with a staff. Leland's laughter had a disquieting effect on them.

"Just hold them in the alley!" the man in the middle said. "The others will take care of them."

Leland took a deep breath, then shouted *"Laal!"* again at the top of his lungs. Beside and behind him, the escort echoed him.

Leland listened for a second, then shouted it again.

This time there was a faint echo. Leland wondered for a second if it was their own cry bouncing off the cliff face of the upper city, but it repeated, out of sync with their own.

"Louder, boys. The Seventh Hundred is drinking out there—help them find us! *LAAL!*" He slid casually forward and thrust suddenly at the other staff wielder. The man tried to block, but only succeeded in guiding the thrusting tip up into his forehead. He fell back. One of the club men jumped forward to slash at Leland's extended arm, but the sword of the soldier beside him flashed out and took the man's wrist. Club and hand fell to the floor.

The remaining man looked at the club in his hand, then at the sword and staff facing him. He turned and ran.

Leland looked around. The other four members of the Eight Hundred were holding their own. The narrow mouth of the passage and the bright steel of their swords kept the men in the yard from bringing their numbers to bear.

ECONOMY OF FORCE.

Leland took a look at the coronet, lying in the passage behind him. Blood oozed from an egg-sized bump at the man's forehead, just under the hairline. He considered checking his pupil dilation, but there wasn't enough light.

His men kept shouting "Laal" at the top of their lungs, in unison. Between their shouts, Leland heard more and more answering calls, coming nearer and nearer. He considered ordering the men to flee down the passage but was afraid they'd be at greater risk than they were now.

Then there was a brief increase in the assault, barely held back, and the attackers fled, running back through the inn or through the stable, as men of the Seventh Hundred poured into the yard through the main gate.

They weren't armed, except for personal knives, but they were numerous and they were enthusiastic. It probably didn't hurt that they'd been drinking.

Leland recognized one of the coronets of the Seventh. "Surround the inn. Let nobody in or out." He pointed at a groaning figure stretched out on the pavement, the victim of his first encounter. "Take that man prisoner and any others you find. Check the passageway." To his armed escort he said, "Search inside. We're looking for any of our men, including Halvidar Gahnfeld and the two men he took with him. Be careful."

He wanted to go in with them but was afraid that they'd try to protect him rather than themselves if it came to more fighting.

He remembered the original messenger, the one they'd tied to hitching post, and he walked carefully between the agitated horses, talking soothingly to them. The man was there and still tied to the rail.

But his throat was cut.

Gahnfeld arrived then, not from inside the inn but on horseback, with the other two soldiers from the escort and several squads from the Seventh Hundred. He found Leland going through the slain man's pockets and belt pouch.

Leland jumped up, surprised and pleased. "You're all right!"

Gahnfeld blinked. "Well, yes, I am."

Leland told him of the message he'd received. "We were ambushed. It would've been worse If I'd actually gone inside. There were men waiting inside, in the passage, and outside the gate."

Gahnfeld looked grim. "Hmmm. I'm afraid both our messages were false. There wasn't any fight—just a loud party that the landlord was quite pleased with. But since their pass was almost up, I collected the men and was heading back when we heard the commotion. Who is *he?*" Gahnfeld pointed his thumb at the body.

"The messenger. We tied him up when we suspected something was wrong. While we were trapped back there, somebody killed him."

"Why didn't they just set him free?"

"And if we ran across him again? He's been silenced. What a cliché."

One of the escort emerged from the inn and saluted. "I see you've found the halvidar, sir. We found the landlord and his family locked in the cellar—otherwise the place is empty."

"Ah. What do they say?"

"The men showed up about an hour ago and chased out the regulars, then locked them up. That's all they know. Shall we let them out?"

"What? They're still in the cellar?"

"You said not to let anybody in or out."

"Well, let them out!" He took a deep breath and lowered his voice. "Show them this man's face. See if they recognize him." He looked down at the blood-drenched clothes and added, "Just the landlord—keep the children away."

The city police arrived then in force, and it was long time before Leland got to bed.

# THIRTEEN

## NANKEN: BAD SWORD

A surprise attendee at the hearing was Zanna de Noram, heir apparent of the high stewardship. She came in alone and unannounced, and those in the room stood in a rippling pattern, as if she were a stone falling into a small pond.

In a loud clear voice she said, "Please sit and continue." She accepted a chair near the front and folded her hands in her lap.

The commissioner of police, presiding, nodded. "We'll hear from Investigator Sherwood, then."

"Yes, Commissioner," said a small man sitting at the back. He strode up and stood in front. "When the guard arrived at the inn, they found members of the Laal contingent in control of the area. There was the partly conscious Simon Grant, the murdered Roberto Dole, killed while tied to the hitching rail, and Pepito Smith, killed as he attacked the warden's party. In addition, a severed hand was found in the passageway beside the inn. The owner, one Jason Li, was found near death down the street at the Winter Inn. He was saved by emergency blood transfusions, but remains gravely ill.

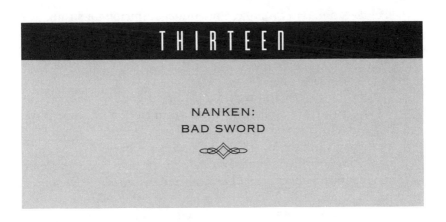

"Pursuant to your instructions, I've questioned the prisoners, Simon Grant and Jason Li, as well as the known associates of the deceased, Roberto Dole. Grant claims he was hired by Dole for the specific purpose of taking 'an unspecified guide prisoner.' Someone that Dole himself would guide to the inn. Without an opportunity to collaborate on their stories. Li says much the same thing, though, of course, I could not question him in great detail in his present condition.

"Pepito Smith is in the police logs, under suspicion for strong-arm activity. Roberto Dole has a criminal record and has served prison time for extortion, threatening innkeepers in the Lower City with gang violence. He is also suspected in the traffic of proscribed goods from hostile and previously hostile countries."

The commissioner frowned, "What sort of goods?"

"Horse tack from Nullarbor, sir. Opium from Kun Lun. Olives from Cotswold."

"Is there any motive established for Dole's actions?"

"Only one, sir. He paid off several debts the afternoon before the attack. One must construe that he was hired. Unfortunately, none of his known confederates knows or is willing to tell us who hired him."

"What about the others who attacked the warden's party?" asked the commissioner. "Any leads?"

"Yes, Commissioner. Gant and Li are cooperating, but the confederates they've named have left the city or are in hiding with the exception of a man in the Lower City infirmary with a damaged larynx. He is unable to talk but, in writing, denies that he was part of the attack. His injury, however, happened late the night of the attack, and we'll move him to the prison when his tracheotomy has stabilized."

The investigator bowed slightly. "We are continuing our efforts, but that is the current extent of our findings."

"Thank you, Investigator. That will be all for now." The commissioner turned to the front row. "Warden de Laal, are you aware of any motive for the attack on you and your men?"

Leland, sitting beside Gahnfeld, stood. "No, Commissioner. No idea. If there had been attacks on any other unit commanders from the expeditionary force, I would've thought it an effort to undermine the military effectiveness of the Noram army, but I seem to have been the only target."

Marshall de Gant's aide, also sitting on the front row, said, "We can't eliminate that possibility. All units have been warned to increase security—especially that of their officers. Dole's traffic in Nullarbor goods is troubling; perhaps he was an agent for them."

"Whoever killed him had to be among the attackers," Leland said. "Perhaps whoever hired him also posed as one of those hired *by* him.

If you run down the other members of the gang, perhaps you can winnow him out."

The commissioner nodded. "Yes. That's the focus of our investigation. Does anybody else have anything to add?"

When nobody spoke, Zanna stood. "I wish to emphasize that my father and I consider this investigation to be of the highest priority, Commissioner."

The commissioner bowed. "Yes, Gentle Guide."

Zanna's father did *not* consider the investigation "of the highest priority" and was not pleased when she reported to him on the findings of the hearing. "Why did you say that? The police have better things to do than chase riffraff all over the country."

Zanna stared at him impassively for a moment, then said slowly, "All right. Someone mounts a concerted attack on an officer in the service of Noram and the son of a Principal of the Council, and you *don't* want to know who did it?"

*Not if it's Cotswold.* "I didn't say that! I said it shouldn't be given any higher priority than usual. Why'd you go to that meeting, anyway?"

"I thought *one* of us should go. Is there something I'm not understanding here? Do you truly think this incident isn't worthy of your attention? What if it had been Marshall de Gant? Or Aunt Margaret?"

"Don't be silly. That would be different."

Zanna shook her head. "I don't understand why. When organized groups of thugs attack *any* of our citizens, it's a signal that something is seriously wrong here."

"An isolated incident. Probably some vendetta brought from Laal. It doesn't concern *us.* Laal is one only one of our many stewardships. It's high time they stopped getting special treatment."

Zanna leaned forward in her chair. "What aren't you telling me, Father?"

He stood and turned his back on her, walking over to the window. "What are you talking about?"

"If Laal gets any special treatment it's because they've earned it. They double-tithed. They've taken the brunt of the Cotswoldian raids for two decades. And Dulan de Laal was instrumental in keeping the country together when Grandfather died." She stood and walked around to where she could see his face. "Has Laal done something you haven't told me about?"

"No." He turned away again, and walked back to his desk. "But it's high time people realized that Noramland is governed from *this* room. Not some backwater town in the southern mountains." He sat in his chair again and said, "Go ahead—conduct your investigation. But don't keep the police from their other duties. For that matter, don't keep *me* from *mine.* I've several people to see."

Zanna bowed. When she rose again her face was composed though her eyes were narrowed slightly as she regarded her father. He had to struggle not to snap at her.

"Good day, Father," she said. "I'll leave you to your meetings, then."

After she left he stared at the door for several minutes, his hands clenched into fists on his lap.

*Was it Cotswold?*

Leland was quiet as he rode back to the estate. The escort of thirty soldiers seemed comfortably large—a force large enough to discourage even thoughts of an attack, much less the attempt itself, but he fretted over the lost training time for the men.

He resolved to stay away from the city for the rest of their stay, though the thought of not seeing Marilyn again was physically painful. Still, there were only three days left until the Eight Hundred was scheduled to march.

*If Cotswold, then why? Especially puzzling were the instructions to capture him. What on earth did they want with him?* He remembered the bodyguard his father had set when Siegfried Montrose was in Laal. *What do you know, Father?*

Phillip had sent a coded report of the incident via heliogram. His father knew of the incident but, the only instructions back had been to increase security.

He found Gahnfeld waiting for him at the front of the estate house, a puzzled look on his face. "A moment of your time, Warden?"

"There's that damn word again. What did I do this time, Halvidar?"

"I've been talking to the soldiers who were with you at the Good Landing."

Leland walked up the steps, into the cool interior of the entrance hall. "Good men. They should be commended—perhaps decorated. By the way, how is the coronet?"

"Coronet Pearson seems all right. He remembers arriving at the inn, but that's the last thing he remembers. He's been examined by the unit medic and by the factor's personal doctor. They're guardedly optimistic. He's on bed rest and under observation."

"Very good. I'm very sorry that I put them in danger. Is that why you've gone back to calling me Warden?"

"No, War—sir. Given the message, I don't blame you at all for going to the inn. In fact, from what I've been able to get out of the men, you seem responsible for getting them out of there alive."

Leland waved his hand. "It was a group effort." He entered the reception parlor, walked over to the bar, and poured himself a glass of water from a waiting pitcher. "A drink, Halvidar?"

"No, sir. Squadman Kantoff said you took out six of the attackers. He also said you were unarmed."

Leland felt his ears turn red. "Is Kantoff blond? Green eyes?"

"That's him."

"Ah—he kept me from taking a nasty blow. Took a man's hand off. I wasn't unarmed. I had a staff—two of them, come to think of it. Besides, it was dark—Kantoff's probably counting people who tripped over each other."

Gahnfeld opened his mouth as if he were going to say something, but he shut it again.

Leland drank. "Well, what *is* the problem? I must've done *something.*"

"I wish you'd told me you had extensive unarmed combat training."

Leland's eyes narrowed. "What makes you think that?"

"I had a conversation with Coronet Jeston. He told me about your mornings at Falling Water Aikikai back in Laal."

Leland frowned. "Coronet Jeston has a big mouth."

"He was very reluctant to tell me. I had to threaten him."

"Threaten him? With what?"

"I told him I'd send him back to Laal before the campaign."

Leland laughed. "That's a *threat?* 'Look, Jeston—you can face death and combat and tell me about the boss's dirty laundry or you can go back home to peaceful Laal.' I don't understand soldiers."

Gahnfeld glared at him.

"Why are you so upset, Myron? Think what you'd be facing now if I'd gotten myself killed or kidnapped. Of course, you'd be rid of an untried commander, but you *would* have to deal with my father."

Gahnfeld blew out hard through his nose, then dropped his shoulders and rubbed hard at his face. "Aiiii. To be honest, I don't know. I guess it's just that I don't like surprises. In war there are too many and they are all too likely to get men killed." He dropped his hands back to his sides and stood at attention. "Is this a Cotswold action? Your father first put the guard on you when Siegfried and Sylvan were in Laal. Sylvan is here."

Leland shook his head. "I don't know. You saw his message. Did Captain Koss say anything else before we left? Did he have special security instructions for here or in the Plain of the Founders that gives you any clue?"

It was Gahnfeld's turn to shake his head.

"Well, then, we'll just have to muddle through."

To call the raised mound a hill would be generous. It rose ten meters above the hot rock waste, a slight bump in the flat desert ten kilometers south of the Black River and well east of Jaren's Ford. On its meager crest, Siegfried sat in a camp chair beneath a canopy, outwardly patient, inwardly seething.

He wished for wind, to cut the heat, but this time of year, all you could really count on was clear weather, hot sun during the day, and cold nights.

Two of his signalmen looked north through tripod-mounted telescopes. Between them, a heliograph with a four-meter exclusion tube pointed at a very specific spot in the mountains across the border. Siegfried's personal guard waited just down the hill, on the southern side of the hummock. His full escort was a kilometer away, in the shelter of a ravine.

They'd traveled in the dark to give the dust kicked up by their horses time to settle before dawn. That much dust could be seen from beyond the border, and Siegfried wanted to keep Laal's attention away from this part of the desert.

He used a horsehair whisk to flick a cloud of midges away from his face, then looked at the sundial set up beside the canopy. The shadow of the gnomon was touching the quarter-after-ten graduation. Unless the signal team in the mountains had mucked up the orientation of their dial, the shadow of their gnomon should be pointing at the same indicator.

"They're sending," one of the signalmen said.

Siegfried looked up, squinting, but without the telescope the flashing light was too faint to see from fifty kilometers. Both signalmen were talking quietly, dictating the message to the cryptographers.

"Message ends," the man at the first telescope said.

The cryptographers compared the message. "I show a match."

"Agreed." One of them took both copies over and bowed to Siegfried.

He took the sheets from the man and set them on the field desk, then took a paper from the pouch at his belt. It was from the traitor, delivered anonymously to his agent in Laal. It purported to be the Laal military code, a sliding cipher that used a complex equation, based on the current date, to encode the message in one long block of letters.

The two sheets of paper held a message sent by his secret signal station agents on the lines-of-site between the Laal's main signal posts. It was an intercepted message, encoded and unreadable, but retransmitted verbatim.

*Hopefully, verbatim.* It took Siegfried twenty minutes to decode the message. When he was finished it said:

> TO: All border posts
> FROM: Koss, Commander Laal Forces
> Siegfried left Montrouge late afternoon by Eastgate. Escort of ninety troops, two water wagons, ten pack mules. If possible determine destination and purpose.

Siegfried didn't know whether to laugh or swear. *The exact numbers! I didn't know they were watching me that closely. But, on the other hand, their code is mine!* He folded the pages carefully and placed them in his pouch, then looked over at the waiting signalmen.

"The message is: Record and transmit all coded traffic."

Unlike the Laal code, Cotswold used a code book for their communications. Hundreds of appropriate phrases had assigned two-letter digit codes. This let Siegfried's message be broken down into DE for "Record and transmit" and 2C for "All coded traffic." Then, in addition, there was an offset based on the day of the month lest one of the code books fall into enemy hands.

The cryptographers encoded the message, checked each other, then gave it to the signalman at the heliograph. The other signalman held a white target before the end of the exclusion tube, to help refine the angle. When they had a clean circle of light projected on the target, they lowered it and the first signalman transmitted the message while the other manned the telescope.

"Message acknowledged, sir."

"Carry on." He walked back to his horse.

His guard fell in with him and they rode their horses at the walk, to avoid dust, back to the ravine where the rest of the troops waited.

Siegfried gestured to the escort commander, and the man trotted over quickly. "Sir?"

"Set up a heliograph relay between here and Montrouge. Exclusion tubes. Offset the last one to the south of the city. I want no chance of interception, so patrol the lines-of-site, as well."

"Yes, sir."

"We leave at dusk. I want to be at Montrouge by morning." *I have some spies to catch.*

Charly, Zanna, and Marilyn came down to see the Eight Hundred off. Gahnfeld put the dignitaries on the makeshift reviewing stand he'd used to direct training in large-scale troop movements. Marilyn and Zanna's mounted personal guard, increased after the recent attack on Leland, formed an impressive backdrop behind the stand.

Charly had a sad expression on her face and Leland asked her what was wrong.

"How many of these children won't come back?"

"Ah. *Hai.*" Leland looked at the troops waiting in neat rows, standing beside their mounts. They were all older than he.

CHILDREN, ALL.

Zanna shrugged. "What can we do?"

"Give the Rootless the plain. We don't need it anymore. We have enough farmland under cultivation."

Zanna looked shocked. "It's not just the farmland. It's the Plain of the Founders. We have a duty."

Charly turned to her and quoted, " 'To win one hundred victories in one hundred battles is not the highest skill. To subdue the enemy without fighting is the highest skill.' "

SUN TZU.

Zanna blinked, staring at the troops again. "It's been tried. Eighty years ago, Pappilion de Noram sent a delegation to Nullarbor. They proposed sharing the plain. The Rootless considered it but eventually refused. 'Give us the plain or defend it. Do not expect us to share it.' "

"But what have you done for me lately?" said Marilyn.

Zanna turned to her younger sister. "Meaning it's time to try again?"

Marilyn had been quiet, listening to her sister and Charly talk to Leland, but she smiled brightly and said, "What could it hurt?"

"Perhaps I should talk to Father," Zanna said.

"Perhaps *I* should talk to Father," Marilyn said. "If you want him to actually consider it."

Charly and Zanna both laughed.

Gahnfeld, who'd been dressing the lines, rode up then and saluted. "At your command, *Warden.*"

Leland glared at him and saw the corners of Gahnfeld's eyes crinkle. He turned to the three women and said, "Ladies, I must leave you."

Charly stepped forward and hugged him, followed by Zanna, who said, "I'll be there in a few weeks." Marilyn hesitated slightly before hugging him fiercely.

"Be careful," she whispered, then stepped back, blushing. There were spontaneous whoops from the troops.

Leland felt a lump in his throat but turned and slid into the saddle of his horse, waiting by the stand. The soldier holding the reins passed them up and Leland said quietly, "Thank you, Collins. Mount up." Leland edged his horse forward until it was by Gahnfeld's. "Pass the men in review, Halvidar."

"Yes, sir."

"And sing something."

"Yes, sir." He raised his signal fan and gestured.

The Seventh Hundred, still leading in the unit competition, went first. As they completed the turn, preparatory to passing before the stand, they began singing:

*One for the Morning Glory,*
*Two for the early dew,*
*Three for the man that'll stand his ground,*
*And four for the love of you, my girl,*
*Four for the love of you.*

On the stand, behind Leland, Charly exhaled. "Children. Glorious children."

The caravan from Cotswold was closely watched.

There were a hundred freight wagons, each with driver and assistant, a farrier's wagon, a portable wheelwright's shop, three cook wagons, a coach for the master, and thirty mounted guards. All together, two hundred and forty-seven men.

Captain Koss shivered. It had snowed the day before, though all of it had melted, and the exposed parapet of the observation tower accentuated the slightest breeze. He shifted the telescope on the rail until it focused on the head of the caravan. "None of them have slipped off? They're all there?"

"Yes, sir," said the intelligence halvidar. "We count them each hour. I had men standing by, to follow, if they hit the taverns in Brandon-on-the-Falls, but they kept to themselves. Except for the Master, and, as you know, he dined with Mr. Pierce." Mister Pierce was the chairman of the Laal Council of Merchants. Four of the wagonloads had been sold to Laal merchandisers.

"Well, they paid the import taxes. That's a lot of olive oil. It should make an interesting splash on the Noramland market." He finally put the telescope down. "Watch them very carefully. Their outriders are moving like cavalry and their order of march is a bit too disciplined for merchants. I don't want that many men loose inside of Laal. Report when they've cleared the pass into Acoma."

"Yes, sir."

Captain Koss handed the telescope to the watchman on duty, then turned and led the way down the many flights of stairs to the ground below. This was Fort Bayard, one of four permanent military installations in Laal. The unit here patrolled the three passes into Noram that were passable in winter and did the occasional bit of mountain search and rescue.

"Any word from Cotswold?"

The halvidar said, "Only the daily troop activity report. They still have no idea where Montrose was for the last two nights. Do we want to push it?"

Koss walked on for another flight of stairs. "No. Some of those agents have been in place for fifteen years. We don't want to risk them. We'll hear about it. Eventually some soldier will talk in some tavern. Just wish I knew what Siegfried was up to, though. It doesn't fit his usual pattern." He reached the bottom floor and walked down the hall to the commandant's office, displaced while Koss was at the fort.

"Shut the door," Koss directed.

"Yes, sir."

There was a map of Greater Noramland on the wall and Koss jabbed his finger at a spot on Laal's eastern border, where the Stewardship of Laal butted up against the Stewardship of Pree. "This is our easternmost heliograph station, at Apsheron village. We're going to set up a series of heliograph stations across Pree and Napa to link up with the Laal forces at the Plain of the Founders."

The halvidar blinked. "But, sir, we have that capability now, routed through Noram City or through the Pree and Napa heliograph systems."

"Guide Dulan is aware of that."

The halvidar stood at attention. "This is the steward's order?"

Captain Koss leaned against the wall and crossed his arms. "It is."

The halvidar stood still for a moment while he thought. Finally he said, "I see. Guide Dulan wants a line of communication that is completely under *his* control. Covert? How heavy will the message traffic be?"

Koss smiled. "Definitely covert. Two men per station, I'd say. Light traffic to be sent twice a day. Be careful with the site lines—we don't want interceptions."

"Yes, sir. We'll send the men in as peddlers, merchants, and perhaps a pilgrim or two. Standard code?"

"No. Break out the next series from cryptography and route all traffic as if it's going to Apsheron—whoever you put there will retransmit on the covert line."

"How soon?"

"Before the first arrow flies. That gives you three weeks."

"It shall be done."

"Good. Carry on."

The halvidar saluted and left. Koss looked at the map again, at the two stewardships between Laal and the Plain of the Founders. Both of them were part of Greater Noram, and Malcom de Toshiko of Pree was so close, he was like family. Napa was also close since all three stewardships shared a border with Cotswold. They'd all come to each other's aid in the years of border fighting.

Laal took the brunt of it, though. The mountains of Pree and Napa went right up to the Cotswold border. Only Laal had low hill country south of the Cloud Scrapers, with only the Black River as a geographic barrier.

*So why does Dulan want to hide communications from his two closest sister states and his own liege?*

They did the march from Noram City to the plain in five days, even though it was the same distance they'd traveled in ten days with Arthur de Noram's party. Gahnfeld was happy. "Now *this* is a military pace."

When they crossed the border between lesser Noram and Napa, the areas of fecundity became more widespread, interspersed with rocky barrens rich in lichens, tough wire grasses, and stubby, gnarled bushes. Villages, farms, and inns were few and far between.

After the midday break, when the Eight Hundred were well under way, "I'm taking the Seventh ahead," Leland told Gahnfeld.

"Sir?"

"Having trouble hearing?"

"No, *Warden.* How far ahead?"

Leland laughed. "Not far. We'll rejoin you before supper. Maintain this pace," he said, then asked his horse for a canter.

Gahnfeld watched Leland's standard-bearer and the two four-man squads of his personal guard fall in behind him. Leland slowed when he reached the Halvidar of the Seventh and called something. The halvidar gave one startled look back at Gahnfeld then raised his signal fan and signaled with series of quick arm motions.

A squad from the front of the Seventh shot ahead down the road, passing the Eight Hundred's point riders, and two other squads went left and right, as flankers. Then the remaining eighty-eight men moved from the trot to a canter, then to a slow gallop.

They kicked up a great deal of dust, and Gahnfeld pulled his bandanna over his nose and mouth until the light breeze carried it away. They were out of sight in ten minutes, beyond the next gentle hill.

Gahnfeld watched the dust of their passage for a few minutes, then gestured with his signal fan: *Order of March: Hostile country.*

Almost immediately the Fourth and First hundreds, traveling at the rear, just in front of the freight wagons, pulled to the side of the road and stopped, making way for the wagons, whose drivers cracked whips to move them ahead, into the main body of the caravan. The First, now at the very rear, detached a quarter of its men to fall back a full kilometer. The Sixth, now leading, sent a quarter of its men up, as point. The Third sent a quarter of its men out on the right flank, and the Eighth sent the same out on the left flank. Archers riding in the body of the caravan strung their bows.

*I don't know what you're planning, young Leland, but you'll not take us by surprise.*

They passed several likely ambush sites over the next two hours, low passes through hills, areas with overlooking high ground or enough scrubby bushes to hide men. The last likely site, a dip through a rocky wash lined with a garden of house-size boulders, was safely past and the entire column was traversing a rocky plain of brown grass and lichen affording little cover. The flankers had moved ahead, racing toward a low ridge in the distance, to check it for hidden dangers.

There was a signal from the forward scouts on the road: *Commander returning.* A few minutes later Leland and his personal guard topped the ridge and rode down toward the column. Gahnfeld rode forward and met them fifty meters in front of the column.

Leland was smiling and Gahnfeld, irritated, saluted and said in his most formal voice, "Did you have a good ride, *Warden?*"

At this, Leland laughed out loud, slapping his knee. "What's the matter, Myron? Afraid I lost the Seventh?"

*Something like that.* "I'm sure the *Warden* knows best. However, if it wouldn't be *too* presumptuous of me, I would like to know where they are."

Leland looked back over his shoulder, at the ridge. "Well, about ten of them are two klicks up the road with all of the unit's mounts."

Gahnfeld nodded. "And the rest of the men?"

Leland gestured left and right. "All around you."

Gahnfeld looked around him at the empty plain. "And where might that be?"

Leland took his battle fan from its saddle sheath and spread it, then gave the distinctive butterfly motion that meant *advance.*

Around them, on both sides of the road, the ground *shifted.* What had seemed to be patches of grass or shrub resolved into poncho-clad soldiers. In addition to the green and tan ponchos, the soldiers wore circles of fish net threaded with tufts of grass and branches of shrub. They held their bows, strung, arrows nocked. Their faces had been darkened with dirt and charcoal.

The nearest one, hidden a mere five meters from the road's edge, was the Seventh's halvidar. He was grinning openly. "One of the point scouts rode right over me," he called, spreading his poncho and pointing to a hoof print near the lower edge. "Luckily, I wasn't under *that* part of the poncho."

Gahnfeld opened his mouth several times but he could think of nothing to say. Finally he lifted his signal fan and gestured forward, *Recall scouts.* The humor of the situation finally overcame his irritation and embarrassment. "Well done. Very well done. I think the scouts, though, will walk the next two kilometers, while your men ride back to their mounts. Perhaps this will get them to examine the landscape a bit closer in the future."

He swung down from his own horse and stepped forward, holding out the reins to the Seventh's halvidar. "And you might as well start with mine."

# FOURTEEN

## SEI: MOTIONLESS, INACTIVE

At the Black River, on the western edge of the plain, Leland and Gahnfeld, riding ahead with the point scouts, surveyed the water running under the bridge.

"*This* is the Black?" The river, a narrow, violent series of rapids, looked nothing like the broad placid river on the southern border of Laal.

Gahnfeld nodded. "Yes. Five major rivers and a host of smaller ones join it before it reaches Laal. The Ganges is a bit bigger, but it's just as wild."

Leland looked at the bridge. The wood was newly milled but the stone breastworks at either end looked old. "Did they just rebuild this?"

"A year ago. Nullarbor held the plain last summer but lost it in the fall. When we hold the plain, we burn all the bridges across the Ganges, on the other side of the delta. When the Rootless hold it, they burn the bridges on this side."

"Sounds wasteful."

"Wastes trees, saves lives." Gahnfeld

A unit of Noram infantry was stationed at the bridge. In addition, a coronet and mounted squad from Marshall de Gant's headquarters unit was waiting to guide them to their station on the Ganges, on the other side of the plain. "Coronet Parker. I'm to be your liaison officer."

"Pleased to meet you. Halvidar Gahnfeld here is my executive officer. He'll introduce you to my unit commanders."

IN WAR, DEFENSE IS HARDER THAN OFFENSE.

*So, we're an expert at war?*

NO. WE SAW *Seven Samurai* TOO MANY TIMES.

*What?*

NEVER MIND.

The sacred plain was really gently rolling hills rising from the Black to the middle of the plain and then settling back toward the Ganges. They hours passed freshly harvested fields of corn, soybean, peanuts, wheat, and maize. Loaded grain wagons, headed east, passed them several times, headed for granaries on the safe side of the Black. Even if the Rootless took the plain, they wouldn't get this year's produce.

At the end of two hours they'd crossed half the plain and stopped for a rest.

"So, that's them, eh?"

Gahnfeld, silent beside him, just nodded.

The ceramic ablative skins of the shuttles were untouched by the passage of time. They stood, squat blunt shapes, vines growing over their landing gear, poking up into the dark empty holes of the spent solid-fuel thrusters. The noses were pointed at the sky, and the doors, large sections of bulkhead, were opened permanently out, revealing cavernous interiors stripped of salvageable materials over three centuries before.

ONE-WAY CARGO PODS. AEROBRAKING—ONLY ONE CHANCE TO LAND. CHRIST! WHAT A RISK, BUT THERE WAS NO CHOICE, WAS THERE?

*If you say so.*

From a large barracks built off to one side, the caretakers came out to answer questions, solicit donations, and keep the wandering soldiers from climbing on the shuttles. Leland wandered closer to one group of young soldiers and listened to the singsong repetition of one caretaker's voice.

"—ty years the Founders lived on this plain in peace, building a golden society in peace and harmony. Rebuilding the population lost during the first winters. Then Josh Townsend had his vision, his infamous revelation. His cult of New Luddites smashed the computers, the imprinters, the four working helicopters. They torched the cultivating equipment and called for the abandonment of technology, the 'demon that destroyed Mother Earth.' It took most of a day for the rest of the settlement to organize and stop them. Before they were captured, the cultists had taken over half the original library and, unable to burn or tear those books, cast them into the Ganges.

"The cultists were over a thousand strong, nearly one-tenth of the population. For their sin, they were cast out, to travel the barrens across the Ganges, where naught but thin grasses grew between rocks and gravel, where no one piece of land would support them, doomed to wander with their flocks and horses lest they deplete the land and starve. To that place without trees, Nullarbor, to be forever without roots."

The Rootless no longer spurned technology completely—they'd added steam tractors to the land they farmed in the south, but they were still largely nomadic and gave lip service to Josh Townsend's original injunction against any technology not powered by human or animal muscle.

One of the recruits asked a question. "What do you do when the Rootless hold the plain?"

"The same. Our function is sacred. The Rootless recognize this."

Leland wondered if Josh Townsend's vision was described as an "infamous revelation" when the Rootless came to view the shuttles, but he didn't ask.

He caught Gahnfeld's gaze and said, "Time?"

Gahnfeld nodded and clapped his hands together, then signaled *assemble* with his fan.

They moved on, reaching the Ganges an hour later, then turned upriver. They passed some of the earlier units already established at the fords, places where the combination of low ground and shallow water would make the river passable in a week or two, when the water fell.

Staff Coronet Parker led them to a place where the ground rose steeply and pointed out a flagged pole sticking in the ground near the road. "Here's where your post starts, Warden. There's another marker a kilometer and a half upstream. They just finished cutting the fall hay in the fields on the other side of those trees." He indicated a thin line of trees running from the river to the road.

They couldn't see the river from where they were—the ground rose toward it and, at the top of the rise, thick stands of pine and birch grew.

"I know this post," Gahnfeld said. "The river is uncrossable here. Even when the water drops, the cliffs make it secure. Why have the Eight Hundred been assigned here?"

"I believe," Coronet Parker said, "that Marshall de Gant intends to use your mounted infantry in reserve. This post is central to fords upstream and down."

"Ah. That makes sense."

Leland stared at the trees at the top of the hill. "Get started on the camp, Gahnfeld. I want to take a look at this cliff."

Parker went with the unit to show them latrine sites and the wells dug by previous units.

Leland, escorted by his guards, threaded his way through the wood at the top of the rise. The trees grew all the way to the cliff, through a trail, several meters back, paralleled the edge. Leland dismounted and walked the last bit.

The river was twenty meters below, a wild cascade of rapids beneath rock walls that rose steeply on both sides. The opposite cliff was slightly higher and about twenty-five meters across the gorge. The trees on the other cliff top were smaller and less dense, accenting the differences in fecundity between the sacred plain and Nullarbor.

Leland leaned over the edge. Below, the gorge was actually wider where the water had undermined the cliffs.

It wouldn't take much, Leland thought, to throw a bridge across the cliff tops, but, he supposed, both sides were probably alert to such an action. As if to illustrate the point, he saw a flash of brown and white downstream and pulled back, slipping behind a tree and waving his escort back into the wood.

Across the gorge, a small party of the Rootless trotted into sight, paralleling the cliff top and scanning Leland's side of the river. He counted nine of them.

*A regular patrol, or are they looking for us in particular?*

They wore leathers and their saddle quivers were full. Their double-recurved bows, shorter than the straight longbows carried by Laal troops, were strung and ready. They continued past, apparently without spotting Leland or his men.

He returned to his men and they rode along the cliff trail, at a slower pace than the Rootless. When they'd reached the point where the hillside dropped back down to join the river, they could see tents on their side of the river and soldiers filling sandbags. He spotted the banner of Scotia.

“Ah—Mildred de Fax’s pikes and archers. This must be where our stretch peters out,” Leland said. He turned back away from the river and rode through the trees back to the road. Sure enough, the second flag was there. They returned to the unit as they were making camp.

Gahnfeld saluted when he rode up. “There’s a small farmhouse in those trees that we’re setting up for you.”

“What happened to the owners?”

“They clear out every fall. If we keep the plain, they’ll come back after the snows drive the Rootless south. In the past, it’s understood that such properties are left in as good a condition or better when the campaign is over. Unless we’re retreating under fire, that is.”

“I see. I want sentries along the cliff, hidden, every fifty meters. Regular posts. Have the watch officer record all enemy activity as he makes his rounds. I want a summary three times a day.”

“Yes, sir. Every fifty meters. We’ve a kilometer and a half so that’s . . . thirty men, plus watch commanders. Three-hour shifts?”

“You know best. I’d like a staff meeting after supper.”

“Yes, sir.”

“And speaking of staff meetings, should I be calling on Marshall de Gant?”

“Next week, sir. Coronet Parker told me there’ll be a staff meeting after the last of the units arrive.”

“So we can do as we like for a few days. Excellent.”

# FIFTEEN

## IRIMI: TO ENTER

Leland had unpleasant memories of the Needle as he climbed the tree. It was a giant fur, thick with needles. In the spaces between the branches, his men had lashed extra steps and handholds. He couldn't see up and he couldn't see down. All around was a sea of dark-green pine needles.

But, unlike the Needle, Leland could feel the tree *move.*

Finally he saw the platform above, the observation post. He stuck his head up through the hole and the two men crouching there saluted but didn't stand—that would be dangerous. One moved aside to make room.

Branches had been bent, pulled into place and lashed, to make a living screen, blocking the platform from observation across the river. They could see out, though, over the lower trees between them and the river, and the still-lower trees on the other side.

The tree cleared its fellows on all sides, rising another eight meters above the platform, but, at this height, the trunk was only as thick as Leland's thigh and the stiff breeze was making it sway noticeably. Leland clenched his teeth and gripped the platform firmly.

"So that's it, eh?"

The coronet in charge said, "Yes, sir. You can see it more clearly in the telescope." He handed Leland his collapsing spyglass.

Leland pulled it out to its full length and peered ahead. A gap between two trees on the far cliff top showed a patch of stretched canvas, probably a tent, and the passage of many men and horses. This wasn't at all unusual. The Rootless had been arriving for the last three days, setting up tents a prudent distance from the river and picketing their horses. Looking upriver and down, Leland could see the dark tents and the rising smoke from fires.

The river was still dropping and not quite passable, but arrows had been exchanged across the water and a sentry from Acoma had been killed.

Leland focused the glass and watched. The tent was large and opulent, about a kilometer back from the river. There were guards and men who waited outside to see someone within.

"Maybe it's a brothel?" Leland suggested.

The coronet laughed. "Haven't seen any women, sir. But there's some big chief in there. A lot of the men waiting are commanders in their own right. See the sashes?"

Leland could see them. The men waiting wore woven sashes across their left shoulders down to their right hips. They didn't carry bows but were often attended by others who did. Unarmed men offered them food and drink while they waited. It was hard to tell from this distance, but they seemed like older men with touches of gray and white in their hair and beards.

*If that's not some sort of staff headquarters, I'll eat my socks.*

He handed the telescope back to the coronet and looked down through the hole in the platform. "Why is climbing down always so much harder than climbing up?"

Leland could tell that Coronet Gahnfeld both liked and hated the idea. "Out of the question. We haven't even been to the staff meeting yet!"

"That's just it," Leland said. "It would be nice to take something, some hard intelligence, *to* the staff meeting. We've got two days and, while the Rootless seem as thick as molasses between that camp and the fords, their pickets seem quite light between the cliffs across from us and that camp."

"Well, yes, but you can detach three squads from the Seventh. Byron can lead them since he's done so good at your camouflauge game. He's familiar with the Rootless, too. He's been in four campaigns."

"I'll need someone who knows their hierarchy. But I'm going, also."

"But—"

Leland held up his hand. "I'll not bend on that point, Myron. Just help pick the right men to come along."

Gahnfeld clamped his mouth shut and stared back at Leland for half a minute, then said, "Very well. I'll pick the men to accompany us."

"Us?"

"I might as well come along. If you get killed or captured I'll never be able to show my face in Laal again."

Leland thought about the improprieties of the commander and second-in-command both going behind enemy lines.

"Well, I won't tell if you won't."

The Pottsdam Engineers, from New New York, were working on several fords upriver, doing their best to make impassable barriers through the use of dams, trenches, and breastworks. Rootless riders, riding in and out of range, were delivering a sporadic shower of arrows. Each soldier working was accompanied by another carrying a large wood-and-felt shield. There were very few shields that didn't have at least one arrow in them, and more than few looked bristled, like a stand of wheat.

Leland found Captain Kuart supervising the placement of rows of sharpened logs in the gently sloping hillside above the river. He looked different without a *hakama* on. There were arrows sticking in the ground a few meters below where he was standing.

"Ah, de Laal. How goes it? Need some engineering at your site?"

"Sort of. I need a field ballista. Would you have one I could borrow?"

"A field ballista? What on earth for? Not exactly a cup of sugar. You need to knock down a wall or two?"

Leland told him. He'd just finished when an arrow, slanted steeply down, struck the ground beside Kuart's foot. The captain frowned down at the projectile then turned aside and shouted, "Halvidar Smith, has the wind shifted?"

A man standing on the top of the bank with a spyglass said, "No, sir. Some of them are riding closer."

"Instruct them in the error of their ways."

"Sir!" The man turned around, raised his signal fan, and gestured to someone on the other side of the rise. Leland couldn't read the signal—it wasn't the codes used by Laal. Smith held his fan straight up then and turned back to the river.

Leland looked across the river and saw another group of mounted Rootless ride toward it, arrows at the ready. He glanced back at Smith in time to see the halvidar drop his arm sharply.

There were three deep *thung* sounds in close succession and something flew overhead, thrumming like a hundred giant bees.

He turned his head in time to see dust fly up on the far bank and horses scream and rear. The charge turned into a rout and several horses fled ahead with empty saddles. Some horses were down, too, but their riders stayed with them, crouched low.

"Why don't they run?" he asked.

Gahnfeld answered him. "They have to tend their horses. If they can't get them up and moving, they'll cut their throats, but the Rootless won't leave a wounded horse on the field."

"What'd you hit them with?"

Kuart scratched his head. "About three hundred kilos of gravel. Well, not exactly gravel—the stones are grated between one half to one kilogram. Those mangonel can throw single rocks at a hundred kilos each, but the Rootless aren't much for fortifications. They prefer to fight in the open with fluid lines of battle."

Leland nodded. "About that ballista?"

"My word," Kuart said. "I don't know if I can justify lending you one of our pieces . . ."

Leland blinked, disappointed.

". . . unless I can come along, too. To make sure it's used properly and all that. Unit property, don't you know."

Leland smiled. "I don't think it will be a picnic, Captain. It could be quite dangerous."

Kuart leaned over and pulled the arrow by his foot from the ground and smiled. "And we engineers don't know *anything* about danger."

"But if you insist on coming along, I can't stop you."

"Well," said Kuart, "you probably could, *Sensei*, but I wish you wouldn't."

They rehearsed the operation in daylight, well away from the river, using trees an appropriate distance apart. Kuart brought a crew to operate the ballista, a horse-drawn giant crossbow with a seven-foot composite bow that was drawn by a three-man windless. It fired steel projectiles seven centimeters thick and two meters long.

They ran through the operation four times, the last two without any problems or mistakes. Leland pronounced himself satisfied and sent the men to rest.

After midnight he couldn't help but think, *We should have practiced blindfolded.*

They waited, in a tree on the Noram side of the river. The cliff was two meters away, and they were four meters off the ground. Below the ballista crew waited, as well.

Leland, his face itching from the charcoal smeared across it, heard a cricket chirp four times in succession—the signal, relayed along the cliff by the sentries. He strained his ears but couldn't hear anything but the roar of the river rapids below. Ring light, filtered by trees, cast dim patches of light and shadow across the other side. Then he saw them, the standard night patrol, about eight mounted men riding down the far path at a trot.

Over the last five days, Leland's sentries had recorded the passage of the patrols. Those at night moved by about once an hour, but that could vary by half an hour either way. Gahnfeld and Leland had agreed that they had at least twenty minutes to cross, though the sentries up- and downstream were primed to alert them if there was any unexpected activity.

Leland hoped there weren't any stationary sentries hidden on the far side, like their own.

They waited five minutes. When there were no unexpected signals from the sentries, Leland cleared his throat and said quietly, "Proceed."

The ballista sent its grappling hook–tipped projectile out into the darkness with a harsh *thwack*. Leland could barely hear the sound of the rope singing endwise off its painstakingly wound spool. He couldn't hear it land among the trees on the far side, but he heard the ballista squad running back into the trees, drawing the rope with them.

Kuart, on the branch below him, called down, "Well? Did it catch?"

"Yes, sir" came the hissed answer. "We can't budge it with six men."

There was motion below and the rope was passed up, from man to man waiting in the tree. Leland took the line and passed it above, to the four men above him. At the top, Gahnfeld fed it through the open-checked block of a pulley, then said, "Take up the slack."

Below the crew took the free end of the rope and pulled it back again, hauling until Gahnfeld called, "Good. Belay it!"

"Belayed!"

"Here goes nothing."

Despite the ring light and cloudless sky, Leland couldn't see the blackened line stretching across the gorge, but he saw the dim shape of Gahnfeld as he slid down the rope, hanging on his well-oiled pulley. The men moved up a branch each and the soldier at the top put his pulley on the rope and waited.

Gahnfeld was supposed to clear the end point, making sure there weren't any dangerous branches to run into, then strike the rope three times to signal the next man. Unless, of course, he'd been impaled on such himself. But the soldier above called down, "There's the signal." Then he launched himself.

The men moved up. By the time each man had properly positioned his pulley, the signal from the previous man thrummed in the rope. When it was Leland's turn, he closed his eyes and pushed out from the tree.

The rope slanted down about fifteen degrees, ten meters off the ground on this side and just about ground level on the far side, he hoped. Above the gorge, the white-noise roar of the rapids seemed to double in volume. Leland vividly pictured the wet rocks far below. Ahead, the dark mass of trees rushed at him and his imagination solidified them, making them a solid wall he'd slam into. Then he felt small branches whipping past and his feet skidded on earth.

He stopped himself, still standing. Hands reached out to steady him, but he said, "I'm all right." The soldier detailed to collect the pulleys held out his hand and Leland handed it to him, then he struck the rope three times with the flat of his hand. The rope thrummed under his hand as the next soldier started across. Leland stepped back away from the line and crouched against a tree.

It took less than two minutes for the remaining seven soldiers to cross. With Leland, Kuart, and Gahnfeld, plus two four-man squads from the Seventh, they were eleven in all. As soon as the last of them were off the rope, they cut the rope where it connected to the ballista projectile. The grappling hook and shaft they threw into the gorge. Leland felt cut off—isolated—but they'd agreed that the rope was likely to attract attention before they got back. Especially if a patrol rode directly into it where it crossed the path at the chest height of a mounted man.

"Ponchos," Gahnfeld said quietly. "Lucien and Laurel—take the point. Remember, we've got over an hour allocated to get there so take it *very* slow. If you guys miss a sentry we're all dead."

Everybody put on the camouflauged ponchos and pulled the hoods up. They'd been supplemented with netting, grass, pine needles, and Spanish moss and, especially in the patchy light of the rings, looked like nothing more than lumps of shrubbery.

They moved through the woods from tree to tree, crouching frequently to listen to the night. As they got away from the gorge and the sound of the rapids faded, the sounds of the night became more distinct: an owl, crickets, toads, and the distant wicker of horses.

The trees thinned but were replaced by patchy bushes and evergreen shrubs interspersed with knee-high grass. They could see the camp now, a collection of eight large tents surrounding a large fire. There were horse pickets to one side and latrines to the other. On the other side of the camp, perhaps another half kilometer away, they could see a much larger camp and more fires than they could conveniently count.

The first sentries were fifty meters out, stationed in pairs every fifteen meters or so and regularly checked by a mounted officer. Other mounted patrols, apparently based at the large camp beyond, occasionally passed the camp. This was probably the source of the men who patrolled the cliff top.

Closer to camp, standing just beyond the tents, was another set of sentries, facing out. These guards were only a few meters apart and challenged all who entered the camp.

Talking in whispers, Gahnfeld, Kuart, and Leland discussed the layout.

"Look," said Gahnfeld. "The sentries are thick as flies, and if they alert the larger camp over there, that's over a thousand men who'll be on us before we get a third of the way back to the Ganges."

Kuart nodded. "It's a point. I can't help but notice, though . . ."

"Notice what?" asked Gahnfeld.

"The bushes are thicker over there, behind the privies. Because of this, there's a spot where the sentries aren't as close together. Also, notice that the guards of the inner circle don't come out as far as the latrines."

Gahnfeld snorted. "Great. We can sneak up to the latrines. If I wanted to pee, I could do it just as well right here, thank you."

Leland smiled. "But the high and low all have to go sometime, Gahnfeld. We might hang around the privy and see what comes to us."

Gahnfeld wrinkled his nose. "As flies to shit? The big fish probably have chamber pots."

"Their aides probably don't," Kuart said. "And couriers with dispatches who want to lighten the load before hitting the road. It's worth a try."

Leland nodded. "It is indeed."

They took thirty minutes to creep around to the side of camp behind the latrines. They sat in clumps, against or in bushes, their legs tucked under their ponchos. Leland, sitting with Kuart and Gahnfeld, couldn't tell where the bushes ended and his soldiers started, even though he'd been watching as they moved. The wind freshened slightly and the stink of urine and feces drifted to them.

"Whew!" breathed Leland. "I see why the sentries aren't standing at just this point."

Gahnfeld replied, speaking, if anything, even quieter. "Yes. You were right about area of the perimeter. I don't think we should take more than three in."

Leland nodded. "Us three?"

"No! I'll take two men in. If we're discovered, get out—don't try to mount a rescue—that'll get all of us caught." He pulled his hand from under the edge of his poncho and showed Leland and Kuart a sand-filled blackjack.

Leland didn't like the thought of staying behind but something about the way Gahnfeld was holding his body convinced him that he wouldn't win this fight. "All right," he said.

Gahnfeld's head twisted, waiting for the "but I'm coming, too," but when it didn't come forth, he nodded and Leland saw his teeth gleam in the ring light. He slid slowly across the ground and tapped the shoulders of two of the other crouching soldiers.

Leland watched them creep forward and then vanish in the bushes, moving centimeters a minute, making no sound. He lifted his eyes and looked at the camp again. Fortunately, a large tent was between them and the fire, keeping the light from their night-adjusted eyes.

There were many awake. Small groups of men sat or stood, holding field cups. Others circulated with skins or flasks, replenishing wine and ale. An intermittent stream of men walked back and forth to the latrines, probably to give off a steady stream. The thought heightened Leland's awareness of his own bladder.

There was a lull at the latrine, then two figures, leaning on each other, stumbled away from a large group by the fire. Leland saw several soldiers seated nearby start to rise, but one of the figures, side-lit by the fire, waved his hand and said something that caused the men to sit back down, laughing.

*Interesting.*

The pair, alternately laughing and swearing, made their way around the edge of the tent and then back toward the latrine. They were backlit by the glow-rimmed tent, but they were alone and no one seemed to follow.

*Now, Gahnfeld,* he thought. There probably wouldn't be a better chance, and they could be the sort of fish they were after.

The bushes around the latrines were the thickest, probably chosen for privacy, so Leland couldn't see what happened when they reached the trenches. When the two figures didn't reappear in a few minutes, he figured Gahnfeld and the men had acted.

He licked his lips and watched the camp, hoping the two wouldn't be missed.

When Gahnfeld and the men showed up a few minutes later, they were still moving slowly, very low, to hide their profiles in the bushes. They were dragging another figure on a strip of netting. When they got close enough, Leland could see that the man was bound at ankles, knees, and waist, his hands tied behind him. He was gagged, as well, but his eyes were closed. The face was lined and bearded, dark hair shot with light streaks. Gold gleamed at his neck and belt.

"What about the other one?"

"We left him tied and gagged in the bushes." He hefted the blackjack. "Neither of them saw us, but if anybody misses them, the cry could go up, so let's get moving."

They spent thirty minutes moving slowly and quietly, to distance themselves from the camp, then, putting three men on each side of the prisoner, they picked him up by the edges of the net and advanced at a shuffle.

They'd just reached the edge of the trees when there was the harsh clanging of a iron triangle being struck repeatedly back at the camp.

"That's torn it!" Gahnfeld said. "At the run, gentlemen." They ran between the trees, the pine needle–covered floor silent under their feet. One of the soldiers carrying the net tripped on a root and three of them went down, spilling the prisoner, but he was snatched up again and they ran on the short distance left to the cliff.

As they listened, they heard the distant clanging spread as if *every* camp was sounding the alarm. They heard more and more hoofbeats as men took to horse, then they were near enough to the river that the sound of the rapids drowned out the clamor. They slowed to a walk and those not carrying the prisoner scuttled forward to check out the trail and look for the patrol.

For the moment, the immediate vicinity seemed safe. Leland reached into his shirt and took out a square of white cloth, oddly bright in the ring light. He waved it back and forth three times, then up and down three times.

There was an answering signal from across the gorge and then he heard the *thump* of the ballista firing. He heard the projectile crashing through the trees overhead. He couldn't see the rope or the projectile but heard branches rustle as the crew on the other side pulled the rope tight.

"Where is it, dammit!" he said.

Kuart pointed to their left and up. "Right here, I think."

The crew on the other side stopped pulling, and Leland looked across for the signal cloth. He held his own out so it could be seen and the cloth on the other side signaled *left.* He moved slowly to his left, the cloth still held out so they could see his position, and then the cloth across the gorge signaled *stop.*

He put away the cloth and spread his arms. The crew on the other side eased off on the rope, and it dropped across his shoulder. He turned and gave a tug at the end in the trees but it seemed firmly stuck.

"Is the prisoner ready?"

The prisoner had awakened and was struggling but ready. A pulley had been tied to the rope holding his ankles. Leland threaded it sideways into the block and slapped the cheek latch shut, then tugged on the rope three times. In response, the rope tightened, lifting the prisoner's feet off the ground, then his entire body. Leland heard his muffled yell from under the gag and saw him twisting harder as the pulley slid along the rope. The soldiers holding on let go, and, upside down, the prisoner slid over the gorge, running down the tightened rope to waiting hands.

After half a minute, the rope lowered again as the crew slacked off the line. The pulleys were passed out and Gahnfeld pointed at Leland, who laughed and pushed one of the soldiers to the line.

It wasn't as quick as their trip across, but it was effective. All but Kuart, Leland, and Gahnfeld had crossed. Gahnfeld made another attempt to get Leland to go, but Leland pointed at Kuart instead. The engineering captain shrugged and set his pulley on the rope. He was sliding on his way when the white cloth on the other side signaled *patrol coming.*

Leland and Gahnfeld shuffled back into the woods and crouched behind a tree, then flipped their hoods up over their heads. Leland hoped the crew on the other side would have the sense not to lower the rope back down.

He felt the hoofbeats in the ground before he heard them, and it seemed like far more than the eight horse of the usual patrol.

It was.

There were more horse than he could count and they came at the gallop, pounding up the trail from downstream. As they rode by, Leland flinched. The hooves were only a few feet in front of them but there were hundreds of them. Then the bulk of the party was past and the ground stilled.

However, they were no longer alone. Individual horsemen, fifteen meters apart, had been stationed facing into the forest. One of them stood a few meters off to their right, a man with long, braided hair who fingered his bow string compulsively while staring back into the woods.

*They hope to cut us off before we get across. Too late for our prisoner, but they don't know that.*

They crouched, still, their heads bent forward so their poncho hoods cast their faces in shadow. There was a rumbling in the ground.

*More?*

More. The next riders came with torches and lances, riding three abreast. The light cast by their torches lit the path and cast flickering light well into the trees.

Leland wanted to pull back but the area around their tree was well lit. He moved his eyes sideways, to look at Gahnfeld, and was relieved to see that, in the flickering yellow light, the vegetation-covered poncho looked no different from the other low brush at the trail's edge.

*Come on. Pass already.*

But they didn't. They just kept coming. After a while, Leland started counting them, then stopped again when he passed five hundred.

He looked up, turning his head very slowly to face the tree trunk, then tilting his eyes up. The blackened rope was visible, barely, in the torchlight, around eight meters above the trail, but so far none of the riders or posted sentries had noticed it.

The riders slowed, reining to a trot and then a walk. Then they stopped and turned their horses to face into the woods, an unbroken line standing stirrup to stirrup.

Leland slowly tilted his face down again, his hood allowing him to see no higher than the knees of the horses facing him, less than two meters away.

There was a spoken command, almost a grunt, relayed down the line of the horsemen, and then they moved, into the woods, at a slow walk.

The blunt end of a lance stabbed down to Leland's left, into the heart of one of the taller shrubs. The horse directly in front of him veered slightly around the trunk of the tree Leland and Gahnfeld were crouching against and put one foot and then another on Leland's poncho. The second foot brushed his calf, pinching a fold of skin between the hoof and the ground.

Leland bit into the cloth of his poncho to keep from yelling at the sudden pain. The horse walked on and Leland released the cloth from his teeth. Sweat broke out on his forehead. He longed to rub the back of his leg but remained still as the line of torchlight receded into the woods.

They left the original sentries, the ones without torches, the closest of whom was only a few meters off to the Leland's left. He shifted slightly until his head was next to Gahnfeld's. The roar of the rapids was a loud as ever and he didn't fear being overheard. "His eyes must still be affected by the torchlight. If we're going to move, it should be now."

Gahnfeld, still frozen, said, "Yes. Climb up to the rope on the side away from him. After you cross, I'll do the same."

Leland looked back at the other sentry, the one twelve meters to the left. He was screened by a spruce, the branches of which came almost to the ground. "No heroes. We'll both go up and cross together. But if it makes you feel better, I'll climb first."

"Yes, *Warden.*" Leland laughed under his breath and stood, slowly, keeping the trunk of the tree between himself and the nearest sentry. The tree was an old fir and the lower branches started about eight feet off the ground. He jumped and hung, freezing to assess any reaction. Then, when he didn't see or hear any reaction to his movement, he pulled himself up and climbed slowly, moving from branch to branch until he reached the lodged grappling hook of the ballista projectile.

It was higher than he'd expected. The cliff top on this side of the river was already higher than the other side, and this rope was at least seven meters off the ground. He looked down. The dark mass that was Gahnfeld's poncho was still at the base of tree, and Leland felt a twinge of irritation. He broke off the end of a small branch and dropped it between the branches to land on Gahnfeld's back.

*Come on, Gahnfeld!*

He felt the tree shift slightly and looked down the other side. Gahnfeld, without his poncho, was starting up the tree. He'd left the poncho behind, probably sliding out from under it as he shifted around the tree trunk.

Leland put his hand on the rope. It was slack, not pulled tight. He pulled on it and felt it shift in reaction, then tighten.

*Good lads.*

THEY'RE ALL OLDER THAN YOU.

*Excuse me. I'm trying to concentrate here?*

He felt something like a soundless chuckle and then nothing.

Gahnfeld joined him beneath the rope.

"Took you long enough."

Gahnfeld laughed quietly. "Ready?"

Leland brought his pulley up, hung it on the rope, and snapped the cheek block shut. Gahnfeld hung his pulley behind. They took hold of the handles.

"On three," Gahnfeld said.

Leland said, "Okay. *Three!*" He launched himself out into the void. Right behind him, swearing, came Gahnfeld.

The rope was much steeper than on their earlier crossing. The air rushing in Leland's ears rivaled the sound of the rapids below. He felt branches whip past him, then his feet struck the ground and he let go of the handle, falling into a forward roll, off at an angle away from the rope. Behind him, he heard Gahnfeld slam into the ground and heard him exhale explosively, the wind knocked out of him.

He came to his feet before the waiting hands reached him. "Did they see us?"

"No" came Kuart's voice out of the dark. "They were still watching the woods."

"Good." He looked at Gahnfeld, sitting on the ground and still trying to catch his breath. "Are you all right?"

The answer was a wheezing intake of breath.

"Oh," said Leland. "Where's Coronet Petroff?"

"Here, sir," a voice out of the darkness said.

"Who's on call?"

"The Third Hundred."

"Get 'em up. I want this rope pulled out of that tree before it gets light. Try thirty men at first, but get it out if it takes the entire Hundred."

"Yes, sir."

"And try to keep it quiet. It's bound to make some noise when it pulls out of the tree or breaks, but other than that, I don't want them to even *suspect* we're here. Carry on."

Coronet Petroff took off at a trot.

Leland turned back to the cluster of dark outlines. "Now, where's the prisoner?"

"We sent him back to camp," said Kuart. "I advised twenty guards and your men complied."

Leland laughed. "At least. Is he who I think he is?" As his eyes adjusted, the head around him were resolving into individuals.

Kuart nodded. "I shouldn't be surprised."

"When is the Marshall de Gant's staff meeting again? Midmorning?"

"Midmorning, with brunch," agreed Kuart.

"Then we needn't get him out of bed." Leland knelt beside Gahnfeld whose breathing was starting to sound normal. "You all right now?"

"Yes." Gahnfeld wheezed, then broke into a paroxysm of coughing.

When it had stilled, Leland asked, "Why'd you choose him?"

Gahnfeld laughed, which brought on another fit of coughing. Finally: "His companion told him, 'Don't fall in. Dobson was back here earlier and his piss would burn even royal skin.' "

"Well, that would explain their response, wouldn't it?"

"Yes," said Gahnfeld. "It would indeed."

# SIXTEEN

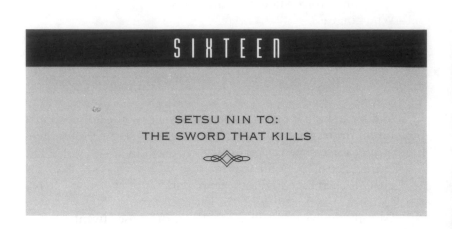

## SETSU NIN TO: THE SWORD THAT KILLS

Dexter was traveling fast, with just ten outriders. The coded message from his father said, "Urgent meeting at Laal Station. Return soonest."

His path, the fastest one, took him from his station in the west to the south, toward Cotswold, to avoid passes already thick with snow, then parallel to the Black for a ways before cutting northeast to the trunk road.

They were waiting for him where the road cut through Potter's Canyon, just before the switchbacks at the canyon's head. It was dusk and at first he thought they must be Ricard's Pikes, but their swords were slung low, not in a back scabbard. He turned his men before they were in bow range and headed back down the road.

He looked back over his shoulder, expecting hot pursuit, but the mounted soldiers were moving down the canyon at a trot, holding formation.

"They're driving us," he shouted to his aide. "They must be at the other end of the canyon, too." He spurred ahead and cut left into one of the many side canyons. It was a twisty dead end, he knew, but, if he remembered correctly, there were scalable spots in the canyon wall.

They rounded two curves, splashed across the shallow creek, and reined up where a series of short waterfalls descended to the join the stream. He pointed at two of the men. "Drive the horses to the head of the canyon and try to climb out there. Get to the Pikes or the militia—get word back to my father of this invasion."

The men paled but said, "Yes, sir." The rest dismounted and spread across the canyon, shouting and clapping their hands to get the horses moving in the right direction. The two soldiers still mounted harried them on from behind.

Dexter's lips pulled back from his teeth, a grin devoid of any humor. *If we can just keep them off us until sunset.* In the dark all things were possible. They scrambled up the hillside, paralleling the falls. One of his coronets whistled sharply and pointed down the canyon. They could see horses turning up the draw.

"Shit." He didn't think his men could reach the ridge top before the enemy arrived, and he was still well within bow range of the canyon floor.

"Sir! Over here!"

One of the men pointed at one of the smaller foliage-lined waterfalls beside him, then ducked behind it. His hand stuck out, beckoning the rest.

The nine men barely fit, crowded together, ankle-deep in water with mist drenching their clothes. Dexter stood at the edge using the shelter of a shrub to hide his head as he peered out at the soldiers passing below. An officer reined to a stop and looked up, then shouted. For a moment Dexter thought that they'd seen him, but then, barely audible over the falling water, he heard someone shout from above.

*They're on the ridge line, too.* Had they been spotted from above? Were the soldiers up top shouting directions to their hiding place? He wished he could hear *what* they were saying, but the officer pointed up the canyon and kept his men moving.

Dexter twisted, trying to see above, but a view of the ridge line was blocked by the lower escarpment. *Well, they couldn't have seen us, then.* If they'd made it to the top, they would've been snared like rabbits.

*Were they waiting for me specifically? If so, how did they know I was coming? And where the hell are Ricard's Pikes!*

Captain de Koss was not wondering where Ricard's Pikes were. He knew all too well. "Show me the message."

Ricard handed him the paper.

On the top of the page was a coded message, meaningless. Below, a signalman had translated it.

*To Ricard de Laal, Commanding Mounted Pikes. From Dulan de Laal. Cotswold crossing in force at Ft. Chavez. Reinforce Falcons there soonest. Militia will cover eastern fords. Best speed critical.*

"It's a fake. There's been no Cotswold troops sighted near here for the last week." Koss's eyes narrowed. *Did you fake this, Ricard? Why would you?* "I'm afraid our code has been compromised."

It was still predawn—the Pikes had traveled all night, waking the Falcons at Fort Chavez two hours before daybreak. Koss was still wearing a bathrobe, grim faced and tired.

Ricard's clothes were dusty and he looked exhausted. "I've got to get back to the eastern fords, then."

Koss closed his eyes and drew in a deep shuddering breath. He felt every one of his sixty-three years.

"Your men and horse are in no condition to travel. Besides, the eastern fords may not be where you're needed. If they've got our code and they've been monkeying with the heliograph stations, they could be *anywhere.* Get your men and mounts some rest. We'll have sunlight in another three hours. I'll break out the emergency cipher and see how much trouble we're really in."

Laal Station was built over the falls that gave Brandon-on-the-Falls its name. The mouth of an underground river opened in the face of a cliff fifty meters above the base. The Station grew up around it, using its output for running water, the community baths, mechanical water wheels for the shops and generators, and the hydraulic piston that lifted the thirty-seven metric tons of the Floating Stone, the main gate of Laal Station.

Carmen Cantle de Laal moved through the lowest passages of the station, a cloak pulled tight around her. These passages were damp with condensate and, while pleasant in the summer, were uncomfortable the rest of the year. It was well after midnight and she hadn't seen anyone. Only the watch on the walls and gate were awake at this hour, and, of course, the man who controlled the floodgate here in the depths.

The watchroom had a small iron stove and a flue that paralleled the speaker tube that led up through several levels to the guard station at the main gate. Carmen stuck her head through the open door and said, "Hello, Max."

Max, one of the regulars on this shift, straightened and bowed. "Good evening, Gentle Guide. Trouble sleeping?"

Carmen smiled. "As always. Spare a cup of tea?"

"As always."

"How's your family, Max? You still look much too young to be a grandfather."

He laughed. "What can I say? I married young and my daughter did, too. You're just lucky that your son hasn't married. He's old enough to have given you a half-dozen grandkids."

She shrugged. "Well, time enough for that later." She stood in front of the stove and spread her fingers to the heat. "No doubt in a couple of years we'll be comparing statistics on teething fevers and first steps." While he poured the cup of tea, she perched on the edge of one of the benches lining the room.

"You look nervous, Guide," Max observed.

Carmen started, then consciously slid back on the bench and leaned against the wall. "You're right, Max. I'm edgy. Whatever kept me from sleeping, no doubt. A premonition of trouble coming."

"Trouble? I shouldn't wonder. They'll be starting the campaign soon, over at the plain. That always means children who don't come back. My daughter's husband is there."

"Well, let's hope he gets back unharmed," she said, lifting her teacup.

He mirrored her movement and said, "Let's hope they all get back unharmed."

They drank the tea companionably. Then there came a voice from the speaker tube—St. George, the watch halvidar. "Max! Stand by the sluice gate. There's something odd going on outside."

Max rose, a surprised look on his face, and put his hand on the locking lever. The sluice gate was an iron door dropped into the channel below this room. The chain rose from a hole in the floor, through a massive block in the ceiling, and then to a counterweight. The locking lever operated a clamp bolted to the floor that held the chain tight, preventing the gate from rising and releasing the water pressure on the hydraulic piston that lifted the floating gate.

The piston arm, an iron shaft a third of a meter in diameter, rose from a hole in the floor to a hole in the ceiling. It had an index mark running up its length that was aligned with one of two marks on the ceiling, the one labeled OPEN.

"Standing by," he said into the speaking tube.

Carmen struck him then with the lead jack. He fell, hard, without a sound, the back of his head soft and red. She threw the lever and the chain rose, clattering through the block as the counterweight dropped into its wooden cradle. Below the sound of water running changed and, from above, came the sound rock grating against rock.

"Max! What are you doing? We haven't rotated the gate yet. It's still open! Get it back up so we can close it!" Carmen put her ear closer to the tube. In the background men were shouting and metal was striking metal.

Carmen held the back of her hand to her mouth then, staring down at Max, her eyes wide. With a shudder, she threw down the lead jack and said, "Sorry, Max. There's no going back now."

She closed her cloak tight around her and left the room.

Dillan sat upright in bed, spilling bedding off. His heart was hammering and his eyes were wide. *A nightmare,* he thought. And then he heard the alarm ringing and knew it was not dreams that disturbed his sleep.

He pushed his window open and looked out. The main court was full of men, more men than he thought were in the station. The alarm, a metal bell on the watchtower, stilled. For a moment he thought someone had ordered the alarm off—then, in the absence of the strident clamor, he heard sword work on the walls. An arrow, fired from above, streaked past a torch and down into the mass of men below. He heard a cry below, then a dozen archers returned fire from the court.

He stared and the most appalling fact of all penetrated his sleep-fogged brain.

*The gate is open!*

He pulled on pants and took his favorite sword from the rack by the door, gripping the scabbard in his left hand and holding the blade in place with his thumb on the guard. With bare feet, chest, and sword, he left the room.

His room opened on a balcony overlooking the west gallery. His study and private reception room were the only other rooms on this level. He took the narrow stairway several steps at a time then turned right, heading for the clamor—the main hall.

The oil lights in the passage were dimmed, turned down for the night by the staff. But one of those same lamps had been smashed in the main hall, and flames devoured curtains on the far wall, casting a yellow light through the room.

The two men closest had their backs to him but they wore their sword belts low over leather breaches—Cotswold cavalry. He killed them before they even knew he was there, drawing the sword and cutting straight across, through the kidney and spine of the first man, then straight down, *shomen,* into the back of the other's head before the dropped scabbard rattled on the floor.

As they fell he saw that most in the room were also Cotswold soldiers except for a knot of kitchen servants fighting desperately to hold the enemy at the passage to the kitchen—carving knives thrust between the cracks of a barricade of tables and chairs.

He took two more out, cutting one extended arm and deep into an outstretched leg behind the knee, before they noticed him, then they turned on him. He didn't stop, didn't let them concentrate their force on him. Three others fell back, cut, one after another, and he moved constantly, shifting so that those coming always had to move over or around the wounded and dying.

They stopped coming then, realizing that they were losing more men in this way. Someone shouted, "Get behind him," and they moved sideways, circling, but this failed when the kitchen staff, taking advantage of the distraction, threw flaming oil past the barricade, disrupting the growing circle.

Dillan took the wrists of two others and killed a soldier plunging by, his clothing on fire. There was lots of blood on the floor now, and he was forced to move more slowly to avoid slipping. A soldier charged him, sword high, and Dillan waited, sword held low and to one side, gripping lightly with both hands, his head slightly forward. The soldier took the bait, cutting down, and Dillan entered fast, going past the soldier and cutting deep into his abdomen. This took him to a drier part of the floor, and he moved on the next two men, one of whom flinched back, giving him time to pull the hip and cut the second man's arm as his sword flashed down past Dillan's head.

The flincher tried to strike then, while Dillan's sword was down, but Dillan slid left, putting the wounded man between them, then thrust over the falling man into the fleshy part of the flincher's arm and twisted. The man screamed and his sword clattered on the floor.

The kitchen staff, shoving the barricade inward, charged into the room. Bartholomew, thrusting a spear made out of a mop handle and a fileting knife, led the way, taking a soldier in the eye, whirling the shaft to block another sword, and then striking a face with the butt end. Irma, a cleaver in one hand and a cast-iron skillet in the other came behind him. One of the Cotswoldian's, thinking her an easy target, jumped at her and cut, but his sword broke on her skillet and she buried the cleaver in his forehead.

Two of the dishwashers, using pot lids as shields and tenderizing mallets as maces, flanked them, and Dillan dropped back beside Bartholomew. "Let's clear the hall," he said almost conversationally, then turned back toward the remaining cluster of enemy soldiers and screamed, "Laaaaaaaaaaaaaaaal!"

The ragtag group charged and the enemy soldiers broke and ran for the main passage. Dillan took one of them from behind, cutting the tendon at the heel, and one of the dishwashers bashed in the hamstrung soldier's head. The rest of the soldiers made it to the passageway.

Dillan charged after them, ahead of the kitchen staff, rounding the corner.

Both arrows struck him together, one in the thigh, the other in the lung. He just managed to shout "Back" to Bartholomew before the collapsed lung kept him from speaking, but it was the severed artery in the thigh that killed him.

Dulan wasn't asleep when the alarm went off but was instead sitting in his study looking over the latest intelligence reports from Captain Koss. He looked out the window and froze. His window was high enough to see over the wall. There were well over five hundred men out there and the gate was open.

He looked down at the reports, then dropped them to the floor—worthless and false. This many Cotswoldians here without warning and the gate open meant only one thing—a traitor inside.

He ignored the current code book lying on his desk and, instead, pulled open a cabinet beside the desk. The Glass Helm, on its stand, gleamed within. He took off his robe and wrapped the Helm tightly within, walking down the hallway as he did. They weren't at this level yet, but, as he passed the stairway, he heard the distant sound of fighting. He entered his bathroom and dropped to his knees on the large ceramic tiles. The one between the washstand and the bath shifted as he pushed *and* twisted, then he was able to tilt it up, revealing the chamber below. There was a bag of coins, some of his dead wife's jewelry being saved for little Lillian, and his father's diary. He pushed them to one side on the floor of the compartment, then pressed the corners of one of the sides in just the right sequence. Another tile, closer to the wall, popped up, revealing yet another hiding place.

The bundled Helm barely fit—Dulan had to stuff the extra cloak material hard into the corners before it would latch. He knocked on it and also on the surrounding tiles. There was a slight difference in sound, but it didn't sound hollow by any means.

He shut the first compartment and then went back to his room and dressed.

Lillian was in the town, in fact, had been since Leland left for Noramland. Her best friend, Odette de Swain, only two weeks older than she, was sharing her bedroom, and the girls were working out a long-shared fantasy about being sisters. Since Odette's mother, Matilda, had breast-fed the both of them when Lillian's mother died on the birth bed, this fantasy had some basis in fact.

The first she knew of trouble was when Matilda de Swain, candle in hand, woke them. "Get dressed, children. Hurry."

It might have been the candlelight, but Lillian thought Matilda white as snow. Neither girl asked questions, though, and they *did* hurry.

Downstairs, at the kitchen door, she handed them each a bag to sling over their shoulders and then leaned forward, putting her face at their level. "We're going up to the shepherd's cabin, but not by the sheep path. As soon as we're to the edge of town, we'll go straight up the hill. Understand?"

"My family?" Lillian asked quietly.

"We don't know. Hopefully they're all fine, but there are Cotswold soldiers in the town and up at the Station. We'll know more later."

Then they eased out the door and through the barn, threading their way through the backyards and stables of the neighbors, then the grove at the edge of the trees.

They paused often, listening, and, though they heard shouting and the clang of steel in the distance, they heard nothing nearby. The hill, after the first few terraces, was steep, and they climbed, digging their toes in and clutching tufts of grass to keep from sliding down.

Then, after half an hour, they reached one of the high streams and followed it into a wooded gully, using the trunks and branches of small trees to keep them from sliding as they climbed beside a series of waterfalls and pools. They used only their touch and the ring light to navigate and, more than once, had to backtrack to get around impassable rock cliffs. Here, in the shelter of the trees, they rested often, unlike their mad dash up the grassy slopes below.

Lillian had been groping from tree to tree for so long that she was surprised when she realized she could *see* her hand as it rested on the rock in front of her. She looked up and saw the gray of predawn sky. Suddenly the lack of sleep hit her and she yawned a great jaw joint–cracking yawn.

"Aunt Matilda, my 'drenaline is all run out. Can I have some more?"

Matilda, working up the slope below them lest one of children slip, laughed shortly, without humor. "It's not far, child. Try to hold on."

"All right."

The cabin was just below the treeline, sheltered in a mixed stand of bare poled aspen and stunted spruce. It was built into the side of the hill, bermed and buried, grass and late flowers sprouting from its roof. Two windows, shuttered, straddled the door, all facing down the mountain. The sheepfold beside it was empty, and there was no smoke from the chimney. The sheep had been moved down to the winter pens the month before, and, at this altitude, snow had already fallen more than once, though the only traces of it were deep in shadowed nooks on the north sides of rocks.

Matilda left the girls crouched behind the low branches of a spruce and went ahead, alone, to check it out. She vanished inside and was gone for so long that Lillian's wish—more 'drenaline—was granted, but then Matilda reappeared and waved them on in.

The cabin was empty, swept clean, the bedding stowed away in the cupboards and the perishables taken away, but wood and kindling were stacked in the fireplace, ready to be lit, and the oil lamps were full.

Matilda put the girls to work making the narrow bunks while she fixed a cold meal from the food they'd brought. When they'd eaten what they could, all three went to wash their faces where the icy stream ran behind the house.

The sun was over the ridge now, and the floor of the valley was well lit. If they stood at the edge of the trees, they could just make out the high bulk of the Station, on the other side of the valley above the falls.

The aspens at the lower altitudes were aflame with color and, in the valley, oak, maples, and fruit trees wore autumn's colors. The sky was patched with gray clouds and the wind was out of the west—where moisture from the sea came when it rained or—Lillian shivered in the chill breeze—when it snowed.

Matilda took a collapsible spyglass from her bag, removed it from its case, pulled it to length, and studied the town and the Station intently. She exhaled sharply, then collapsed the instrument and put it away. She turned back into the wood and led the way back to the cabin without speaking.

"To bed, girls."

"What did you see?" asked Lillian.

Matilda looked from Odette to Lillian, her face blank, still silent. Finally, after weighing it, she said, "I couldn't see much, but the banner of Laal on the Station Tower is down. Cotswold's hangs in its place."

*It's like throwing stones into an abyss.*

The Fort Chavez heliograph station was on the west tower, exposed to the wind and cold. The operator was dressed for it in heavy woolens and a long sheepskin coat, but Koss crouched behind the shelter of the north balustrade and held his hands next to the charcoal brazier.

They'd been at it for thirty minutes, but, aside from the acknowledgments of the first relay, thirty kilometers away, they'd heard nothing.

*They've got one of the towers between here and Laal Station and they're not passing the coded messages on. Well, not the new code. The old messages, though . . .*

He heard hoofbeats, coming fast, and lifted his head over the parapet. Three horseman were tearing down the road to the fort, trailing dust. "Lend me your glass," he said to the signalman. The operator put the spyglass in his outstretched hand, and he focused on the approaching group.

They had the shoulder badges of Anthony's couriers and, *yes!* Anthony himself was in the lead.

*Now maybe we'll find out what the hell is going on.*

Anthony stood before the fire in the main hall of the fort, staring at the flames but not seeing them. He didn't have any notion how they'd done it, but he was terrified that it was somehow his fault. *Damn you, Father—why do you always have to be right?*

He heard steps on the flagstones and turned. Captain Koss entered the room one step ahead of Ricard. Anthony blinked when he saw Ricard.

"Why are you *here?*" he said, voice rising.

Koss held up his hand. "A false message, supposedly from your father. The current code was broken or stolen, and they must've taken one of the signal stations in the past few days—one between Laal Station and Fort Lucinda probably, though the way this morning's messages are going, I'm afraid they have one between here and Laal, too."

Anthony closed his eyes. "There's over eight thousand Cotswold soldiers stretched along the trunk road. They stretch all the way from the Black River to Fort Bayard with most of them concentrating in the Tiber valley."

He took a deep shuddering breath. "There are very few refugees getting out, but the few who have claim that Laal Station has fallen."

# SEVENTEEN

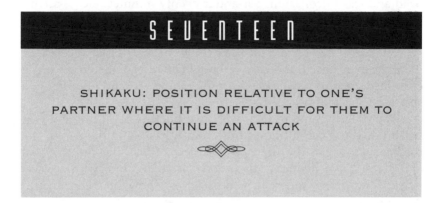

SHIKAKU: POSITION RELATIVE TO ONE'S PARTNER WHERE IT IS DIFFICULT FOR THEM TO CONTINUE AN ATTACK

When Leland limped into the back room of the small farmhouse, the four guards, one in each corner, came to attention but didn't take their eyes off the man sitting on the edge of Leland's cot. The prisoner was resting his elbows on his knees, his fingers supporting his head, but Leland saw his eyes gleam, watching the guards, then Leland.

Leland dropped to one knee and bowed his head briefly before standing again. The man sat up, narrowing his eyes.

*Yes, I know who you are.*

"How is your head?" Leland asked.

The man didn't speak, just glared.

Leland caught a glimpse of himself in the small mirror over the fireplace. His face was still blackened with charcoal and grease. He turned to the guard nearest the door. "Send for the unit medic, then ask my orderly to get us some hot water and wake the cook. We'll want tea and a simple sort of breakfast."

The man on the bed paled, then turned slightly green. Leland took the wash basin off the stand and set it on the floor near the bed.

The man glared at him and began taking deep breaths. His color improved. Leland put the basin back on the stand.

The guard returned, followed, after a few minutes, by the unit medic and his assistant.

"Are you hurt, Warden?" the medic asked, saluting.

Leland thought about the flesh on the back of his calf, where the horse had stepped on him. "Our guest was struck on the back of the head and was unconscious for about twenty minutes. Please attend him. Be thorough. If he's got a cerebral hemorrhage, I want to know *now* while we can still relieve the pressure."

The medic bowed and moved over to the seated man. For a moment the man tensed, and Leland thought he was going to resist being examined, then he acquiesced, turning to one side and pointing to a spot at the back of his head.

The orderly came in then with two buckets of steaming water. Leland diverted half a bucket to the wash basin and the rest to the medic, then began the tiresome business of washing the charcoal and grease from his face. His orderly presented him with a towel when he was done, and he turned back to see how the medical exam was coming.

"You're just a child!" The man's voice was rough. His first words had clearly been surprised out of him.

"A babe wandering in the wilderness," Leland agreed. "But then, most of us are, aren't we? Except for officers, how old do your men tend to be?"

"They're all old enough to fight," the man said mildly. Then his eyes narrowed. "To kill themselves a Noramlander."

The corners of Leland's mouth turned down. "Well, we're all old enough to die, that's for sure. Children included." He turned to the medic. "Prognosis?"

"Pardon, Warden?" The man looked puzzled.

"His injury. How's he doing?"

"Ah. Perhaps a slight concussion. He's got a very respectable knot but his vitals are good and I don't think he's more than bruised. Cold compresses and willow bark as needed. He shouldn't sleep for several hours and he should be watched, just in case."

Leland smiled. "I can assure you that he will be watched. That will be all, thank you."

The man didn't move. "Uh, sir. I noticed you're limping."

Leland sighed. "Oh, very well." He pulled off his boot and rolled up his pant leg. The cloth had stuck to the skin.

"Oh. How did you manage to do that, sir?"

Leland twisted to look at the leg. A massive bruise, seeping blood on one edge, spread across the back of his calf. Looking at it made it hurt more than it had. "A horse stepped on me," he said. "I suppose it should be cleaned."

"Yes, sir."

While the medic washed and bandaged his calf, his orderly and one of the cook's assistants set up a breakfast table. Leland replaced his boot and thanked the medic again. This time he and his assistant left.

Leland looked at his orderly, standing there with a towel draped over one arm. "We'll handle things," Leland said, and tilted his head to the door.

The man bowed and left.

Leland eyed his guest, then pointed to each of the guards in each of the corners and jerked his thumb to the door. "Gentleman, please wait outside."

The coronet in charge protested. "Sir! Are you sure this is wise?"

Leland considered throwing him out the window but said instead, "It's my call, isn't it? Please see that we aren't disturbed." The coronet started to open his mouth again, but something about Leland's steady gaze deterred him.

When the door had shut, Leland returned to the table, drew out a chair, and held it. "Your majesty?"

Roland, Master of Nullarbor, King of the Rootless, head of the Mantis Clan as well as all the confederated clans, glared at him, then stood slowly, one hand feeling the back of his head, and shuffled a few cautious steps across the floor.

WATCH IT!

Leland was already moving when the warning came, feinting at Roland's face as the man suddenly lunged for him, arms extended, then Leland dropped to his knees and pivoted into Roland's legs. The man flew forward completely off the ground. He didn't know the *ukemi* and slammed down onto the floor, breaking his fall with his arms, but still hitting the side of his face and shoulder on the floor before collapsing in a heap.

The door opened and a guard looked in, a worried look on his face. His eyes went from Leland, standing, to Roland, on the floor.

Leland frowned. "I do *not* want to be disturbed." The door shut, quickly.

Leland bent over Roland, worried. *Not the head!*

Roland's foot shot out, aimed at Leland's good leg. Leland shifted and the kick grazed his boot. He slid back, out of range, then picked up the chair, which had fallen over. He held it again.

"Please, your Majesty. You should rest. The last thing you need is *another* injury."

Roland stood and stalked Leland, walking carefully, catlike, across the room.

Leland sighed and pushed the chair back under the table, then slid forward, his head slightly forward. Roland took the bait, lunging forward to punch at Leland's face. Leland slid off the line and forward, then swept his arm over the extended punch as it just missed his chin, took the wrist in his other hand, and twisted and dropped, letting his weight come down on Roland's upper arm, locking the elbow and driving him to the floor again.

This time the fall was gentler, but Roland's arm was locked, the elbow at the limit of his extension. He tried to straighten the arm by brute force, and Leland expanded his chest. Roland grunted in pain as his elbow hyperextended and stopped resisting. Leland backed off, then released the arm suddenly and whipped his elbow over into Roland's exposed back, striking him over the kidney.

NOT TOO HARD.

*No.* Leland moved quickly away as the man spasmed, then stood again. He watched Roland get up, more slowly this time, a hand on his lower back. "Really, your Majesty. There are twenty guards around this house and around *them* are seven hundred and eighty more. What good will it do you to attack *me?*"

"I had over a thousand. It didn't stop *you.* Besides, I'll have a hostage." He was moving forward again.

Leland eyed the breakfast longingly, then moved well away from the table, to protect it. "It's not the same," he said weakly. "They didn't know I was coming."

Roland shifted closer, flexing his big hands. Leland extended his arm and Roland grabbed it with both hands. Half a second later Roland was facedown on the floor, his arm pinned to the floor at the elbow and wrist by all of Leland's weight.

YOU ACTUALLY DID THAT RIGHT. The inner voice sounded surprised.

Leland, irritated, said, "I would like your parole, sir. I'm hungry and I don't have time to play these games. If I don't get your parole, then I'm afraid I'll have to have you tied to a chair. Where's the courtesy in that?"

Roland tried one more time, pushing up against Leland's weight. Leland rolled the elbow forward slightly and Roland grunted. "Enough. Parole."

Leland didn't move. "On your clan name."

Roland gritted his teeth. "I, the Mantis, Roland Otis Felts, do give my parole. I swear by clan, family, and self."

Leland released him immediately and backed away. When Roland stood, this time rubbing his elbow and shoulder, Leland remained kneeling. "Would it please his Majesty to take tea?"

Roland frowned, then sat in the waiting chair. "It would."

Leland poured. "May I join you, your Majesty?"

"Why so polite?"

Leland frowned. "I sincerely apologize for any breech of courtesy you may have experienced."

"Oh, sit down. Who the *hell* are you?"

Leland sat opposite Roland. "Thank you. My name is Leland de Laal."

Roland groaned. "de Laal. Your father is Dulan?"

Leland nodded. "His fourth son."

"You don't look much like him."

"They say I take after my mother."

Roland drained the teacup and held it out for more. "Well, you are a lot of trouble, Leland de Laal. And in this, you *definitely* take after your father."

It was raining lightly when it was time to go to the meeting. They wore ponchos, even Roland, the green-and-brown oilcloth covering his finely embroidered leathers. Leland took Gahnfeld and an escort of four men. Kuart had returned to his unit before dawn but swore he wouldn't miss the staff meeting for any amount of love or money.

Marshall de Gant's headquarters was in the middle of a granary, most of the storage bins temporarily converted to housing of one kind or another. The headquarters was swarming with activity, couriers leaving and arriving, unit commanders and their aides arriving for the staff meeting, and soldiers filling sandbags and stacking them against walls.

Kuart and one of his halvidars rode up while Leland was arguing with Marshall de Gant's chief of staff.

"I'm sorry, Warden, but de Gant is meeting with his intelligence staff and told me he'd have my head if I disturbed him for anything short of the arrival of Roland and all his forces."

Roland began to laugh, earning a glare from Leland. Kuart,

in hearing, also started laughing. "But, Captain Pearson, you don't realize—"

Captain Pearson interrupted. "What I realize is that I've got too many things to take care of in the next five minutes to listen to jokes. You can talk to the marshall during the staff meeting." He turned abruptly and left, leaving Leland with his big news unsaid.

Roland said, "Close your mouth, boy. Something will nest in it. It's probably not too late to take me back to the river and let me go."

Leland shook his head. "Too late for that, I fear. Ever been to a Noramlander staff meeting?"

Roland grinned. "No."

"Well, then, it should be educational."

Gahnfeld closed his eyes. "For everyone."

Inside, Leland checked in with the halvidar at the door to the large conference room. "de Laal, Gahnfeld, and, uh"—he grinned suddenly—"Otis from the Eight Hundred."

Roland, beside him, laughed again.

They took seats near the front and Leland sent Gahnfeld over to the buffet for food. Roland's appetite had improved from the morning, and Leland surmised his head must be doing better.

Roland swallowed the last of a hard-boiled egg and washed it down with cider. "You did this on your own, eh, boy?"

"I'm afraid so," Leland agreed morosely.

"Why?"

"Well, to tell you the truth, we were just trolling for intelligence. If you hadn't ended up at the latrine when you did, it would've been somebody else."

Roland got a bleak look on his face. "And here I was wondering how the hell you targeted me. Well, you're scary, child, but not quite as scary as I thought."

Leland shrugged. "An opportunist."

"What do you expect to get out of this?"

"It would be nice if we could stop the fighting."

"Easily. Just vacate the Plain of the Founders," Roland said.

Leland started to say something when the staff halvidar at the door cleared his voice and said, "gentleman and ladies, the Gentle Guide Zanna de Noram."

Everyone shot to their feet—though, Leland noted, Roland rose slowly. Zanna came through the door with Marshall de Gant. She looked preoccupied but smiled briefly and raised her hand.

"At ease, please. I'm just a midge on the wall." She took a seat off to one side.

de Gant continued to the front and stood. "This was supposed to be a simple staff conference, a preliminary event before the real thing began, but we don't have that luxury anymore."

Leland stood.

de Gant glared at him. "Sit down, de Laal. Captain Pearson's told me you wish to speak to me. It'll have to wait."

Leland opened his mouth, then closed it. Sitting, he said, "As you wish, sir."

Beside him, Roland said quietly, "*That's* telling him."

de Gant went on. "As those of you who aren't blind know, the Rootless have been stirred like a swarm of bees. Sometime early this morning, they mobilized and began patrolling their side of the river vigorously. Our agents in their forces now inform us that King Roland has disappeared from his encampment, apparently without *anybody* knowing how or why."

Roland raised his eyebrows and looked at Leland. "Agents? How *interesting*."

Leland thought about the proprieties of an enemy commander listening in on a classified staff conference and closed his eyes.

de Gant was still talking. "—the disappearance has resulted in a schism in their forces. The Cricket Clan is claiming the succession and the Mantis Clan, accusing the Cricket of assassinating Roland, has stepped forward with their claim."

Leland looked at Roland.

First smiling, Roland was now pale and his face a grim line. He muttered, "I'm going to *kill* that bastard Dobson."

"So," de Gant continued, "we have before us a golden opportunity. Do we strike now, while their command structure is in chaos, or do we wait and see if they'll come to open combat and do our work for us?"

"This has gone far enough!" Roland said loudly.

de Gant narrowed his eyes and looked from Roland's poncho to Leland's. "Is this man with you, de Laal? If you can't control him, I'll eject him from these proceedings."

Leland stood. "That, sir, would be a grave mistake." Aside to Roland he said, "Take off your poncho."

Roland pulled the poncho off and let it drop to the floor. At first, de Gant only saw the embroidered leathers and the sash of a Nullarbor commander, then his eyes moved to the face.

"Roland! My god. What are you doing—"

There was an outburst from the assembled officers and the rest of de Gant's question was drowned out. Only Leland heard Roland mutter "Slumming" in reply.

de Gant held up his hand for silence. "—iet! That's better. What are you doing here, your Majesty?"

Roland shook his head and gestured to Leland. "I'm this child's pri—"

"Guest," interrupted Leland. "His Majesty is here secretly in hopes of initiating certain negotiations with Noramland. He crossed the Ganges this morning"—very early this morning—"and requested safe passage."

Under his breath, Roland said, "What are you pulling, child?"

de Gant asked, "What sort of negotiations?"

Leland gestured to the room at large. "With no disrespect to my fellow officers, this large an audience does not lend itself to *secret*."

de Gant frowned. "Perhaps you're right. Gentlemen, please return to your units. I want everybody on full alert status. Even with his Majesty talking to us, I don't want to risk an accidental invasion by one of those out-of-control clans." He turned back to Roland and Leland. "His Majesty, de Laal, myself, and the Gentle Guide de Noram."

Leland looked around at Kuart, two rows back. The engineer was glaring at him. *Trust me,* he mouthed. Kuart rolled his eyes up and sighed heavily, then nodded.

de Gant tilted his head toward the door, almost bemused. "This way, please."

Roland stood but let the others precede them before he said to Leland alone, "What are you doing, child?"

"Would you rather be here as an envoy or as a prisoner of a . . . *child?*"

"Not a great choice. Either way, I look the fool what with my clan chiefs squabbling among themselves."

"Yes, but a prisoner doesn't have the ability to return quickly and settle that. An envoy does."

Roland stared Leland, his brows furrowed. "What do *you* get out of this?"

"As I said, an end to the fighting."

Roland shook his head. "If I were to lead our forces away without a fight while Noram still held the Sacred Plain, I wouldn't last a week.

They'd depose me, pick that bastard Dobson, and attack in force, wastefully, killing thousands on both sides. Do you want that?"

Leland shook his head. "Of course not. But who said you had to walk away with *nothing?*"

Three hours later Leland and his men escorted Roland to the Ganges, a ford in Captain Kuart's area that was close to Roland's camp and, most important, patrolled by members of Roland's clan, the Mantis. Leland rode down into the river, alone, a flag of truce resting in his stirrup and streaming sideways in the wind. *If they can't see that, they're blind.*

OR THEY CHOOSE NOT TO.

The Rootless on the other side rearranged themselves, and after a moment a commander rode slowly down and out into the shallow water. "We have nothing to say to you," he said harshly. "And you have nothing to say that can interest us."

*Then why are you here?* "I understand. However, one awaits above whose words *will* interest you." He waved the flag from side to side without taking his eyes from the Nullarbor officer. The man's eyes narrowed as he watched something over Leland's shoulder, then widened and his mouth dropped open.

Roland rode into the water and stopped beside Leland.

The Nullarbor officer swung down off his horse into knee-deep water and dropped to one knee. Leland winced. This water was snowmelt two days old, but if it bothered the officer he didn't show it.

"Get up, McCain," said Roland.

"Are you all right, sire?" McCain asked as he swung back into the saddle.

"Well enough. I need an escort back to headquarters and a cloak, to cover my head. I have a surprise for Dobson that he'll remember for the rest of his brief life."

McCain grinned savagely. "Yes, sir!"

"Right, then. Go along and get things organized. I'll be right up."

McCain frowned and looked from Leland to Roland.

Roland sighed. "I've been safe in his company for the last twelve hours. Another minute won't hurt."

"Sir!" McCain splashed his horse through the water and galloped up the hill.

"Well, boy, it's started. Tomorrow we'll continue the negotiations on my side of the river—a good touch, that." He looked down at the water. "You might not get what you want out of this."

Leland nodded. "But you'll try?"

Roland sighed. "Yes. I wouldn't mind a winter without mourning."

Leland bowed his head. "That's all I can ask. I release you from your parole."

Roland laughed. "Oh, don't tempt me. Perhaps you'd like to be *my* prisoner for a while, child."

"I'm sure it would be interesting, your Majesty."

Roland got a sour look on his face. "I don't think I have enough guards. I'll pass. Tomorrow, boy."

Leland watched him ride all the way up the bank and into the waiting group of horseman before he turned his horse and rode back up the hill.

*That was either the wisest or stupidest thing I've ever done.*

"Confess."

"Excuse me, Gentle Guide?"

They were alone in Zanna's quarters. She'd ordered Leland brought to her after he'd escorted Roland back to the river. She was sitting on a *zafu,* cross-legged, her knees touching a thick carpet. Rich cloth hangings, the product of Charly's looms, covered the walls, turning the utilitarian room into something familiar and warm. Zanna kept her back straight and cupped her hands in her lap, thumbs touching in a posture she'd copied from Charly.

"Come on, Leland. I was watching Roland's face. These negotiations were as big a surprise to him as they were to us. What was he really doing over here?"

Leland, seated *seiza* on the hard stone floor at the edge of the carpet, licked his lips and cleared his throat. "Um. I was surprised to see you, Gentle Guide. I thought you weren't coming up here until next week."

*That does it! See if I offer you a cushion.* "I changed my mind, just like *you* just changed the subject." She leaned forward slightly and narrowed her eyes.

"Well, I was out walking last night with Captain Kuart of the Pottsdam Pikes and a few of my men when we ran across his Majesty. We offered to escort him here." Leland face was still—almost frozen—but there was a slight tic in his right cheek.

Zanna crossed her arms and said, "Uh-huh. And where was Roland when this chance meeting occurred?"

"We ran into him in a latrine."

"Oh, so you guys were just standing around your unit latrine comparing dicks and his Majesty walks in?"

Leland cleared his throat again. "Well, it wasn't our latrine, actually."

*Now we're getting to it.* "Whose was it then?"

"Uh, Roland's. I mean, it was his camp latrine, not the chamber pot he keeps in his tent." The tips of Leland's ears were turning red.

Zanna blinked, surprised despite herself. "Roland's—on the other side of the river? In enemy territory?"

Leland shrugged. "Well, I admit we might have been a little *lost,* but we managed to find our way back without losing anyone."

"You kidnapped him!"

"A prisoner of war," Leland amended. As she continued to stare at him he said, "Well, yes. We kidnapped him."

"Why didn't you say so? That's what Roland was going to say, wasn't it, when you interrupted him?"

Leland spread his hands apart in a vague gesture, then let them drop back into his lap. "I believe so."

"Why did you turn it into a diplomatic mission?"

"I didn't know someone would try to seize power the minute he was gone. I realized he couldn't do anything for us if the powers in control on the other side *didn't want him back.*"

Zanna shook her head. "What use is he to us now? He'll be back in control and have the clans united under him. We could have kept him and attacked while they were still confused."

Leland shook his head. "Nothing ends internal squabbles faster than external threats. They would've forgotten their differences long enough to fight hard. Hundred, maybe thousands, would die."

Zanna sighed, suddenly tired. "This *is* war, Leland."

Leland looked at her. "Why?"

She deliberately misunderstood him. "Why is it war? Because it's an armed conflict between nations."

Leland refused to be distracted. "Why are you at war? Is it because you want access to the Sacred Plain, or because your father wishes to funnel the military aggression of Noram stewardships at an external rather than internal target?"

Zanna narrowed her eyes. "The plain, of course." But her brow furrowed as she thought of the implications of his statement.

"So, if you can get access to the plain without bloodshed, wouldn't that be a good thing?"

She stared past him, considering. Finally she said, "What makes you think it's possible?"

"It only takes one to make war, but it takes two to make peace. Roland will try. We have an . . . understanding. It's not a guarantee. He has to get something out of this negotiation that will satisfy his people, but he is not . . . inflexible."

Zanna tapped her chin meditatively. *What sort of understanding?* She waited for him to squirm, to show some sign of discomfort, but he sat there calmly, as if his shins rested on feathers instead of flagstones. She made up her mind.

"I wanted to talk to you before I heliographed my father," she said. "Marilyn's been working on him about this very thing, perhaps starting some sort of dialog during the prisoner exchanges that always follow the fighting. But that was going to be *after* the conflict.

"If you really think there's a chance that Roland will treat this seriously, I'll recommend giving it a shot to Father. de Gant will also endorse it. He thought this morning's session was very promising, mostly because Roland has a good reason to devote some attention inward rather than outward just now."

Leland licked his lips. "I think it's a good risk—not a sure thing, but worth pursuing. If I may suggest, however, I wouldn't mention my name in your report."

She'd already reached the same conclusion but said, teasing, "Afraid it'll turn into a fiasco and you'll get the blame?"

Leland shook his head. "No. I'm afraid your father will react negatively if I'm associated with it. He doesn't seem to like me. I'd hate to see this fall just because I've displeased him somehow."

Zanna sighed. "Yes. I know. I don't know what sort of knot he's got in his dick about you, but I agree. Let's see if we can get him to do the right thing despite it."

Gahnfeld was talking to a woman in dusty riding clothes, a sword carried in a back sheath, as the Falcons did. Leland didn't recognize her but something about her made him think of home.

Gahnfeld turned to look at the door leading into Zanna's quarters and saw Leland. His expression showed a quick flash of relief before going back to brow-twisting worry.

"Something wrong, Myron?"

Gahnfeld nodded, then gestured toward the woman. "This is Halvidar Miyamoto—she's one of Captain Koss's intelligence operatives."

Leland returned her salute. "Pleased to meet you, Halvidar. What are you doing here?"

Gahnfeld interrupted before she spoke. "Excuse me, sir, but may I suggest we move someplace less *public?*"

Zanna de Noram's guards were standing three meters away from them and de Gant staffers walked past frequently. Leland nodded and led the way toward the stables, stopping by a corral full of horses but empty of humans.

Gahnfeld said, "Tell him what you told me."

The woman glanced around, then said, "Captain Koss had us set up a direct heliograph line across Pree and Napa to link with your forces here. We've been in place about three weeks."

Leland blinked. "Why? What's wrong with the main line through Noram City?"

"Captain Koss did not say. However, two hours ago we received word, over the line, that Cotswold has invaded Laal in force. Preliminary estimates are crude but the numbers seem to indicate over nine thousand men are in the stewardship with a third of them concentrated at Fort Bayard."

"The passes," Leland said flatly. "Nine thousand men? But that means he has only a thousand left in Cotswold. What about the Station? My father?"

"We don't know. Any traffic sent from Apsheron into Laal on the established stations is suspect. When using the emergency code, they get no response. Using the old code gets messages back but they're flat-out wrong, saying everything is fine, what invasion? It seems as if they must have some of the Stations and they broke the regular code."

Leland turned to Gahnfeld, "You haven't heard anything about this? There are no rumors flying around camp about trouble in Laal?"

Gahnfeld shook his head.

"Excuse us a minute, please." Leland led Gahnfeld several meters to the side. "You're sure of this woman?"

"I worked with Miyamoto—very, uh, closely." Gahnfeld blushed. "Koss trusted her with his most sensitive material."

"Shit. Take her back to the unit and wait for me."

Gahnfeld called after him, "Where are you going?"

"I'm going to see what I can find out from de Gant's signal office."

Zanna sat in de Gant's desk chair and watched Leland pace back and forth across the room. "We've sent queries. There's no reported trouble in Laal," she said. "Surely my father would've said something when he sent instructions to proceed with the negotiations."

"I'm sure Miyamoto is right. Cotswold broke the treaty and is occupying one of Noram's stewardships."

Zanna frowned. "Surely this is questionable? How could he expect to get away with it? Even if he could hold the passes until the spring, we'd get in there eventually. He couldn't hold it."

"No, but he could loot it and retreat back across the Black."

"We just don't know," said de Gant, standing to the side of Zanna. "Maybe there's weather in the mountains. It *is* getting on to winter."

"Then Miyamoto's signal line couldn't reach Ashperon. I've got to get back to Laal," Leland said.

"Wait until you know for sure," said Zanna. "Think about the talks. Roland listens to you for some reason."

"Roland will deal fairly whether I'm here or not."

de Gant shrugged. "Very well. Who will you leave in charge, Gahnfeld?"

Leland looked at de Gant, eyes wide. "I won't leave a single man behind. If Cotswold has invaded Laal, I'll need every one of them there."

de Gant looked tired. "And I'd have to arrest you for desertion in the face of the enemy."

"What! Roland's not the enemy. Siegfried is."

"We don't know that. Wait until we know more," the old soldier said. He turned to Zanna. "I don't know why, but your father told me to strictly control the units here at the front. He specifically told me not to let any units leave the front without his permission."

Zanna stared at de Gant, eyes suddenly wide. *Father? Did you know about this ahead of time?* She licked her lips. "Send a message asking permission for Leland's unit return to Laal."

de Gant nodded. "Yes, Gentle Guide. And if he says no?"

Zanna looked at Leland. "We'll just have to see."

Leland was preternaturally still, staring past them. After a minute he said almost absently, "Yes, we'll just have to see."

Leland left one of his men at headquarters to bring the results of de Gant's query when it arrived, then rode back to his unit. His face was still but his mind was flooded with images and thoughts.

"Gahnfeld, get the unit ready to move. Then come get me when we hear what Arthur has to say. I'll be in my room. I don't want to be disturbed until then."

"Yes, Guide."

Leland chased his orderly away and took off his boots. Then he put a cushion on the floor and sat *zazen,* legs crossed, knees just touching the floor, his hands cupped together. He did timed breathing, exhaling to the count of ten, then inhaling at the same rate.

LET GO OF THE WORRY, THE PANIC, THE FEAR FOR YOUR BROTHERS, YOUR SISTER, YOUR FRIENDS, AND, YES, EVEN YOUR FATHER.

The thoughts were still there but he let them drift across his consciousness without following them, without attaching to them. He was surprised when the knock came at the door.

"Enter."

It was Gahnfeld.

"I thought I told you not to come until we've heard from Marshall de Gant?"

"Yes, Guide. We have. Tobias just returned."

Leland blinked, then started to stand. His knees were very stiff. "How long have I been in here?"

"Almost an hour."

"Oh. What's the word?"

Gahnfeld's mouth twisted like he'd tasted something foul. "Permission denied. No forces to leave the front until a negotiated peace is ratified by Arthur personally or the winter snows end the fighting."

Leland nodded, not surprised at all.

"Shall I have the men stop preparations to leave?"

Leland shook his head. "No. Have them ready to leave by morning."

Gahnfeld blinked. "We won't do Laal any good by fighting the forces of Noramland."

Leland shook his head again. "Don't worry. We'll save our swords for Cotswold." He sat on the edge of his bunk and said, "I have to go speak to his nibs."

"Marshall de Gant?"

"No. Roland."

It was dusk when Leland and Gahnfeld led the Third Hundred, on foot, to the cliff's edge. Leland pointed to a thirty-five-meter tall fir tree three meters back from the edge. "That one."

Four soldiers with axes walked forward. Two of them began chopping into the tree on the side away from the cliff, alternating blows evenly. The other two chopped into the side facing the gorge lower than the first and the noise became a staccato beat. When the higher notch was about a third of the way through, those two soldiers turned to a younger tree, ten meters high, and felled and trimmed it.

Twenty men took up the smaller tree and braced it against the first, pushing against the larger tree five meters above the cut, pressing toward the gorge. The four axmen continued cutting on the lower notch, stepping in and out as their turn came.

Leland watched the far side of the gorge. As he'd suspected, it was better patrolled now. A few moments after the chopping began, he saw a head looking from behind a tree and, a few moments later, several men rode up on horseback. They had bows and Leland watched carefully, worried about an incident.

He eyed the progress of the tree. The bottom notch was almost halfway through the tree and the pushing was having a noticeable effect, swaying the tree slightly.

The men on the other side, also watching the tree, had moved to both sides, out of the way.

The segment of trunk between the notches parted with a deep groan and all involved scrambled away from the tree as it fell over the gorge. It crashed down on both sides and, on Leland's side, a meter-deep section of cliff top crumbled and dropped into the gorge. Its impact on the other side was softened by the breaking of branches, and it stopped, wedged on the far side between trees.

The officer on the other side motioned, and all his men drew arrows and nocked them.

Leland got out the flag of truce and waved it.

He could see the officer frown, then say something to his men. They pointed their bows at the ground and waited.

Leland handed the flag to Gahnfeld.

Gahnfeld took it. "Are you sure it's all right? That tree hit awful hard."

"Do you see any cracks in the trunk?" Leland asked.

Gahnfeld shook his head.

"Good. If they try to cross, burn it, right?" Leland hopped up on the trunk and walked out over the gorge. The first half was the hard part. Though the trunk was broader, the branches didn't start until later and Leland had nothing to hold on to. He thought seriously about sitting down and scooting across, straddling it.

IT'S WIDE AS ANY PATH. JUST WALK.

He sighed and did that, putting his mind two inches below his navel. Still, when he reached the branches and had handholds, he felt much better.

The Nullarbor officer waiting on the far side was suspicious and Leland didn't blame him in the least. "Why didn't you do this at one of the fords?"

Leland shrugged. "I don't control a ford. I need to talk to his Majesty, King Roland."

The officer shrugged. "Then come to the meeting tomorrow."

Leland sighed. "I have information for Roland that can't wait and, if he has to wait until tomorrow, he will *not* be happy."

"And if this turns out to be some sort of trick, he'll stake you to the plain and stretch your entrails ten meters."

Leland smiled. "Just be sure they're not *your* entrails."

They brought him into camp on foot, hands tied behind his back and a rope around his neck leading to the officer's saddle.

They made him wait while the officer went through his chain of command, ending up with a commander Leland recognized—McCain, the officer who'd met Roland at the ford.

"So it *is* you," McCain said. To his captor he said, "Bring him."

McCain didn't say anything about untying Leland so Leland shuffled along trying to walk as if he were just clasping his hands behind his back. The rope around his neck spoiled the effect, though, especially when the man at the other end kept jerking him to a halt, then shoving him forward again.

They entered the largest tent in the camp, a multipoled affair over five meters high and fifteen meters across. Oil lamps hung on the poles and a few tripod-mounted braziers heated air already warm from the body heat of its occupants.

Roland was sitting on a field chair at one end of the space. There were perhaps thirty men, commanders and clan chiefs, inside, standing around the sides of the tent listening to a large man in the open area.

Leland focused on what he was saying.

"—and why didn't anybody know of this negotiation ahead of time? I say it's because it's not a negotiation—it's treason. He's selling us out to the technocrats—not negotiating, but betraying!"

Leland blinked and turned to McCain. "Let me guess—Dobson?"

"The Cricket," McCain corrected.

"He's *not* Dobson?"

"He is. But the clan chiefs are referred to by the clan name."

"Isn't he in enough trouble without this rhetoric?"

McCain exhaled sharply. "This is his only chance of *not* dying. If he convinces enough of the clan chiefs that his charges are true, they'll depose Roland and his premature coups will become a reality."

"—is this the king you want? This old man who hasn't the courage to fight for the plain?"

Roland, watching Dobson with something akin to boredom, yawned pointedly. His eyes strayed and he saw Leland.

Leland expected him to call them forward, but instead a speculative expression appeared on Roland's face. After a moment he stood as Dobson finished another sentence.

"Fitness, is it? I would challenge you for that, if I were allowed to, just as you would have long ago challenged me. However, I can think of a . . . *fit* . . . test. Let's see how fit *you* are to rule."

Dobson spat on the grass between them. There was a dark mutter from many of the men in the room, but Leland could see some of the others nodding in approval.

"Name your test," said Dobson.

Roland gestured then at McCain. "Bring that prisoner here."

Leland blinked and swore to himself.

I BET I KNOW WHAT, OR *who*, THE TEST IS.

*Oh, shut up.*

McCain, the guards, and Leland walked across the grass. Leland tried to look as unthreatening as possible.

Roland pointed at the rope. "Cut him loose."

Leland felt a knife slide between his hands and the ropes fell away. He rubbed his wrists while the rope was removed from his neck.

Roland gestured at Leland as he said to Dobson, "Think you can take him?"

Dobson looked at Leland.

Leland smiled weakly.

Dobson snorted contemptuously. "What is this, one of your Noram masters? Are you led by children?"

Roland said clearly, "I'm led by the interests of our people. And I say *you* can't even defeat this child, much less lead our people against his."

Leland looked at Roland and said quietly, "Is now not a good time? I could come back later. No trouble, really."

Roland ignored him and said to Dobson, "Would you like a weapon? He looks pretty dangerous."

Dobson turned to the crowd and said loudly, "Does a warrior fight *children?*"

Roland said, "Do you fight *anybody?* Or do you always wait until their backs are turned or they're away?"

This remark raised a reaction from the audience and Dobson shrugged. "Very well—I'll spank this child for you."

Roland prodded Leland from behind.

*May as well get it over with quickly.* He stumbled forward, as if Roland had shoved him.

Dobson laughed and stepped forward, reaching out for Leland's shirt front.

Leland took the man's wrist and elbow and pushed across slowly, as if doing *ikkyo.* Dobson sneered and pushed back, easily overcoming the motion, but that's what Leland wanted. He stepped in under the arm and across Dobson's front, turning and dropping to his knees while he extended his arms forward. Dobson's forward push became a fall, totally unexpected, and, rather than roll, he tried to stop himself.

BIG MISTAKE.

Dobson's shoulder and the side of this head crashed into the grass floor and his body folded on top of him, landing in an awkward heap.

Leland stood and backed away from the man, waiting for him to get up, but he didn't.

Roland gestured and McCain went forward, bending by Dobson's side. "Dobson? You can get up now." He frowned when there was no response. He moved forward slowly, then eased the body over.

Leland felt the blood drain from his face. *I didn't mean to . . .*

Dobson stared at the ceiling with unseeing eyes, his neck folded over at an unnatural angle.

IT WAS AN ACCIDENT . . . BUT I KNOW HOW YOU FEEL.

McCain looked at Leland and raised his eyebrows before standing and saying loudly, "His neck is broken. He's dead."

Roland brushed his hands together as if removing dust and said in a voice suddenly iron hard, "Thank you for coming. That will be *all* for now."

Leland remained standing by the body as the chiefs and commanders filed out. Then, when the guards pulled the tent flaps closed, leaving only Roland, McCain, and the guards who'd brought him into the tent, Leland turned to the side and vomited.

McCain took a step toward him and Leland's voice was savage. *"Get away from me!"*

Perhaps he was afraid of getting vomited on or, perhaps it was the clear reminder of Dobson's body, lying there—in any case, McCain blinked and took a step away.

Roland walked back to a small table by his chair and poured liquid from a pitcher into a tall mug. He brought it back and held it out to Leland. "Rinse your mouth," he said.

Leland thought about striking the mug from his hand but the taste in his mouth changed his mind. He took it and filled his mouth—wine. He swished it around his teeth, then spat it onto the grass.

"So," said Roland, "didn't mean to kill him, eh?"

Leland shook his head.

Roland nodded. "Well, I'll not lie to you. You just saved me a great deal of trouble. Humiliation is more what I had in mind, but this works on so many more levels. He's dead and, in a sense, it was in combat, against the enemy. Not an execution. His clan won't be an inclined to make trouble with me, and I *know* his heir won't—the man couldn't stand Dobson."

Leland stared at the body and didn't say anything.

Roland slapped Leland on the back. "Don't look so glum, boy. The world is a better place without him—he was the most aggressive of my chiefs. If he had his way we would be at war with your people year around on all borders—not just the plain."

Leland swallowed convulsively and looked away.

Roland said, "You'd think you'd never killed a man before."

Leland said bitterly, "Thousands. One a day, before breakfast, to get the blood . . . flowing."

Roland stared at him. "Your first, was it?"

Leland shrugged.

Roland pointed to the corpse and said, "McCain, have these men deliver the body to his heir. Put him on a litter and hold it high, like a returning hero. You go—tell him that the funeral will be at daybreak, all clan chiefs attending. Send notice to them all, then join me in my quarters."

McCain nodded toward Leland. "Do you want me to fetch more men?"

Roland shook his head.

One of the guards opened his mouth, as if to protest, and Roland pointed at Leland and snarled, "Go! You want me to sic *him* on you?"

The guards lifted Dobson's body and left.

Roland sighed and looked down at the spot Dobson's body had occupied. "In a way, child, you brought this on yourself. Dobson wouldn't have moved for the throne if you hadn't snatched me away. All our actions have unexpected consequences."

Leland gritted his teeth. *You didn't have to create that confrontation.*

Roland may have sensed the thought. "You've used me to your ends. Now I've done the same to you. See how *you* like it." He led the way through the back of the tent into a smaller tented room. Here the floor was covered with a patchwork of carpet and sheepskins.

"Now," said Roland, letting the tent flap close behind them, "tell me why you've come."

Leland was escorted back to his makeshift bridge on horseback by McCain and a troop of archers.

The trip across the log was easier this time. Leland had too many things on his mind to worry about falling. Gahnfeld watched him as he stepped off the trunk, worried, and Leland said, "Go on to step two."

"They'll let us?" He sounded surprised. "You looked so grim coming across . . ."

"Just the bridge, so far. They want independent confirmation of my information before we go to the next stage."

Gahnfeld's face fell. "That could take days!"

Leland smiled. "Hours. They have heliographs, too, and agents-in-place. We should have an answer by the midmorning conference."

Gahnfeld turned. "Coronet Sanchez!"

"Sir!"

"My compliments to the halvidars of the First, Second, Fourth, and Eighth hundreds. I need them and their men for some engineering work. On the double."

Zanna took a deep breath before guiding her horse into the ford. She remembered a story about an Italian river that, once crossed, committed one to an irreversible course.

*Is this my Rubicon?*

She, de Gant, and Leland had a small escort consisting of de Gant's aides and some of her personal guard—nothing, really, when compared to the forces waiting them on the other side. They rode out of the water and up the bank to where McCain waited with an honor guard of two hundred.

He bowed in the saddle and indicated the way. The party moved on and the honor guard closed around them like a hand.

Zanna remembered that their first meeting with Roland had been the result of a forcible abduction. Had the tables been reversed?

McCain dropped back beside them, by Leland, and Zanna heard Leland say, "Quite an honor guard."

McCain nodded. "You are our guests. It wouldn't do for anything to happen to you while in our care."

Leland lowered his voice and Zanna edged her horse closer. "—any danger of that?"

"I doubt it, but, just in case . . . If some faction, however small, wanted to spike these talks, violating your safe passage would do it, no?"

Leland glanced back at Zanna and smiled thinly. In a normal voice he said, "And how was this morning's . . . ceremony?"

McCain laughed. "Well attended. All honors due a great man. His Majesty expressed his hope that no *other* clan chiefs would die this year. The bier was like a mountain." He pointed to the southwest. "You can still see the smoke."

Zanna followed his finger and saw a dark smudge of smoke rising beyond a gentle hill. "Who was the deceased?" she asked.

The corners of Leland's mouth turned down and he said, "The Cricket Clan has a new chieftain."

Zanna blinked. *Roland didn't waste any time. I wonder if that mes-*

*sage is also for us?* "My condolences on your people's loss," she said dryly.

McCain bowed in the saddle. "We'll bear up somehow."

They were taken to a heavily guarded encampment with several large tents, but most of them were being dismantled. As she dismounted Zanna caught Leland's eye and inclined her head toward the latrines at the edge of camp. "Are those . . . ?"

Leland nodded.

McCain pulled back the flap on the largest tent and Leland groaned out loud. "It would have to be this one."

de Gant frowned. "Something the matter, Warden?"

Leland took a deep breath. "No, Marshall."

Zanna entered first and straightened as she saw the men assembled around the edge of the tent. Leland and de Gant were right behind her. McCain motioned them to wait, just inside the door.

Roland entered the tent from the far side, a younger man, dressed in the sash and leathers of a clan chieftain, just behind him. Everyone in the room bowed and he walked across the space, spreading his arms. "Welcome."

The three bowed in response and Zanna said, "Your Majesty honors us."

Roland grinned widely and said, "It costs me nothing to be polite." He turned to the young man beside him. "Allow me to present the Cricket, Donald Dobson, newly come to his office." To the new clan chief he said, "The Gentle Guide Zanna de Noram, heir to the Stewardship of Noram, Marshall Cornelius de Gant, Commander of the Noram Allied Forces, and Warden Leland de Laal, Captain of the Laal forces and"—Roland cleared his throat—"architect of these talks."

Zanna looked around at Leland and found him staring at a spot on the grassy floor. He looked up, though, at Roland's words and blushed.

The Cricket bowed to them. "Honored." He turned specifically to Leland and said, "My thanks."

Leland sputtered, "It was not my intention—"

The Cricket interrupted him. "I know. His Majesty explained this to me. Nevertheless, thank you. My great-uncle was a dangerous man and almost threw our people into a civil war."

Zanna frowned. *What on earth are they talking about?*

Before she could ask, Roland said, "If we had the time, I would introduce the rest of my clan chiefs. I'm afraid our talks today will have to be very brief."

Zanna's frown intensified. "Has your Majesty reconsidered negotiations?"

Roland laughed. "Oh, no. In fact, as a gesture of goodwill, I'm removing my forces from this front and will also commit to no offensive actions against Noram for the remainder of this winter."

Zanna's surprise was total. "That is generous, your Majesty. What do you expect of Noram in return?" She glanced sideways at her companions to gauge their reactions. de Gant was watching Roland with narrowed eyes. Leland's head lifted suddenly, as if he were drawing in a large breath.

Roland shook his head. "Nothing, really. Refrain from any offensives of your own. And give serious consideration to my proposal for the future dispensation of the Sacred Plain."

de Gant a suspicious look on his face, said, "And that is?"

Roland looked at Leland and smiled slightly. "Well, if this were a long, protracted negotiation, I'd start by asking for all of the Sacred Plain and, in a couple of months, end up settling for half. Instead, I propose the creation of a neutral free trade zone consisting of the entire plain, farmed by representatives of every nation on Agatsu, who would be free to sell their produce to any customer, regardless of origin."

de Gant frowned. "We have the entire plain right now. Why should we give up portions to other countries?"

"The cost," said Roland. "In blood. The cost of holding the plain year after year after year. If I lead my people away from the plain this year without a fight, without a single square kilometer of the plain, next year we'll be back with our full forces—not just the young coming to be tested, but our veterans, our reserves, *serious* men, slow to start, impossible to stop. And we'll not stop at the Black, either. Such an effort would require more reward than the plain itself."

de Gant said angrily, "If you think—"

Zanna held up her hand. "Gently, Marshall. His Majesty isn't talking about what *he* intends to do. He's talking about what his people are likely to do if this negotiation yields nothing for them. I suspect Roland does not expect to be in power if that were to happen."

Roland smiled. "You have it, Gentle Guide. My people are just as serious about the Sacred Plain as yours. If I give it up without a fight, it could mean my downfall. The offensive would follow."

de Gant subsided. "I see. Still, why should it be anybody but Nullarbor and Noramland?"

Roland glanced at Leland before saying "It was suggested to me that the plain is the heritage of all humans on this planet." He looked back at de Gant. "Besides, as a practical consequence, the more involved in keeping it a neutral zone, the better. If it were just the two of us, a conflict could cause the outbreak of hostilities. Add Yukifuri and Kai Lung and Neuveau France to the mix and you end up with a more stable configuration."

Zanna said, "And Cotswold?"

Roland's eyes crinkled. "Sure. *Any* national entity that exists when this agreement is finalized."

"How much of the plain goes to each country?" Zanna said.

Roland shrugged. "This will have to be settled, but Yukifuri is tiny and Noramland is large. Nullarbor is almost as large as Noramland but your population is greater. If you agree to the first part of my plan, then the division would be the subject of our next meeting. I suggest we meet at the solstice—three months from now, where the shuttles stand. And we invite every nation."

Zanna took a deep breath and held it, thinking hard. Unless the Rootless broke this agreement, it definitely secured the plain for another year and, if Roland was serious about his proposition, maybe it ended the perennial conflict for good. She exhaled sharply and said, "Very well. I'll submit your proposal to my father with my full support."

Roland spread his hands apart. "I couldn't ask more."

*You most certainly could.* "Does that complete our business?"

Roland bowed and offered his arm to Zanna, escorting her out of the tent. The rest followed. There was another exchange of courtesies and then the horses were brought up.

As Zanna mounted, she saw Leland just coming out of the tent talking to the new clan chieftain of the Crickets. Leland looked around, saw Zanna and de Gant mounting, and bowed quickly to the Cricket, then hurried to mount.

Except to thank McCain, who commanded their escort back to the Ganges, Zanna didn't speak until they were well across and surrounded only by their own troops.

"Do you think he means it?" she finally said to de Gant and Leland, riding to each side of her.

Leland said, "I believe so."

de Gant said, "I've faced him during prisoner exchange talks five times—twice when they took the plain and three times when we took it. He's never said one thing and done another. He's always kept his word. I think he'll do as he says."

Zanna rode on for a while without speaking. When they made the turn into the headquarters lane, she finally spoke. "Okay. I'll ride for the capital immediately, using the relays. Marshall, report my departure to my father and tell him I'll brief him completely on arrival. Monitor Roland's forces and report any movement." She turned to Leland. "I'll make inquiries about Laal. Surely there'll be *some* news if Cotswold's broken the peace."

Leland nodded. "I appreciate that. If they have invaded and this is not common knowledge in Noram City, someone is blocking the news . . ."

Zanna completed the sentence in her head. *Like my father.* She didn't say anything though. If Cotswold broke the peace, then Noram's reserves should be moving to Lall's relief. If this cease-fire with Roland succeeded, *all* of Noram's forces could march to their aid.

*Unless my father's done something incredibly stupid.*

Leland and his escort left the headquarters compound at the trot, but the minute they were out of sight, Leland put his heels to his mount's sides and shot ahead. The troops behind struggled to catch up. They reached their camp in twenty minutes.

Except for a few perimeter sentries and a row of empty wagons, the camp was deserted, tents gone, firepits filled. Leland pushed on into trees and found the men resting, in ranks beside their tethered horses. He passed them and came to the cliff.

Another tree, parallel to the first, stretched across the gorge. Saplings, cut and trimmed, had been spiked and lashed across, forming a flooring for the bridge. Next, hay and straw had been packed into the crevices, and last, dirt carried on shields by a long line of men was being dumped onto the straw. Four men with a makeshift roller, a short section of tree trunk almost a meter in diameter, were packing the dirt into the cracks.

Gahnfeld held the head of Leland's horse as he dismounted, eyes asking the question.

Leland just gave him a sharp nod and said, "When can we cross?"

Gahnfeld made a fist and raised it in the air. "*Yes!* Twenty minutes. Let them finish tamping it down and get the guard lines strung."

Leland looked across the gorge. When he'd left this morning, the Rootless had lined the other side, bows strung. Now there were only four of them, dismounted, watching the construction as they rested.

For a brief paranoid moment he pictured Roland's forces, waiting, hidden by the trees, until the Eight Hundred crossed, and falling on them, then using the bridge to launch a surprise attack on the Noram troops.

RELAX. WHAT CHOICE DO YOU HAVE?

*None.*

"Halvidar Miyamoto," he called.

The woman approached him and saluted.

"Have you coordinated with my signalmen?"

"Yes, sir. I've sent the instructions. My people are moving south, near the border. The line will still be intact back to Ashperon and, if you're within fifty kilometers of the Black, you should be able to signal us."

"Right. And we're using the new code?"

She nodded. "With an offset. Even if they capture it in Laal, without the offset they won't be able to break it."

He held out his hand and she shook it. "Get going. Once we cross this bridge, we're deserters. I don't want them to pick you up as one of us."

"Good luck, sir."

"And the same to you."

She mounted her horse and left, walking it quietly through the woods.

The men with the roller finished, then Gahnfeld detailed four squads from the Seventh to march back and forth across the bridge while another group of men strung rope along both sides, using branches left on the tree trunks for this purpose.

There was a moment of excitement as one of the marchers found a hole and his leg dropped down through the bridge, showering dirt into the river below. His mates pulled him out and the hole was patched with large rocks, then covered again.

Coronet Sanchez threw his poncho over his horse's head and led the mount across. The flooring held.

Leland covered his horses head and said to Gahnfeld. "Space them four meters apart but double-time them. It's probably going to take over an hour as it is. Recall the sentries when we're down to the last fifty men."

Gahnfeld rolled his eyes. "Of course, *Warden.*"

Leland winced, then jogged across the bridge, leading his horse at a trot. The bridge bounced slightly, and he hoped the vibrations wouldn't shake the dirt and straw out. The last thing they needed was to have a horse put a leg through a gap. Besides the danger of breaking a bone, the animal could panic and go over the edge. The rope railing was purely visual—structurally it might as well not be there.

Across, he haltered his horse and tied it to a tree, then took his saddle off and laid it on the pine needles just beyond. He took the poncho and spread it on the ground, then lay down, his saddle for a pillow, staring up through the branches.

IT'S GOING TO WORK.

*It's got to work.*

He closed his eyes.

"Warden."

Leland sat up, surprised. He hadn't expected to sleep, but there'd been little enough the night before.

Gahnfeld stood there. Beside him was one of the Rootless. He peered closer—it was the Cricket, Donald Dobson.

Leland stretched. "Good morning—afternoon?"

"Afternoon," the Cricket said.

Leland climbed to his feet and looked at the bridge. There were still men crossing it, this time leading the unit's draft horses—converted from wagon teams to pack animals. "The sentries?"

"They've crossed. Twenty more animals and we're done. None of the other units seems to have noticed." Gahnfeld nodded at the Cricket. "Apparently we're ready to leave as soon as we cross."

The Cricket nodded back. "True. I've the honor of escorting you to our gathering point. Or, as Himself said, to make sure you won't hold us up."

"We'll need a torch," Leland said.

Fifteen minutes later, hot flames rising into the sky, the bridge tumbled into the river, smoke and steam rising where the glowing embers splashed into the water.

Leland mounted his horse and said almost absently, "Well, let's get going. I've burned my bridges behind me. There's no turning back."

# EIGHTEEN

## SUTEMI: TO THROW AWAY THE BODY

*Where is it?*

The guard at the holding cell said, "Good morning, sir," and it took great effort on Siegfried's part not to slam him against the wall.

"Just open the door," he said.

The guard's tentative smile dropped from his face and he pulled the bolts and swung the door wide, moving quickly.

Siegfried gestured to the side and his personal guards dropped off, stationing themselves on the opposite wall. Then Siegfried stepped into the room and pulled the door shut behind him.

Dulan was noticeably thinner. It had been a week since his capture, and Siegfried was allowing him only water. He was sitting cross-legged on his straw pallet, back against the wall, hands resting in his lap. The leg irons weren't visible and for one paranoid moment, Siegfried thought Dulan had gotten out of them, but then he saw the chain running across the pallet and under his legs.

The two oil lamps that lit the room were on this side of the room, out of the prisoner's reach, as was a large chair from Dulan's own study. Siegfried sat in the chair and watched Dulan impassively.

*Where is it?*

Dulan opened his eyes then and looked at Siegfried without surprise. "Ah. You." He straightened his legs, letting blood flow back into his lower legs. He didn't ask what Siegfried wanted. Siegfried was interested in only one thing.

"Me. Where is it?"

"What do you think?"

Siegfried narrowed his eyes. "I think you hid it."

"I can think of other possibilities. I could've sent it into Noram. I could've sent it with Leland. I could've floated it down the Tiber in a reed basket. Or I could've destroyed it."

Siegfried felt a twinge of panic at the last but said, "Don't be ridiculous. I could dream up possibilities all day long if I had nothing to do. I don't care about possibilities. I care about actualities.

"Where is the Helm?"

"Ask Dillan."

Siegfried sighed. "You know that was a mistake."

The night of the attack, Dulan had been taken in the main hall, after seeing Dillan's corpse. He'd been unarmed but had killed or disabled eight of Siegfried's men before being knocked unconscious. The chains that held him were very strong, and Siegfried had no intention of coming within his reach, half starved or otherwise.

"No. I'm sure you wish you had him alive, to use as a lever against me." Dulan's eyes strayed to the wall on the other side of the doorway and Siegfried looked, despite himself, at the irregular brownish stain.

Siegfried wondered if having Dillan alive would make any difference. He'd gone through five of Dulan's closest staff without results, starting with the household manager, Martin, and ending with the companion of Dulan's daughter, the Gentle Guide Bridgett.

Dulan had wept at each cut, openly, but remained silent even in the face of their screams—each death.

Siegfried snarled, angry. "Do you want more blood on your hands?"

Dulan stared at Siegfried. "*My* hands? Don't kid yourself."

Siegfried narrowed his eyes. "You know, don't you? You know what I intend. That's why you didn't spare them."

Dulan didn't say anything. Instead, he crossed his legs again, rattling the chain, and folded his hands back into his lap. He let his eyelids half close and unfocused his eyes. Siegfried had the irrational feeling that the man had left the room.

Siegfried stood. "We'll see how you handle this when the delirium sets in. When your tongue swells in your mouth and your throat feels like sandpaper."

He stood and banged on the door. When it swung open he said to the guard, "No more water for the prisoner. Not a single drop."

The door shut with satisfying finality.

His guards fell in behind him and he walked through the Station to the main hall. Most of the staff and residents were either dead or crowded into the servants' wing, under guard. He entered the small family dining room and greeted the one exception.

"*Gentle* Guide."

Carmen Cantle de Laal was also thinner, though Siegfried hadn't limited her food. Except for a constant escort, she'd been given the run of the Station. He wondered if she was having second thoughts about her treason. *Too bad.*

She bent a knee. "High Steward." Her face was blank, an expression Siegfried was used to—one he cultivated in his own servants.

"Please be seated." Siegfried sat at the other end of the table, one of his guards holding the chair. Another guard held Carmen's chair then stood back against the wall.

Lunch was grilled mutton, saffron rice, and a salad of hothouse tomatoes, cucumbers, and basil. Siegfried's cook was delighted with the produce of Laal and had a troop of Cotswold infantry fully occupied in supplies confiscation. He wanted Siegfried to relocate his capital to the Tiber valley.

*Too cold.*

"I've given some thought to your request, *Gentle* Guide."

She stirred at the end of the table, looking up from food that she'd disarranged on her plate but hardly tasted. "My portion," she corrected. "Of our agreement."

He waved his hand as if shooing midges from his face. "I can hardly give the governorship of Laal to someone who is currently leading troops against me. Your son and Koss are fighting my men in the southwest."

"After you've won, choosing Ricard will do much to pacify the area. If he was with you now, he wouldn't be an effective governor later. The people would rise against him."

Siegfried pretended to consider her words. *If I can just find that blasted Helm, I won't need* any *of you.* "I'll consider it. I don't want a rebellious province sucking up troops."

There was a knock at the open door and one of the signal runners paused there.

Annoyed, Siegfried gestured him on in. His staff knew not to bother him with routine traffic, so it must be urgent.

FROM: Dickson, Commanding Eastern Division
TO: High Steward Siegfried Montrose
SUBJ: Nullarbor invasion
Sir. Rootless Clan Forces numbering over seven thousand calvalry have taken or besieged all seven of the border forts before proceeding northwest, toward Bottleneck. Our losses at the border number over eight hundred dead, wounded, or captured leaving only three hundred and fifty troops under my command. Initial attacks on heliograph stations prevented our report until now. We are running before them, maintaining contact, but cannot possibly engage them without relief. Please advise.

Siegfried stared at the message until the words blurred. Those troops should be fighting the Noramlanders over the Plain of the Founders! He'd counted on that when he'd pulled his forces west for the invasion of Laal. Now, between the ragged remnant of Dickson's forces and the militia left in Montrouge, there were fewer than seven hundred troops between the Rootless and his capital.

*Should I move my forces back to Cotswold?*

If the Rootless weren't fighting the Noramlanders, then where were Arthur's troops? Still on the plain or moving west, toward Laal? He had a deal with Arthur, but had Arthur double-crossed him?

Since Siegfried planned on double-crossing Arthur, the thought came easily to him.

No, he wouldn't run back to Cotswold. Perhaps the Rootless would stop at Bottleneck, the narrow section of Cotswold between the Bauer Rent and the Bay of Sorrow, then consolidate their hold on the peninsula, territory that had belonged to them in the previous century.

Even if he had to take his capital back, he was staying. With the Helm, he could do anything. However, Arthur could still be a problem if he acted too soon.

"Two messages," he said to the runner. "First, to Dickson: Maintain contact and report movements. Second, to my son in Noram City: Execute Operation Commitment immediately."

* * *

*Dillan is dead. Father is their prisoner.*

The news had leaked out of the Station, passed mouth to mouth, hand to hand, in the way that bad news travels. A man driving confiscated sheep to the station under guard heard it from the station butcher. Ejected from the fortification, he told it in the market. It traveled up into the woods with a deadwood collector who left the news on a sheet of paper under a certain rock. Matilda collected the paper at sunset and held it two days before finally telling Lillian.

She'd cried herself dry and now, a day later, she couldn't cry any more. She'd retreated—packed cotton wool around her being—certain that the next message would be the death of her father or the capture of her brothers.

Now she did what Matilda told her or sat in the corner, huddled in blankets. Siegfried's patrols swept farther and farther up the hill, and Matilda was afraid that the sight or smell of smoke would give them away, so they ate cold meals, bundled their clothing around them, and, at night, slept together to share their body heat.

*Will I ever be warm again?*

"Again? What does he want this time?"

Marilyn's maid, Dora, said, "He didn't say."

Marilyn frowned. Until Zanna reached the capital the next morning, she was just waiting. She'd done all she could to prep her father, to incline him toward negotiations, and sensed further efforts would backfire, annoying him. She really had no excuse not to see Sylvan.

"All right. Please ask him to wait in the conservatory. Ask the kitchen for tea." That was public enough. Lately Sylvan's attentions had become both more forceful and more intimate. A month before she would have welcomed them, but now . . . Anyway, the conservatory should be safe. She wasn't worried about handling him, particularly. She just wanted to avoid the necessity.

She dressed in one of her old dresses, from those days when she practically lived in the drafty halls of the Great Library, a high-necked velvet gown, with long sleeves, and a long enough hem to comfortably tuck one's feet under while reading. It was an almost-black dark purple with an appliqué of the Stewardship's Crest worked over the heart in royal blue and scarlet.

It didn't make her look at all sexy, but it reminded, ultimately, of who she was. It made her feel like *someone.*

Sylvan was pacing along the long glass wall that gave the conservatory its name. He turned when she entered and smiled briefly. "I was beginning to think you were a figment of my imagination. There was this girl I was betrothed to, but try as I could, I couldn't find her."

Any sympathy she felt was wiped out by his use of "girl." Still, she was polite. "I've been assisting my father in affairs of state. For the first time in two hundred years, it looks like we might have peace with Nullarbor. In fact, because of the peace with Cotswold, nobody seems to be at war on the entire planet."

Sylvan nodded. "I've heard the rumors. Imagine, peace. Who would have thought it?" He turned and walked toward a couch and a group of chairs around a low table. "I brought something you might be interested in."

He picked a package off the table, a book-shape object wrapped in cloth, and opened it. It was, not surprisingly, a book. She took it from him carefully for it was not one of the Prime books, the indestructible volumes brought by the Founders, but a copy—a very *old* copy—missing the front cover and several pages.

The running header said *Pharmaceutical Processing from Scratch.* It was one of the missing volumes, the ones listed in the colony indices but never found, probably thrown into the river four hundred years before by Josh Townsend's New Luddites. *Someone* had found it, though, if the copy existed.

"Where did you get this?" She didn't attempt to hide her excitement.

"There's a used goods shop on Stellar Way. The man sells furniture, dishes, and other junk, but he also sells copies of Prime books, original works, and old magazines. I don't think he knows what he has, though. This was in a pile of last year's newspapers. Got him down to half a soy because of the damaged cover."

"Half a soy? This is priceless!" The tea service arrived and she started, annoyed. "Did he say where he got it?"

Sylvan helped himself to a handful of cookies. "Got it? Um, didn't ask. Had to get to lunch—keep up my strength. You going to sit down, Gentle Guide?"

She frowned and sat. "I've got to see that shop. The missing pages might still be there. There might be other lost volumes."

Sylvan blinked. "Well, I suppose I could run you over there after tea."

She poured a cup, threw sugar and lemon into it, and thrust it across the table. "While you drink that, I'll get my cloak."

She'd expected complaint. Instead he just nodded. "As you wish, Gentle Guide."

His father had sent the bait all the way from Montrouge, earlier in the month, from his private library. Not the library that he'd let Marilyn see when she was there, but the truly private one, the one that he kept from everybody.

She'd gone for it like a trout after a caddis fly.

He walked her across the city, taking the narrow, winding walkway that avoided traffic. Two guards followed—hers.

"Since the attack on Warden de Laal," Marilyn said, explaining the guards.

He nodded. "Wise." It didn't matter. He'd planned for guards. He turned onto the Appian Stair, just short of Stellar Way.

"I thought you said it was on Stellar Way?"

"Well, near there. I'm new to your city. I couldn't really remember the name of this one, but it's near Stellar Way." He'd been careful *not* to tell her, lest she tell someone at the palace.

The shop was on an alcove off an alcove, and Sylvan saw the guards checking the shadows. It was much as Sylvan had described it, though, a junkshop selling the secondhand goods of the well off to the not so well off.

Marilyn stooped like a hawk on a rabbit to the double shelf of books outside the door, skipping her finger across the titles and pulling out the volumes without covers.

The gray head of the proprietor stuck through the door and eyed the party, then said, "The good books are in the back. These are the ones that I can risk the elements with."

Marilyn stood. "I'd reached that conclusion myself. Please show me."

One of the guards pushed through, to screen the interior, then stepped back outside, nodding to Marilyn. "It's a single room with no other exits."

Sylvan almost laughed but controlled himself. *Idiots!*

Marilyn followed the proprietor back inside and Sylvan came behind, lagging. He stationed himself just inside the door and loosened his dagger.

The proprietor pointed at the "good" books, two low shelves at the rear of the shop, near a gas lamp. Marilyn said, "Thank you," and knelt before the shelves.

The proprietor turned and looked at Sylvan, who nodded. The man reached out to the wall and pulled a knob.

"Wha—!" The floor beneath Marilyn dropped, a swinging trapdoor, and she dropped out of sight. There was the sound of a bottle breaking and the door swung up. The knob was pushed back in.

The first guard stumbled through the door and fell to all fours, an arrow in his back. Sylvan kicked him in the head, using his boot heel, then carefully looked outside.

The other guard was slumped against the wall, two arrows in his chest and another in his neck.

Sylvan looked up at the four archers in the second-floor windows across the alley. He gave the hand signal and they unnocked their backup arrows and pulled the window shutters closed again. Sylvan stepped out, grabbed the ankles of the dead guard, and dragged him into the shop.

As soon as the body was clear of the door, the proprietor stepped past Sylvan with a bucket of water and sluiced the blood off the wall and cobbles, then hung the BACK SHORTLY sign on the door and bolted it shut from within.

Sylvan started to pull the trapdoor knob and the proprietor said, "Not yet. She could still be holding her breath and you'll disperse the ether vapors. Give it another five minutes and you know she'll be out." He began shaking the flour from his hair, turning from the aged proprietor to the Cotswold agent-in-place.

Sylvan dropped his hand and snapped, "Very well." He hated waiting. Still, in ten minutes the horses would be there and he could leave on his "hunting trip."

The shop would remain closed and the bodies of the guards would go into the oubliette. It was tight enough to contain the ether fumes so it would contain the smell of decomposing bodies for quite some time.

Operation Commitment was proceeding nicely.

Dexter's small remnant of fugitives was down to five men. In the last four days they'd moved barely thirty kilometers, and Cotswold forces were still combing the district. Twice they'd almost been taken; the second time it took sunset and the lives of five men to buy them the distance necessary for escape.

*This can't go on.*

They'd eaten only twice, once a sheep missed by the invading troops and the second time, partially burned ears of corn taken from a torched storage crib. This part of Laal was rain shadow barrens with tiny, scattered pockets of fecundity suitable for single homesteads at best. Very few people lived here, and those who did were captured, dead, or driven into the mountains, their dwelling places burned, their livestock and stores taken.

*Where are the Pikes?*

His men weren't dressed for the high country. In fact, every night was a trial as the temperatures dropped after dark and they couldn't risk fires.

The night before, unable to walk any farther, they'd found an overhang and, stuffing dried grass around themselves, had huddled through the night. It was the coldest night yet. Now, in the morning, if the enemy were to come across them, they couldn't even run. Their muscles were cramped from the cold and they moved like arthritic ancients, seeking a sunwashed slope where they could warm themselves without being detected.

A half hour later they found a boulder field on an eastern slope and crept into the maze. The rocks not only caught the sun but intensified it, reflecting the light into warm spots. They crept in gratefully and collapsed, spread like lizards in the sun.

*Someone should keep watch,* Dexter thought. He considered asking one of the others but they'd already given so much. He struggled to his feet and leaned against one of the boulders, raising his head just above the rock.

The slope overlooked a shallow valley, rocky, with sparse yellow grasses and thorny succulents. There was a wagon track, two thin lines weaving between boulders, paralleling the dry wash at the bottom. He checked the ridge tops, watching each section carefully, looking for any movement, before checking the next section.

He was about to sit again when he heard hoofbeats.

It was a small patrol, seven mounted men, moving their horses at a walk because they had prisoners, three women and a man, hands tied behind their backs with a rope up to their necks, as they couldn't lower their hands to their waist without choking themselves.

*Cruel.*

He dropped back down. "Simon, Leon," he whispered. "Are your bowstrings dry?"

Only two of his remaining men were archers, but they were good ones—district champions who'd been assigned to his person for that skill alone.

His men had heard the hoofbeats now and crouched, moving closer to him.

Leon said, "They're dry, but if we don't get our muscles warm, we won't even be able to hit the ground."

Dexter nodded. "We'll need some time to set up. They've got prisoners and they're moving even slower than we are—especially if we cut over the ridge. By the time we get in position, we'll *all* be warmed up."

His cornet said, "Are you sure we should risk it? From the way they've kept after us, it looks like your capture is a priority with them."

Dexter shrugged. "They've got clothing, horses, and food. And their prisoners are civilians—a man and three women.

"*Our* people."

The message came uncoded, over the heliograph network, and, even though it was addressed to Arthur directly, it took awhile to filter up through the network of clerks and secretaries. He read it after entertaining friends from the country for dinner.

> Arthur,
> I've been thinking about the wedding plans. Marilyn's input would be invaluable. Arrangements already made should stand, of course, but close consultation with Marilyn would enhance that.
> Siegfried.

Arthur frowned as he looked at it. *What on earth is he talking about?* He thought about sending back a note asking for clarification but didn't want to appear stupid. He'd been thinking about the events in the Plain of the Founders, and it took him a minute to shift perspectives.

*Arrangements?* Ah, the agreement—to wipe out the house of Laal. *What does that have to do with Marilyn?*

Marilyn hadn't been at dinner but Arthur suspected her of not liking some of his guests, whom she called yes-men, so he wasn't surprised. She'd probably eaten alone or at the library.

He'd never intended to let the betrothal stand. He planned to break it in outrage when he *officially* found out about the invasion of Laal, but by that time, the snows would cover most of the passes and he'd be forced to wait for the spring. Then Siegfried's forces would give him a token resistance and fall back to the black and the status quo would be preserved.

*Except Dulan will be dead, Noram City will again be the center of technology and culture, and I'll have my own man governing Laal.*

He sent a servant for his daughter. When he learned that she'd left Noram House with Sylvan, he sent for her maid.

"To a bookshop, High Steward. On Stellar Way. Guide Sylvan found a rare book and the gentle guide wanted to see if here were others."

"What's the name of the shop, Dora?"

"She didn't say, she was getting her cloak. I asked her if she would be back for supper and she said she would."

Dulan looked at the darkness outside his window. "She didn't?"

"No, High Steward." The woman was worried. Even Arthur could see that.

"Don't worry, Dora. I'll make inquiries."

After she'd left, he sent for Sylvan. The servant he asked told him, "Guide Sylvan left this afternoon to visit Guide Lance de West."

"Oh, that's right. Hunting, wasn't it?" de West's estates were north, about forty kilometers. Perhaps Marilyn had decided to exercise some of the latitude shown betrothed couples. *Without Dora?*

He considered the message again.

*Arrangements already made should stand, of course, but close consultation with Marilyn would enhance that.*

It was after dark so messengers had to be sent rather than use the heliograph. By the time they returned from de West's estate with the news that Sylvan had never arrived, Arthur felt he knew what Siegfried meant by "close consultation."

*What have I done?*

*I should just end it.*

PERHAPS YOU SHOULD.

Dulan lifted his head from the straw mattress, surprised. Against all odds—despite his capture, the deaths of his son and friends, the occupation of his land by Siegfried—he felt the corners of his mouth tug up. It hurt.

*Long time, woman. Thought you were gone.*

JUST DORMANT.

*After all this time, I'd begun to think you weren't really ever there.*

THEN YOU HAD SOME VERY STRANGE "NOTIONS" WHEN YOU WERE TWENTY-EIGHT.

*I guess so. Lillian certainly thought so.*

IT'S HARD TO SHARE YOUR HUSBAND WITH ANOTHER WOMAN. THAT'S ONE OF THE REASONS I WITHDREW. BESIDES, I COULDN'T DO THAT MUCH WITH YOU—YOU SHOULD'VE WORN THE IMPRINTER YEARS BEFORE YOU DID.

*Depends on which agenda I wanted to follow—yours or mine. I could barely resist you as it was.*

OUR AGENDAS WEREN'T DIFFERENT AT ALL. IT'S OUR METHODS.

Dulan shook his head. He didn't know. Would doing things her way have led to this same place?

*I'd be willing to go back and try it your way.*

NOT EXACTLY POSSIBLE, IS IT?

Dulan sighed. He rubbed a dry tongue over cracked lips. His temperature was up and he'd hadn't been able to summon saliva since the day before, something that happened between six and eight percent of body weight loss from dehydration. He felt a stab of paranoia. *You aren't the beginning of my delirium, are you? The first psychotic episode?* After ten percent, physical and mental incapacitation waited.

NO, BUT IT'S NOT THAT FAR BEHIND. THE LOOSENING OF YOUR SELF-IMPOSED BARRIERS IS WHAT BROUGHT ME AWAKE. THE BARRIERS BETWEEN YOUR CONSCIOUS AND SUBCONSCIOUS WILL FALL SOON.

*And I won't be able tell reality from fantasy—won't know who I'm talking to or what I'm saying. That's what Siegfried's waiting for.*

WE BOTH KNOW WHAT HE WANTS WITH THE HELM.

*I can't let him get it.*

THAT WOULD BE BEST.

He tried to laugh but it came out as a painful rasp. *You pacifists are always the most bloody-minded.*

YES.

*You can depend on me.*

I KNOW.

*What about the key?*

FOR LELAND?

*Yes.*

GIVE IT TO SIEGFRIED.

Dulan thought about it. Yes. Make anybody who came into this cell a messenger, willing or not.

*Well, it's nice to have someone to talk to.*

I WON'T LEAVE YOU AGAIN.

Dexter had a light cut on his shoulder, but it was bandaged and he was warm. He wore a full set of enemy clothing over his own, and his stomach, filled with captured trail rations, wasn't grumbling.

The prisoners let them know the worst of it.

"Yes, I'm sure. My cousin came through three days ago. They occupy the station and Brandon-on-the-Falls and hold the passes into Noram. He said the Pikes and Falcons are together, pushing up from the southwest."

Dexter asked all the obvious questions, but they didn't know the answers. "No, Guide. I don't know about your father, brothers, or sister."

Dexter gritted his teeth. *I thought I knew what fear meant these last five days.* And from fear came rage. *I'll kill that double-dealing Siegfried.*

His first impulse was to go north, straight to Laal Station.

*And straight into the enemy's teeth.*

They had seven horses, relatively rested, and they could double up on the two largest.

"We go west—to the army."

"Why me?"

Siegfried smiled. "He doesn't know you betrayed him." *You* and *Arthur.* "By now he'll be completely disoriented, delirious, but your voice, familiar and, most important, not *mine,* can mislead him. Comfort him. You'll take water in with you. Bathe his face and give him enough to drink so he can talk. Tell him that Dexter's troops are in the castle but the fighting is hot and he needs to know where the Helm is, to keep it safe."

Carmen shuddered. "I don't want to do this."

The smile dropped from Siegfried's face. "Don't even imagine you have a choice." He spread his hands. "Well, perhaps you do. I can let it be known what part you played in the current state of affairs *and* put you out of the Station. How long do you think you'll last?"

Carmen paled. "All right. When?"

"Now, *Gentle* Guide."

He led her to the cell without further conversation, then provided her with a small pitcher of water, a cup, and a rag. "Do you understand what I want?"

"Yes!" She spat the words, her face contorted.

Siegfried nodded. *Who do you hate more—me . . . or yourself?* He motioned to the guard to open the door and stood back, out of sight, while she entered. They left the door ajar, to listen.

The first sound was Carmen's scream. The second was the sound of the earthenware pitcher breaking on the cell floor.

*What the hell?*

His guards went first, to make sure, but there was no danger.

Carmen, hysterical, had to be taken up to her rooms. Siegfried waited until her sobs had ceased echoing down the hallway before he asked, "How did he do it?"

The guard who'd examined Dulan stood. He was pale and he looked sick. "He chewed through the brachial artery on the inside of his elbow. The mattress is soaked with blood."

"Well, not all of it," Siegfried said tightly.

"No," agreed the guard. "Not all of it."

They fell silent, staring at the wall. In meter-high letters of his own blood, Dulan had written NON OMNIS MORIAR.

Siegfried sent the Guard commander up to the library for the Latin dictionary. When he returned, Siegfried sat in the chair across from the body and looked up the phrase.

Loosely translated, it meant "I shall not completely die." Siegfried said it aloud, shut the book, and dropped it to the floor, disgusted. "I don't want any word of this getting out—not to his people and not even to ours, 'cause they'll talk. You make sure about your men!"

"Yes, sir." The man glanced back at the bloody words. "Was he mad? What possessed him?"

"I don't know." Siegfried ground his fingernails into the palms of his hands and clenched his teeth together until his jaw muscles bunched to rock-hard clumps on the side of his face.

*Where is it? Where is it? Where is it?*

# NINETEEN

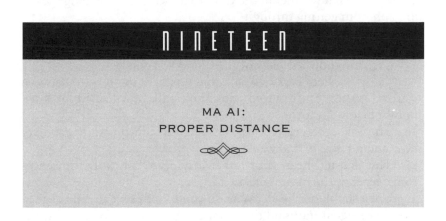

## MA AI:
## PROPER DISTANCE

Zanna waited for Charly in the private parlor of Charly's townhouse. She wanted to pace, to stretch, perhaps even to break something, but held herself still, in *seiza,* arms crossed.

There were footsteps on the stairs and Charly entered, serene and smiling. "I saw the guards."

Zanna's frown finally faded and she smiled. "How could you miss them?"

They entered each other's arms like coming home. Zanna inhaled deeply, her face hidden in Charly's hair—woodsmoke, a touch of incense, and a whiff of sweat. "You didn't bathe after class, did you?"

"No. And you've been riding all day." Charly held Zanna out at arm's length. "What's the matter?"

Zanna sighed and the corners of her mouth turned down.

Charly pulled her close again. "I know that look. What has your father done now?"

"I'm not sure . . ."

Charly led her over to the couch and sat, pulling Zanna's head down to rest on her shoulder. "You suspect something. Is it merely stupid, or is it awful?"

"I think he's betrayed an entire stewardship of Noram."

Charly stared at Zanna, silent for a moment. "That would be in the 'awful' category. Laal?"

Zanna nodded. "I think he cut a deal with Siegfried. Leland said he'd received word that Cotswold has invaded Laal, but my father says it's not true. That weather in the Cloud Scrapers is just keeping the heliograph from getting through."

"Maybe he really believes that?"

She shook her head. "I sent a message to Perry Sensei, in Acoma, and asked him how the view of the Cloud Scrapers was."

Charly nodded. Perry's small dojo was near the border between Laal and Acoma. She'd stayed with him on the way to Red Rock ten months before. "And?"

"The weather is crystal clear. They have a high-pressure zone over them and no hint of bad weather."

"This doesn't mean your father is lying. What do the messages from deeper in the mountains say?"

Zanna shook her head. "Why do you think I sent the message to Perry? The signal staff said that no messages were to go to Laal without my father's authorization."

"Oh. That does look bad. What does Marilyn think?"

"I don't know. She's disappeared. Apparently with Sylvan. My father thinks they've eloped."

"Eloped? She doesn't even *like* him." Charly shook her head. "Where are *her* guards?"

"Nobody knows. Father didn't want to but I finally got him to start a quiet investigation using the city police."

Charly frowned. "Marilyn said she would be at practice tonight. She wasn't, but I just thought something came up." She stood and stared absently at the corner.

Zanna, curled in on herself, watched Charly. *Did you do this thing, Father?*

Charly turned back to Zanna. "My father is in the city. I want to tell him about this."

Zanna flinched. Charly's father was the current chairman of the Council of Noramland and, after Dulan de Laal, the man the most respected by the council members. "It feels like betrayal," she said.

"Whose? If your father is merely mistaken, the council can save him from disaster. If your father is right about Laal, then it can do no harm. If your father has betrayed Laal . . ."

Zanna closed her eyes. ". . . then the council should know." She wrapped her arms around herself.

"Very well—do it."

* * *

*If I don't get out of this land soon, I'm going to dry up and blow away.* Leland licked his perpetually dry lips and tasted dusty grit. He felt like a sun-dried tomato, leathery and weathered. *With all my sugars concentrated.*

The farther west they rode into Cotswold, the drier the conditions. After taking the forts along the border, the main task of the Rootless army had been to find enough water and fodder to continue their ride into Cotswold.

Gahnfeld, beside him, pointed. "There he is."

Roland's scouts arrived first, followed by his personal guard, then Himself and the Cricket, Donald Dobson.

"Your Majesty." Leland bowed in the saddle.

"Sure you won't change your mind?" Roland asked. "Your Eight Hundred going up against Siegfried's nine thousand aren't going to do much, but helping us take his capital will surely hurt him."

Leland shook his head. "It's not that desperate. My father's forces are nearly intact—over five thousand men. And we're fighting on *our* ground. We know our mountains better than these southerners." Leland's signal staff had been able to keep contact with Miyamoto's secret heliograph line and, the second day of their journey, started receiving messages from Captain Koss himself.

Leland didn't mention the bad news also received over this line—Laal Station and his father captured, his brother Dillan dead, his brother Dexter and sister Lillian's fates unknown.

He just wanted to get home.

"Well, the worst of Cotswold, the Anvil, is between you and the river. This"—he gestured at the scrub and sand around them—"is wet in comparison."

Leland looked at Gahnfeld and said, "My senior halvidar has spent weeks on the Anvil. We'll rely on his experience."

Roland nodded. "Very well. We've outpaced our intelligence and we're advancing faster than we can get information on the areas we're entering. If you get wind of Siegfried's forces moving back this way, please get word to me."

Leland said, "Gladly. How much of Cotswold are you going to keep?"

"The jury is still out. If worse comes to worst and you and yours don't seriously hurt Siegfried's army, we'll settle for the lands east of Bottleneck. That's several times the size of the Plain of the Founders.

My people will be pleased and you don't have to worry about us coming after Noram."

"What are the casualties so far?"

Roland shrugged. "We've lost a hundred and fifty-seven men. Nothing, really. We outnumber the locals by a huge margin. We can play it safe."

"And their dead?"

"Twelve hundred or so."

Leland closed his eyes. There was twice that number dead in Laal so far.

MORE TO FOLLOW.

*Yes.*

"What about the noncombatants?"

Roland laughed. "You're talking about future citizens of Nullarbor. We're not going to make this land too hot to hold. We've been talking with them—they know what they have in Siegfried and they seem willing to give us a chance. We're treading as lightly as we can."

*That's something.*

"Good luck, then, your Majesty." Leland lifted his hand in salute. "Long may you reign."

Roland returned the salute. "Long may *you* reign."

Leland shuddered and shook his head. "Not me."

Roland turned his horse and started to ride away. Over his shoulder he called, "We'll see," and then the dust of his party's passage swallowed him.

Marilyn's face was resting on something hard and bouncing. She shook her head and found out that it was her own knee. Her head hurt, her mouth tasted foul, and she felt packed in cotton wool, disoriented and dizzy.

She was in a basket, she realized, knees folded to her chest. Tiny specks of sunlight shone through the lid and danced on the cloth of her dress, back and forth, with the motion. She tried to pull her hands up, but they were stuck on something. It took her a moment to discover that both her wrists and ankles were bound and a short rope connected the two. Someone was drumming somewhere.

She shouted, "Hey! Let me out of here!" Her world jolted and she realized that she was in a pack basket, one of a pair mounted on a mule or horse. Her shout had started the animal. The background noise resolved itself into hoofbeats, not drums.

The earth stilled as the animal carrying her basket was halted. Another horse rode close and there was a fumbling at the top of the basket. Bright light stabbed down and Marilyn winced as it set off an intense headache behind her eyes. She squinted up at a silhouetted figure and then Sylvan's voice said, "Awake? All cozy in there?"

She drew breath for a scathing reply and his hand darted in, covering her mouth and nose with a cloth. Fumes strong and searing bit her throat and lungs.

"We'll fix that, won't we?" Sylvan said, and then she dropped back into darkness.

"This is the last water for fifty kilometers."

It was early afternoon and though the temperatures weren't intolerably high, the air sucked the moisture from their skin. The water in question was a midstream pool formed by a rock and clay dam. The water level was well below the spillway, and the bed, downstream and up, was dry as dust.

Leland eyed the pool, a mere seven meters across, then looked back at the string of men and animals. He dismounted and took the unit banner from the standard-bearer and probed the bottom with the shaft. It was a little deeper than it looked.

"Start filling the bags. And break out the shovels. We'll be digging before we're done."

Gahnfeld addressed the assembled Eight Hundred. "Each man will carry water for his horse and himself, plus corn fodder for two days. Trail rations for six days. Weapons, ponchos, one blanket, and two changes of socks and underwear, winter gloves and hats. Tents will be taken from the packhorses and split, one per squad. Five spare horses per Hundred carrying their own water and fodder." He paused looking from unit halvidar to unit halvidar. "All other animals, equipment, and supplies will be abandoned here."

He turned to Leland and said, "Anything to add, Warden?"

"I want the nets." Leland shook his head. "Other than that, you know best." He hoped that they'd have enough supplies and equipment to survive the mountains.

THEY HAVE TO SURVIVE THIS CROSSING BEFORE SURVIVING THE MOUNTAINS.

*True.*

They cooked a large meal, a feast, really, and fed the horses well. By late afternoon the water hole was a wide, muddy dish and ten men stood in the middle, digging down into the bottom while buckets of dirty water were passed to the shore, filtered through cloth, and given to the horses.

"Who uses this water?" Leland asked. "I mean, who made the dam?"

"Shepherds, usually. Fortunately, they won't need it this winter. Roland's commissary officers bought their flocks."

"Bought?"

"Well, promissory notes. If Roland holds this part of Cotswold come summer, they'll be redeemed."

"Hope they make it through the winter."

Gahnfeld said, "They did let them shear them first."

Leland looked at the muddy bottom of the water hole. It was already drying at the edges, the mud cracking into plates. "Waste not, want not."

They left after sunset, not so much to avoid the heat of day but to endure the cold of the desert night. There was a path, fortunately, since the Anvil was mostly broken rock and treacherous to horses. The formation of soil was limited to dust blown from outside the region and gravel created by temperature fluctuation stresses.

"When we went after the bandits, we lost ninety percent of our mounts the first week," Gahnfeld told Leland. "We lost thirty percent of our men before we ever drew bows." They were leading their horses on foot, side by side. The path was wide enough only for two horses. They walked twenty minutes out of every hour.

In ring light the Anvil was cold silver, a rough plain stretching in all directions. Their eyes, accustomed to the dark, could make out the glimmer of snowcapped mountains seventy kilometers north.

It was well after midnight and they were wearing their ponchos and gloves. Gahnfeld stared out into the waste, his head wreathed in exhaled fog. "I hate this damn place."

Gahnfeld kept them moving, with very short breaks, until the sun was two diameters above the horizon. Then he passed the order, "Tether your horses, feed and water them. Wet your mouth with your own water but no more. Rig shade and rest."

By noon heat waves were dancing off the rock and distorting the horizon. Despite walking and riding all night, Leland was restless and had trouble sleeping. He longed to keep moving, to rush to Laal.

AND KILL YOURSELF, YOUR MOUNT, AND THESE BOYS WHO FOLLOW YOU. HASTE MAKES WASTE.

He sought refuge in *zazen,* seated on a folded saddle blanket, knees crossed in a half lotus, back straight, counting his inhalations and exhalations. After two hours he was able to sleep. Gahnfeld woke him when the sun touched the horizon and they started moving again.

"It doesn't seem quite fair, does it?" Leland said as he put on his poncho as the temperatures dropped again near midnight. "I would've welcomed this cold in the afternoon. And now I'm wishing I had the heat we had then."

"Bitch, bitch, bitch, bitch," Gahnfeld said. After a moment he added, "Sir."

Leland smiled. "How are we doing on water consumption?"

"We'll be completely out by sunset tomorrow."

Leland frowned. "Is that bad?"

"We'll see. We're going to make the river sometime tomorrow night. I just don't know when. The last hours will be thirsty ones."

"What if we're attacked? Kept from advancing?"

Gahnfeld shrugged. "Then we'll take *their* water. But only fools would be out here."

Leland frowned. "What does that make us?"

"Don't ask."

It was by far the strongest push into southwest Laal, five thousand of Siegfried's troops under Marshall Plover sent down to deal with the increasing annoyance of Koss's army. With the Falcons, the Pikes, and the steadily increasing militia forces, Koss was still a thousand men short of their number, but he didn't intend to fight them man to man.

This was their land they were defending and the land itself would fight.

The Pikes and half the militia waited on the high plain, camped in the open where the Cotswold scouts found them and reported. The Cotswold column moved in, through Hindman Pass, intending to take advantage of their clear numerical superiority.

"I bet Plover would like to flank them. I know I would in his shoes," Koss said to Anthony.

They were almost two kilometers above the Cotswold column, in a rock pocket that sheltered them from the worst of high winds. They were bundled to their eyebrows and Koss's voice was muffled, coming from under his scarf.

They had a clear view of the pass below and the plain. To their left was a snowfield, a cornice just below the bare rock ridge above. Fresh snow was piled high up here but it had melted in warmer regions below, where the Cotswold troops moved.

Anthony nodded. "He could divide his forces but it would take the flanking unit a couple of days to get in position. Through the pass, he can close in one hour. Plover probably plans to split his forces once he gains access to the plain."

Koss nodded. "So he plans. We'll help him split his forces, eh?"

The column below moved inexorably through the pass. Koss smiled in satisfaction. These Cotswold troops knew the desert well, but none of his own troops would move through a pass this late in the year without checking above.

"Now, I think," he said conversationally to Anthony.

Anthony took the red flag and stepped out of the pocket, bracing himself against the wind. He didn't bother to wave it. Once he held it aloft, the wind flapped it wildly. He looked up to the ridge, above the cornice.

Figures appeared, dots of men spread all along the rock edge, moving from whatever shelter they'd been able to find. He saw the first boulder roll down, gathering scree as it went, before it kicked up snow at the upper part of the snowfield and disappeared within.

Nothing happened at first, but then the second boulder and the third hit, and then they came too fast to count.

Koss, also standing out in the wind to watch, clenched his jaw. *Come on, come on!*

Then they heard it—a crack, sort of half break, half oomph—and the snowfield began to move. Koss could *feel* it move, through his feet, grinding against the face of the mountain. He backed back into the pocket, pulling Anthony with him and checking above him for any rock debris that might start sliding from the vibration. A large boulder rolled past and then their backs were against rock, the overhang protecting them.

The avalanche picked up more rock and snow on its way down, a mass of white shot with specks of dark rock and hazed by a fog of airborne snow.

The troops below broke from a solid snake winding through the pass into scattered dots, but there was no place to go. They were knocked head over heels by the compressed air traveling before the avalanche, then enveloped by the white wave. When the airborne snow had settled, fully a third of the Cotswold column had *disappeared,* swallowed whole. The rear third was stuck in the pass, behind a wall of rock, snow, and the bodies of the dead and dying. The front third, in shock and disorganized, was between the blocked pass and the forces on the plain.

Koss's lips pulled back from his teeth and, for the first time since the fall of Laal Station, felt like something was going right. He turned back to Anthony and said, "The green flag, if you please."

Anthony was already bending to pick up the other flag pole. He held it up, in the breeze.

Farther up the pass, too far to see with the naked eye, figures appeared above *another* snowfield and began rolling rocks down the hill. The Cotswold troops who weren't caught in this new avalanche would be trapped between the two snow slides.

Out on the high plain, Ricard's Pikes and the militia started forward, at the walk, steadily, keeping in formation. The lead element of the Cotswold forces tried to regain some semblance of order, but they didn't really stand a chance.

Koss patted the icy rock beside him.

*Thank you.*

They reached the river at midnight, dry as dust. The horses had to be restrained, to keep them from racing ahead when the scent of the water came to them across the rock. When they came to the edge they found they were still short. The river was fifty meters below them at the bottom of a shear rock face. They were at the Bauer Rent, where the Black cut through a thirty-kilometer canyon.

"Don't worry," Gahnfeld said. "We're near the western end." He turned them due west, parallel to the river. Two more hours of gradual descent brought them down to the water itself.

The shores at the canyon mouth were marshy and the mud, after their crossing of the rock Anvil, seemed alien. Papyrus dominated the shore along with low brush.

It was not a good point to cross the Black for the bottom was treacherous, with quicksand common. In addition, they were only opposite Pree, still quite some ways upriver from Laal. Even though Pree bordered Laal, cutting across would put them in mountainous areas far from Laal Station.

"There's a good crossing fifty kilometers downriver," Gahnfeld said, "but there's one of the Cotswold border posts there. Or we can try a swimming ford once we're past the marsh. It peters out about fifteen kilometers downstream."

It was an hour after dawn now, and the horses were being watered again. More than one soldier hadn't been so careful—drinking too much and vomiting it out again.

Leland was standing by the water's edge looking out through the papyrus to the main channel. A piece of deadwood was drifting by in the current, faster than a man could walk. "How are the horses?" he asked.

Gahnfeld shrugged. "Not great. They'll need a day's rest, and the fodder around here isn't that good. We'll have to go easy on them."

Leland nodded. "Easy indeed. We're leaving them here."

"What?"

"Have the men start cutting reeds. Bundle them in rolls half a meter in diameter and four meters long. Then we lash these together."

Gahnfeld was still staring at him.

Leland stepped down to the water's edge, drew his dagger, and began sawing through the reeds at water level.

"We're taking to the river."

By spreading their harvest over three kilometers, the Eight Hundred left a good third of the papyrus standing and still had enough of the reeds for their purpose. The Eighth Hundred included the son of a rope maker who was soon supervising the weaving of a portion of the reeds into ropes for the binding.

At noon the signal officer gave Leland a message from Miyamoto's heliograph line. He read it by water's edge, watched by Gahnfeld.

"What is it? You look so grim."

Leland exhaled. "Five thousand more dead, in Laal."

Gahnfeld's eyes went wide. "Our troops? Our people?"

Leland shook his head. "No. Siegfried's troops. Koss lured them into Breathless Pass and dropped avalanches on them."

"But that's *good.*"

Leland tried to smile but it was a sorry effort. "Siegfried has a lot to answer for. You can tell the men if you think it'll cheer them." He looked downstream, to the activity on the banks. "Keep them going. I want to be on the water by sunset. They can rest as we float."

Gahnfeld left.

Leland composed his response.

To: Koss, Commander Laal Forces
From: Leland de Laal, 800
News of Breathless Pass recvd. Our current position western end of bauer rent. Taking to the river. Will join you in the tiber valley ASAP.

Zanna waited with the council in her father's formal staff room. He was late and they stood around the conference table, waiting, some fidgeting, some, like Zanna, perfectly still. Arthur was known for making people wait.

He finally entered, his secretary at his elbow, taking in the faces and pausing when he saw Zanna. "Gentleman. Daughter. I am here as requested. What business is so urgent that it can't wait until the next council meeting?" He didn't sit, so the others in the room continued to stand.

Charly's father, the Guide Michael de Rosen, inclined his head briefly and said, "I'll come straight to the point, High Steward. Cotswold has broken their treaty and invaded the Stewardship of Laal."

Arthur blinked and looked surprised. "How do you know this? Are you going by the word of the deserter, Leland de Laal? He maintained this, but he was with de Gant's forces on the plain and no such news came through Noramland."

*Is that an act, Father?* Zanna stood. "We have confirmation from Guide Kevin de Toshiko of Pree. A steady stream of refugees, mostly children with caretakers, have crossed into Pree at Apsheron. Cotswold troops have entered Laal in force."

Arthur's shoulders dropped. "Well, then. We must take action. What does the council propose?"

Michael de Rosen spoke. "Send the central reserves to Laal at once. Also recall the forces from the plain and have them make best speed."

Arthur shook his head. "de Gant's forces are engaged."

Zanna shook her head. "Father, de Gant reports that Roland's army is deep inside Cotswold." *Dammit, I* know *that report got to you!* "Roland is currently closer to Laal than the plain. He's also given his word to leave the Plain alone for the remainder of the season."

Arthur looked annoyed. "We had Siegfried's word, *too.* What about Kai Lung? What about Yukifuri? If I move the reserves, we'll be ripe for an attack from either of them—or from Neuveau France."

Michael de Rosen frowned. "We are at peace with all three of those countries. Why should they attack us now?"

"Opportunity!" Arthur said stridently.

The council representative from New New York cleared his throat. "Excuse me, High Steward, but am I correct in my understanding? You don't want to respond to Cotswold, who *has* attacked one of our stewardships, because we *might* be attacked by countries with whom we have peaceful relations?"

Arthur shook his head. "That's not what I said!"

"Then you'll give the order?" de Rosen asked. "Speed is imperative. There are only two passes open through the Cloud Scrapers right now."

Zanna held her breath, watching her father with narrowed eyes. *If you fail to take action, you'll lose the high stewardship. If you fail to go to Laal's aid, what stewardship will trust you?*

Arthur pulled the chair at the head of the table back and sat. His secretary jumped to scoot the chair back in. He leaned forward and rested his elbows on the table and briefly covered his face with his hands. When he removed them Zanna was shocked to see how old he looked.

"I have reason to believe that Siegfried coordinated this action with his son, Sylvan, who has disappeared. He seems to have taken Marilyn with him, apparently as a hostage. I have instigated an investigation, but there are no results yet."

Michael de Rosen pulled out his chair and sat. The others, with the exception of the secretary, followed suit. de Rosen said, "I see. We must do everything we can to keep her safe . . . and still come to Laal's aid."

Zanna nodded. *One person versus the thousands in Laal.*

Arthur clenched his jaw for an instant, as if he were going to argue, but then he sighed and covered his face again, rubbing at his eyes. "Very well—I'll give the orders."

Zanna exhaled. "Father, may I carry your orders to the signal staff?"

Arthur glared at her for a moment but she kept calm, still. Then his expression changed and he looked at her as if she were suddenly a stranger, an unknown quality. His eyes narrowed and he pursed his lips. Then his shoulders squaring slightly, he said, "My secretary can carry the orders. I want *you* to find Marilyn."

They didn't take Marilyn out of the basket as much as spill her rudely onto the ground.

It was dark and the pressure on her bladder was prodigious. Her eyes were used to the dark, though, and she saw men—seven of them—making camp or unloading horses in the shelter of a stand of oaks. The mustached man who spilled her onto the ground bent to her legs and she thought about kicking him, but then realized he was untying her ankles.

Her feet and hands were numb, completely without feeling, and she knew she was about to pay the price of restored circulation.

The man took the resulting length of rope, still connected to her bound wrists, threw it over a tree limb, and tied it off with just enough slack that Marilyn's wrists hung in front of her chest when she sat up.

She tried to curl her feet, then release them, flexing the muscles to hurry the blood flow—then the first sensation started and she wished she'd left well enough alone. Her eyes were clenched shut when she heard Sylvan's voice.

"Resting?"

She opened her eyes to narrow slits to look at him but didn't trust herself to say anything—not until the needles-and-pins throbbing in her feet stopped.

"Enjoying the journey, love?" Sylvan said. He squatted before her, sitting on his heels, and drew idly in the dirt with his finger.

She wondered if she could get the rope around his neck if she moved fast enough. *Not enough slack and I'd probably just fall on my face trying.* Better to wait until she'd had a chance to stretch her limbs.

Sylvan smiled again. "I'll wait until you're more talkative, my dear." He stood and started to turn.

Marilyn spoke between clenched teeth. "What did you do with my guards?"

Sylvan turned back and drew his thumb across his throat.

Marilyn squeezed her eyes shut again and inhaled sharply, through her teeth. She wanted to hurt him—an elbow lock, perhaps—only continuing until the bone broke or cartilage and tendons tore. But he was out of reach and it wouldn't bring them back.

"I need a bathroom," she said.

Sylvan paused and looked around. After a moment's thought he said, "I'll send a spoon over. You can dig a latrine behind the tree—the rope should reach that far if we loosen it a bit."

She didn't reply and, after a moment, he walked off.

The mustached man returned a few moments later with a wooden spoon and some toilet paper, then lengthened the rope tied to the tree branch overhead. *Damn. I could've sharpened a metal spoon on a rock.* Clenching it in her numb hands, she hobbled behind the tree trunk and managed, with great effort, to accomplish the task without wetting herself or her clothing.

The effort restored enough circulation to her hands that she repeated the agony she'd just finished with her feet. She sat back in front of the tree and clenched and released her fists, trying to get it over with.

She tried to reach the knots of her wrist bindings with her teeth but they were not amenable to such manipulations. She suspected they'd have to use pincers to untie the rope or cut it off. *Or,* she thought morbidly, *they'll just bury me in them.*

Seeing her business behind the tree was done, the mustached man came back and shortened the line again. "If you have the need again, call."

She eyed his belt dagger longingly but her hands were still in pain and she doubted she could cut herself loose before the others closed in on her.

There was the sound of hoofbeats and another horse entered the camp. Sylvan, seated by the new fire, stood.

"They've closed the border, Guide," the new arrival said, swinging down from his horse. "The local militia, perhaps fifty strong, are stationed at the pass."

Sylvan shrugged. In a voice that barely carried to Marilyn he said, "Well, it was a bit much, expecting Arthur to do nothing when we took his daughter. He's *fine* about betraying thousands of people in Laal but draws the line at his kin. Don't worry. My father has a contingency for this. He *always* has a contingency. One way or the other, we'll be in Laal this time tomorrow."

*That can't be true. He must be saying that to upset me.* But Sylvan was so far away from her that surely he couldn't count on her hearing? She remembered her father's odd behavior when they were in Laal and back in Noram concerning anything to do with Leland.

*Father, what have you done?*

Siegfried sat in Dulan de Laal's study and stared blindly at the mountains through the open window. The cold air swirled through the room, and he felt the chill but couldn't be bothered to shut the window or add fuel to the cast-iron stove in the corner.

He wished Commander Plover were alive. He wished it very much. *If he were alive, I could kill him.* For a moment he actually saw the mountains and shuddered. *I hate this stubborn, vicious place.*

The chill finally overcame his shock and he looked around for a servant, momentarily annoyed, then remembered. He'd thrown the last one down the stairway shortly after the news reached him.

*Plover, you deserved to die, but taking half my army with you!*

He stepped out into the hallway and saw his guard straighten at the other end of the hallway, at the head of the stairwell.

"Get some charcoal up here for the stove!" he shouted, and they all jumped.

The guard commander pointed at one of the men and then pointed down the stairwell. The man went down the stairs two at time.

Siegfried walked down the hall and into the bathroom. He looked into the mirror hung over the basin and snarled. The lines in his face had deepened in the last month and there was an edge of panic in his eyes that he didn't like at all.

*Where is it?*

He picked up a carved stone soap dish and threw it into the mirror. The glass shattered, scattering glittering shards across the floor, and the soap dish dropped into the wash basin with a harsh clatter.

The guard commander knocked on the door. "Are you all right, sir?"

"Yes!" he snarled.

He picked the soap dish out of the basin and tossed it aside, hard, to bang against the wall, then drop, with a clatter across the tile floor—bang, bang, thump, bang.

*Thump?*

He used his booted foot to sweep the worst of the glass shards from that side of the room, then dropped to his knees and began knocking on the tiles with the soap dish. *There.* He raised the dish higher and smashed down, cracking the tile and the thin wood panel it was bonded to. He used his dagger like a pry bar and, ripping up pieces of tile and wood, uncovered a box-shape cavity filled with a cloth-wrapped object.

*Could it be?* He fumbled the cloth—a cloak, he realized—off the object, unwinding it as fast as he could. Then, with a clatter, it slipped out and rolled across the floor, coming to rest on its side near the door.

*Yes!*

He picked it up carefully, inspecting it for any sign of damage. A streak of blood from his cut finger dripped down the glistening surface and he laughed.

*They don't have any idea what's in store for them.*

# TWENTY

## AI UCHI: MUTUAL KILL

They fed Marilyn cold camp bread in the predawn light. Her teeth clattered so hard in the cold that she was having trouble chewing and, in the night, her bound hands had gone to sleep again, causing the now-familiar pins-and-needles agony of renewed circulation.

After they'd all eaten, they put her on a horse and tied her hands to the saddle pommel, then ran a rope from ankle to ankle under the horse's belly. The man who held the reins of her horse grinned. "Don't give me any trouble, Gentle Guide. We'll be on mountain trails all day and if your horse goes over the side, you go with it."

Sylvan, overhearing this, laughed long and hard.

Marilyn indulged herself in several fantasies involving Sylvan and pain but paid no outward attention to either man. The column moved off, through the trees, and she kept her eyes open, waiting for whatever chance might come.

They came out of the woods as the sun cleared the horizon and rode across fallow farm fields. Now she could see the Cloud Scrapers, snow-topped and sharp like teeth, standing high above the trees, much closer than she'd realized. *No wonder it was so cold last night. We're already into the foothills.*

It bothered her that they no longer hid her in a basket even though they were still this side of the mountains. *Does he plan to buy passage with my well-being?* The thought of being used in that way deeply disturbed her. *Surely Father has given orders not to let me out of our territory no matter what the threat. Why else is the militia blocking the pass?*

They rode through more fields and Marilyn caught a glimpse of the main road on the other side of the line of trees. She experimented with leg aids, to see if her horse would respond to the seat alone. He did, both in turning slowing and once, transitioning from the trot to a canter, but the man leading her horse yanked viciously at the lead rope and Marilyn stopped confusing the poor animal.

Finally, as the ground rose higher and higher, they cut over to the main road and joined it. It was empty of traffic and the few houses along this way were abandoned for the winter. After a bit, the road hugged the face of a hill, turning this way and that as the switchbacks climbed higher and higher.

"How much farther?" Sylvan asked the man who'd joined them the night before.

"Two more hairpins, Guide. They've set up a post at the traveler's aid station."

Sylvan nodded. "I remember it." He reached behind and took something from his saddlebag. "Who pulls the strongest bow?"

There was some argument over that but the matter was solved when Sylvan said, "Shut up! I don't care." He pointed at one of the three men claiming superiority. "Come here and give me one of your arrows."

"Yes, Guide."

Sylvan tied a small tube to the shaft of the arrow, just behind the head. Then, using a match, he lit a projecting fuse. Smoke, thick and white, poured from the tube. He handed it quickly back to the archer. "Straight up. Quickly."

The archer fitted the arrow to the string and, coughing, loosed it high. The smoke made an easily seen arch across the sky.

"Let's go!"

Sylvan started up the road again, moving at a walk. They rounded one hairpin and then another. Ahead, at a rare flat spot on the hillside, a large timber building stood surrounded by soldiers. As Sylvan's party moved into sight, the soldiers spread across the road.

Marilyn frowned, wondering who the signal had been for.

Then she heard the sound of hoofbeats, hundreds of them, and she knew.

There must've been two hundred of the Cotswold cavalry thundering down the road. The militia at the station were seriously outnumbered. Sylvan moved his party forward, to the beginning of the flat, then, taking Marilyn's horse's reins, said, "Block their retreat." He led her horse back down the road and waited.

It didn't take long.

The captain in charge of the calvary rode up to Sylvan and saluted. "A handful of them barricaded themselves in the aid station. Should I pry them out?"

Sylvan shook his head. "Not necessary, Captain. Not necessary." As they rode by the traveler's aid station, he pointed to it and said, "Burn it. Burn it to the ground."

Zanna saw the fire from twenty kilometers away, but it took half the day to close the distance. When she and her men finally rode around the last bend, she saw one man with soot-blackened skin and clothing lining up bodies in neat rows besides the still-smoking embers of the former aid station.

She immediately dispatched twenty men to replace him and had her medic look him over.

"Some minor burns and he's a bit shocky but he'll be all right," her medic reported.

"What happened here?"

The survivor looked at her, his face blank and his eyes very strange. This had been a militia unit so the dead were almost certainly his village neighbors and relatives. When he talked, his voice was a harsh croak. "There was a party coming up the road and we were getting ready to turn them back when they fired a smoke arrow into the sky. Several hundred calvary came out of the pass above us and we ended up being trapped between them.

"I was knocked off the road by a horse, early on, and fell down the hillside, but a bush caught me before I went off the cliff farther down. By the time I climbed back up to the road, the fighting was over and they were torching the aid station."

Zanna asked, "Why?"

"To kill them that was in it." He held up his blistered hands. "After they rode off, I tried to get to them, but the roof collapsed and I was forced away by the flames."

Zanna closed her eyes briefly. "Did the party coming from Noram have a prisoner?"

"Yes. A woman in a dress." He looked up at Zanna, his eyes going over Zanna's uniform, her vest of scale, her helm, then, finally, her face.

Zanna pulled the helmet off and let her hair show in the sun.

The man grunted. "Yes, she looked like you."

The Eight Hundred put to shore just east of Jaren's Ford two days after entering the river. They left six destroyed Cotswold riverside border posts behind them, a relatively easy task since they'd been stripped of manpower for the invasion of Laal and their skeleton staffs were easily surprised.

Gahnfeld came to Leland. "What about the prisoners?"

There were twenty-three Cotswold prisoners, many of them wounded. They huddled at the riverbank watched by four squads from the Third Hundred.

"What do you suggest?"

"Put them across the river and harry them south for an hour."

Leland shook his head. "It's still the Anvil. Might as well shoot them here."

Gahnfeld shrugged. "Can't leave them here where they can report our presence. We need all the surprise we can muster."

"True."

Leland looked at the papyrus rafts pulled up on the shore. "Tie them up and put them on one of the rafts with two of our men. They can float five hours downstream, cut one of them loose, then try to join us. The prisoners will be thirty kilometers away from us—longer by the time they're all untied and get the raft to shore—but where they can get water. We only decrease our strength by two."

Gahnfeld thought about it. "Sounds good. I'll pick someone from that part of Laal.

"Wait," said Leland. "We're going to have company so there may be more prisoners. Save five rafts."

"Company? How do you know? And what about the other rafts?"

"Tear them apart, drag them into a pile, and burn them. Someone will come looking. Company. Hopefully," he added, "on horseback." He fingered his poncho. "And if we use our training properly, they won't see us until it's too late."

Almost immediately after the occupation of Laal Station Siegfried had the plating workshop cleared of everything but the banks of lead acid batteries. He'd known, since his original visit when the peace treaty was signed, that he wouldn't have to haul his own from Montrouge.

"I'm guessing at voltages here," Siegfried said to Sylvan, still dusty from travel and the only other occupant. Siegfried connected a series of cells together and took leads off at strategic points. His voltmeter, brought from Montrouge, was a needle cantilevered to a pivoting electromagnet coil with a mercury column resistor. "If I'm right, these are the values we need. If only I could be sure that what I'm calling a volt is the same as the manual's."

Sylvan blinked. "Don't the books tell you what a volt is?"

Siegfried laughed. "Sure, in terms of things I can't duplicate! If I had cadmium, I could make a Weston cell and calculate it that way, but I don't. And I don't have a scale fine enough to calculate current based on how much silver is deposited per second. Roughly, perhaps."

Sylvan shook his head. "I don't understand."

Siegfried turned back to the Helm, muttering "Why doesn't that surprise me?" He looked at his copy of the manual once again to identify the contact points.

This was handwritten on paper. The original had been found by clay harvesters, buried in a riverbank. It was sealed in an airtight case but wasn't one of the permanent books—it was an original paper manual, cracking and disintegrating. Making his copy had required destroying the original page by page.

He took his ground, a solid copper wire with an end that had been painstakingly filed down to almost hair thinness, and inserted it into an almost invisible hole in the helmet's interior surface. The ground poised no risk and he wasn't worried about it, but the next step, the five-volt wire, quickened his breath and brought sweat to his hands. He wiped them carefully on his pants before inserting the wire.

A previously clear portion of the Helm suddenly darkened, and Siegfried held his breath as it resolved into Arabic numerals.

5.73

"High, but well within tolerances," he breathed. He put the next wire in.

The display changed.

5.73 13.42

He inserted the last probe.

5.73 13.42 –11.92

Then the three sets of numbers blinked and disappeared replaced by the words DIAGNOSTIC MODE. There was a crystalline tone, like fine glassware ringing and then a stream of words.

PHOTOVOLTAIC CELLS SELF-TEST: FAIL MARGINAL

CAPACITORS AT .01 CAPACITY

CHARGING CAPACITORS WITH LINE CURRENT

TIME UNTIL FULL CHARGE: 15.4 MIN

CHECKING MEMORY . . .

CHECKSUM OK, FULL P MODE, 96% FULL

DIAGNOSTICS OFF

TIME UNTIL FULL CHARGE: 14.7 MIN

Siegfried's laughter filled the room. "They waited decades for it to charge in the sun and we'll do it in a quarter hour!" He flipped through the pages in the manual until he came to the next section. "This is where you come in, son." He gestured at the pendulum clock set on the wall. "When I say 'go,' begin counting off seconds. Understand?"

"Yes," Sylvan said shortly.

"Good. Ready? Go."

As Sylvan began counting, Siegfried pulled the five-volt lead from the helm. When three seconds had gone by, he put it back in. The display changed:

MENU

1 CLEAR IMPRINT SET

2 CHANGE IMPRINT MODE

3 DOWNLOAD IMPRINT SET

4 EXIT

"Yes! It works."

Sylvan winced at the words, which were more shouted than spoken. "Should I keep counting, then?"

"No."

Working through the menu using pulses from the five-volt lead, Siegfried selected Change Mode. The display changed.

Basic >>Full P<<

With another pulse it changed to:

>>Basic<< Full P

Then:

Confirm? Yes >>No<<

He confirmed. There was a series of five beeps and the display read:

Basic Mode Enabled
Download Imprint Set Now? >>Yes<< No

He selected "no." There was a loud prolonged beep.

Setup Incomplete!
Download Imprint Set Now? >>Yes<< No Other

He selected "other."

WARNING! Manual Mode is NOT recommended!
Confirm Manual Mode? Yes >>No<<

"Stupid machine! I don't have the equipment to do an imprint download." He selected "yes."

There was another series of five beeps and the machine read:

Manual mode selected
Select length of imprint
>>1 min<< 5 min 15 min 20 min

He selected one minute. The display changed.

Manual Imprint Mode, 1 minute cycle

It returned him to the menu and he exited.

TIME UNTIL FULL CHARGE: 11.7 MIN

"Sylvan," Siegfried said, his lips drawing back from his teeth, "bring me a prisoner."

The Cotswolders scouts scanned the riverbanks around the pillar of smoke and steam before waving in the rest of the troops. The cavalry split into three elements, one on the road, one swinging wide to the downstream bank, and one upstream.

It did them no good.

The archers loosed their first arrows prone, invisible, from under brush and ponchos. It must've seemed like the very ground vomited missiles. They stood for the next volley, converting the ground from brush-covered rock and gravel to overwhelming hostile forces.

Those at the rear tried to flee, only to find their paths blocked by more earth-colored soldiers with pikes, swords, and bows.

None escaped.

The Eight Hundred now had one hundred and fifty horses though they lost ten men in the ambush. Eighty-five of the Cotswolders died before the rest surrendered. The resulting prisoners were told of the Nularbor invasion of Cotswold before they were sent floating downstream with guards.

Leland looked at the bodies strewn across the slope, his mouth a tight line. He shuddered and forced his attention away from the dead.

Gahnfeld, just up the hill, was shouting orders. "Mount the scouts. Dress them as Cotswolders and get them out there. We may have just taken out the entirety of the local forces, but we must know for sure." He turned to Leland and raised his eyebrows.

Leland added, "Also mount a signal squad and get them to high ground. We need contact with Koss."

"Yes, Guide. Shall we start the rest along the main road?"

"Yesterday, Myron. Yesterday."

When the guards came for him, Bartholomew thought it was another problem in the kitchen, as when Siegfried's chef wanted to consult on the draft controls of the ovens. But the guards, after taking him from the cell, went away from the kitchens, toward the workshops. *Maybe it's another work detail.*

They wouldn't trust the old staff to prepare food but they did use the prisoners for general labor—hauling firewood, cleaning the stables, and laundry.

But they usually took more than just one prisoner, and it wasn't Siegfried's son who commanded the guards.

The hairs on his neck stood on end when they entered the plating workshop. The smell of sulfuric acid and silver nitrate was strong. He recognized Siegfried immediately, even though he was turned away from the door, doing something at a workbench.

Siegfried looked over his shoulder and said, "The chair." He nodded at a heavy oak armchair brought down from the main hall and fitted with a set of leather straps and metal buckles, ex-horse tack by the look of it.

*Is this what happened to Martin? Dame Bridgett?*

He started to resist when they pushed him down into the chair but stopped when Sylvan put a dagger to his throat. "Sit!"

They closed the straps around his biceps, wrists, ankles, chest, and lap. Finally they placed a loop of wire around his neck and pulled it taut against his skin.

"Don't move," Sylvan said, "or you'll choke yourself."

Bartholomew wondered what the alternative was, but held himself still.

"There, all charged," Siegfried said from someplace behind Bartholomew. "Everybody out but Sylvan."

*Me, too?* Bartholomew thought. He doubted it.

The guards filed out and Sylvan closed the door behind them and threw the bolt. He turned and leaned against the door, arms crossed, face impassive.

Siegfried's steps walked closer and he spoke again. "Remember—don't say anything during the imprint period or you'll mess up the process."

Sylvan nodded. "As you wish, Father."

"Okay. Here. We. Go."

Something cold and hard slid onto Bartholomew's head and he jerked, surprised, but the wire loop around his throat brought him short. Then the thing settled onto his head and he felt a burning sensation on his scalp, then . . .

He had to listen and watch. Something was about to happen. Something important. Something more important and urgent than anything he'd ever seen or heard in his entire life. His eyes were wide open, unblinking. His ears heard every scrape of movement, every breath of air. His spine was erect, rigid, totally fixed.

A man stepped in front of him and bent over, putting his face in front of his. Siegfried. He spoke.

"You exist only to serve *me*. You will obey *me* before all others and obey those *I* direct you to obey. You will do nothing that might harm *me*. If necessary, you will die to protect and serve *me*. Serving *me* fills you with joy. Disloyalty to *me* causes you pain and sorrow."

And then Siegfried repeated it.

Each word riveted Bartholomew, etched itself in his memory like a chisel carves letters from granite. He silently echoed it when Siegfried repeated it, each word matching Siegfried's and building, building, building. By the third repetition he was repeating the words aloud, first in a croaking whisper, then in a stronger, firmer voice. The voice of a man with a purpose.

"—ving *you* fills me with joy. Disloyalty to *you* causes me pain and sorrow."

Siegfried looked up at the clock, then back into Bartholomew's face, then the force, the force that had held Bartholomew's eyes open, his spine erect, left him, and he slumped into partial darkness, unable to control himself, sagging down against the wire and choking.

He felt a hand push his head back, relieving the bite of the wire, heard a voice, a wonderful voice, say, "Dammit, this wire was a mistake—get it off him, Sylvan!"

The pressure came off his throat and he coughed uncontrollably for a time. Slowly control of his muscles came back and he straightened, looking around, trying to find the source of that marvelous voice.

There, watching him, Siegfried searched his eyes. Bartholomew waited, expectant, hopeful.

"How do you feel?" Siegfried asked.

Bartholomew smiled. "I feel good, Guide." Guide—yes, this was his *guide*. And his guide *cared* about him. He cared about how Bartholomew felt.

Siegfried gestured to Sylvan. "Let the guards in. And get me another prisoner."

"Don't you have to charge the Helm again?"

Siegfried nodded. "Yes, but that's not why I want a prisoner. Go on!"

Sylvan opened the door and left. The guards came in and Siegfried pointed back at Bartholomew. "Release him."

One of the guards held his arms from behind the chair while another knelt and undid the buckles. When all the straps were free, Siegfried waved them away from the chair.

"What is your name?" he asked.

"Bartholomew Kwiats, Guide."

"Stand up, Bartholomew."

Bartholomew stood as quickly as he could.

Siegfried pointed to a glass vat on the bench and said, "This is full of sulfuric acid, for the batteries. Do you know what sulfuric acid is?"

"Yes, Guide."

"What would happen if I were to stick my hand in it?"

Bartholomew became very uncomfortable. "It would burn your hand, Guide. Please don't."

Siegfried nodded. "You look worried. What's upsetting you?"

"You aren't going to stick your hand in the acid, are you?"

"No. That was a hypothetical question."

Bartholomew exhaled and his face relaxed.

Siegfried continued. "However, I would like *you* to put your hand in the acid."

"Now, Guide?"

"Yes, Bartholomew. Now."

Bartholomew smiled and walked over to the bench, then plunged his hand into the glass jar without hesitation. He kept his eyes on Siegfried's face, lest he miss an instruction. Somewhere, in the back of his mind, a voice screamed out, but Bartholomew ignored it, irritated, afraid it would distract him from his first duty.

"Very good, Bartholomew. You may withdraw your hand."

He pulled his hand from the jar and glanced at it. It was wet but otherwise unharmed. "Guide, this is not acid."

Siegfried smiled slightly. "Water."

The door opened and Sylvan came back in with two guards and a prisoner. Bartholomew looked. It was Sven, one of the junior kitcheners.

"Do you know this boy, Bartholomew?" Siegfried asked.

"Yes, Guide. He worked for me in the kitchen."

"Ah, excellent." Siegfried turned to the guards. "Strap him in the chair."

Sven didn't try to struggle but his eyes darted back and forth, returning always to Bartholomew. When he'd been secured, the guards stepped back to the door.

Siegfried pulled his dagger from its belt sheath and held it out to Bartholomew, hilt first. The guards tensed.

Bartholomew took the dagger and held it briefly to his forehead with both hands as he bowed, then held it loosely beside his leg.

Siegfried pointed at the chair. "What's his name?"

"Sven Hilltopper, Guide."

Siegfried nodded. "Kill him."

Bartholomew raised the knife to waist level and tightened his grip. "Yes, Guide."

"I've a message from my mother, from Laal Station."

Koss looked up at Ricard, surprised. "Oh, really? How did it come?" The army was camped in the barrens, southwest of Laal Station. It was cold but dry and they'd met little resistance in their march. They talked in Koss's staff tent, by a charcoal brazier.

"Apparently, it was floated in a bottle down the falls and picked up downstream. Refugees brought it out of the valley and passed it to one of our scouts."

Koss was skeptical. "Are you sure it's from her?"

"Aye. It's not signed but it's in her hand and ostensibly from Petronius."

"Who is Petronius?"

Ricard blushed. "A cloth rabbit I had as a child."

Koss chuckled. "I see. What does she say?"

"She has intelligence and can pass it to us."

"Let me read it."

To: Commander Mounted Pikes
From: Petronius, Same old place
Have News of here. Need reliable path for future messages.
Meet contact in Kitchen of Birthday Party midnight Thursday.
Contact knows your face.

"What does she mean by 'Kitchen of birthday party'?"

"We celebrated her last birthday at the Blue Whale Inn."

"Ah. Very clever. Even if this was intercepted, it only identifies you, safe with your troops." He held it to his chin and pursed his lips.

"Risky rendezvous, though. We now outnumber his forces in Laal, especially with the Eight Hundred marching from the south, and, with the Nullarbor invasion of Cotswold, he's unlikely to be reinforced. I'm not sure I want to risk one of our experienced commanders in an intelligence operation we don't need."

Ricard spread his hands. "What about Guide Dulan and all our people still in Laal Station? What if she can get us inside without a protracted siege? It could mean the difference between taking the Station intact or destroying it, not to mention the lives saved."

Koss closed his eyes. Hostages slaughtered was one of his recurring nightmares, especially after the recent destruction of the Cotswold forces under Plover. He kept expecting to hear of a bloodbath at Laal Station from the refugees or his agents scattered around the Tiber valley.

"Well, you have me there. Heavens knows *Siegfried* did it. I wonder how?" *A traitor?* His spies knew nothing about it. He returned to the matter at hand. "Could she have written it under duress?"

Ricard shook his head. "Then she wouldn't have used Petronius and *they* wouldn't know about that."

Koss grunted. "Well, we can try it. I'll send you over the mountains the way our couriers have been traveling, weather allowing. It's snowshoes and frostbite, but the Cotswolders don't stray there. You can just make it by Thursday if you leave today."

Ricard nodded and started to turn, but Koss stopped him with his next words.

"If you don't make it back, I'll give command of the Pikes to Dexter." He paused, waiting for that to sink in. Dexter and Ricard did *not* get along. "So be careful, dammit! If there's any hint of a trap, run for it. No risks. Understand?"

Ricard grimaced, then spat in the brazier. "I understand."

Marilyn had been installed in a guest bedroom with its own bathroom and newly mounted set of throw bolts on the wrong side of the door. There were three windows but they were arrow slits, too narrow for her body. At her request, she'd been provided with warmer clothes, since they didn't trust her with fire for the stove that heated her suite.

When they brought her meals, armed guards stood without while a servant brought the tray in and fetched the tray from the previous meal. In the three days since their arrival these were the only faces she'd seen. She'd asked for reading materials and a chance to exercise outside but if these requests had been passed on, they'd been ignored.

She was almost wishing that Sylvan *would* come force his obnoxious presence upon her. It would give her something to do.

*Be careful of what you wish for,* she thought when Sylvan arrived at dinnertime with more servants. They put candles on the table and set two places. A servant remained behind, for table service, when the guards shut the door and threw the bolts.

She expected him to exult in the situation, to glory in his role as her jailer, but he seemed subdued, preoccupied.

"Mmmm. Good mutton, eh?" he finally said. "These mountain grasses are good for that. And this wine!" The wine was from the Station cellars.

Marilyn, eating to maintain her strength, didn't comment. She didn't touch the wine, wanting a clear head. He was inoffensive enough at the moment, but she remembered her guards, the slaughter on the mountain road, and the flames from the aid station.

"You're not saying much, my pet." Sylvan took a deep breath and narrowed his eyes. Wherever he'd been, he was back now.

*I'm not your pet,* she thought, but said nothing, chewing mechanically.

He leaned back in his chair and sucked on his teeth, probing at a piece of mutton stuck between his molars. "I wonder what sort of wife you'd make," he finally said. "You're not very pretty and you're flat-chested but the rest of you isn't too bad. I could always keep a mistress on the side."

Marilyn put down her spoon. "Marry the mistress."

"No, Father is still set on you."

"Did you do something to upset him?"

Sylvan misunderstood. "Well, you're not *that* ugly."

Marilyn smiled grimly and didn't enlighten him. "I won't marry you, you know."

He shook his head. "What you desire isn't an issue anymore." He looked oddly disturbed. "More's the pity."

"You'd marry me against my will? Do you plan on never sleeping?"

Sylvan shook his head again. "If I marry you, you'll want it more than I. A lot more."

Marilyn kept her mouth closed. *What on earth is he talking about?*

Sylvan stood and looked at her, eyes narrowed. "I wanted to do it myself, however long it took. Now, though, it looks like that won't be an issue. Unless you're willing now?"

Marilyn frowned. "What are you talking about?"

"Willing to be mine in body and soul, without my father's little device."

"What kind of device are you talking about?" She didn't like the sound of this at all.

"Never you mind. Are you willing?"

"Not in a million years."

He sighed. "I thought so." He turned and knocked on the door. The bolts rattled and it opened inward. He looked back once more. "You will be."

The door shut and the bolts thudded home. She stared at the wood and worried.

Ricard spent two hours waiting for dusk just below the timberline, with Lillian. Of all his cousins, she was the only one he'd ever felt comfortable with. His mother had tolerated her in a way that she hadn't her older brothers. Perhaps it was because Lillian had also lost a parent while a baby, like Ricard.

"Dexter and Anthony are fine. I left them with the army though they almost caught Dexter with a false message, just as they decoyed me to the west. Leland is in Laal and coming up from the south with his troops. The armies will converge here."

"What about Father?"

Ricard shook his head. "No news, but I might have some soon. My mother's found some way to send messages out of the Station. I'm meeting a contact of hers tonight in the town."

"Well, good. I'm glad she's alive. Did you hear about Dame Bridgett?"

Ricard nodded but said nothing, watching Lillian carefully. Her eyes were clear of tears but had dark circles below. News of the deaths of Martin, Bridgett, and a few others had come before the battle of Breathless Pass. The bodies had been burned but rumors of horrible wounds had still gotten out of the station.

"Will they kill us all?" Lillian asked tonelessly.

"No," Ricard said firmly. "We outnumber them now and, thanks to the invasion of Cotswold by the Rootless, we'll continue to. In fact, we've been funneling news of the Rootless invasion to every level of Siegfried's forces. Before we attack again, we'll let it be known that deserters won't be harassed if they want to go home to protect their families. Well, not by us. Siegfried is probably pretty tough on his deserters—there haven't been that many." He stared out the tiny window to the darkening sky and remembered burned farmsteads near the borders and families dragged from the homes and slaughtered in the snow. "And they have reason to fear us, too. Without some sort of assurance, I'd not want to be a lone Cotswolder in the Laal countryside."

Pearson, his guide, drinking hot tea on the other side of the cabin with Matilda de Swain, drained his cup and stood. "It's time, Captain." Pearson was a small man, serious, worry lines etched into his face. He was responsible for every covert agent and courier working under the enemy's eyes.

Ricard swallowed the last of his own tea, cool now but still wet and sweet. "Keep well, cousin."

Lilian smiled slightly and said, "I'm not the one headed into enemy territory.

Ricard grinned, gave her the empty cup, and shrugged into his outer clothing.

It was dark and snowing when the reached the outskirts of town, a fact that pleased Pearson. "If you have to run, this'll hide you."

"What about you?"

"They know me here—I'm a well-known collaborationist. They won't even bother me for being out past curfew. As long as *you* don't blow me."

Koss had been clear on this. Pearson's network's continued intelligence was crucial to the upcoming fight. "I'll die first."

Peason nodded. "I depend on that."

They passed by the front of the Blue Whale Inn twice, walking casually, then again on the street behind. Ricard kept his eyes on the shadows. The guide watched the windows. Finally Pearson left him waiting in the barn down the street and dared the interior.

Time stretched on and Ricard's imagination pictured troops closing on the barn. He spent his time peering through a crack into the barn wall, but all he could see were the dim outlines of the neighboring buildings through a fog of swirling snowflakes. *Relax. He probably bought a glass of ale, to explain his presence. It would be odd if he didn't stay to drink it.*

Finally a single figure appeared, walking through the dark, resolving into Pearson just before he opened the door. He was smiling and the worry lines were gone. "All clear. Your mother's in there. Let's go."

Ricard followed him back to the inn shaking his head. *And I thought he was worried about his entire network, not just this mission.*

They shook off the snow in the mudroom off the kitchen, stamping their feet and flapping their coats, then, head bared, Ricard pushed through the inner door.

And into a trap.

Yes, his mother was there, smiling. So was Siegfried Montrose and ten armed men.

He bolted backward but someone shoved him from behind, before he could get out the door, giving the guards time to round the worktable at that end of the room and take him. Two held his arms while another pulled his dagger and the hidden short sword from their scabbards. Ricard looked over his shoulder to see who'd stopped his exit and saw Pearson standing there, blocking the door, unmolested, unguarded . . .

"How long?" he asked him.

Pearson looked at him, still smiling that almost serene smile. "What?"

"How long have you been theirs?" he spat out.

The answer came from his mother standing beside the central brick ovens. Someone had overstoked the oven, probably some of Siegfried's men. Why should they care if they set the inn on fire? The oven interior was white hot and the partially open iron door glowed red at the hinges. "Ten minutes, son. Only ten minutes."

He turned his head back. "Impossible." His mother's smile was eerily like Pearson's. "Did you take his family?" he asked to the room at large.

Siegfried had turned away as soon the guards had removed Ricard's weapons and was fiddling with something set on one of the far counters. Now, though, he laughed and turned back toward Ricard. "Really. Ten minutes ago he was fighting like a wildcat." He pointed at one of his soldiers, standing over a sink.

The man turned his head. He was holding a cloth-wrapped bundle to his face, which Ricard presumed held ice or packed snow. The top of the cloth was red with blood.

Siegfried stepped to one side revealing what he'd been fiddling with.

Ricard stared at it for a moment before realizing what it was. "What are you doing with the Glass Helm?"

His mother explained. "The high steward knows how to use it to, ummm, *adjust* attitudes."

Ricard shivered. He'd never seen his mother look so *calm* or happy. She'd always been edgy and angry, all his life. "He used it on you, didn't he?"

She nodded. "Yes. Though we were working together before that. But not for the *right* reasons."

Ricard stared. *No, don't tell me . . .*

"Your mother has been an enormous help to me." Siegfried said. "Between giving me your military code and keeping the Floating Stone grounded she was worth five thousand men. However, she's been even *more* helpful since wearing the Helm." He glanced back at the bench. "As you will be, as soon as it finishes recharging."

Ricard stared at his mother. "Why?" His anguish and disgust showed in his voice and expression.

For an instant the smile faltered, then returned. "I did it for you. You should've been steward here. Your father was the heir. He would still be ruling if not—" She stopped herself. "I've got better reasons now."

Ricard squeezed his eyes shut and ground his teeth together. *No, no, no . . .* He opened his eyes again. His mother's treason was at its limit—the damage maximized, but Pearson behind him could betray Lillian's hiding place and the entire network of agents in the valley or, worse, use it to feed false information back to Captain Koss. And then there was the damage that Ricard himself could do, if the Helm worked as well as they claimed.

He slumped in the grip of his guards, apparently overcome, and they shifted, surprised, pulling him back up. He surged with them, stamping down into the instep of one, then kicking into the knee of the other, all the time watching Pearson, still behind him, out of the corner of his eye.

Pearson surged forward, reaching for Ricard's shoulders. Ricard let him close, then surged back against him, smashing back with his elbow with all his might and focus. Pearson's larnyx took the bony point and collapsed, cartilege breaking. His neck folded forward and he dropped, choking, to his knees.

The guards surged back toward him and he vaulted forward, over the worktable, temporarily gaining breathing room, but no more. He was trapped between the guards at the door and more coming around the brick ovens to ring him in.

His goal, however, was not escape. On the end of worktable was a five-liter ceramic jug labeled olive oil. He picked it up and threw it at the guard between him and the ovens. The jug was heavy and the man had plenty of time to duck.

Then the jug smashed against the red-hot iron door and the oil splashed into the white-hot interior. Flame gushed from the door like a dragon vomiting, spreading burning oil and cinders across the floor and over his mother.

The advancing guards threw themselves back, scrambling toward the door. Ricard took one look at Siegfried, wondering if he had a chance to get him or the Helm, but the high steward was being helped out a smashed window, one hand clutching the Helm and the other beating at a smoldering patch of cloth on his thigh.

His mother was down, motionless, in a pool of burning oil, her hair already gone, her clothes nearly so. The ceiling was on fire, casting a lurid glow over everything. Ricard's own clothing was smoldering and a gust of hot wind seared his face. He turned again and saw one of the guards reaching back into the kitchen, trying to pull Pearson from the interior.

They might be able to get a tube into Pearson's throat. Even if he couldn't talk, he'd be able to write the names of his agents. Ricard moved that way, ignoring searing pain, then stopped when a spear poked through the doorway. He looked around for a weapon, something to parry with, and spied a half-full four-kilo sack of flour. He grabbed it and, holding it by the bottom, flung his arm out, scattering the flour into the air between himself and the door, trying to snare the spear tip with the cloth bag so he could get by and finish Pearson.

The cloud of fine flour ignited, turning the air around them all into a sea of flame.

It was the last thing he saw.

Siegfried sat in the snow surrounded by his guards and held packed snow against the burn on his thigh. *So close!* He'd nearly lost everything: the Helm, this war, his life, all from the actions of one supremely insane man acting against all odds. One minute Siegfried had *everything* going his way, and the next . . .

Despite the curfew a crowd of the townspeople was manning a pump wagon and spraying water over the buildings closest to the inn. Others shoveled snow, flinging it past gouts of flame thrusting out windows or through the gaping hole where the back door used to be.

That fireball had killed two of his men standing *outside* the building as well as those in the antechamber, trying to recover the spy, Pearson.

In his present mood, Siegfried would've liked to let the entire town burn to the ground, but he clamped down on the impulse to order the firefighters slain.

He struggled to his feet, still clutching the Helm. "Back to the Station! Hurry!" He was feeling especially vulnerable just now. An arrow from the dark, lead shot from a sling, a thrown knife—he wanted thick stone walls between himself and his enemies.

Never again would he risk the Helm. He should've had Ricard de Laal tied down the moment he was in the room. And the Helm should have never left the Station. *Are all these mountain people like that madman?* Impossible. Or he wouldn't hold as much of Laal as he did.

Still, his next subject would be completely immobilized before Siegfried or the Helm entered the same room. Someone who could influence and betray his enemies. Someone like . . . the younger daughter of Arthur de Noram.

# TWENTY-ONE

## KAESHI-WAZA: REVERSALS

The first units to reach Zanna's temporary camp were reserve militia, followed closely by the professional reserves stationed at Noram City. Her father, after several contradictory messages, finally sent a heliogram indicating his intent to join the expedition in a few days.

*Damage control,* Zanna thought cynically. *He can't put his interpretation on it without being here.* She asked herself the question again, the one she'd asked over and over again in the last week: *Why did he ignore this invasion for so long?*

There were barely three thousand troops with her so far. Marshall de Gant and the majority of her professionals were barely a third of the way from the Plain of the Founders, and their advance units wouldn't arrive for another four days.

She knew what her father would say, *if* she asked! *Stay put until you can advance in force.*

She sent the scouts out and called her unit commanders to her. "Start on the pass."

One of the professional commanders said, "We're not waiting for Marshall de Gant's forces?"

"No. With luck, we'll have the way open by the time he arrives and he can proceed directly into Laal. In the meantime, large numbers mean nothing in the pass—some spots are less than four meters across—so waiting for the rest of the army is pointless." She narrowed her eyes. "Unless there's some other reason you're reluctant?"

The officer looked embarrassed. "No, Gentle Guide. We'll begin immediately."

Leland's troops advanced up the Tiber carefully, taking outposts by stealth and surprise whenever possible. The slow pace galled him, but Gahnfeld pointed out that they were not so large a force that they could afford to leave enemies at their back.

He remembered running up this road three months earlier, covering the entire distance to Brandon-on-the-Falls in less than ten hours. They'd spent two days covering a third of that same distance, and it was harder now to take the outposts by surprise.

*What's happening in Laal Station?* He wondered what Siegfried had done with his father, with the other hostages in town. He was surprised that Siegfried hadn't started a withdrawal from Laal. News of the Nullarbor invasion must've reached him by now. *Doesn't he realize his people need him?*

I DOUBT IF HE CARES. HE STRUCK ME AS INTENTLY SELF-FOCUSED.

Leland shook his head.

The latest message from Captain Koss put the majority of Laal troops only a day away from the valley facing light opposition.

"Pick up the pace, Myron," Leland said. "Or we're going to be late for the party."

Marilyn found the piece of wood just before breakfast.

She'd started early, before dawn, and, unable to sleep, went through every dynamic and static stretching exercise she knew. That killed forty-five minutes and brought a rosy predawn glow to the eastern sky. She meditated after that, taking, as her focus, the picture of a bird flying from a cage.

When she opened her eyes, she was staring at the bed.

The frame was oak, rectangular, with a cotton mattress perhaps six centimeters thick. She pulled it away and found thin planks running from the head to the foot. Lifting one of these, she found oak dowels, perhaps three centimeters thick, running perpendicular to the planks and supporting them. They were almost exactly the length and thickness of a *jo*, the short staff she was so familiar with, but they were firmly glued into the long frame members.

She removed all the planks, then lowered herself down, midway down the bed, between two of the dowels, and put her foot against one side of the frame and her shoulder against the other. She took a deep breath and then pushed. The bed was extremely well made. After four attempts, all she had was a bruised shoulder.

She took a towel and folded it into a pad for her shoulder. The bed gave on her next attempt, the glue releasing from the two dowels on either side of her. Some vertical wiggling and the glue gave on the other end of her chosen dowel. She left the other one in place and put the bed back together, then spent some time smoothing the dried glue off the ends by rubbing it on the stone floor.

The result wasn't perfect but the wood was good—nice even grain without any warp. She tried a few *tsuki,* thrusts, with it, then ran through some of the *jo* basics. The wood sang in the air and she stopped, satisfied.

She took the pillows from the bed and the extra blanket and formed the semblance of a sleeping body beneath the bedding, then she kneeled, to one side of the door, the staff resting across her lap.

*It's time to leave.*

"What do you mean, she's gone!"

Sylvan, satisfied that the fault wasn't his, replied calmly. "She's not in her room but her guards and the servant who brought her meals were tied up and locked in her room. The servant has a broken arm and the other two are still unconscious. The servant says she had a staff. We found a cross member missing from the bed frame."

Siegfried stepped away from the workbench. They were back in the plating lab, and he'd given the order to have Marilyn brought to him after breakfast. Sylvan watched his father's hands. The fingers were locked together and, though Siegfried's voice was calm, Sylvan could see the knuckles turning white.

"Are you searching the Station?"

"Yes, sir. We've doubled the guards at the gates, too."

With a visible effort, Siegfried untwined his fingers and dropped them to his sides. "Was she trained or just lucky?"

"We're not sure. She took out both guards while the servant was still putting the tray down so he didn't see what happened. By the time he'd got back to the door, she was coming back in. He tried to resist and got his arm broken and a poke in the stomach that put him down. The guards are still out so we can't ask them what she did."

"And you're not sure? You have no imagination. Pass the word to approach her with caution."

"Well, we did. She took a knife and a sword—she's armed now."

Siegfried rolled his eyes. "She was armed before. She was probably armed *without* the staff. I still want her alive . . . if possible. If she's a martial artist, she'd make a wonderful assassin. Perhaps I could use her to take out her father and sister."

Sylvan shuddered.

Siegfried turned back to the bench where the Helm sat connected to the battery cells. "I have a mission for Bartholomew. Get him."

The Cotswolders drew the line four kilometers south of Brandon-on-the-Falls at a place where the Tiber valley narrowed, fortified by a snow-and-wood blockade that stretched from cliff face to cliff face. The Eight Hundred could have forced their way through, but only at a cost Leland wasn't willing to pay. They were already down to seven hundred fifty-three, and Leland carried every one of the forty-seven deaths, as if their stone grave markers rested on his shoulders.

*What are you doing, Father? Are you still alive? Healthy? Or are you torn and bleeding and hanging on to life by a thread?*

DON'T DO THAT TO YOURSELF. YOU DON'T KNOW SO DON'T MAKE THINGS UP.

Leland paced back and forth, behind the lines, unable to stay still. His communications with Koss were temporarily cut off by snow in the heights, blocking heliograph transmissions, so he couldn't even advise him of his current halt.

They'd discussed slipping back and up into the mountains, bypassing the blockade, but their clothing was barely adequate for the weather in the valley. Going into the heights would be risky without better gear.

At the very bottom of the valley, where the Tiber was frozen over, the snow was meters deep. Leland's path across this section was now a trench, shoulder deep. In early morning, he led Gahnfeld to the spot.

"Yes, Guide?" Gahnfeld asked, puzzled.

"We're over the river. Dig that way"—he pointed down at an angle toward the enemy barricade—"until you reach the ice. Then follow it upstream. Dig quietly."

Gahnfeld grinned suddenly. "I understand."

* * *

Marilyn waited, lying on her back, in the best hide-and-seek place in the Station, the chest beneath the window seat in the library revealed to her by Leland so very long ago.

They'd already searched the library three times. Each time she'd expected the panel above to be lifted and men, armed and ready, to seize her. Each time, though, they'd gone on without finding her. She'd sneaked into the toilet in the hall once. The rest of the time she tried to ignore her stomach's rumbling. She'd only snatched a bite of breakfast when she left the bound men in her room and fled down a flight of stairs and over one wing to the library.

She planned to wait until the wee hours of the morning before moving again.

*"Excuse me, do you work here?"* That's what she'd said, the first time she saw Leland. He'd stared at her, frozen, and she remembered wondering if she was wearing her breakfast on her chin.

Finally, though, he'd blinked and stirred, a statue returning to life. *"I suppose you could say that. I work everywhere else."*

Lying in the dark she replayed that first meeting in her head, a totally unexpected, wonderful encounter that still brought a smile to her lips. Then the dinner and his sudden inexplicable hostility, and their later arguments when she'd returned from Cotswold.

*Well, he was certainly right about Cotswold.*

Thoughts of Sylvan entered her head and she clamped her teeth together until her jaw muscles stood out like rocks. She forced herself to relax, counting her breaths, and turned her mind back toward escape.

She'd become familiar with a few parts of the Station when she'd last stayed here, but there were whole sections she'd never entered. She needed a plan of the Station and a map of the surrounding area. Where would she get them?

*In Noram City, I'd go to the library.*

Silently, lying in the darkness, she began to laugh.

They were well under the barricade now. Gahnfeld was having the men tunnel around the clock, changing units every half hour.

The tunnel was just wide enough for two men to walk abreast, one entering with an empty shield, one exiting with a shield piled with snow. The temperature in the tunnel was almost balmy, and the walls and ceiling were continuously melting and refreezing, forming an icy shell that was stronger than the snow.

A single candle burned near the ever-moving end, but otherwise the men shuffled forward in darkness, moving quickly, almost holding their breaths until it came their turn to scoop out the next shield of snow and hurry back out into the fresh air.

"As long as they keep moving," Gahnfeld said, "they should move enough fresh air in . . . I hope."

After sunset he and Leland took a quick inspection.

Gahnfeld emerged, taking deep breaths. "It's foul."

Leland nodded. "Too much $CO_2$—the candle is dimming. Send some spears in. I want shafts to the surface every five meters on this side of the barricade."

"Right away."

Leland returned to his headquarters, a makeshift hut with snow walls, a pine-bough roof, and a constant haze of smoke waiting to exit a vent hole. The door was a hanging blanket, to keep the heat in, and his bed salvaged pine needles well away from the fire. He took a deep breath before entering, then sat quickly, on the bed, to duck under the smoke haze.

The warmth was welcome. He'd grown chilled watching the work. He thought about taking a turn at the tunneling. The work would keep him warm, but he'd been up most of the night before and was exhausted.

He pulled a blanket up to his chin and tried to push everything away—the responsibility, the worries, the worst-case nightmares, but the harder he pushed, the harder they came at him.

NOT LIKE THAT.

He sighed. *How then?*

LET THEM COME, BUT LET THEM GO, TOO. YOU'RE GIVING THEM THEIR STAYING POWER. OBSERVE BUT STAY DETACHED. GET OFF THE LINE. WOULD YOU STAND STILL BEFORE A STRIKE? SLEEP WILL COME.

And so it did, eventually.

Gahnfeld woke him. The fire had died to embers and it was still dark outside.

"An attack?" Leland asked.

Gahnfeld laughed. "No. A refugee from the Station, one you should talk to. He came around the barricade, down the mountainside."

Leland followed Gahnfeld out into the cold, pulling the poncho hood up to keep his ears warm. A crowd of men stood around one of the closest warming fires, their attention on someone seated. As Gahnfeld and Leland approached, the group opened up and Leland saw who it was.

"Bartholomew." Leland's grin was so wide it hurt his face. "You've lost weight."

Bartholomew stood, smiling, and threw his arms around Leland and pounded him on the back. He pushed Leland at arm's length, looking him up and down. "Thank god you're all right.

"I've a message from your father."

Marilyn came to the opinion, reinforced by her experiences in Siegfried's capital, that Cotswolders were not readers. After the library searches she heard only infrequent traffic on the stairway at the far end of the hall. The library itself was quiet and still. She took to leaving the lid of her hiding place open and ready, but strayed from its confines to explore the library shelves.

She found what she was looking for in the "new" books, books printed or handwritten on paper since the Founding. The treasure was contained in an ongoing record of architectural changes to Laal Station.

> *. . . the invalid Athelia having died two years before, Lemuel de Laal ordered her rooms converted to a study. The elevator shaft was left in place against future need and the opening covered with shelves and cabinets in the study and on all the floors below with paneling to keep the unwary from falling.*

A current floor plan of the Station didn't show the elevator, but it did show the study up by Dulan's rooms and there was a small two meter–by–two meter gap that had to be the shaft. The other floors weren't to the same scale so it took some juggling to figure out where the shaft would be on other levels, but by working back from the stairwells she worked it out.

Dulan's study was in this wing but two floors up. The shaft, if it used to open on this floor, should be six meters down the hallway outside the library. Three floors down from this one (and her stomach rumbled at the thought), it should open near the kitchen.

She took a quick, timid foray out into the hallway and located a section of wood paneling midway down a stretch of stone wall. A woven hanging covered most of it, and when she pushed the cloth aside and tapped gently on the wood, it sounded hollow.

She took her stolen knife and went to work.

Bartholomew led the way, and Leland and a bodyguard of four followed, fighting their way up snow- and ice-covered slopes, into the heights.

It was snowing, which was a blessing and a curse. A blessing, for it hid their passage effectively from those in the valley below. A curse, because, even with the extra clothing scavanged from the dead, the blown snow abraded their exposed skin like a rasp and coated their clothes, making it heavy with ice. For Leland, the clothing had started out heavy.

*The naked dead.*

THEY HAVE NO EARTHLY NEEDS.

*And whose fault is that?*

DO YOU THINK THEY CAME JUST BECAUSE YOU GAVE THE ORDER? THESE ARE THEIR HOMES, THEIR FAMILIES. THEY WOULD'VE COME ON THEIR OWN.

This didn't comfort Leland. His internal marching song was an inventory. The extra socks on his hands came from Peter Merkle of the Seventh, second son from a family in Fort Lucinda, who took an arrow in the head twenty kilometers inside Laal. The extra poncho came from Coronet Desmond Mann, father of two girls waiting in the village of Oasis, near Fort Chavez, who was trampled by Cotswold cavalry. The extra pants came from Vince Carey, only child of a family from Brandon-on-the-Falls, gutted by a spear and two days dying. The scarf wrapped over his lower face came from a Cotswolder soldier, cut down in one of the Eight Hundred's camouflaged ambushes. His full name and origin were gone with him, but his sword belt had "Zeb" burned into it.

They came back down into the shoulders of the valley again, when it spread and had room for shoulders. This also put them in the trees and gave them some shelter from the bitter wind, but the snow lay in deep drifts and they had to take turns breaking a path in waist-high or deeper snow.

*Peter, socks* step *Desmond, poncho* step *Vince, pants* step *Zeb, scarf* step. *Siegfried has a lot to answer for. And you, too, Father. How could you let him surprise you like this?*

They avoided unnecessary talk. "Siegfried's moved the majority of his men into the passes so his occupation troops are spread very thin, but he moves them constantly," Bartholomew told them. "But they're not very good in the snow."

Leland took a stint as pathbreaker, wading into the snowdrifts and tramping them down. *Peter's socks and Desmond's poncho, Vince's pants and Zeb's scarf. Damn you, Siegfried, damn you, Father. Too much fuss and too much bother.*

"If you don't get your father out soon, he won't last much longer. However, he is more concerned about getting the Glass Helm out of Siegfried's reach. I think we can do both."

"But why Leland?" Gahnfeld had asked.

"His father won't trust the Helm to anyone else," Bartholomew had answered. "He was very specific."

"Why do you think they won't have found your escape route and be waiting?"

"Because I left a rope hanging off the west wall, but I didn't get out of the Station that way."

"Why not more men?"

"We'd be seen. The steward would die and Siegfried would get the Helm."

Gahnfeld hadn't liked it, but it was Leland's decision. "Continue as we planned," Leland told him. "Link up with Captain Koss and follow his direction. We'll join you as we are able."

"Yes, *Warden.*"

Leland had left laughing.

Outside of the Brandon-on-the-Falls the small group took to the hills again, working their way from steep forest to brush and scrub and then, finally, rock and ice, barely crossable. They went roped together now.

It never stopped snowing and Leland never stopped his litany. *Peter's socks and Desmond's poncho, Vince's pants and Zeb's scarf. Damn you, Siegfried, damn you, Father. Too much fuss and too much bother.*

THIS IS GETTING MONOTONOUS.

*You don't have to walk.*

Leland felt his knees buckle and he stumbled forward, steadying himself against the rock face.

WHO DO YOU THINK HAS BEEN KEEPING YOU UPRIGHT WHILE YOU TALK ABOUT DEAD MEN'S CLOTHES? DO IT BY YOURSELF FOR A WHILE.

Leland found himself too busy concentrating on his footing to continue the litany. The slope had gradually steepened into a cliff whose limits vanished into the falling snow above and below. It was clear that one could fall but unclear how far. The imagination stretched the drop to infinity.

They heard the falls long before they saw them, thundering out of the east face of the station. It grew out of the mist, resolving slowly, wreathed in a fog of ice crystals. Above, the bulk of Laal Station loomed large and dark, its lines blurred by the snow. They couldn't see the guards on the walls far above, and, they hoped, the guards couldn't see them.

"This better work," Leland said in Bartholomew's ear. "It's not like it's been tested."

Bartholomew shrugged. "True. Coming down I had a rope, but . . ." He suddenly clapped Leland on the back. "Well, you had to climb to get the Glass Helm the first time, too."

Leland shuddered, and not from the cold.

When it wasn't winter, the water pouring out of the Station was a tremendous gout, a torrent could be felt throughout the Station. When he was very young, his first night spent outside the Station, he'd been unable to sleep, missing something. When he returned, he felt it then, aware and unaware at the same time.

The rock below the falls was water smoothed and hollowed out, a face steeper than vertical.

With the frost and snows higher in the mountains, the water volume diminished to a quarter of its late-spring levels. As it grew colder and colder, the ice began to coat the rocks around the falls, layer upon layer.

The sound of the ice ax was barely audible to Leland over the torrent, and he had little fear it could be heard above. It was slow going—the ice was very hard and slick. Twice he fell when vigorous ax blows shook him from slick hand- and footholds, but the other five were tending his rope and pulled him up again, dangling helplessly above the ice and water below.

As he progressed, he moved both up and sideways, vectors converging on the mouth of the fall itself. During the first of many rest breaks, the others offered to spell him, but tentatively, their eyes wide.

"I'm the lightest. When I drop, you guys can hold me. And, as Bartholomew has pointed out, I've some experience with this."

As he worked, a mist of ice crystals swirled around him, stinging his face and layering his clothing with ice. With each rest break, he changed his outer poncho, and Bartholomew would pound the ice off the spare one.

Several times he wished for Bartholomew's escape rope, but Bartholomew had brought it with him, needing it to get down the rest of the mountain.

The last three meters before the mouth were the worst, the spray the wettest, soaking his clothes and threatening hypothermia. With each stroke of the ax he resorted to his litany, a syllable per blow. *Pete . . . er's . . . socks . . . and . . . Des . . . mond's . . . pon . . . cho . . .*

VIN . . . CES' . . . PANTS . . . AND . . . ZEB'S . . . SCARF.

*Damn . . . you . . . Sieg . . . fried.* DAMN . . . YOU . . . FA . . . THER.

*Too* . . . MUCH . . . *fuss* . . . AND . . . *too* . . . MUCH . . . *bo* . . . THER.

He could barely lift the ice ax and he was perched there, more than half frozen, staring dumbly to his left to pick out another hand- or foothold when it finally penetrated his head that he was inside the edge of the mouth and, finally, out of the worst of the mist. Also, the rock there wasn't coated with ice and the air coming out of the tunnel was almost warm or, at least, above freezing.

It took him several attempts to move his left foot over, to step down onto damp stone, then swing around, to crouch tiredly at the edge of the rushing water on a tiny ledge that looked like a soccer field after the footholds in the ice.

His eyes adjusted slowly and he spent the time rubbing his face, trying to restore the circulation to his bare skin. His fingers ached in the cold and he felt arthritic in all his joints.

GET A MOVE ON, CHILD.

He groaned and moved forward, splashing down into the very edge of the stream, in ankle-deep water. He moved quickly, before the water soaked through to his skin, and, hunched over, scrambled up the stream, deeper into mountain. After a moment the ledge appeared and he climbed onto it, teeth clattering. He looped the rope around the ice ax without untying it from his own waist, then wedged the ax between the wall and a slight irregularity in the ledge. He sat down, his feet braced against a crack, and tugged the rope four times.

It took twenty minutes for all of them to join him and, for a while, all they could do was sit there on the ledge, shoulder to shoulder, and rest. Leland took off his wet socks and replaced them with the ones from his hands. *Peter's socks.* Then rubbed them until restored circulation made them throb.

Bartholomew led the way then. Leland had been down here before, though it was forbidden, of course. Still, when the winter snows were falling, his brothers and he had ranged the entire station, forbidden or no. But Bartholomew had passed this way only two days before and he knew the disposition of the guards, so it was he who lit the candle and led the way.

Another hundred meters and the walls went from water-smoothed stone to mortared blocks, then they were on paving-stone steps and climbing up a narrow stairway. Bartholomew stopped at the top and blew out his candle. He stood before a door outlined in thin cracks of dim orange light.

Leland joined him, one step down.

"Shhh," Bartholomew said. He leaned forward, pressed his ear against the door, and froze. After a moment he took a thin piece of wire from his belt and used it to hook the bar on the far side, then, laboriously, work it out of its brackets. After several minutes he grunted and said, "Gently now—push the door open while I hold the bar."

Leland reached past him and eased the door open. The hinges squealed softly and then the gap was wide enough for him to slip through. There was a wall-mounted oil lamp at the far end of the hall but no one in sight. He turned and took the drop bar before it clattered to the floor, then the rest of them joined him in the hall and they closed the door behind him.

Bartholomew pointed down the hall away from the lamp and tiptoed in the same direction. Leland vaguely recognized the hall as the one outside a series of storerooms near the baths. The dampness from the river permeated this wing and ruined anything that couldn't take the wet.

Bartholomew made a left at the next turning and they moved toward the "dry" wing, the more modern side that, due to its distance from the river and an improvement in ventilation, was far more usable for storage. "Though," Bartholomew had told Leland the night before, "Siegfried made us prisoners move all the stores and turned those rooms into holding cells. That's where your father is."

*My father.*

WHERE ARE THE GUARDS?

Leland tapped Bartholomew's shoulder. "Where are the guards?" he whispered.

Bartholomew held his fingers to his lips sharply, then pointed ahead and crooked his fingers to the right.

*Around the corner?*

Bartholomew stopped, however, well short of that point, outside an old door with two freshly installed bolts mounted upon it. Again he held his fingers to his lips, then pointed at Leland and the door before them. Then he pointed to each of the others and pointed down the hallway, held up two fingers, and pantomimed striking down on something with his closed fist. Finally he held his finger to his lips one more time.

Leland looked to see if his men understood. The men drew their daggers and Leland, sickened, started to say something, but then their halvidar reversed his dagger so the heavy pommel projected, a potent club. Leland flipped his hand forward and they crept down the hall.

Bartholomew went to work on the bolts, easing them back with only the slightest scraping, then pulled the door open. It was pitch black within and Leland could see nothing. Bartholomew handed Leland the candle and his packet of matches, then pointed to himself and down the hall, after the others.

Leland slipped inside the dark room and felt the door shut behind him. He was fumbling with the matches, preparing to light the candle, when he heard the bolts thud home.

WHY DID HE DO THAT?

*To make it seem undisturbed if anyone came along?*

HMMM.

Into the darkness he said quietly, "Father?" His voice was quavering and he hated himself for it. There was no answer, no sound. He knelt and scraped the first match against the stone floor. It broke.

CALMLY.

The second match lit and he blinked in the sudden flare, then concentrated on getting the candle alight. Then, when it was well lit, he finally looked across the cell.

They'd used quicklime, which was why there wasn't much odor. There wasn't much left of the body but bone, buttons, and some iron-gray hair. They hadn't tried to take the ring from the left hand, though, a ring Leland remembered playing with in his father's lap, and the manacles were still there.

It was well he hadn't stood for he would have surely fallen.

THIS DID NOT HAPPEN OVERNIGHT.

Leland clenched his teeth. *Damn you, old man! I did everything you asked! How DARE you die on me.* He dropped his other knee to the floor and slumped. The candle splashed hot wax on the back of his hand and he jerked. He dripped more wax on the floor, then pressed the candle base into it. He became aware of that other voice.

BARTHOLOMEW HAS BETRAYED YOU.

*Excuse me. Can I have a moment here?* He took a deep shuddering breath. *Bartholomew? He'd die first.* The anger was leaching away replaced by overwhelming numbness.

NO. NOT IF SIEGFRIED HAS THE IMPRINTER.

Leland wiped tears from his cheeks with the back of his hand. *What are you raving about? What's the imprinter?*

YOU CALL IT THE GLASS HELM.

Leland stared blankly back at the skeleton. The eye sockets stared up, almost as if they were looking at something. Leland lifted his head up, at the wall above, and saw the dark, brownish letters: NON OMNIS MORIAR. *What?*

I SHALL NOT WHOLLY DIE. OH, YES, I REMEMB—

There was a brilliant flash behind Leland's eyes and he gasped out loud, both hands going to his head. He staggered to his feet and felt every muscle in his body suddenly spasm. He knew he was falling backward and that he should do something about it, but he couldn't.

Darkness followed.

# TWENTY·TWO

## KENSHO: ENLIGHTENMENT

"*Non omnis moriar.* Well, someone has a sense of humor." Dr. Herrin resisted the urge to rub her scalp. The electrodes were easily dislodged and they'd been calibrating them all day.

The technician holding up the sign snorted and Dr. Guyton frowned at him before turning back to Herrin. "Well, we've tried it with or without the key and the key seems to work better. It gives them a chance to assimilate the other personality over a period of time instead of overloading their sensorium and sending them into shock."

"What happened to your test subjects?"

Dr. Guyton looked uncomfortable. "The last one is doing all right. The first two . . ." He shrugged. "We hope they'll recover, in time."

"So there's no shock with the key?"

Guyton licked his lips. "Not as *much.*"

Dr. Pearson, the neurologist, turned from his workstation and said, "We're as ready as we ever will be."

Dr. Guyton nodded. "Are you ready, Michaela?"

Dr. Herrin laughed. "As ready as I ever will be."

The technician held up the sign and Dr. Herrin stared at it, as instructed. Then they threw the switch and she was—

* * *

Ten years old, racing over the waves, taking the hovercraft from Seattle to Victoria, weaving between the San Juan Islands. She spent the entire trip with her nose pressed to the glass, looking for the sharp black dorsal finds of killer whales. She didn't see any.

Mommy was home on leave and Daddy actually turned off his workstation for the day, though he checked his e-mail once every ten minutes, on his portable.

Fifteen years old and a street gang almost caught her down by the docks and she pulled the screamer off its clip, dropped it, and ran, shielding her eyes from the glare of the strobe and holding her ears against the shriek of its siren. A police unit dropped from the sky, and the gang scattered like the debris blown before the turbofans.

The woman officer who drove her home complimented her on the timing of her reaction. "Most people with screamers don't use them or pull them too late. Have you considered studying a martial art?"

Twenty-three years old and, even before they handed her the diploma, Ph.D. magna cum laude, she knew economics wasn't the field for her. Still, she worked for Barclay's Bank in Tokyo for a year because it let her continue her study of Aikido at Hombu dojo. At the end of that time she was invited to become an *uchideshi,* an inside student, and quit the bank. She stayed for three more years.

Thirty years old and she met William in Amherst while working for her Ph.D. in social systems. He was seven years younger than she was, bright, attentive, and, most important, an *aikidoka,* someone who knew what the hours on the mat meant. They married the day she graduated.

Thirty-five years old and chief investigator in the Mexico City riots. So many people in such a small space. She'd predicted it in a paper three years before but it didn't help. She talked to her girls every night, safe in Colorado, but to four-year-old Carmen's questions she could only say "Yes, it's as bad as they're showing on the tube." It was far worse, actually, and she was having trouble sleeping.

Forty-nine years old and she cried when Carmen left for Rice. "Mom, we can vid! Stop it, you're embarrassing me." But Carmen's eyes were red, too, and, when she lifted off in the collocopter, she wiped at them with the back of her hands.

Fifty-three, a very bleak year. William was attending a seminar at New York Aikikai when the Ramapo Fault let go. It rained at the funeral and it was all she could do not to rage at the coffin. *Damn you, you were supposed to live longer than me!* Her cradle-loot, her child-groom. Carmen and Mallory were dazed, tight-lipped, helping when they could and being cried upon by William's parents. *One's husband should outlive one's parents.*

Everyone was helpful, but especially the students from the dojo, bringing food, running people to and from the airports, and just being there. It was her dojo but William had been dojo cho for so long that she wondered if her own death would've hurt them half so much.

Fifty-seven and Carmen cried at the launch. "Carmen, dear," she'd said, "We can vid!" She didn't add, *Stop it, you're embarrassing me,* because she wasn't embarrassed. She was touched.

Mallory said, "Take your meds, Mom. Bone loss is a problem at your age anyway, and in a sixth of a gee . . ."

"Two years of med school and already a doctor! It's only six months—just long enough to do these interviews. The research has all been done in Antarctica, anyway. I'm just confirming its applicability to extraterrestrial habitats."

"Ice is not vacuum, Mom. People have been going to Antarctica a lot longer than they've been going to the moon."

"Or the stars, child. These studies are important for Project Giant Leap. If I were young enough for *that* trip—"

Both of her daughters looked horrified and she laughed.

Fifty-eight.

A *very* bleak year. Carmen dead. Mallory dead. Six billion dead on Earth. Bauer dead on the floor before her.

*What have I become?*

The rest of the committee was staring at her. Novato, the NASA/ESA rep, said forcibly, "It had to be done. Don't resign."

She shook her head. "And what happens the next time somebody wants to disagree with me? There's a certain chilling effect. 'If I tell her what I think, will she kill me?' I really think I've gone over the line here."

She excused herself and waited outside in the packed corridor, while they discussed it.

When they called her back, someone had moved Bauer back into the corner and covered his face with a handkerchief. She could've predicted the way they'd realigned themselves, Stavinoha at their head, Novato beside him. She approved—her efforts would not be undone.

Stavinoha spoke. "We don't think you should die. We don't know if you've insured our survival or doomed it, but whatever, you may go with the colony."

And Novato added, "But there is a condition . . ."

Fifty-eight.

The technician held up the sign and Dr. Herrin stared at it, as instructed. Then they threw the switch and she was—

*Oh.*

OH.

Leland felt something hard beneath him, something holding up his arms, his back. He opened his eyes and blinked. The room was well lit with gas lamps and smelled of something familiar.

Sulfuric acid. The plating workshop.

He tried to lift his hands to shade his eyes and found they were tied to the arms of a chair. No, he realized, as his eyes adjusted—strapped to the chair. His legs, waist, and chest, too. Someone had removed his outer clothing, but not his extra shirt. He was warm and still dazed from the awakening.

He knew what kiwi fruit tasted like, a plant that didn't grow on Agatsu. He had body memories of countless hours on the mat. Of having sex as a woman. Giving birth. Growing old. Dealing death deliberately. Incredible grief and loss.

*So that's what you are.*

SO THAT'S WHAT WE ARE.

There were two guards standing against the wall. Leland turned his head and saw Bartholomew standing against the other wall.

He felt a flash of anger and then understanding. "What happened to my men, Bartholomew?"

"They're bruised but alive. The high steward doesn't kill if he can avoid it. He prefers to convert." Bartholomew's smile was serene, peaceful. "I'm glad you'll be joining us."

"I find it painful to know that you've betrayed our people. Betrayed *me.*"

Bartholomew shrugged. "You will feel differently, after."

DON'T BOTHER. THEY TRIED EVERYTHING TO DEPROGRAM THE IMPRINTEES IN TURKEY AND IRAQ, BUT ONLY THE IMPRINTER CAN UNDO WHAT THE IMPRINTER HAS DONE.

*Then what about me?*

The door opened and the guards snapped to attention. A guard stuck his head in, then said, over his shoulder, "Secure, sir."

The guard withdrew and Siegfried came in carrying a case.

He looked at Leland with narrowed eyes. "Good morning. Did you have a nice rest?"

"Morning?" It had been late afternoon when they entered the mouth of the falls. "Oh, yeah. Very restful. How long did I sleep?"

Siegfried put the case down on the workbench and Leland had to crane his neck to see him. Siegfried shrugged. "I'm not sure if sleep is the word. My men tell me it looked more like a seizure. You're not epileptic, are you?"

*Would it interfere with the imprinter if I was?*

I DOUBT IT.

"No," Leland said.

Siegfried removed the Helm from the case. "I expect it was something of a shock finding your father that way." He looked over at Leland and raised his eyebrows.

Leland, stone-faced, said, "Shock. Yes."

"Enough to cause a seizure?"

Leland shrugged.

"It doesn't matter. You'll answer my questions soon enough." Siegfried was doing something with wires. "Blast! The charge is down again. We'll have to wait a bit for it to recharge." He walked over to stand before Leland.

"Fetch me a chair," he said to the air in general.

Bartholomew reacted first but the guard next to the door left quickly and Bartholomew leaned back against the wall.

Siegfried continued. "Tell me what happened at the Plain of the Founders."

Leland blinked. "Zanna de Noram negotiated a truce for this year. Then the Rootless found out you'd poured all your men into Laal and decided to invade Cotswold."

Bartholomew cleared his throat. When Siegfried looked over at him, he spoke. "According to his men in the Eight Hundred, Leland took King Roland right out of his own camp, forcing negotiations, and later, he was the one who told Roland that you'd shifted your forces." He beamed at Leland like a proud father.

Siegfried frowned. "Oh, really?" His chair arrived and he sat, hands steepled before him. "Very resourceful. You will have to use some of that resourcefulness on my behalf . . . for a change."

Leland licked his lips. "One man, more or less, won't make any difference. You're seriously outnumbered here in Laal. Convert me if you will; the forces of Laal and Noram will still walk all over you."

Siegfried laughed. "One man, more or less, is exactly what I need. They have to be the *right* men, of course. Captain Koss is next on my list, as well as your remaining brothers and sister. I had your cousin Ricard, but he chose death before conversion." He tilted his head to one side. "You don't have that choice, by the way. You'll get me your siblings and the good captain and then we'll see who's outnumbered. Arthur and his girls, perhaps, after that. Then I'll work my way back through the Nullarbor clan chiefs."

He tapped his fingertips together. "I'm going to rule this planet before I'm done, without bloodshed or violence."

Leland shook his head.

Siegfried smiled. "You disagree?"

"It's the ultimate violence—the destruction of personal volition, the loss of choice."

"I will give them direction and purpose. Ask Bartholomew if he's happy."

Leland glanced at Bartholomew. Bartholomew's eyes were on Siegfried, following his every breath and movement. Leland felt bile rise in his throat and forced it back. He didn't speak.

There was a crystalline tone from the workbench and Siegfried straightened. "Ah. The point is moot. You'll know what I'm talking about in just a moment."

*What can we do?* He tested the straps, straining, summoning *ki*, legs, arms, chest, but the straps were thick, new leather, more than adequate to contain him. Perspiration formed under his arms and soaked his shirt. His breathing rate increased.

Siegfried walked over to the bench, humming to himself lightly, as if he were engaged in some mundane chore—not the destruction of a human being.

GET OUT OF MY WAY.

*What?*

GIVE ME CONTROL. REMEMBER WHEN YOU WERE FIRST TAKING UKEMI? YOU RELAXED AND MY BODY MEMORIES TOOK OVER. I WANT YOU TO GO AWAY, THINK ABOUT SOMETHING ELSE. DON'T TAKE THIS HIT—GET OFF THE LINE.

Siegfried lifted the Helm and disconnected the leads from the battery. "I'm looking forward to working with you, Leland. I was impressed by your loyalty to your father."

Leland clenched his teeth together. *My father? You have no idea.*

Siegfried continued. "Any last thoughts? Of your own, that is?"

Leland shut his eyes and searched frantically for a focus, something worthy of concentration. He heard Siegfried step behind him and pushed his feelings about his father away. He thought of . . . Marilyn.

*Okay, do it.*

Something cold and hard touched his head and he went away.

The ropes from the old lift still hung in the shaft, but Marilyn had no intention of trusting her weight to them. Instead, she worked down the shaft using a series of hand- and footholds formed by offset bricks.

Once she'd closed the wall hanging over the hole in the paneling, it was pitch dark in the shaft. She carried a candle and matches with her, but needed her hands to climb, so the candle stayed behind with her knife, wrapped in a cloth tied around her waist. Her staff hung across her back, tied with another piece of cloth. Fortunately, the footholds were regular, probably deliberate, and she felt her way down, slowly, in the moldy dark.

She passed three different sets of paneling, old openings closed, before she came to the top of the old elevator, rotting ropes still attached to its frame. According to the plans, they were down to the levels of the baths, the bottom of the shaft. She wondered what they'd done to the opening on this level.

*Hopefully, they didn't brick it up.*

When she pried open a corner of the elevator roof and lowered her lit candle, she found just the opposite. The elevator had been converted to storage, with barrels and shelves. The door to the hallway was wide open and she saw the glow of distant gas lights.

She put out the candle and listened for a good ten minutes. She could hear the distant sounds of running water, but no footsteps or human voices. She dropped down into the closet, then stood on a barrel to replace the roof panel.

The barrels contained salted fish; the shelves, paraffin-encased cheeses.

*Life is good.*

Zanna's advance troops were reinforced when they'd made the top of the pass but before they'd reached the fortifications at Fort Bayard.

Her losses were heavy, both in number and on her mind, and the last thing she needed to hear was her father's voice.

"You could've waited for the rest of us," he said, when he heard the figures.

Marshall de Gant was the only other person present and she had no compunctions when she snapped, "Don't speak to me about waiting! You delayed us *weeks*. How many people have died in Laal while you denied the invasion?"

Arthur's face went from petulant to vicious. "I can still disinherit you. Don't take that tone with me."

Zanna crossed her arms. "That threat doesn't work anymore! You're rapidly ruining anything I'd want to inherit. I don't want control over our people—I want their trust, and you're destroying that."

de Gant intervened. "None of this gets us into Laal. Surely that's the current problem? You can finish . . . assessing the situation *after* we've kicked Siegfried's butt out of Greater Noram."

Arthur looked ready to explode, but Zanna chose to take the hint. "You're right, Marshall. What do you propose?"

"I suggest we isolate and bypass Fort Bayard. Now that your forces have gotten us past the worst of the snow, we can move around the fort on the southern route." He tapped the map on the table.

"It's still in bow shot," Arthur pointed out.

"We have shields," said de Gant. "We're going to be moving quite fast, and Captain Kuart's ballista will be operating from the top of the pass, a height advantage that greatly increases his range." He put the tip of his index finger on the pass, then lifted it in an arc that dropped down on Fort Bayard with an audible *thunk*. "They'll be too busy to bother us."

Koss moved his forces carefully through the high passes, alert for the same sort of trap he's used on Marshall Plover's forces. Dexter commanded the Pikes and Anthony was directing his couriers as scouts.

It was cold but the weather was below them, low clouds in the valleys. *Let it snow on the bastards.*

Dexter, Captain Koss, and Anthony came together on horseback, in the lee of the pass, as the troops moved past.

"No traps, Captain," Anthony reported. "They had some sentry posts but they're running before us, pulling back."

Dexter asked, "Any word from Leland?"

Anthony frowned. "No—we know roughly where the Eight Hundred is, er, are, but there's snow falling between here and there."

Captain Koss blew into his mittened hands, then banged them together. "Well, let's get moving. Once our forces are down in the valley, Dexter can send a unit to link up with them."

They began the descent.

Gahnfeld signaled the attack when the sun hit the valley floor.

They burst out of the snow-covered tunnel end to find that over half the opposing troops had pulled back in the night. Those remaining didn't stand a chance. The Eight Hundred took no casualties.

The prisoners were disarmed and sent south, roped together, under a small guard. "Get them below the snow line, then turn 'em loose," Gahnfeld said. "Then join us."

He mounted a captured horse. "The rest of you get moving! We've got a date in Danbury."

"*Excuse me, do you work here?*" That's what she'd said, the first time he saw Marilyn. He'd looked up, transfixed by an angel.

Finally, though, he'd blinked and stirred, embarrassed by his moment of stupefaction. "*I suppose you could say that. I work everywhere else.*"

He'd been buried, hiding, deep in the book, anything to get away from the bleakness his life had come to. Her very existence had shown him there was more in the universe than his own pain.

He kept that memory before him like a cold man holding his hands before the fire and basked in its glow, no, he watched the memory just as he'd stared at Marilyn that faraway morning—as if it were the most important and wonderful thing in the universe.

It was the sound of his own voice speaking that brought him out of it—his own voice, but it wasn't him speaking.

Just his body.

"—protect and serve *you*. Serving *you* fills me with joy. Disloyalty to *you* causes me pain and sorrow."

Two voices, actually. Siegfried's, too, but all Leland could see was Marilyn's face, feel his attraction to her intensifying, fixating.

Then there was a moment of extreme disorientation and the sunny library ledge disappeared in waves of vertigo. He was slumped over, blinking, and he could feel his body struggling to sit upright. Again, not Leland, just his body, that other—Michaela. He started to help, but other hands were there, lifting his head, unstrapping his limbs.

Leland waited, floating.

Siegfried's voice. "How do you feel?"

"Not bad for an old bag of bones" came the answer. Michaela's inflections were different, an accent unmarked by three hundred years of phonetic drift. Leland's head swiveled sharply and stared, unblinking, at Siegfried.

"Old?" Siegfried frowned. "How old?"

"I was born four hundred and eighty-three years ago."

Siegfried took a step back from him. "What are you talking about? You're not even twenty years old!"

*Just barely eighteen.*

"Leland isn't, I am. But that's not important," said Michaela. "How may I serve *you?*"

Siegfried peered at her, somewhat calmed. "What is your purpose?"

"To protect and serve you." Leland could feel that smile on his face, a matching version of the one on Bartholomew's face, and longed to wipe it off. Instead, he tentatively took control of his hands, rubbing the areas where the straps had bitten into his wrists.

Siegfried relaxed even more, setting the Helm down on the bench by the batteries. "You were born on Earth?"

"Yes. Tacoma, Washington."

Siegfried's expression was blank.

"In North America. I suppose that's where the name Noram comes from."

"Ah." Siegfried nodded. "And was Cotswold a mighty country back on Earth?"

Leland felt his head shake. "It was a small region of England, but pretty." At Siegfried's expression she added, "At one time, England *was* the mightiest empire on Earth."

Siegfried shrugged. "It doesn't matter what happened on Earth. What became of Leland?"

"Oh, he's here, too," Michaela said.

Siegfried nodded. "And you came from the imprinter, eh? Do you have any knowledge of Earth technology?"

"Oh, yes," Michaela said. "What do you want to know?"

"Imprinters. Could you make more?"

Michaela sighed. "No. I know the theory, but the many support technologies are beyond me."

Siegfried scowled. "Well, then, how about weapons of war?"

"Yes, I know about those."

Leland began flexing his toes inside his boots.

Siegfried smiled. "Enough knowledge to direct their manufacture and use?"

"Yes. Poison gas, projectile weapons, Greek fire, even explosives, though I understand their use is forbidden in this culture."

Leland shifted his hips in the chair.

Siegfried waved his hand. "A superstition. Don't worry about it. You are a pleasant surprise, much more useful than the boy Leland. I suppose it was you who directed his accomplishments back east?"

"Not really. I wasn't fully awake then. Leland is surprising, but he's not to be trusted."

Siegfried laughed. "I hardly think that's the case now. Is it? I mean, doesn't he share your purpose?"

As Michaela said, "No," Leland moved, darting out of the chair and to one side, directly at the leftmost guard. He left his voice to Michaela who echoed Siegfried's "Stop him!" in almost perfect unison.

The guard reached for him with both hands, and Leland brought a cupped hand up from his waist, almost gently contacting the man's chin, and extended out. The man's head met the wall hard and Leland turned, taking the other guard's reaching arm in the first teaching, Ikkyo, and doing the *ura* version, which brought the man's head down and into the chair before he'd fully reached the floor.

"Stop! Submit! Don't do this!" his own voice in Michaela's accent protested. "I'm sorry, sir, he's not very biddable!"

Leland threw the bolt on the door before the guards outside responded to the noise and turned back to the room.

Siegfried was backed into the corner, holding the Helm in one hand and a dagger in the other. Bartholomew stood between Leland and Siegfried, a knife in his hand. Leland recognized the blade, the same one Bartholomew had given him so long ago. Bartholomew held it low, with his hand back, and advanced with the other hand forward, to block and check.

"Good, Bartholomew," Michaela said through Leland's mouth. "Hold the blade back. Strike and pull back. Don't let him get your knife hand."

*Careful. You don't want to confuse him.*

STOP THIS! DON'T YOU SEE THAT SIEGFRIED MUST BE OBEYED? THIS IS WRONG.

Leland lunged to the left and Bartholomew struck out, a slashing chest-high blow from the outside in. Leland entered, checking a return slash with a hand on Bartholomew's elbow. And extending, propelled Bartholomew away from him, to tangle, briefly, with one of the fallen guards.

Before he could take advantage of Bartholomew's momentary imbalance, Siegfried lunged at his exposed side.

"Don't!" warned Michaela.

*Thank you,* thought Leland. He pulled his hip, took the wrist, and pivoted, taking his other arm over the Siegfried's, then up under, grasping his own wrist and locking Siegfried's elbow. He expanded his chest and heard a creaking sound. Siegfried gasped and let his dagger clatter to the floor.

Bartholomew recovered his balance and turned back. "Let go of him!"

"Yes!" Michaela seconded with Leland's voice.

*I don't think so.*

Siegfried dropped the Helm onto the bench with his free arm and tried to strike, across his body, at Leland's face. Leland leaned back, putting more pressure on the elbow, and Siegfried shot to his toes, trying to get away from the pain, twisting. Leland let him pull back into the corner, exposing Leland's back to Bartholomew.

He heard Bartholomew move and Leland smiled.

"Look out, Bartholomew!" Michaela cried.

Without changing his grip Leland raised Siegfried's captured arm, then twisted his hips hard, one hundred eighty degrees, dropping abruptly to one knee at the end. Siegfried's feet came off the ground and his entire body flew over Leland and into Bartholomew's charge.

Siegfried's scream cut short at impact in an anguished, desperate gasp for air. Then Bartholomew began screaming.

*He didn't get hit that—*

Michaela began screaming with Leland's mouth.

Bartholomew's knife was buried to the hilt in Siegfried's left kidney and blood was spreading across the floor at a prodigious rate.

Leland felt sick. *Enough!* He took control of his voice away from Michaela and his own throat stopped screaming. "Enough!" he shouted out loud.

Bartholomew dropped to his knees, his hands to his head, his face twisted in unimaginable pain. His scream dropped to a closed-mouth keening and he began rocking back and forth.

*You will do nothing that causes me harm. Disloyalty to me causes you pain . . .*

The guards in the hallway were yelling and pounding on the door. They pounded, first with their fists, then with their shoulders and the hilts of their swords as they tried to break in.

Michaela was dealing with her pain better. HELP HIM. WE CAN STOP THE BLEEDING. GET A DOCTOR TO HIM. A TRANSFUSION.

Leland reached down and felt for a pulse at Siegfried's neck. He felt three beats, each weaker than the one before, then nothing.

He looked at Bartholomew and said, "He is beyond harm. He is beyond pain. He is beyond need."

He could feel the internal keening lessen and knew he was on the right track, but the pain on Bartholomew's face was frightening in its intensity.

I WONDER IF HE LEFT ANY WRITTEN INSTRUCTIONS?

*Spare me.*

# TWENTY-THREE

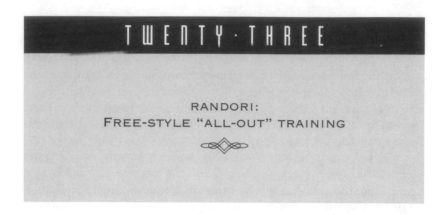

## RANDORI: FREE-STYLE "ALL-OUT" TRAINING

Sylvan led a large contingent from the Station down the snow-covered road. They were coordinating their advance with other Cotswold forces retreating up the valley and hoped to encircle the town before their purpose became known.

A part of him wished he were back in the Station, watching what happened when Leland wore the Helm, but another part of him was glad to be out in the clean, cold air. He shuddered. Even this mission was designed to further his father's plan—conversion of enemy commanders.

As they neared the edge of the town, his signalmen reported that Captain Emmet's down-valley troops were in position. Sylvan raised his arm. "Remember—women and children. Let the men run or kill them if they want to fight. Gather the hostages here. We're taking what we have back to the Station in one hour."

He dropped his arm and the hunt began.

Pickings were slim—the town was nearly deserted.

"There are tracks leading up into mountains," a coronet reported. "Halvidar Samson wants to know if he should pursue."

"No! Keep searching *in* the town." Sylvan looked at the twenty hostages found so far. Most of them were elderly, over sixty, unable to brave the frigid heights. There was a young woman with a newborn infant and two pregnant woman due, apparently, any day now.

"When did everyone leave?" he asked the prisoners.

One of the old women stepped forward. She looked into Sylvan's eyes without a trace of fear. "They started three days ago, but most of them left yesterday."

"Why?"

She looked pointedly left and right, at the prisoners and guards. "Because you're losing. Desperate men do desperate things."

*We are not losing!* He thought about striking her with his riding crop but controlled himself. Negotiations over hostages was just the bait to lure Captain Koss into the Helm's embrace, and he didn't want to make the prisoners more difficult to control than necessary. He narrowed his eyes and leaned forward in his saddle.

"What is your name?"

"Dru Druza."

"Well, Madame Druza. We are getting desperate. Very. Do keep that in mind."

At the end of the hour, they'd added a mother with three children under four, but that was it.

"Get them moving," Sylvan said. Scouts had spotted Laal troops in the valley and there wasn't much time.

Marilyn heard the screaming as she neared the corner, oddly muffled, punctuated by the sharper sound of fists pounding on wood. She peered around the corner.

"Open this door! High Steward? Are you all right?" The muffled screaming stopped and the guards increased their efforts, slamming shoulders to the door, then pulling their swords and slamming the hilts against the wood.

There were three of them and they looked scared. As she watched, one of them left at a run, probably to fetch help.

*I should leave. This is going to be a very popular spot shortly.* But she walked forward instead, holding her *jo* at the ready. They didn't notice her until the first one dropped. The second one parried her first thrust, and she was forced to step back to avoid his counterthrust. She feinted high and he thrust low, as she hoped, and she dropped her center and the *jo* on the blade, just above the hilt. There was a metallic bell sound and the blade broke, then clattered to the floor. He tried to block her thrust with the hilt and the stub of a blade but managed only to lift it from his solar plexus to his throat.

The guard fell back, choking. She heard the creak of door hinges and twisted, raising one tip of the *jo.*

The figure inside was silhouetted by the gas lights within but there was something familiar about him. When he spoke, she couldn't help but laugh.

He said, "Excuse me, do you work here?"

"Oh, Leland, you idiot! What are you doing here?"

"I was wondering the same thing about you." He pushed the door completely open and she saw limbs sprawling, and blood. She took a step closer.

"*Malnutrition,* is that Siegfried?"

"Yes." Leland was watching her with an intensity that reminded her of that first encounter, so long ago in the library.

She looked at the other two bodies and a man crouched before Siegfried, face knotted in some deep emotion. "Did you do all this?"

Leland looked back at the room and the intensity of his expression faded, became weary. "Yes, sort of." He waved a hand at Siegfried's bloody side. "Bad *ukemi.*"

Ukemi? *Well, he's a friend of Charly Sensei. I should've realized he studies.*

He stepped back to the corner of the shop and picked up a translucent headpiece from the workbench. "I suspect we should leave now."

Marilyn nodded. "Yes—one of the guards ran for help. What's that?"

Leland looked down at the object in his hands and said, "A great deal of trouble." He crouched beside the kneeling man and said, "Bartholomew—it's time to leave."

Bartholomew looked at him with wet eyes and said something that Marilyn couldn't catch.

"Very well," Leland said, standing. "Bring him, then."

Bartholomew leaned forward and gathered Siegfried into his arms, unmindful of the blood. He staggered to his feet.

"Are you sure you can manage?" said Leland. "We'll probably be too busy to help."

Bartholomew nodded. His face was calmer.

Leland studied Bartholomew's face for a second, then nodded, satisfied. "How many of our people are in the Station?"

Bartholomew looked confused and Leland amended the question. "Natives of Laal. Prisoners."

"Oh. Perhaps thirty-five. They're all in the old kitchen staff quarters."

Leland blinked. "That's only five small rooms."

"Yes. It's very crowded," said Bartholomew.

"We'll have to do something about that." Leland looked down at the object in his hands. "But first I need to hide this."

Marilyn thought about the elevator shaft.

"I know just the place."

Sylvan came back into Laal Station and had to wait for the guards to notice they'd returned. When the gate finally opened he screamed at the guard commander. *"What the hell is going on here!"*

The man flinched. "Your father, sir. Something's happened down in the plating shop!"

Nothing anybody said made sense so he took two squads down into the lower levels. He found men treating two unconscious guards, a guard breathing painfully through a damaged larnyx, and a guard with a scalp wound. There was blood all over the floor.

"Where is my father?"

"We don't know," said one of the uninjured men. "Except for Graves," he said, pointing at the man with the throat injury, "they were all unconscious when we got down here. We've searched this level and we haven't found him or the prisoner."

"de Laal. What about Bartholomew?"

The man shook his head. "No sign."

"What happened here?" he asked Graves.

Graves tried to say something, but it came out as a rasping noise.

"How about you?" Sylvan said, tapping the man with the scalp wound. "What happened?"

"Uh, the prisoner attacked us. He slammed Rael's head into the wall and then threw me. My head hit the chair."

Sylvan stared. "Before he was strapped into the chair?"

"No, Guide. After."

*"After?* Didn't my father use the Helm?" He looked around suddenly. "Where is the Helm?"

The man shook his head. "It was here. The high steward used it on the prisoner, just like he did to the spy in the Blue Whale."

"And de Laal still attacked you? After?"

"Yes, sir."

"What happened to my father?"

The man shook his head. "I don't know. He and Bartholomew were here. I was knocked out." He pointed to his scalp wound again.

Sylvan looked at Graves. "Did Leland attack you, too?"

Graves shook his head.

"Who, then?"

Graves pantomined long hair and breasts with his hands.

"A woman?" He frowned. *Oh!* "Was it Marilyn de Noram?"

The man looked puzzled.

Sylvan said, "Was it the woman I brought with me when I came from Noram?"

Graves nodded.

*Marilyn and Leland. And whose blood is this?* He looked up from the puddle on the floor. "Find them. Find them right now."

They had to wrap Siegfried's midriff several times to keep the body from trailing blood everywhere they went. Marilyn guided Bartholomew from fish barrel to shelf, helping boost the body up through the gap she'd made in the ceiling planks. Leland followed, replacing dislodged items and dusting the more obvious footprints away.

Perched on the elevator roof, in darkness, Leland replaced the planks while Marilyn lit her candle. "I didn't know this was here," he said, watching her every motion.

"Then you haven't read every book in your own library. I found it in the *Station Renovations Log.*" The candle caught and she shook out the match, then looked at Leland. "What?"

"Pardon?" Leland said.

"You were staring at me like . . . like you'd never seen me before, or something."

*Like I might never see you again.* "Sorry. I'm very glad to see you, Marilyn. Why are you here?"

"Treachery. Betrayal." Her eyes narrowed and her mouth became a straight line.

Leland hazarded a guess. "Ah. Sylvan?"

She nodded.

"But you escaped?"

"They think a warrior is a large man with weapons. This puts them at a disadvantage."

Leland laughed softly. "They should be more flexible."

"You never said how you got here."

"Treachery. Betrayal. Bartholomew, here, lured me into a trap."

Bartholomew, crouched beside Siegfried's body, nodded matter-of-factly without taking his eyes from Siegfried's face.

Marilyn frowned. "And you brought him with us?"

Leland looked back at Bartholomew and nodded. "Yes. It wasn't his fault. Which reminds me—" He lifted the Helm and looked at it. "Lend me your candle."

Marilyn handed it to him. He twisted to the back of the shaft and held the candle down behind the elevator cabin. There was a large gap at the back, perhaps half a meter, and he could see that it extended below the elevator itself. He handed the candle back to Marilyn, then pulled off his extra shirt and wrapped the Helm with it.

"You're right—this is a good hiding place." He pushed the Helm into the gap and held it down as far as he could reach, then let go. It fell with a slight clatter and stopped with a soft *thump*. He sat back upright and looked up the shaft. "I'm trying to picture where it opens on the kitchen floor." He remembered scrubbing the floors around the kitchen countless times.

"By the library, the shaft is covered by paneling. There's also a woven rug hanging over—you're doing it again."

Leland shook his head hard, as if to clear it. "Sorry. There's a stretch of paneling in the passageway between the Great Hall and the kitchen. That must be it. How are the prisoners contained, Bartholomew?"

"They've reinforced all the doors with iron bands and installed drop bars. They never open more than one room at a time and, when they do, they have bring in extra men. They feed them through a slot and let one prisoner empty the chamber pots once a day."

"How many guards are there now?"

After a moment Bartholomew said, "Perhaps three, in the kitchen. Siegfried stripped the Station to reinforce the passes, so they let the doors do most of the work."

Leland and Marilyn exchanged glances. "Just how many Cotswolders are in the Station now?"

Bartholomew tilted his head to one side. "Depends how many troops have come in. They're retreating up the valley and it could end up being a considerable number. It was down to forty-five this morning, and Sylvan took most of those with him to collect hostages in the village. He's probably back."

"Hmmm. What shape are the prisoners in?"

"So-so. Until last week they were using them as work crews so they were feeding them. When Siegfried sent troops up into the passes, they stopped because it took too many to watch them."

Leland looked at Marilyn. "It's a lot of people to get out of the Station."

Marilyn nodded. "So we'll just have to take the Station, instead."

One of the searching men found a bloodstain, a drip that had been walked upon, in one of the hallways, but all the rooms and storage areas nearby proved empty of the fugitives or further signs of their passage. Sylvan stormed through the passages shouting at the men. "Damn your hides! Find them!"

He'd stationed two squads at the entrance to the underground river, lest Leland leave the way he'd arrived. Both stairways up were guarded by a squad, and four more squads were scouring the floor. There were barely enough men left to man the lookout posts on the walls or watch the prisoners.

There'd been a man on each stairway all day and the fugitives hadn't passed, but still, after thirty minutes of vigorous searching, they couldn't be found. "Dammit. There must be secret passages or hidden rooms. Keep guards on the stairways and the lower passage, but widen the search to the rest of the Station. Find them!"

*Just how trained is he?* Marilyn thought.

They'd left Bartholomew in the elevator shaft with Siegfried's body and forced open a section of panel outside the kitchen. She'd expected him to talk about some strategy for dealing with the guards, but he'd just set her staff against the wall, pushed the panel roughly back in place, then walked casually down the hallway. She'd scrambled to keep up.

As he entered the kitchen he began talking to Marilyn in a normal conversational voice. "What are you going to do after all of this? When it's all settled, that is?"

There were two guards sitting at the kitchen table near the ovens, and they looked up at the sound of Leland's voice.

Marilyn, glancing at the guards, said, "I, uh, hadn't really thought about it." *What are you doing?*

Leland kept walking, toward a passage at the back of the room, presumably the rooms where the prisoners were being held. "I suppose you'll be going back to Noram City. I wonder if I could find a position with the university—"

"What are you doing here!" one of the guards said, standing.

"—maybe a janitor or something," Leland said, ignoring the guards. "I've got lots of experience." He turned toward the guard and waved his hand airily. "Don't mind us. We'll just help ourselves."

Both guards were up and moving now, and Marilyn started to wish for her *jo.* "Cornelius would love to have you on his staff. But not as a janitor."

Leland said, "Well, anything that let me be near you."

Marilyn felt her ears heat suddenly and, despite the two closing guards, she couldn't help smiling.

"I said"—one of the guards spoke loudly—*"what are you doing here?"* They drew their swords.

*That's torn it.* Marilyn was wondering if she could protect Leland when he turned suddenly, leaning slightly forward, his eyes suddenly fierce and wild.

The first guard flinched, then lifted his sword and cut at Leland's head, but as the sword dropped he found Leland standing beside him, away from the second guard, Leland's hand between his own on the sword hilt. As the sword dropped, Leland extended that arm ahead and the guard flew forward, without his sword.

The second guard cut sideways at Leland and Leland pulled his hip, increasing the gap. The tip of the sword whistled past, then Leland moved in before the sword came back, blocking the man's elbow, then moved in and threw the man down hard with *kokyū-hō,* using the back of his upper arm first to lift the man's chin, unbalancing him, then continue the motion over in an arc. The guard landed on his back, hard, and Marilyn could hear the air rush from his lungs.

*Okay, I don't have to protect him.* She took the sword from the second guard's nerveless fingers and placed its edge against the neck of the first guard, struggling to rise. "Just lie there, why don't you?" He dropped back to his stomach.

"You really think Cornelius would give me a position?" Leland asked.

"Leland, *I'd* give you a position, if you'd come live in Noram. But is this really the time to talk about this?"

"Well, soon, then." He gestured at the guards. "Can you manage?"

"Certainly." She winked, then said slightly more loudly, "If necessary, I'll just kill them."

Leland laughed and went on, to the back of the kitchen.

She kept her eyes on the two guards but heard a *clunk* followed by the sound of a timber clattering on the floor. Leland's distant voice came to her. "Well, are you going to just lie around all day?"

There was a explosion of voices stilled suddenly, and she heard Leland say, "Release the others. We've things to do."

Returning to the basement level was the last thing Marilyn wanted to do.

"Well, I'd go alone, but I can't bear to be away from you."

She looked for some trace of irony or sarcasm in Leland's face but he looked perfectly sincere. "What's wrong with you?"

Leland looked confused for a moment. "Is this feeling wrong? It feels like the best thing that's ever happened to me."

"Get over it."

Leland sent Bartholomew with the freed prisoners, making sure they all understood what was to be done. Bartholomew nodded affably, then trailed after the group, staggering slightly under his load.

Marilyn shook her head. "He can't carry him around forever."

Leland shrugged and said, "That's okay, he'll drag him." He looked at Marilyn with that intense stare again. "We all carry our burdens. Are you coming?"

Marilyn shifted, uncomfortable. "I don't know. What's your dan ranking?"

Leland shook his head. "What's that have to do with anything?"

"I want to know if this is a suicide run."

Leland blinked. "I'm unranked. If it matters, Denesse Sensei awarded me a *shidoin* certification."

"And you're unranked? But only the—" She shut up abruptly. "I'll go."

"What were you going to say?"

Marilyn shook her head. "Later." Under her breath she added, "If there is a later."

They descended the elevator shaft again in darkness, not bothering with the candle, then down into the storage closet.

Leland turned left out of the old elevator, away from the plating shop, a direction Marilyn hadn't explored. She tried to remember where this passage went, from her study of the station floorplan, but could recall only that the baths lay this way. They moved quietly past rows of storerooms and shops, many with their doors ajar, contents disarrayed from the recent search or earlier looting.

Leland talked quietly. "How often do you think I could see you if I moved to the city?"

Marilyn, trying to listen for Cotswold soldiers, shook her head. "Can we talk about this later? Did you get hit on the head or something?"

Leland laughed. "Something." He checked a cross passage before moving on. "You know how Bartholomew is carrying Siegfried around?"

"Yes."

"Siegfried used the Helm on Bartholomew, to compel him to obedience. That's why Bartholomew betrayed me to him. It's irresistible, really. He was going to do it to lots of people—you, your father, your sister, my brothers."

Marilyn stopped walking, horrified. "That's awful."

Leland stopped and faced her, nodding. "Siegfried tried to do the same thing to me."

Marilyn took a step back. "But it didn't work, obviously."

"Not as he intended. Instead, thanks to a previous experience with the Helm, I was able to focus on something else. Something I was already obsessing upon, anyway."

Marilyn shook her head. "I don't understand."

"I focused on you."

"You were obsessing on me before?"

Leland shrugged. "A crush. Nothing abnormal, really."

Marilyn frowned. *Just a crush?* "And now?"

Leland waved his hands vaguely in front of him. "Now I'm obsessing."

There were footsteps from the far end of the hall and Leland pulled her into an open storeroom. They slipped behind the door and stood quietly while booted feet walked briskly in their direction. Leland peered through the gap by the hinges and Marilyn stood behind him, suddenly aware of the warmth radiating from his body, the line of his neck.

He needed a bath.

*Obsession? Is that like love?*

She tensed as the soldiers, several of them by the sound of the footsteps, passed. After a moment Leland said, "I think we can go now."

She checked the corridor. "Yes." They moved on.

They were in a damper section of the cellar, and the vibrations from the river were more evident. Leland paused at the corner and held up his hand. "Hmmm. There are guards. Oh, well. Let's go."

She stepped around the corner with him. Ten meters down the hallway stood two men on each side of a door. "What are we going to do?"

Leland looked at her. "Do? We're not going to do anything. This isn't practice. If they attack us, something will happen, that's all. That's what aikido is really about. I wonder if we could get an apartment near the university. I don't think I want to live in Laal House. It's not close enough to the dojo."

Marilyn stared at him.

"Are the rents high?"

The guards saw them or, more likely, heard Leland, and turned, then drew their swords and walked toward them.

Leland kept walking. "You will live with me, won't you? I didn't really ask."

She shuddered. "*Now* is not the time."

The guard in the lead said, "Stop right there."

Leland smiled at the man. "Why?" He walked faster, closing the gap between them and pulling slightly in front of Marilyn.

The guard looked worried, then said, "I'll give you a reason!" He stepped forward and thrust his sword at Leland's midsection.

Leland pulled his back hip off the line and skipped in, suddenly standing beside the soldier as the blade passed him. Leland's near arm swept over the guard's and his bicep slammed into the soldier's face. The man went over backward, his feet flying out from under him. Leland kept moving, bypassing the other soldier before he could react. "Take care of him, would you?" Leland called over his shoulder. He turned into the gate room.

The remaining guard looked both directions, torn. Marilyn moved in toward him, offering her head as a target. The guard jerked his blade up and cut down reflexively. She entered, sliding off the line, and turned, *tenkan,* trapping his sword hand by her hip and twisting around to take his balance. He stumbled forward and she reversed, stepping back as she swept his hand and sword across her front in a wrist lock and turning again.

He screamed and dove over his own arm to relieve the pressure, slamming into the wall and leaving the sword in her hand.

Her heart was beating fast and she wanted to jump up and down and say, *Look what I did!* But he wasn't there to see it. *Or to catch you if you failed.* She found herself grinning like an idiot.

The man she'd just thrown tried to get up again and she lifted the sword.

"You look tired," Marilyn said. "Why don't you *rest?*"

The soldier settled back against the wall, cradling his wrist.

There was a shout from the room Leland had entered and the sound of something breaking, then a series of grunts and crashes. She held her breath, listening. There came a clanking sound followed by the rattle of a chain and the sound of something dropping. The ever-present sound of rushing water increased momentarily, followed by the sound of grating stone.

Marilyn backed away from the man until she could see into the room. Leland was standing by a speaker tube that came down from the ceiling. There were three men scattered around the room either groaning or unconscious. One of them was upside-down against the wall, his legs folded back over his head.

Leland glanced at her and smiled without taking his ear away from the tube.

"What now?" she asked.

"We wait."

Sylvan came back into the courtyard to find the hostages shivering against the wall, watched by three squads. "What are they still doing here?"

"We didn't know where to put them, sir."

Sylvan cursed under his breath. The watch captain who'd been privy to his plans was supervising the search for his father, Leland, and Marilyn. "Put them—"

There was a groaning from the front gate, the sound made when it lifted on its hydraulic pivot.

*What now?* He yelled up to the gate captain, at his post on the gate tower. "Who ordered the gate opened? Is someone coming?"

The gate captain yelled back. "Nobody on the road. I didn't order it, sir!"

*The fugitives.* Well, it would do them no good. It wasn't as if they had someone outside waiting to take advantage of the unlocking of the gate.

He pointed his finger at the coronet in charge of the hostages.

"Take two squads down to the watchroom and lock the gate. If the fugitives are still there, capture them."

"Yes, sir! My squad and Chumley's. Peterson, your squad has the hostages." He led them off at a run, using the stables entrance to the main structure.

Sylvan looked back up at the gate captain. "Are you sure there's nobody out there?"

"Yes, sir. They're fighting in the village but nobody's headed this way."

"Any word from Fort Bayard?"

"I'll send a runner to check."

*Dammit. I should've brought all the troops with me.* His father had directed him to leave them in the valley to slow the enemy advance. If Laal calvary broke through at the village, they could be here in ten minutes. He yelled up at the gate captain. "Get some timbers and wedge the gate, just in case the—"

Both halves of the main door slammed open and a howling mob—that was the only word for it—of men and women charged forward armed with a motley collection of weapons, gardening tools, and kitchen implements. They made straight for the gate, sweeping over the four guards stationed there and, while the majority of them, perhaps twenty, formed a perimeter around it facing out, six of them threw themselves at the gate, pushing it open.

The guards on the walls opened fire, but immediately other arrows shot from the slits on the side of the main door, dropping two of the archers and forcing the others above to take cover in places where they couldn't shoot down into the yard.

*Where did—the prisoners. They let all the prisoners out.* Poorly armed as they were, there were almost as many of them as there were Cotswolders in the entire station.

The hostages struggled to their feet and Sylvan, about to order their guards to attack the forces at the gate, drew his sword and screamed, "I'll kill the first one of you that moves." He was about to turn, to use this same threat to force the mob to close the gate, when the massive stone half cylinder dropped into its locking grooves with a thud he could feel all the way across the yard.

*Damn you, Father. How could you let this happen?*

"Through the stables. Get them inside," he shouted to the squad. "If any of them give you trouble," he said deliberately, "kill the children."

* * *

The index mark on the great iron shaft rotated to the OPEN mark and Leland threw the lever. The rushing water sound changed and the shaft dropped. For a second Marilyn thought the grinding noise overhead was a prelude to the ceiling collapsing, but then it stopped. Leland jumped away from the lever and started rummaging through a chest in the corner.

"What are you do—sit down!" The guard with the injured wrist was trying to stand and Marilyn skipped forward, raising the sword. He subsided. She backed up again to see Leland turning a clevis pin on the heavy chain where it joined the top of the sluice gate.

"Are you going to drop it back in?"

"Yes."

"Won't that let them close the gate again?"

He shook his head. "No, there's a slot below the channel. It'll drop all the way down, past the water. It'll take days to fish it up even if they figure it out." He got the pin loose but the weight of the iron sluice gate kept it from releasing. Leland stepped back and, using the wrench as a hammer, slammed into the link, once, twice; then, on the third blow, the pin flew across the room, the chain flew up through the block, the gate fell into the slot, and the counterweight smashed its wooden cradle to pieces.

Leland dropped the wrench and said, "Time to go?"

Marilyn looked back down the hall—there was movement at the corner. "Yes."

They left the room, moving down the hall in the other direction at a run.

# TWENTY-FOUR

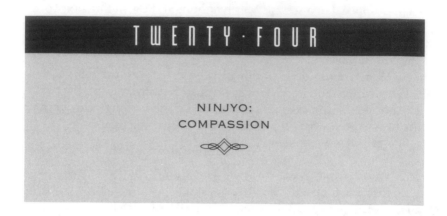

## NINJYO: COMPASSION

When they were finally in touch, Koss detached his headquarter's unit and rode with them to the edge of Brandon-on-the Falls to meet the Eight Hundred. He already knew of Leland's decision to infiltrate the Station and feared the worst—that, like Ricard, Leland had fallen into a trap.

Gahnfeld assembled his units on the snow-covered soccer fields south of town. With a slight shock he remembered seeing them there in just this formation, the evening they'd frog-marched back from the Black after escorting Siegfried out of Laal—the night of the fall Harvest Festival.

They were wearing ponchos, turned light side out, and their breath steamed in the cold air.

Koss searched their faces, looking for children they'd sent out to the plain, but the faces stared back, unimpressed. These weren't children anymore.

"Myron."

"Uncle."

They saluted formally, then Koss studied Gahnfeld's face. "Rough trip?"

Gahnfeld nodded. "Rough enough."

"Any word from Leland?"

Gahnfeld sighed. "I was hoping you could tell me."

Koss shook his head. "We've heard from Marshall de Gant. They've bypassed Fort Bayard. Their advance units will be here by the end of the day.

"Hmmm. That's faster than I thought. To tell you the truth, I'm surprised they came at all."

Koss looked at the lines of men. "No comment. I don't know what happened. I'm reserving judgment."

Gahnfeld said nothing.

"You did well, Myron. You brought far more of them home than I'd dared hope."

Gahnfeld's voice broke. "It *wasn't me!* Leland did it *all!*" He straightened and cleared his throat. "I want permission to advance on Laal Station."

Koss looked out at the men again. Those within earshot were watching him intently. *Did they all come back alive to die at home?*

"Permission granted. We'll be right behind you. Hit them hard."

Leland went through two guards at the back stairway. Marilyn, a step behind, didn't see what happened, only that she had to jump sideways suddenly, flattening herself against the wall as the first body came down the stairs, then the second. Leland never stopped and Marilyn struggled to catch up.

They emerged into the main corridor to see some of their own people closely following a group of Cotswolders as the enemy backed into the Great Hall.

Irma, one of the Laal kitchen staff, saw Leland and said, "They've taken hostages into the Great Hall. Women and children from the village."

Leland walked forward. "What do they want?"

Irma looked at him doubtfully. "Well . . . they want to talk to you. It's Sylvan."

Marilyn felt her lips draw back from her teeth. She remembered her guards and the troops at the aid station. Sylvan would kill without hesitation.

Leland said, "How many hostages? How many soldiers?"

Irma said, "Perhaps twenty-four hostages. Twenty soldiers."

Marilyn stepped up to where she could see Leland's face. It was a blank mask, devoid of emotion.

"What's happening in the rest of the Station?" Leland asked.

"Well, there's a group of them holed up in the gate tower and a bunch of them down in the cellar. It's hard to say how many others are around, but they're individuals, scattered, and we've been picking them off as we go."

"Where's Bartholomew?"

Irma shuddered. "He's in the back courtyard. He wanted to cool the corpse off in the snow."

"Did you tell Sylvan his father is dead?"

"Hell, no! I was afraid if he found out, he'd start killing for sure."

*Good call,* Marilyn thought.

There was the sound of fighting from the stairway behind them, the one Leland and Marilyn had just climbed from the basement.

Irma smiled grimly, the worried look on her face dropping briefly. "Looks like Robert and Allen caught up with the crowd in the basement."

Marilyn blinked. "Only two of them?"

"No. They've got half our guys. Robert and Allen also have bows."

Leland, seeing a look of incomprehension on Marilyn's face, said, "Those two . . . well, they know how to use a bow."

Irma laughed shortly, then looked back at the entrance to the Great Hall.

Leland said, "Send somebody to fetch Bartholomew and the body. Also, we need somebody with axes to go get the Glass Helm. Marilyn will show them where." He glanced at her for confirmation.

She nodded.

He smiled briefly and said, "As soon as they're done below, get Robert and Allen up into the musicians' gallery. But have them hide and wait unless I point at someone like this." He held out his fore and index fingers together.

Irma duplicated the gesture.

Leland clapped his hands together and said, "Please hurry."

The first thing he noticed was how scared the soldiers looked, even more scared, it seemed, than the hostages. The second thing he noticed was a piece of bamboo, still leaning in the nook behind his father's chair. It was yellower than the last time he'd seen it, less green.

AREN'T WE ALL?

*Tell me, Michaela, do you feel any compulsion to obey this man?*

He finally turned to face Sylvan, standing stiffly before the right fireplace behind a living barrier—an arc of guards with drawn blades themselves standing behind another living barrier: the hostages.

NOT REALLY. THE IMPRINTING WAS QUITE SPECIFIC. SIEGFRIED IS . . . WAS A VERY "ME" PERSON.

"Where is my father!" Sylvan's voice was a touch strident, and Leland noted how it made the soldiers even more nervous.

*Is it his voice or his missing father that bothers them most?* Leland kept his voice light and calm. "Hello, Sylvan. Did you enjoy your stay in Noram?"

Sylvan didn't take it well. After stepping down from the dais and pushing between the guards, he grabbed one of the hostages, a young, extremely pregnant woman, by the hair and put his dagger to her throat.

*"I asked you a question!"*

Leland took a deep breath. "I've sent for him. He'll be here in a moment." He wondered how long it would be until Robert or Allen was in the gallery. "What are you trying to accomplish here?"

"Where is the Helm?"

WELL, NOW WE KNOW WHAT HE'S TRYING TO ACCOMPLISH.

"Oddly enough, I've sent for that, too."

Sylvan took his knife away from the woman's throat but still kept his fingers entwined in her hair. "What happened down in the cellar? When my father put the Helm on you?"

The woman's eyes were wide open and she was breathing rapidly, her face beaded with moisture. There was fire in both fireplaces but it wasn't *that* warm in the room.

Leland shrugged. "It didn't work."

"I *know* that. Why?" He raised the knife again.

"Perhaps it's broken."

Sylvan's face paled.

*He was counting on the imprinter to get him out of this mess.*

APPARENTLY.

"We'll see if it's broken," Sylvan said. "Where's Marilyn?"

Leland felt a palpable blow in the pit of his stomach. *He'll try it on Marilyn.*

TRY IS THE OPERATIVE WORD. IT HASN'T BEEN RECHARGED.

"Marilyn is bringing the Helm."

Leland heard the door hinges creak and turned.

It was Bartholomew with the late High Steward of Cotswold. Siegfried's face was drained white, and the cloth they'd wrapped around his midriff was soaked in blood. He was starting to stiffen, either from rigor mortis or his time out in the snow, and there was no doubt in anybody's mind that he was dead.

HELP HIM. He could feel Michaela's urge to walk forward, to share Bartholomew's burden.

*No.* He turned back to Sylvan. "So, what now, High Steward?"

HIGH STEWARD?

*He's his father's heir.*

Sylvan exhaled slowly. Under his breath, so low that Leland almost didn't hear him, he said, "I thought he couldn't be killed."

Leland thought about his father's bones in the cell below. "Believe me, I know the feeling."

He waited a moment, then said, "It's over, you know. Your enemies are closing in from all sides. My troops from the south, Koss from the west, de Gant from the north, Toshiko from the west. But you might still live after this.

"But not if you harm a single hostage."

He raised his voice. "None of you will live if a single hostage dies."

Sylvan laughed harshly. "Ignore him. He'll sing a different tune in a—ah, my fiancée."

Leland turned. Marilyn had entered the room carrying the Helm still wrapped in Leland's extra shirt.

"Bring it here!" Sylvan said loudly.

Marilyn ignored him, bringing it instead to Leland.

Sylvan raised the knife again, wrenching the woman's hair back to expose her throat. The woman gasped, then cried out suddenly, her hands going to her abdomen.

SHE'S GOING INTO LABOR!

*"Bring it here!"* Sylvan snarled.

Leland accepted the bundle from Marilyn and pulled the shirt from it. It gleamed in the light from the windows and the fireplaces.

*"BRING IT HERE!"* Sylvan screamed.

Marilyn flinched, her eyes on the woman, and she started to reach for the Helm. Leland stepped forward instead, before she could touch it, and walked slowly toward Sylvan, carrying the Helm at waist level.

"What good will it do you, Sylvan? You did know that you can't even go home, right? Roland is closing on Montrouge even as we speak. By this time next week, the nation of Cotswold won't exist. What you should ask yourself is 'Will Sylvan Montrose exist next week?' "

"Shut *up!*" Sylvan said.

Leland stopped two meters in front of Sylvan and held it out, gripping the slight bulge where it covered the neck.

The hostage jerked and Sylvan swore. "Hold still! Do you *want* me to cut your throat?" The woman whimpered, then groaned deeply.

There was a splashing sound and Sylvan said derisively, "Did you just wet yourself?"

"Her water broke," Leland said, speaking slowly and emphasizing each word as if he were talking to a mental defective. "She's having a baby."

"What?" Sylvan looked down, taking the knife back from the woman's throat. Leland let the Helm drop slightly then whipped it back up and down, smashing it into Sylvan's wrist. The knife fell to the floor and, swearing, Sylvan shoved the woman forward, at Leland, while he stepped back and drew his sword.

Leland caught her and stepped back, first pulling her, then pushing her behind him. "Take her to Irma," he said without taking his eyes off of Sylvan. He heard Marilyn helping her across the room, talking in a low soothing voice.

Sylvan turned to one of the other hostages and raised his sword. *"Is this what you want? How many of them will I have to kill?"*

Leland stepped forward again. "You want the Helm? Or do you want to kill women and children?" He dangled the Helm by one finger.

DON'T DROP IT!

*Why the hell not?*

"Or are women and children the only thing you *can* kill?" He let the Helm drop back to his side and deliberately turned his back on Sylvan.

He saw Marilyn come back in the door, her eyes widening as she took a breath to shout. He heard Sylvan's foot scrape the floor, then, using both hands, raised the Helm abruptly over his head, concave side up.

Sylvan's blade, cutting down, slammed into the Helm. There was a sizzling sound and Leland stepped forward as he felt the Helm jerked from his hands. He turned to see Sylvan staring, horrified, at his sword.

The blade had cut halfway into the Helm and a small wisp of white smoke was rising from it.

HOW COULD YOU!

*Well, you're not immortal anymore.*

IT WASN'T THAT—IT WAS THE KNOWLEDGE . . .

*I'll try to write things down.* To Sylvan he clucked his tongue and said, "Well, if it wasn't broken before . . ."

Sylvan looked murderous. He tried to shake the Helm off his sword but it was wedged. He put one booted foot on it and shoved it off.

"Give it up, Sylvan," Leland said.

Sylvan raised his sword again. "You killed my father." He took a step forward. "You tell me I'm surrounded." He took another step. His voice increased in intensity. "You tell me I can't go home." Another step. More volume. "You destroy the Helm, my last chance." His voice raised to a shout. *"And you expect me to quit? Tell me what I HAVE TO LOSE!"* He charged Leland.

Leland froze, waiting. Sylvan closed and cut *kesa,* a diagonal slash down toward Leland's neck. Leland slid forward, deep, striking in at the hilt of the sword while he turned sharply, moving away from the blade. Sylvan found himself falling forward, the sword pulling from his hands, but he twisted at the last minute and kept the sword, falling hard on his shoulder. He scrambled up, holding the sword out, pointed toward Leland.

Leland walked away from him, toward the dais. He heard Sylvan's halting steps following him. He took the bamboo from the nook and turned again, to face Sylvan.

"Better look out," Leland said. "I'm armed now."

Sylvan lunged forward and cut across at Leland's stomach. Leland slid back and the sword tip cut cleanly through his shirt, missing his skin. Almost as an afterthought, Leland struck down with the bamboo, hitting the back of Sylvan's hand. The sword clattered down upon the floor.

Leland walked away from the sword and Sylvan. He heard metal scrape on the floor and turned to see Sylvan pick it back up. Leland stopped, then raised the bamboo over his head.

Sylvan approached more cautiously this time, his face contorted with rage.

Leland moved suddenly toward him and Sylvan jerked the sword up and cut down. Leland slid just off the line and, as the blade just missed his elbow, struck Sylvan in the head with the bamboo.

Sylvan fell back, stunned. The sword clattered on the floor again.

He put his hand to his hair and it came away bloody. Growling inarticulately, he reached for the sword again.

Leland's foot reached out and kicked the sword away, which surprised him, since he hadn't willed it.

STOP TOYING WITH HIM.

Leland screamed inside. *What about* MY *father? What about the thousands dead in the stupid war? Shouldn't* someone *pay?*

THEN KILL HIM, BUT THIS . . . IT LACKS DIGNITY.

Leland sighed. He gestured toward Sylvan with his hand. "Marilyn, watch him."

"*Hai!*" He heard her move closer, then turned back to the hostages.

The soldiers looked more frightened than before.

AND MORE DESPERATE.

"Why are you still holding weapons?" Leland asked. "Didn't you hear what I said? Anyone who hurts a single one of them dies."

One of the older men, probably an officer, said, "But *first* they'll be dead." He was holding an older woman by the hair and threatening her throat with a knife. "We have control here."

There was something about the woman—

Leland heard a scuffle behind him and looked over his shoulder. Apparently Sylvan had tried something with Marilyn. His face was grinding into the floor and she was kneeling beside him, his arm locked into a Nikkyo pin by her knees and arms. Leland looked back at the officer and his hostage.

*Who?*

DRUZA. THE sandan FROM THE VILLAGE.

"Control?" Leland started laughing. He saw movement in the musicians' gallery and thought, *I could kill you with a gesture.* Instead he said, "You are mistaken." He tilted his head to the woman, Druza. "Please explain it to him."

The old woman took the wrist holding the knife and backed under his knife arm, twisting her hips while she applied Sankyo to his wrist. Despite his hold on her hair, the knife and his wrist twisted back into him and he had to jump back, both to avoid the point of the knife and to relive the sudden pressure on his wrist.

Druza cut down, bending the man over, then cut down into his elbow with her free hand. She did the standing pin, pressing the palm of his twisted wrist against her knee and leaning in. He screamed and the knife dropped onto his back.

Druza picked up the knife with her other hand and held it briefly to the back of the pinned man's neck. She said dryly, "Control is an illusion." She threw the knife into the fireplace, gave the wrist one more twist, then dropped the arm.

The officer yelled again, then lay there, groaning. Madame Druza stepped to the next hostage in line and pushed her out into the room, away from her guard, then the next, and the next. The guards looked confused and Leland tensed, ready to point two fingers at any of them who threatened violence, but Druza's matter-of-fact manner seemed to calm them, and the hostages were soon standing on the other side of the room from the guards.

"Put down your weapons now," Leland said.

Some of them looked stubborn and Leland pointed his two fingers at his father's chair on the dais. Two arrows buried themselves in the back of the chair, the impacts so close together they made one longer sound. He held the two fingers up again, pointed at the ceiling. "The weapons?"

The swords clattered to the ground, followed by daggers.

"Go sit against that wall," Leland said, pointing to a spot away from the swords but within sight of the balcony.

He turned back to Sylvan and Marilyn. Sylvan was groaning. Leland raised his eyebrows.

Marilyn shrugged. "He keeps trying. He's going to damage his elbow or shoulder, I think."

Leland nodded. "Let him up?"

"I guess." She took Sylvan's wrist and pressed it down against his back as she stood and slid away.

Sylvan tried to scramble up, but it took him a minute because his arm still wasn't working right. His face was bloody from the scalp wound and his eyes were wide, showing white all around the iris.

"*You!*" He lunged at Leland again, his good arm extended to grab.

Leland sighed, then dropped the bamboo and entered, sweeping Sylvan's arm down and around, cutting into the back of Sylvan's shoulder as he dropped and pivoted.

Sylvan ended up facedown, his own arm a crowbar forcing him down. Leland reached across Sylvan's head and cupped his chin.

THAT'S THE TECHNIQUE I USED TO KILL BAUER.

*I know.* He paused a long moment thinking about his father, the thousands of dead, including his oldest brother, Dillan.

WILL IT BRING BACK ANY OF THEM?

Leland transferred his left hand from Sylvan's chin to his nose, pinched it, and said, "BEEEEEEEEEP."

From somewhere down the hall came the distant wail of a newborn baby.

Marilyn, sitting exhausted on the bench above her hiding place, watched the troops enter the Station from the library window. Leland, opposite her, glanced at the soldiers, smiled when he saw Gahnfeld ride past the Floating Stone, then looked back at her.

Still looking at the window, she said, "You're doing it still."

Leland laughed. "Sue me. It makes me happy to look at you. Is that so terrible?"

Marilyn looked back at him. "I don't know." She shook her head and looked out beyond the walls. "I see my sister's banner and de Gant's. Father won't be far behind. It's going to be crazy."

Leland sighed. "Yes. We could always hide." He tapped the bench beneath him.

Marilyn smiled slightly and shook her head, then frowned suddenly as she remembered. "No. I've got to talk to Zanna about Father. Quick, before they get here: Why did you destroy the Helm? Because it's so dangerous?"

"I didn't destroy it—Sylvan did."

Marilyn tilted her head to one side. "Don't feed me that! You made that decision. When you blocked with Helm it was as deliberate as any other move you made."

Leland closed his eyes. "Okay, okay. Yes, the Helm was dangerous—look how close Siegfried came. But really, I destroyed it because it's time. Time we went on."

"Is that what your father wanted?"

Leland opened his eyes again. "My father? My *father?* He never used the Helm the way it should've been used. He used it in the other meaning, to steer . . . to steer, to, well, guide. But he never took all that knowledge and disseminated it, did he? He hoarded it like a miser."

He held his fisted hand out and slowly opened it. "It's time to let go. I'll do my best to document what I've gotten from the Helm, to teach, but it's time we sent that knowledge out into the world, to be used in ways we never anticipated, never even thought of."

Marilyn tilted her head to one side. "You didn't do it just to spite your father?"

Leland shrugged. "Maybe. Or to spite Michaela."

Marilyn straightened on the bench. "So, you're two years younger than I am, you have a four-hundred-year-old woman in your head, your attraction to me is artificially reinforced, and you want me to get involved with you?"

Leland's smile dropped. "What I *want* is to marry you. But I'll settle for just being near you. Following you around on the street, sleeping on your doorstep, annoying you at parties, sending notes, serenading your balc—"

"Stop it!" she said. A tear slid down her cheek. She looked back out the window, up the mountain road, and wiped at her face with the back of her hand. "My father's banner."

There were running footsteps on the stairway, still several floors down, but climbing. She stood abruptly and started to walk away.

Leland held up his hand, to stay her. "What can I expect?"

She looked down at the floor, refusing to meet his eyes. "How can I answer you? I don't know myself."

Arthur walked down the hall with a smile on his face. So the family of Laal still existed and the looting he'd expected hadn't been carried out. Dulan was still dead and he was getting used to the role of rescuing hero. True, that brat, Leland, was getting the lion's credit, but there was plenty to go around.

He pushed open the door of the study and the smile dropped from his face. "What's this?" he demanded.

Zanna, Marilyn, Marshall de Gant, Leland, Dexter, and Anthony de Laal, and Leonid Koss were standing in a semicircle around a solitary chair.

Zanna's and Marilyn's eyes were red. Dexter and Anthony looked furious. The rest of them were impassive.

Marilyn spoke. "Please sit down, Father."

*They know.* He looked for weapons. Koss, Anthony, and Dexter were armed. The rest weren't. From what he'd heard of Leland, he didn't need weapons. An even more terrible thought entered his head. *Neither do my daughters.*

"It would be rude of me to sit when there's only one chair."

Zanna said, "Sit. Down. Father."

He sat, trying to do it as naturally as possible, as if it were his choice. He crossed his legs. "What is all this? A trial?"

Marilyn stepped slightly forward. "The trial is over, Father. This . . . this is the sentencing."

"And the accused?" Arthur said lightly.

*"DON'T!"* said Anthony. *"Don't even pretend!* Do you want me to drag Sylvan up here and have him say it to your face?"

Arthur flinched. "I really don't kno—"

Zanna started crying openly.

Marilyn said, "Father, that you conspired with Siegfried to betray Laal is *not* in question here. The evidence has been heard. The orders you gave to your signal staff. Sylvan's admissions while he still thought Cotswold was winning. Your orders to de Gant keeping the Laal contingent from coming to Laal's aid. Don't make it harder."

Arthur sagged. It was Zanna's tears, more than anything, that broke him. *I just wanted to be looked up to.*

He croaked, "What do you want?"

Marilyn continued. "Your abdication."

He glared back. "Never!"

Dexter started to draw his sword. "Fine. I didn't want to do it like this, anyway!"

Leland stepped between Dexter and Arthur, pushing Dexter's sword back into its sheath. "Wait," he said to both of them. Then, to Arthur: "My brother wants you dead and I can't blame him. However, we Laals had our own traitor, but she's dead and it's unclear which of you did the most damage.

"If you stay on the throne we will make sure that all Noram knows of your role and Noram, as a country, will cease to exist. The center will not hold—who'll trust you? Laal will certainly not stay a part of a Noram that you rule, and I'm sure several other stewardships will secede. We'd rather trust Roland than depend on you."

Arthur was white now.

Anthony spat out, "If our troops find out what you did, you won't live to see the border."

Leland held up his hand before Anthony and gestured to Marilyn with the other.

She took over. "But if you abdicate in favor of Zanna, no one outside of this room will know of your role in the invasion and you can retire to your estate in Merida with some dignity."

Dexter, his hand still on his sword hilt, said, "Let's be clear about this. Your choice isn't between abdication and staying in the high stewardship. Your choice is between abdication and *death.*"

It was reflexive, really, his subsequent protests, but in the end, he agreed.

* * *

They buried Siegfried in the Laal family cemetery, in the central court. It was Leland who'd pointed out that "If you put him in a town plot his gravestone will be desecrated daily."

They put Siegfried next to Carmen's grave. All Carmen's plot held were some random ashes collected from the remnants of the Blue Whale. A similar grave, ashes only, was next to hers, for Ricard.

The story of his death had come from one of the Cotswold soldiers. When Leland contemplated the tenuous chain of events that kept Siegfried from success, he shuddered.

Bartholomew supervised the Cotswold prisoners who did the excavation, a massive effort in the frozen soil, and it was Bartholomew who read the rites of the dead. Sylvan was there, in chains, and some of Siegfried's officers, but, besides the guards, Leland was the only Laal in attendance.

THANK YOU.

*You wouldn't have given me any peace otherwise, right?*

DAMN RIGHT.

Leland left when the dirt was mounded high above the grave, despite internal protests.

Late that night he awoke, bare feet on packed snow, shivering, standing before the grave, alone beneath frozen stars. He shook his head and beat his arms, then, fully awake, realization hit.

*Damn it! What are you doing?*

SAYING GOOD-BYE.

*What you're doing is giving me frostbite!*

IT'S OKAY. WE CAN GO NOW. I'M DONE.

It took him an hour, huddled before a fire under blankets, to warm up.

It was Michaela's memories that supplied the phrase.

"What part of 'no' don't you understand?"

Dexter shook his head. "Really—you should take the stewardship. Dillan was the one trained for it, but he's dead. I *never* thought I'd have to. Besides, you're the one who wore the Helm."

Leland searched for words.

Anthony, sitting silently in the corner, stirred. Lillian, fresh come from the mountain, and the three brothers were in their father's study trying to separate his papers from Siegfried's. Anthony spoke. "He's right, you know. I think Father even intended it, after you wore the

Helm. What else was all that business with the sticks for, if not to toughen you up—get you ready?"

Leland shook his head violently. "I will *die* before I sit in that man's chair. I don't care what he intended, I'm going off to Noram to study and teach."

"Laal needs you," said Dexter. "None of us wore the Helm."

"And no one ever will again. Get used to it." Leland pointed his finger. "Laal needs *you.* And Anthony. And Lillian, for that matter. It needs time to recover from this invasion. It needs time to heal and rebuild and—" His voice caught and he looked away for a moment before saying "Grieve. Time to grieve."

Leland rubbed at his eyes fiercely. "I'll do what I can." He gritted his teeth. "Zanna's asked me to serve on the council and I'll look out for Laal's interests in the city, but *that* is where I'll be. Not here.

"None of us expected to wear these shoes. Maybe they'll chafe for a while, but we'll break them in . . . in time."

He left abruptly, before they could muster more arguments.

Eventually he found Marilyn, walking with Zanna in one of the upper courtyards, their heads wreathed in ice fog.

"Am I interrupting?"

Zanna shook her head. "No. We're just . . . well, just trying to make sense of things."

Marilyn had shadows under her eyes and looked at Leland gravely, without reaction.

Leland froze, holding his breath.

After a long moment, she stepped up to Leland and pulled him close, laying her face against his shoulder as he hugged her back. He saw the worried look on Zanna's face drop briefly as she smiled at them.

"Marilyn tells me you're looking for an apartment near the dojo."

Marilyn swung around to face her sister but kept an arm around Leland's waist. He soaked up her warmth and felt pure contentment. "Yes," he said to Zanna. "Do you know of something?"

She nodded. "Yes, I do. I'm going to have to live in Noram House so Charly is going to have to move." At Leland's look she said, "She may be my sensei, but I'm her steward. It's a double-check. Besides, we belong to each other. She can go to the dojo all day, but at night—" She turned her head to the northwest briefly. When she turned back to face them again, she said, "I'm sure Charly would want you and Marilyn to use the townhouse. You can't get closer to the dojo than that."

Leland looked at Marilyn. "That would be very . . . good." He remembered something. "What were you going to tell me, that time I told you about my *shidoin* certificate? When you said, 'I'll tell you later.' "

Marilyn looked at Zanna, then back again. "In Aikido, there's only one person who teaches yet is unranked. I was just wondering if Denesse was . . ."

Zanna blinked. "Interesting thought, sister. Very interesting. Maybe that's what he had in mind."

Leland looked from one sister to the other, then one of Michaela's memories came to him. "Oh, no. No way."

Marilyn shrugged. "It's just that the *Doshu* is considered beyond rank. After all, you contain the woman who brought Aikido to this planet. She lived thirty years on Agatsu in the flesh and, from what I now understand, made frequent reappearances via the Helm, to keep Aikido on track."

"Which will never happen again, thank god!" Leland shook his head violently. "It was never O-Sensei's intention that Aikido be a fixed and static thing. He wanted it to evolve, to grow. And I'm not at the point Michaela was. She was a fifth dan when she arrived on Agatsu but she trained for thirty more years. I don't have that experience."

Zanna looked at him. "No, not yet—it's like a lot of things in life. We'll see."

He looked at Marilyn for support, but she just shrugged.

"We will see."

# EPILOGUE

## Kachihayabi: Victory at the Speed of Sunlight

Vulcan Probe Message #2563: Epsilon Eridani II

$CO_2$: .278% $O_2$: 22% $N_2$: 77.5%

Chlorophyll reflective spectra: 30% surface area, 3% in organized fields. Atmospheric hydrocarbons in trace amounts. Some patterned electromagnetic activity. Concentrated thermal zones unrelated to geologic phenomenon.

Est human population: 500K ± 25K

Prognosis: Population Viable

Repeat

Prognosis: Population Viable

Message Ends